]

Love Storm

*For Pam + Jan—
We hope you'll like
this book.*

Peter Sonderegger

Peter Sonderegger

ISBN : 1-4196-5086-6

To order additional copies, please contact us.
BookSurge, LLC
www.booksurge.com
1-866-308-6235
orders@booksurge.com

Love Storm

PROLOGUE

Maine is the most magnificent state in America! Period!
No other state has such an incredible array of lakes, ponds, rivers, streams, mountains, forests, ski hills, whitewater harbors, ocean scenery and on and on. No other state even comes close to what Maine physically offers its citizens and quests.

Few states have as many beautiful lakes as does Maine. North in the state is Mount Katahdin, which is over five thousand feet high with marvelous hiking paths leading to its peak. In addition this area is the starting points for two super rivers, the Kennebec and Penobscot that flow down to the Atlantic Ocean. Both offer fly fishing for salmon and trout as well as canoeing, kayaking and rafting

Throughout Maine are all sorts of camping sites around land owned by paper mills and forest owners. People are accepted in these areas but they have to be careful around the large trucks hauling logs down to the paper mill factories.

To the south are located the major cities...Portland, on the Atlantic Ocean, state capital Augusta, Lewiston and Waterville...all of which contain about two-thirds of Maine's population. The furthest city up north is Bangor with a population of over thirty thousand.

One of the reasons for Maine's beauty is its lack of people. For instance the Boston Metropolitan area has over three times as many citizens as the entire state of Maine, even though Maine is considerably larger than all of the eastern states.

There are very few multi-storied condominiums in any part of Maine so this allows the state to offer water frontage to the public.

Highway ninety-five north of Waterville has strange problems... Moose, which have a habit of standing in front and damaging cars and drivers. Drivers also have a tendency to take a nap while boringly driving up northeast. Both of these are caused by nothing on the sides of the highway except trees.

To the east of Bangor are some of the most beautiful ocean frontages in America with Acadia National Park as the most famous of all and where Bar Harbor, Northeast Harbor and Southwest Harbor are located.

When people look at a map of Maine, they can see why traveling in mid Maine is basically going east and not north, though the direction is basically called "Northeast." In fact the most popular magazine in Maine is "Down East."

So when you travel to the ocean frontages in Maine you are going east and not north.

"Northeast" is also used to describe the viscous storms that often attack Maine, particularly in the winter. Though these storms do not compete with the dangerous hurricanes in the southern states they do create serious problems in the winter months. Five years ago most of Maine was clobbered with a northeastern storm that knocked out electricity and telephones for 10 days. The snow added to the ice also prevented vehicles from moving on all of Maine's roads.

Two couples in the Bangor area were about to have their lives changed by a northeastern storm that was sneaking into northern Maine. They were not prepared for this massive storm, or what was about to happen to their marital relationships.

CHAPTER 1

On Thursday afternoon, Rita Dubois sat waiting in an orthopedic surgeon's examining room on the fifth floor of the Eastern Maine Medical Center hospital complex in Bangor, Maine. It seemed to be taking a long time for Dr. Forster to determine what was wrong with her right knee since she had arrived in his office to have her knee examined. All sorts of illustrations were hanging on the wall, showing what problem hips and knees looked like.

She didn't quite understand what they were showing, but they looked horrible to her. There were drawings of what was under a human's skin and where knee and hip problems were located. This room didn't have a window so there was nowhere else to look except at the body illustrations or some old magazines.

The pain in her knee was constant even though she was able to walk, but she had to stop jogging and playing racquetball since the pain accelerated when participating. Her husband told her she should get her knee checked out by an orthopedic surgeon, so she set up an appointment with Dr. Eric Forster who was recommended to her by a friend, Jean Jensen, Dr. Forster's nurse.

Dr. Forster was recommended to all sorts of potential customers, as he was young, talented, and successful in correcting ailing body joints such as hips, knees, and shoulders. So Rita, while nervous about a potential operation, was looking forward to a meeting with him.

She was afraid Dr. Forster would suggest some sort of operation and maybe even a knee replacement. The thought of such an operation worried her. Maybe, she prayed, there was nothing really wrong with her knee and some painless medication cure might get her knee back to normal.

Rita was approaching her fifty-third birthday and was finding it a bit more difficult to keep her body in shape since the knee problems started and her athletic functions stopped. She began to gain weight. She stood at a tall five foot eight inches and her weight was getting into the 140-pound range. Her short brown hair was also beginning to show a little grayness.

While waiting for his meeting with Rita Dubois, Dr. Eric Forster was on his cell phone confirming the evening's dinner date with his wife Susan and two of their friends, Jack and Janet Meacham. While he talked, his nurse, Jean Jensen, knocked on his door and opened it before he could answer her. She pointed to her watch, which told him their patient was waiting.

"Susan," he quickly told his wife, "I've got to see a patient right now. I'll see you at the Pilot's Grill Restaurant at five." Eric had planned a three-day vacation at the Benoit Lodge in Bethel, Maine starting Friday afternoon. He had hoped to spend the weekend alone with his wife, but she insisted on inviting the Meachams. Eric and Susan were having problems with each other and he thought a long weekend together would do much to improve their marriage that was beginning to fade away. But having the Meachams at the Benoit Lodge would probably take away the togetherness he was looking for.

"OK," she replied, "I'll contact Jack and Janet. See you there. Bye."

She hung up before he had a chance to answer.

Without a smile, nurse Jensen told him, "Doctor, Mrs. Dubois' x-rays are ready and she's in the third examining room." She placed the x-rays on Eric's display box to the left of his desk.

Jean Jensen was a middle-aged lady who had been a nurse with this group of doctors for about 15 years. She was extremely careful with their patients and with the four doctors in the clinic. She stood about five and half feet tall and her body was in excellent shape as she worked out on a continuous basis and played racquetball with a group of friends at least once a week. She was married and had two teenage boys, who were equally active as she and her husband, a purchasing agent with a paper mill located north of Bangor.

She was extremely fond of Dr. Forster as she was always impressed with his kind attitude toward his patients and, should an operation be needed, his talent in surgery. This is why she recommended him to her friend Rita Dubois and then set up an appointment with him to check out Rita's knee.

Dr. Forster stood about six foot four inches tall with a slim athletic-looking body. He had long arms and legs with a handsome face. His light brown hair was beginning to fade back on his head. His smile was very attractive to those who created it and as a result he was quite popular. He'd been an orthopedic surgeon for a little more than three years, but his reputation was more like that of a surgeon who'd been operating for many years. He had a great love for the state of Maine and spent considerable time with his patients.

"Doctor, Mrs. Dubois has been waiting almost fifteen minutes in room three. She's very nervous about what you're going to say about her knee."

Eric studied the x-ray and asked, "How old is she?"

"Fifty-three. She's a good friend of mine and when she started to have problems I suggested she come and see you, but she didn't want to think about a knee replacement."

"Well," he commented after looking at the x-rays, "She's got a serious-looking problem, so let's go see her." Nurse Jensen led him into the examining room where Rita Dubois was sitting on the examination table staring at the floor.

"Sorry, I'm late," said Eric Forster as he entered the examining room. He held out his hand to her with a smile on his face. He sat down next to her and looked into her eyes. "Now tell me about your knee."

Rita quickly felt comfortable as she was immediately impressed with him, so she began to tell him about her problems. He patiently listened to her and made a few notes. He didn't interrupt her comments as he felt it important that Rita relate her feelings without interruptions.

When she finished relating her problems he stood up and looked at the x-rays displayed on the wall case. Eric pointed to the x-rays and began to explain what was happening to her knee. "Well, Rita, your knee is suffering from osteoarthritis," he said while stroking Rita's right knee, "and there is no way it's going to cure itself. It will get worse and your pain will intensify and your mobility will lessen. How's that for sad news?" he said with a smile as he sat down in front of her.

Rita's eyes began to mist as she thought of how she could exist the rest of her life with such pain. Dr. Forster was aware of what she was thinking.

"Now, Rita, the good news," he calmly told her. "We can correct this problem with a knee replacement. With a new knee you'll be able to continue your activities without any pain. Knee replacement is a rather common answer to the arthritis that begins to attack humans who are aging or suffering from over use. And I think your knee is giving up after all your years of physical activities. I understand you do a lot of jogging and you play racquetball with Jean." He looked at his smiling nurse

She nodded as she looked into his eyes, and then asked, "You're sure there's nothing else I can do?"

Eric shook his head. "I'm afraid not. If you did nothing your knee will get worse and your activities will be further limited due to the pain. Eventually you might find it difficult to even walk. If you have your knee replaced, you'll enjoy a relatively normal lifestyle with almost no problems."

Eric Forster understood the feelings that patients brought with them. It was obvious that she didn't want an operation, much less a knee replacement. Eric understood this without a word being said. It was obvious in her gaze at him.

He then explained the procedure to her in a quiet, yet serious, tone. "If you have concerns about this operation, Jean could put you in touch with other patients who have undergone this same operation."

He further explained to Rita Dubois the healing time she'd experience. "You will have pain, but not as bad as I think you're thinking." He smiled at her as she nodded. "Right after the operation the therapy staff will get you out of bed so you can practice walking."

"How much pain will there be?" asked Mrs. Dubois.

"Everyone is different on how long and how bad the pain will be, but within three weeks you should be free of any significant pain. You'll undergo therapy in your home. You'll also need to use a walker for about three weeks, depending on how quickly you heal. After that you'll use a cane until the strength gets totally back in your knee. You should stay indoors if we have a snowfall, as you just cannot take a chance on falling while you're healing. There are also do's and don't's while healing to protect the replacement. You'll need to follow these rules without question." He looked seriously at Rita who in turn nodded her approval.

"How long will that take?"

"I don't have an answer for that because every patient is different. You'll be able to move about sooner than you might think, but when is generally up to the patient and how quickly the therapy works. You're in good physical shape so your healing process should take less time than normal"

Rita looked over at Jean Jensen and asked for a name of someone she could talk to about the operation. She looked back at Dr. Forster and asked him if she should seek a second opinion.

"That's entirely up to you," he replied. "Jean can give you a list of orthopedic surgeons here in the Bangor area. To reduce your cost, you can have these x-rays sent to whomever else you might want to see." He then took her hand and told her that this operation was not as difficult as it once was and that many thousands of people all over the country have it performed every year.

Rita Dubois looked at both Eric and Jean with a very concerned look.

"Can I go skiing again?" she asked with a worried voice.

Eric nodded his head. "Probably, but we would need to have you build up your muscles before trying skiing again. Most of my patients have continued their outdoor activities, but you'd have to be more careful on how difficult the ski hill might be." He looked over at Jean Jensen who did a lot of skiing. "Isn't this true?"

She looked at Rita and nodded her head with a smile. "Dr. Forster has replaced all sorts of knees and hips for people who are now enjoying life as they did many years ago. One is Jack Meacham whose left hip Dr. Forster replaced last year, and now he can do everything except play football again. He is now coaching football up in Orono." Meacham was a former all pro halfback for the New England Patriots.

Rita was not aware of this and looked at Eric Forster with a surprised look.

Eric Forster smiled at Rita. "I'd recommend participating in as much outdoor and indoor activity as you'd like. The only thing I'd suggest stopping is jogging as this has a tendency to put too much pressure on your real and artificial hips and knees. Jack Meacham can never play football again, but he can coach a team as long as he doesn't get into any physical contact.

"Well I don't do that but I enjoy being somewhat active in the outdoors. I don't want to be stuck in the house the rest of my life," Rita answered in a worried voice.

Eric looked directly into Rita's eyes and answered in a soft voice. "I understand," Dr. Forster said, "but if you don't have this done, you're not going to be able to continue your activities anyway. This knee is not going to improve itself. With the replacement you will be amazed at how little difference there is between the real and artificial knee, and your current pain should vanish." Eric got up from his chair and took Rita's hand in his. "Let us know what you want to do. In the meantime, if you need some pain medication let me know and I'll write a prescription for you."

"OK," Rita answered, "maybe it would help to get rid of this pain."

Eric leaned over the table and wrote a prescription. "Now, these pills should help with most of your pain, but they are not going to cure the osteoarthritis.

"I understand," said Rita as she took the prescription from him.

Eric left her with Jean so they could set up appointments with former patients and second opinion doctors if she felt it necessary. He also told her if she wanted him to do the surgery, an operation could be done in about four weeks. She thanked him with the first smile she had made since arriving at his office.

When he left the examination room, Rita thanked Jean for setting up the appointment with her boss. "He's really quite a guy, isn't he?" Rita said to Jean.

"Yes, he is. He's very talented and he's also very concerned for his patients. I've worked with all sorts of surgeons, but he's by far the best of the bunch."

Rita smiled back at Jean. "Yeah, and he's certainly very handsome. His wife must be ecstatic to be married to him. I know I sure as hell would be." She broke out in laughter at that thought and rolled back and forth while Jean Jensen agreed with a smile.

Rita stopped laughing and got up from her chair. "Jean, I don't think I need to talk to another surgeon about replacing my knee. I really don't want it to happen, but Dr. Forster has made it quite clear that I don't have a choice. This damn knee really hurts and I guess he's right about what needs to be done." She sat back down in a chair and put her hands on her aching knee. "Let me talk with my husband first, and then I'll give you a call so you can schedule the operation."

"Rita, you'll be OK. After you've decided what you want to do, let me know. In the meantime I can give you the names of all sorts of people who've had their knee replaced so you can get an opinion." Jean found it somewhat difficult working with her best friend, as most of her patients were people who she didn't know.

Rita smiled as she shook her head. "No, I don't think I need to do that. If I change my mind I'll let you know." She stood up again and wrapped her arms around Jean. "Thanks very much for getting me here. I really appreciate it." She kissed Jean on her forehead, and then headed out the door. She turned around and smiled at Jean. "If I agree to this operation, I expect to get several points in our next racquetball games."

Jean didn't say a thing. She just smiled at Rita and pointed her out of the office.

After rearranging the examining room, Jean went across the aisle to Dr. Forster's office. She knocked on the door and then opened it before he could answer. She found him sitting at his desk with his hands over his face and his elbows resting on the desk.

Jean was somewhat shocked by it and quickly asked, "Are you all right?"

Eric leaned back on his chair and smiled at Jean. "Yep, I'm fine. I think I'm just tired." He quickly changed their conversation. "Rita Dubois seems to be a very nice lady. Do you think she'll accept the operation?"

"Yes, I do. She's just scared about having it done, but then most of our patients feel the same way." Eric nodded in agreement as he stretched out his arms around his chair. His office had two chairs and a large window overlooking the Penobscot River. The sky was very gray and it was beginning to get dark even though it was only three thirty; Maine was so far northeast it really should be part of the Maritime time frame.

Jean finally sat down to go over Eric's schedule for Friday. The details of the operations were on his desk. "You've got two operations tomorrow morning in Waterville. Don Taylor is going to have a left hip replaced and Kent Douglas is having his right knee done. All the equipment has arrived at the hospital and the ball and socket sales rep will be there to oversee the hip operation."

Eric picked up Taylor's details and read them again. "Yep, we're going to use a new hip replacement part that has done quite well. It's our first use of it."

He leaned back again with his hands over the back of his head and closed his eyes. "I'm having dinner with Susan and the Meachams at five o'clock at the Hillsboro restaurant and then I'm heading down to Waterville."

Jean Jensen looked with concern at Dr. Forster. "Maybe you need to take some time off," she suggested as she felt he was in need of some rest.

"Well, we're going to spend the weekend at the Benoit Lodge in Bethel. The Meachams are going to join us. It should be fun. We're bringing our snowshoes, skis and a book or two in case we can't go outside."

Jean grinned at this thought. "That should be fun. When are you going?"

"Tomorrow afternoon when I leave the Waterville Hospital after these two guys have recovered from their operations. Then I'll head over to Bethel."

Jean Jensen was happy to hear what Dr. Forster was planning. She was aware that he and his wife, Susan, were not getting along, so maybe a weekend together might help. She also could not believe that Susan had problems with Eric. He was too nice a person not to love.

"I'll be back here Tuesday morning," he told Jean.

While she walked out the door, Eric got up from his desk and walked over to the window. He leaned his right hand on the side of the window and gazed down at the Penobscot River that flows from northern Maine into the Atlantic Ocean. His thoughts were of his wife Susan and what he hoped would be a recovery of their marriage.

Eric was very much in love with Susan, but he knew their relationship was beginning to come apart due to a fading day-to-day feeling between the two of them. Eric loved living in Maine, while Susan had a real problem with the lifestyle in Maine. She wanted to move back into a market like Boston where their affair started, but Eric couldn't see living in Boston.

Eric had hoped that he and Susan could work out their problems by spending the weekend together in Bethel, but that vanished when she insisted on inviting Jack and Janet Meacham.

He had planned to spend the weekend with just Susan, but she wanted to invite Jack and Janet Meacham, their closest friends. Maybe, he thought, there was something going on between Susan and Jack, but the more he thought of it the less he believed it. They were just good friends.

CHAPTER 2

The University of Maine is located in Orono, a small town a few miles north of Bangor. In relation to major state universities, Maine is relatively small but has a good reputation.

Sports are at best average, except for hockey, where Maine is recognized as one of the consistent best in the U.S. The hockey arena holds about 5,000 fans and seats are sold out for every game. They're part of the Hockey East conference that has other high quality hockey teams such as Boston University, Boston College, New Hampshire, and others of slightly lesser year-by-year talent. Maine has won the national title several times, while other Maine college sports don't do anywhere near as well as the hockey team. The attendance for football and basketball and other sports also doesn't come anywhere near the hockey attendance.

Dr. Eric Forster's wife Susan had been the women's soccer coach for the past three years. She was hired as the assistant coach five years ago, just after she married Eric, with the understanding she would take over as the soccer coach when the current head coach retired. This occurred two years after she accepted the job.

Susan stood about five and a half feet tall with short brown hair and brown eyes. She was a very attractive woman who was also in remarkable physical shape from her years of playing soccer and her continuous workouts. There wasn't any excessive fat in her body. By being in this shape she was able to convince her team to follow the same routine.

She was becoming very pleased with how well she was doing in improving the winning percentage of her soccer team. She was getting more girls to try out for the team and their attendance was increasing. Not like the hockey team, but very competitive with other women's sports, including basketball.

However, Susan wanted to coach a major college team located in a large city. She was not happy with living in the Bangor area and didn't like the move down to Lake Lucerne It was about a forty-minute drive to Orono that was miserable in the winter.

Susan walked down to Jack Meacham's office to make sure he knew about the dinner date, knocked on his door, and opened it when she heard his voice.

"Hi, Jack."

"Good afternoon, Susan, how are you?" he asked while getting up from his chair to reach for her hand. Jack Meacham was a well-built athlete standing just less than six feet tall. His brown hair was thick, but short with no appearance of balding. His arms were extremely muscular as was his body and he still looked young though he was in his mid thirties.

Jack Meacham was an assistant football coach who got this job when, as a professional halfback with the New England Patriots, he suffered a career-ending hip injury when he was tackled on the sideline. It occurred when he was in his prime and the end of his career created a mental problem. He couldn't handle not ever being able to play football again and it negatively affected his marriage to Janet even though she had nothing to do with his problems. In the meantime Maine was lucky to have gotten him to assist a team that rarely had a winning record, but now with a former all pro halfback on staff, potential high school running backs wanted to be taught by him.

Susan liked Jack as they both enjoyed the same lifestyle. Both were excellent athletes who continued exercising on a frequent basis even though their competitive days were history. Since arriving at the university they had become good friends.

She sat down and leaned forward on his desk. "Can I get a ride with you to dinner tonight? I'm going to leave my car here."

"Sure you can," Jack replied with a smile. "What time?"

"Well, dinner's at five so we'd better leave here about four thirty. And Eric is going to drop me off at our house. I'm coming back tomorrow with a neighbor. Then Eric is going to take my equipment and Janet's to Bethel.

Jack's eyes widened as he tried to figure out what he was just told. "Sounds confusing but no problem. I understand Eric's going to take Janet with him to Bethel since they'll both be down south tomorrow morning, so you'll be stuck with me." Jack was looking forward to spending more time with Susan and the ride over to the western part of the state should be a good beginning.

Susan grinned, then nodded her head. "That's right, you're going to suffer with me." She got up from her chair and headed out the door. "See you in half an hour."

The Pilot's Grill Restaurant was a classic place that had been in Bangor for over 50 years. The tables all had white table clothes with white napkins. The chairs were reasonably comfortable and for several customers there were cushioned seats for two. The waitresses all had been employed at Pilot's Grill for many years and in turn they knew their customers. The atmosphere was generally quiet since their customers were considerably older than those at most other restaurants.

The food was excellent and varied from fresh fish, shrimp, lobsters, and scallops cooked in a variety of ways. Their beef was thought to be the best in the city. The men had steaks while the two ladies ate fish.

If there appeared to be a problem it was that the patrons were mostly elderly people. Young people seemed to have ignored Pilot's Grill. The owner, Cliff Manchester, was conscious of this and tried hard to encourage young, married couples to have dinner at his restaurant. To date Manchester was somewhat disappointed at the outcome of his promotion.

During dinner Eric confirmed what was going to take place Friday. He would pick up Janet in Augusta and then head over to Bethel. Susan and Jack would go together sometime in the early afternoon, so they would probably be the first to arrive in Bethel.

Eric and Susan's marriage was beginning to disintegrate due to the differences in lifestyle. They still loved each other, but more like friends than husband and wife. Eric's mother was a lady who didn't hold back her feelings. She told him that he goofed in marrying Susan because she felt there was not enough common ground except for bedroom activity. She told her son that sexual encounters generally lasted less than an hour and then you'd have to find something else in common for the next twenty-three hours. His father excused himself to go outside during that conversation.

Eric wanted to get away with Susan for a long weekend to see if there was any hope of correcting their marital problems. He selected the three-day Presidents Day weekend in mid-February to go to the Benoit Lodge in Bethel, Maine, located in the state's western foothills. He reserved two rooms, each with a double bed, for arrival late on Friday afternoon and a checkout Monday afternoon.

The second room was for Jack and Janet Meacham, whom Susan invited in case Eric and Susan couldn't get along with each other; at least they'd have friends to deal with. Nonetheless, all four appeared to be looking forward to the weekend at the Benoit Lodge.

Eric first met Jack Meacham when Jack's hip began to deteriorate and Susan suggested he make an appointment to visit her husband to see what could be done to correct his problem. The answer was simple. He needed to have his hip replaced. He had heard the same suggestion in Boston, but he had ignored it thinking that it would heal itself. After several months of painful waiting he finally agreed to the operation. The result was dramatic. Jack was now able to walk without pain, but Eric told him that his competitive days were over and that he had to be careful not to get too close to the playing field. There was also the possibility of the hip coming apart if it was mistreated or hit by some of his football players.

During the summer and into the fall and early winter, the four became close friends and quite often had dinner together either at a restaurant or at one of their houses. And several times during the past summer the Meachams joined Eric and Susan at their house on Lake Lucerne.

As they finished dinner and the set-up for Friday, Eric grinned at Jack. "Let me warn you, Jack, that Susan will backseat drive you all the way over to Bethel," Eric said, receiving a responsive slap on his back from Susan. Then he told Janet, "I'll pick you up whenever you're ready."

"OK, I should be finished around two. I'll know more tomorrow." She pulled out her cell phone. "You can reach me on my cell phone." She wrote down her cell number and gave it to Eric.

"Eric nodded his head in agreement and replied, "That's OK. It will let me spend time with the patients' families and then get a quick lunch."

They all agreed, then Eric and Susan went to the Meacham house where he picked up Janet's equipment and then drove Susan down to their home on Lake Lucerne. Susan did not like driving this road in winter as it was two and a half miles down a hilly, winding, narrow road. Eric wanted to be sure she could handle the road. Since there hadn't been any snow for a while, the road was clear and relatively easy to drive. When they got to their house Eric loaded his SUV, hugged and kissed Susan as she urged him to drive carefully. He then headed off to Waterville about an hour and a half drive. Susan would get a ride to Orono from one of her neighbors, so she wouldn't have to drive her car up the hill.

Eric knew Susan did not like living on the lake, particularly in the winter when driving was a challenge. She had slid off the road more than once and had to get towed out by one of their neighbors. This led to more confrontations that negatively affected their marriage. She felt as though they were at odds end with too many subjects, and certainly their house location led the way. They were just not happy doing things together so the hope was this weekend at the Benoit Lodge would give them some time together and with friends to see if their problems were correctable.

She often stayed in a bedroom at the university instead of driving down to the lake. This made her mad. On occasion she would drive to Eric's office and then go down to the lake with him, so she didn't have to drive.

Eric preferred that they go by themselves to the Benoit Lodge but Susan was adamant about inviting the Meachams.

CHAPTER 3

On Thursday night, the Weather Channel's Friday forecast for Maine was for light snow by late afternoon with a pleasant weekend, perfect for outdoor winter activities. "Enjoy the weekend," announced the national weatherman as he signed off. "There's a storm way out in the Atlantic, but don't worry about it. It won't reach Maine."

However at about four o'clock Friday morning, Tom Siegel, Channel 2's secondary weatherman, was studying the weather facts pictured on his computer and then became concerned about the low that was scheduled to fade in the Atlantic after maybe brushing by Nova Scotia.

His concern was with a high that appeared to be preventing the low from moving to the east. The more he studied this, the more concerned he became. He thought about reaching the head weatherman, Sam Gunther, because he wanted to run his theory past him before he announced it on the air, but it was too early in the morning.

He couldn't find him or anyone else who might listen to his pending forecast. He still didn't buy the Weather Channel's forecast so when it came time to give his announcement early Friday morning, Siegel decided he'd better let his viewers know what he was thinking.

At five o'clock Friday morning the newscaster gave her report, and then turned it over to Siegel. "Good morning, Maine," he announced in an unusually serious voice. "I think we've got a potential problem heading our way." He pointed to his computerized map where the low was positioned. "There's a powerful low east of Massachusetts that appears to be a potential problem."

Tom Siegel was a handsome, articulate weather forecaster who had graduated from the University of Minnesota a year and a half ago. Since Bangor was a small market, it became the starting point for all sorts of TV personalities who had visions of eventually working for a network or in a large TV market. Thus the turnover at Channel 2 was relatively high since the young staff members seemed to spend as much time on their resumes as they did working.

Siegel was very popular with the younger audience and probably the older female viewers. However, he was not very popular with management, particularly, Doug Felty, the station manager. Felty had been with Channel 2 for many years and too often suffered the effects of his trainees. Siegel was of particular concern since he too often gave an incorrect forecast that created all sorts of internal and external problems.

Siegel continued with his forecast. "Now there's a high out in the Atlantic that is strong enough to push the low back toward Nova Scotia." He pointed to another storm that was coming across from upper New York. The Weather Channel had indicated that this storm would fade away before it got to Maine. Siegel shook his head. "I think this storm will increase in strength and will hit us sometime early this afternoon. I think it will start with freezing rain, then a lot of snow."

He explained what he thought would happen if certain conditions occurred. He also had the electronic maps showing the track of the storms. The first was a storm heading east across upper New York that was scheduled to fade before it got to Maine, but Siegel felt this storm was underrated. He felt it would actually gain strength as it came over Vermont and New Hampshire.

Next he described the massive low over the Atlantic Ocean that was forecast to miss Maine and end up east of Nova Scotia. If the low came under Nova Scotia, it would create a powerful northeaster that would hit all of Maine. If these two elements collided in western Maine that area would suffer with freezing rain, heavy winds, and a massive snowfall with significant drifting snow. The remainder of Maine would get a large snowfall and heavy winds with some possibility of freezing rain.

Tom Siegel believed the low would come through Nova Scotia and into northern Maine as a northeaster and slowly come across the state from the northeast. He showed these possibilities to his viewers by tracking a situational storm, first across northern and western Maine and then clobbering the remainder of the state.

Since Siegel was a newcomer to Channel 2, he was in charge of the morning weather forecast starting at five o'clock when very few people were watching TV. Later in the morning Siegel's audience dramatically increased as he warned his viewers to be cautious for the remainder of the day and said he would be back with more details later. He said, "I might be wrong, but there is a distinct possibility of a major storm heading toward us, so I'd suggest getting home early this afternoon, checking your firewood, hooking up your generators, and doing some grocery shopping because if this storm hits us, you might be stuck at home for a few days."

He related the story of the last major northeaster to hit Maine in the winter. It was 1998 when the entire northern two-thirds of Maine was clobbered by a major storm that knocked out power for up to ten days. That storm was also not forecast properly.

Next Tom Siegel illustrated the coming storm on the computerized map of the state of Maine and the Canadian Maritime Provinces. He again showed how the low in the Atlantic would gather moisture and strength as it hooked around Nova Scotia and then pelted Maine with a monster snowstorm.

He then illustrated the western storm that was headed across Vermont and New Hampshire Friday morning and how it would collide with the northeaster to create a significant snowstorm, particularly in the western part of Maine.

For those who were watching TV Friday morning, the concern was real. Was this storm going to hit Maine and if so, when and how bad? Good or not, the number of viewers at seven in the morning was relatively large so many people heard Siegel's forecast, though many ignored it. However, a majority of the viewers paid attention to what he was saying and many contacted family friends. Tom Siegel continued on with his discussion about the storm. He turned to the TV audience and warned his viewers. "I think this is going to be a major storm, larger and with more snow and ice than anything we have seen for a long time. There will also be significant drifting of all this snow because of all the wind that's accompanying the storm." His voice conveyed his concern over what would be happening later in the day.

Siegel stood just less than six feet with abundant black hair and a thin body. He was young and handsome, with a voice that could best be described as somewhere between a tenor and a baritone. He was relatively new to Channel 2 and he too often misinterpreted the weather facts, giving a rainy forecast when the sun was shining. There wasn't anyone on staff that early in the morning who could dispute his forecasts and this had put his job in jeopardy more than once. However, he was popular with the morning viewers, particularly women, and his ratings were the highest in the Bangor market for morning and noon news reports, so any negative move on management's part could possibly hurt the station.

Since Bangor, Maine, was a small TV market it was a training spot for young graduates who had majored in weather and climate or television reporting. To succeed as a weatherman, you had to be articulate, good looking, and knowledgeable about the causes and effects of weather. Siegel was one of these young and aggressive reporters. He had specialized in climate and weather forecasting at the University of Minnesota and was offered and accepted a job as the alternative weatherman at Channel 2. He was given airtime when few people were watching TV such as early in the morning and on weekends when there was no one in management to check his forecasts.

The station manager Doug Felty was a longtime employee at Channel 2 who had a reputation for sticking to the facts when reporting a story as he didn't want something to come back to his station should one of his reporters get the facts wrong. Felty was in his early sixties and what hair he had was white. He was tall, just over six feet, heavy, and always looked as though he'd slept in his clothes. He had suffered through the training programs of his reporters, weather people, and anchor personnel, and when he was getting dressed at home, he was shocked to hear Siegel's latest forecast since their prime time weather expert hadn't forecast anything like a northeaster.

When he got to his office it was well after seven. Doug was shaking with anger as he yelled at his secretary, "Jill, track down Siegel and have him come to my office. Now!" It didn't take much thought on Jill's part to see that Doug Felty was madder than hell.

Jill Hudson nodded her head and ran to the end of studio where she found Tom Siegel studying his weather maps and the Internet. He had a puzzled look on his face. "Tom, Mr. Felty wants to see you."

"OK, but let me finish this project first," Tom answered without looking up from his printouts. "Man, have we got one hell of a storm heading our way!" He sounded excited.

"Tom, he wants to see you now." Jill emphasized the word "now." The tone of her voice indicated that she was carrying Doug Felty's anger.

"Why? Is he mad?" Tom looked a little worried as he refastened his tie and put on his green TV jacket.

Jill was concerned with what Tom had forecast because what he was predicting would probably affect their TV time buyers. "That's an understatement. I think he's concerned about your forecast this morning," answered Jill with a concerned look.

"Hmm," answered Siegel, frowning, still studying his data before looking up at an insistent Jill. "OK, let's go."

Siegel was somewhat worried about what would happen when they reached Felty's office. Felty was on the phone, but glared at Tom when he knocked on his door. Felty waved him into a chair in front of his desk while trying to soothe an advertiser who was on the other end of the phone line.

"Sam, if Tom Siegel says there's a major storm coming, I am certain he means it, so it's best we warn our viewers about this possibility. OK? If there is any change in this forecast, we'll let you know. Thanks for calling." He hung up the phone and glared at Siegel.

"I hope to hell you're right about this storm. This guy," he pointed to the phone, "is the owner of the Maine Seaport Lodge in Bar Harbor and he's already getting cancellations for this weekend because of your forecast. So, tell me, how can you say this storm is going to do what you say it is when channels 5 and 7—even the Weather Channel—are not saying anything about a major storm?"

Felty continued, "Did you check your forecast with Sam Gunther?" Gunther was the lead weatherman who had been at Channel 2 for seemingly a lifetime. He was also very conservative in his forecast so he wouldn't frighten his audience.

"No, I couldn't reach him. It was too early in the morning to call him," answered a nervous Tom Siegel. He had never seen Mr. Felty this angry.

Doug Felty got out of his chair, went to his window, and looked at the sky, which was cloudy but inactive. He brushed his balding gray hair with his right hand and noticed that his head was damp, all from worrying about Siegel's forecast.

Tom Siegel slinked down in his chair. "All I can do is report the facts and that's what I did." He proceeded to explain the potential movement of these two storms and the effect they could have on the state.

"There's a low off in the Atlantic that everyone seems to think will head for Nova Scotia and totally miss us, but I think they're all wrong. There's a high way out in the Atlantic that I think will force that low into us as a northeaster." Siegel was still excited about this coming event and how he figured it out before anyone else. The more he talked the higher he sat and for a moment it looked like he might fall off the front of the chair.

Doug Felty frowned and began to turn red. Tom thought he looked something like Santa Claus in a business suit. "Damn it, if you're wrong you'd better update your resume. You could add this in with all the other wrong forecasts you've passed on to our viewers." He banged the desk with his fist and increased his volume. "I sometimes think that you're our version of the comic weatherman and this is why your ratings are so high. No one believes you but you're entertaining." *Damn it,* Felty thought to himself, *how could we have hired this jerk?*

Siegel hung his head and answered Felty's comments, "I'm sorry, but if I didn't warn our listeners and they got caught in what I believe is coming, they'd be in deep trouble." He sat up in his chair and looked at a mad boss who was at a loss for words.

Felty finally banged his desk again. "Have you any idea what this forecast will do for our advertisers if you're wrong? There are all sorts of President's Day promotions going on with our car dealers, the lodges on the coast, and the restaurants here in town and at the Bangor mall. If you're wrong I wish you luck in your next employment." Doug was starting to get an ache in his stomach so he reached for a Tums in his desk drawer.

Damn it, Doug thought, *why don't I retire from all this crap? I don't need this.* His daughter Janet was married to a former football player who certainly had enough money to properly support her and she was also a very good grammar school teacher. His wife had died several years ago in a car accident, so he only had to support himself and that shouldn't be a problem. The problem was putting up with these young kids who figured they were destined to rule their viewers.

Siegel shrugged his shoulders and had no answer for Doug Felty's anger, so the room became silent.

Felty started to calm himself and then asked in a quiet voice, "Why haven't the other stations figured this possible...and I emphasize, possible...storm is coming?" Felty sank back in his chair, loosened his tie, and closed his eyes, hoping Tom Siegel would disappear.

He didn't. Doug Felty leaned his head on his hands as Tom Siegel continued his reason for his weather forecast. "The other weather guys have a habit of waiting until noon to give a forecast and then they usually use what the government's computers are telling them." Siegel spread his hands to emphasize his thinking. "I think the government forecast is wrong."

Felty looked out his window. "So, everyone else is wrong and you're right. It's eight o'clock and there isn't any snow falling." The sky was cloudy but it didn't look any different to him than any other cloudy day.

"It will start between two and three here but earlier in the west," commented Tom Siegel with confidence that he knew what he was forecasting was correct and that no one else saw the same thing.

Felty turned back to Siegel. "My daughter Janet Meacham, her husband, and a couple of their friends are headed over to the Benoit Lodge in Bethel for the weekend. What am I supposed to tell her?"

"She's probably heard the forecast," answered Tom Siegel, "so she must have made other plans." Doug Felty shook his head and went to his phone to call his daughter Janet.

As he picked up the phone and started to punch in her phone number, his secretary Jill rushed into the room. "Before you make a call, Mr. Babcock is on line two. He is most anxious to talk with you."

Felty lowered his head and murmured in an angry voice. "Damn it, Tom, if you're wrong, you're fired. I can't have inaccurate forecasts coming out of here. This is another advertiser who has a special promotion this weekend. I can imagine what he wants to tell me." Felty pointed his finger at Siegel and waved him out of his office. *This is all that I need now,* he thought. Babcock was the owner of several auto dealerships in Bangor and his largest advertiser.

Tom Siegel quickly got out of his chair and headed for the door without saying anything. He understood the look Doug Felty was giving him, so he wanted to get back to his desk so he could further track this potential storm.

"Hi, Doug, it's Phil Babcock. Now about this storm..."

Doug Felty knew he'd be on the phone for a long time so he slouched back in his chair and put his feet on his desk and promptly forgot to call Janet.

CHAPTER 4

The Friday morning sky was overcast and looked somewhat ominous. Janet Meacham had already left for her meeting in Augusta with another teacher at six o'clock so they hadn't heard Siegel's forecast; even if they had, they wouldn't have put much faith in it. Her teacher meetings started at eight and would run until noon when they'd all have lunch and then head back home.

Eric called Janet on her cell phone at about nine thirty after his first operation was completed.

"Hi, Janet, it's Eric. What time do you want me to pick you up?"

"Hi, Eric. I've got a lunch date I can't miss so I'm looking at sometime after one thirty. Is that OK?"

Eric answered with an OK. "Where do I pick you up?" He had pen in hand, waiting for the name of the building.

"It's the building next to the Capitol. I can't remember its name." Janet searched her papers for the name of the building.

"No problem. I'll find it."

After Janet hung up, her cell phone rang again. "Hello, this is Janet Meacham."

An aging, tired voice answered, "This is your father." He sounded different than usual.

"Hi, Dad." She was concerned at the sound of his voice. "Are you OK?" she asked.

"I'm fine, but I forgot to call you earlier. Are you still planning to go over to Bethel today?"

Janet thought he sounded worried. "We sure are. Why?" She started to become a little worried about her father.

"Well, our weather guy, Tom Siegel, says we're in for a northeaster storm sometime this afternoon, even though I don't completely buy it."

Janet thought for a while and frowned to herself. "Do you think it's true, Dad? You know he's been wrong before with forecasting storms while the sun was shining."

Janet, I don't know. Siegel's adamant about it, so I wanted to pass it along before you leave."

"Thanks, Dad, I'll check with Eric Forster. He's driving me over to Bethel."

Janet hung up and went to a window to check the sky. Nothing spectacular was happening and it was already about ten o'clock. *I don't want to miss this weekend,* she thought. *We all need time away from work.* Jack was to pick up Susan at her office around two this afternoon. She tried Jack's cell phone, but got a busy signal.

At the Waterville hospital, Eric performed his second operation, a left hip replacement. The operation was on a middle-aged worker with Champion Paper in Skowhegan, a town to the west of Waterville. The operation was successful and when finished he waited until he could meet with the patient's family to let them know everything went well and it would be another hour before the anesthesia wore off. He was right on schedule. He met with the nursing staff to go over what both men would need. Then he met with the therapists who would work with both men to get them out of bed and walking by late afternoon.

After meeting and comforting both patients' families, he went out to his SUV and was surprised at how gray the sky was. He then headed over to a Wendy's where he picked up a cheeseburger with fries, then drove down to Augusta, about 15 miles south, to pick up Janet. A light snow was falling as he parked his SUV and waited for Janet to arrive.

He thought about Janet and how much he enjoyed being with her. She and her husband Jack had come down to the lake several times during the past summer and he and Janet often went sailing together since Susan and Jack didn't enjoy boating. It was obvious that Janet enjoyed sailing as she learned very quickly how to sail his boat, a relatively small 16-footer.

Her appearance in a bathing suit was something that caught his attention. She was tall and well structured, topped by beautiful long blonde hair. But what impressed Eric the most was her attitude. She was very positive and friendly, but Eric also had the feeling that something negative was happening between Janet and Jack. They just seemed to be very cool to each other.

When Janet finished her meetings and lunch at about two she exited the building with several other teachers. Her presence impressed Eric as he was waiting for her. She stood out from all the other teachers at the meeting. He got out of his car to greet her with an embrace, and then put her luggage in the back of his SUV.

Janet was a sixth-grade teacher who truly loved working with young children, particularly those in her class as they were all beginning to mature.

She enjoyed teaching them and, in turn, she was popular with her students and with their parents. Her good looks made visits by the students' fathers quite a bit more frequent than normal.

"Are you ready for the weekend?" he asked while arranging her luggage and equipment.

"You bet," Janet answered with a relaxed smile.

"Did you have good meetings?" Eric asked as Janet fastened her seat belt and stretched out her legs.

"It was all right, but there was all sorts of bickering about class sizes for next year." She related how everyone wanted to reduce class sizes, and no one seemed to know where the money would come from, but she said it was still a good meeting and everyone got their two cents in. She smiled and looked over to Eric, who was waiting for traffic to open up so he could get on the main street. "But it's really fun to be a teacher and most of the people at the meeting have the same feeling. Kids need all the help they can get from us."

She then realized she had done a great deal of talking, so she settled back in her seat and said, "However, I'm looking forward to this weekend. I really need the time off and I know Jack does as well. It's been a long winter and I'm tired of the snow and cold even though we're headed for more. At least this will be a fun time in the snow," she offered as she looked at Eric. "Oh, I forgot to ask, how did your operations go?"

"OK. They both went well and there should be no complications. They'll both recover on schedule. I did a left hip and a right knee." Eric glanced over at Janet as he spoke. He had always been impressed with Janet for her good looks and body, as well as her mind. He figured she had to be an outstanding teacher. *Maybe,* he thought, *I'd go back to sixth grade if I could have Janet as my teacher.*

Janet laughed as she said, "Maybe one day you'll transplant entire bodies. Want a new head? Call Dr. Forster." She grinned then asked, "Has anyone ever replaced the wrong hip?"

He laughed and answered with what seemed to be a kidding remark. "It has happened so we mark the knee or hip, 'yes' or 'no' when the patient's fully awake. That way we don't replace the wrong one." He looked over to Janet who couldn't believe what she just heard. "No, it's true," explained Eric. "It has happened where the wrong hip or knee got replaced."

"You're joking." Janet could never seem to know when Eric was serious or kidding. So she assumed this was a joke.

"Nope, we do it all the time. Seriously!" He seemed serious as he looked over at her, but the smile on his face made it questionable to Janet.

Eric joined Janet in laughing about that possibility and then changed the subject as she looked out the side window. "Boy, it's really beginning to snow hard."

She looked over at Eric with a concerned expression. "Dad called me this morning and said his weatherman predicted a major storm for this afternoon. Everyone else said we'd just get a few flurries."

Eric headed northwest on Route 27 to the junction of Route 2. These were all two-lane roads that were somewhat dangerous because of the large amount of traffic going east and west. There were no east-west freeways in Maine, New Hampshire, and Vermont although the politicians had talked for years about building one.

From the junction of 2 and 27 Bethel would be about 50 miles away, but with the amount of snow falling it would probably take them over an hour to get to the Benoit Lodge.

Janet related her conversation with her father about Tom Siegel's forecast for a major storm. "I just didn't give it much credence," Janet added, staring out at the snow getting heavier. "But maybe he's right this time. Golly, I hope not!"

Traffic was slow but Eric felt comfortable in his SUV as he placed the Jeep in four-wheel drive to give him more stability on the road. What cars were on the road were moving slowly and even the trucks had slowed down to avoid spraying snow on the cars behind them. The wind was beginning to pick up, which made the visibility more difficult.

Janet was staring out the front window. "Boy, I'm glad you're driving. It's really nasty. "All I can see is white," said Janet.

Everything was quickly turning white including the road and that concerned Eric. "Let's check the radio to see if there is anything happening we should know about," he said.

The weather report came about 10 minutes later when Eric had driven past the junction of highways 27 and 2 to a small logging town called Wilton . The reporter sounded worried about the change in weather. "We've changed our forecast," he said. "As we indicated to you this past hour there appears to be a major storm headed into Maine that will hit the western hills first, so if you are headed in that direction, drive with caution because there will probably be a combination of snow and freezing rain falling along with significant winds in the foothills."

The announcer was quiet for a moment and then came back on the air. "I understand the state police are stopping vehicles from going on interstate 95, so if you're headed that way, turn around and head home. We fully expect westbound highways are also going to be shut down. It is important that if you're on one of these highways, or any road for that matter, get back to your house as quickly as possible," suggested the radio announcer in a very calm, yet serious voice. He continued, "From all indications this storm is going to be a very nasty and dangerous one, so please get home. You might want to make a quick stop at your grocery store to stock up with a couple of days' food, because I will be surprised if we don't lose power later this afternoon."

"Damn it!" Eric said as he pounded his hand on the steering wheel. "This is all we need. It's too late to turn back so we'd better head for the lodge."

"Whatever you think is best," Janet answered without committing herself to any alternative. She was concerned about the condition of the road in front of them as it was becoming thick with snow, but so far Eric's SUV was handling it quite well. The windshield wipers began to freeze so Eric had to reach out while driving to bang the ice off the blades. Janet tried to do the same on her side of the front seat but couldn't reach the blades.

"It would take us at least a couple of hours to get back to Bangor, but Bethel's about thirty miles from here so we should get there about four. Jack and Susan probably left about two and a half hours ago and they are probably on this road, if they're not already at the lodge." Jack checked his odometer so he could plot out the distance they needed to travel.

Janet gazed over at Eric and with a worried voice said, "I hope the ladies who came down to Augusta will be able to get home before they close 95."

"Well, if they left about the same time as us, they should be home by now. If not, I hope they can find someplace to stay." Eric was also very concerned about anyone driving anywhere in Maine.

He pulled the road map out of the storage compartment and passed it to Janet. "Check and see if I'm right about the distance and then you might want to call Jack and even the Benoit Lodge." It was a few minutes before four and the atmosphere was getting dark, making driving even more difficult because the headlights were reflecting off the snow.

Janet studied the map and came up with the same estimate, about thirty miles. She dialed Jack's cell phone and got nothing, then tried her cell and got the same response. "Nothing," she said, "Maybe they're in an area where cell phones don't work. I'll try the lodge and see if they've heard from them."

She dialed and got nothing but static. "Nothing, Eric. I can't believe this. It feels as though we're all alone on this road. Maybe even the state." And looking out the window she didn't see another car.

Eric drove very slowly on Route 2 as the snow and rain pelted his SUV. Janet began to get nervous. Eric felt the same but he couldn't let her know his feelings. Everything was blanketed in white and the wind was actually moving the SUV. It was now getting dark and difficult to see what side of the road he was driving on, but at least he was alone on the road. There were no other cars or trucks on the highway and that gave Eric an eerie feeling. But at least it made the driving safer.

The snow was mixing with freezing rain so Eric lowered the SUV to its lowest gear and the four-wheel drive also to its lowest drive. They were moving slowly but at least they were moving and going reasonably straight. "Janet," Eric explained, "there isn't an alternative to continuing. If we stop it might be difficult to get moving again. We're going to get to the lodge soon. OK?" He looked over to Janet with a confident smile and patted her knee.

"OK," she answered in a very positive voice.

About a half hour later Janet asked, "Eric, how much farther do you think it'll be?" Janet asked with a nervous voice. It seemed to her that they might have passed the entrance to the Benoit Lodge.

"It's just a couple of miles till we get to their entrance and then it's up hill to the lodge. We'll be OK," he said, while again patting her knee. "It's just harder than hell to see where the damn road is." The snow was getting deeper and the freezing rain was occasionally falling, which made driving even more difficult. They hadn't seen another car for the past half hour. The windshield wipers were starting to get coated with ice again so Eric reached out to grab the wiper in front of him to bang the ice off it. It worked fairly well, but the wind was getting stronger and it sent the rain and snow hard onto the car and it began to pile up as snow banks along the road.

It was as though someone on the road was shaking Eric's SUV. Eric began to worry about what might happen if they didn't get to the Benoit Lodge before the Jeep stopped running. At the same time he felt concern for Janet, who was fighting off her fear over what the northeaster was doing to them.

Eric began to worry about getting stuck somewhere on this road. If that happened it might be a long time before someone rescued them, so it was vital that they get to the Benoit Lodge as soon as possible. There was no way he and Janet could possibly walk to some house since there was nothing visible on this road.

Janet began to talk. "Dad told me that his weatherman, Tom Siegel, forecast this storm this morning but no one believed him. The weather forecast last night said it should be OK today. Boy, did they screw up. I've never seen it this bad. I wonder where Jack and Susan are. I hope they're all right." She looked as though she was about to cry and she couldn't stop talking. "Do you think we should maybe stop?" she asked, knowing what the answer would be.

"Hang on, Janet. I think I see the lodge sign." Off on the right was a sign nearly covered with snow and ice so Eric stopped the car and Janet ran out of the car through the snow and wiped the snow off the sign. It read: *Benoit Lodge, Left ½ mile*. "OK, Janet, we're going to make it." Eric breathed a sigh of relief and thanked God for getting them off Route 2.

Janet told him about the snow and ice she encountered while walking over to the sign. "Eric, that snow really hurt my face. It felt like a flurry of needles. It's horrible out there."

After he had gone the half mile, Eric could barely see the Benoit Lodge entrance since the sun had just about set and darkness was beginning to take over. There were no other tracks on the drive so obviously no one had driven up recently. He made the turn onto the lodge's driveway at about as slow a speed as the SUV could handle to prevent it from sliding off the road. He then accelerated to gain momentum to make it up the incline to the lodge. Even with his four-wheel drive he was spinning wheels because of the depth of the snow and the ice beneath the snow. He got the car up about a quarter mile when his SUV stopped going forward and began to slide back down the hill. To prevent it from going all the way down, Eric put the SUV in reverse and steered it off the road.

The Jeep clunked into a mass of what appeared to be bushes and quickly came to a stop. Janet was tensed out as she bounced forward and hung on to the dashboard, breathing deeply. She was close to tears, but was relieved to have the Jeep stopped.

Eric turned off the engine and all they could hear was the snow and rain pelting the SUV. He reached his right hand over at a very relieved Janet and said with a smile, "Welcome to the Benoit Lodge. I don't think we're far from it so if we put on our snowshoes we should be able to walk there in a few minutes." He said this hopefully because he didn't want to worry Janet anymore that she already was. Eric was concerned about the walk up to the lodge in this snowstorm. They had to make it to the lodge to be safe.

Janet was struggling to get her down jacket on and finally got her arms through the sleeves punching Eric in his chest in the process. Eric added with a grin, "Anyway, this is what we planned to do this weekend so we'll get an early start on snow-shoeing. Janet didn't say anything and Eric could feel she was beginning to panic. He needed her to get involved quickly before she worried too much about the weather. "The people at the lodge can probably come down here with a snowmobile to get our suitcases."

Eric asked, "Can you reach the snowshoes?"

"I think so," Janet turned around in her seat and slid over the back of the front seat into the back seat so she could reach the equipment in the back of the SUV. She handed Eric his snowshoes, opened her door and started to put hers on. The snow and sleet were coming down so hard it was nearly impossible to see anything.

Eric opened his door and put his snowshoes on. "Do you see our ski poles?"

"Yep."

"We might need them."

"OK"

After she got her snowshoes on Janet opened her door and stepped out into the storm. "God, this is horrible! I hope we don't have far to go." She turned her head away from the snow and sleet that were blasting directly down the driveway. There had to be at least a foot of snow on the driveway. Eric asked her if she had something to cover her face. She didn't.

Eric thought for a moment before telling Janet, "At least it's not really cold but the wind is horrible, Janet, so walk behind me, hang on to my jacket and keep your head facing the ground looking at the back of my snowshoes. It'll keep the snow and ice off your face. We'll be OK," he said, holding his right arm around her shoulders. She put her ski poles back into the car. It was reasonably easy to pick out the driveway because it was the only area without trees, but their vision was limited from the snow and darkness at the end of the day.

Both Janet and Eric were in good shape but the elements put all sorts of roadblocks in their way. The snow was still roaring horizontally and was mixing with freezing rain. They were both tired, but they knew they had to keep going. After about fifteen minutes Eric shouted into the wind, "I think I see the lodge." Janet raised her head and she too could see the lights from the Benoit Lodge about one hundred yards ahead. Even with the miserable weather, the lodge was impressive.

It seemed to take forever to walk the last distance, but when they finally reached the porch they collapsed on the snow-covered steps. Then Eric fell down on his back. After resting for a minute or so, he took off their snowshoes while Janet looked at Eric's face and began to laugh. "You look like Frosty the snowman. You're covered with snow and ice." She fell backward laughing. "And thank you for getting me here." She sat up, hugged him around his shoulders, and kissed him on his snowy cheek. "Now, let's see if Jack and Susan are here," she said as they headed to the front door.

CHAPTER 5

At two o'clock Jack Meacham finally got to Susan's office. He had an embarrassed look on his face. "Susan, sorry I'm late.

"What happened?"

"Oh, hell, I got stuck interviewing a potential recruit and it took longer than I anticipated. We really want this guy because he's a good kid, a good student, and a hell of an athlete. He thinks he wants to stay in Maine, so maybe we'll get him." He sat down in front of her desk and discussed what the recruit would do for the team.

"Did you get him to commit?" asked Susan.

"I think so," replied a grinning Jack Meacham, who pounded his hand on her desk. He was very pleased with himself over the prospect of signing up this potentially good halfback.

Susan Reddy got up and looked out her window at the snow that seemed to be getting heavier. "That's OK. It's just after two. We should be there well before dinner, but God, the weather looks terrible. I've heard that we're in for a major storm today."

Jack came over to the window. "Maybe we should call Janet's dad before we start. Have you heard from Janet or Eric?"

"I tried to call, but got no answer on his cell phone or from the lodge."

Jack frowned as he sat back in his chair. "Maybe the storm caught them on the way over. Cell phones don't work in that area, but you should have been able to reach the lodge by telephone. Let me try it." He dialed the number and got nothing, not even a ring.

Susan picked up her phone and gave it to Jack so he could call Janet's father. Doug Felty finally answered, "Hi, Jack. You're still here? I thought you'd be at the lodge by now."

"No, I got hung-up, but now we're wondering what the weather is like on the way over." He doodled with a pencil while talking, glancing up at Susan. "We can't reach Eric on his cell phone and we can't get through to the Benoit Lodge."

"It's hard to believe this, but I think our jerk weatherman's got it right this time. There's a hell of a storm out there, Jack and it's going to get worse, so you'd better get home as soon as you can. I can imagine her road is going to be like a ski hill." The Forster house on Lake Lucerne was down some two and a half miles on what was called the Lodge Road. The road started with a very steep and long hill that when icy became, as residents called it, the toboggan slide.

Doug Felty offered another thought. "Jack, let me get Siegel on the line so he can fill you in on this storm and what might be happening out west. OK?"

"Yeah, thanks Doug." Susan looked at Jack and shrugged her shoulders. "I guess we might not be going...damn it! I've been looking forward to this weekend. Now it sounds like it's not going to happen." She looked out the window again to see the snow getting heavier and the wind stronger. He then turned on the speaker so Susan could hear what was going on.

Felty was back on the phone. "Jack, Tom Siegel is here and he can better explain what's happening. I'll put us on the speakerphone if I can figure out how to do it. Jill!" Jack heard Doug Felty get his secretary Jill to connect him to the speakerphone.

"Hello, Mrs. Forster, this is Tom Siegel. Mr. Felty wants me to tell you about this storm." Siegel hesitated for a moment before relating what the storm was doing. "Well, the worst is yet to come, though the western part of the state has been getting a taste of this storm for at least the last two hours. We got a lot of snow falling now and shortly we'll be getting some freezing rain that should create some very bad driving conditions. When it's finally over it will take the snowplows a couple of days to get rid of all this snow and ice. I expect we might get as much as three feet of snow in certain parts of the state, particularly the west. And I have a feeling that we'll see a lot of trees falling over because of the ice buildup and this can bring downed power and phone lines. With this heavy wind there are going to be some massive snowdrifts.

"We're about to go on the air with a special weather report to tell our viewers what they can expect and it isn't good. I also think the state will soon be telling Maine citizens to get off the roads and into their homes. It's going to be one of the worst storms to hit us in a long time."

Jack Meacham asked, "What you're saying is that there is no way we can get over to Bethel this afternoon."

"Not even just now, but for a couple of days. I would suggest getting home as soon as you can before the roads become completely impassable.

This storm is a wicked one. I think we'll get over three feet of snow, mixed at times with freezing rain." Siegel sounded joyful as the storm was saving his job and the more snow that fell, the better his chances of hanging onto his job and the more popular he was becoming.

Jack said, "Doug, I'll drive Susan home. We should be OK. It's about a forty-minute drive in good weather." Susan had gotten a ride to work with one of her neighbors this morning since Eric left for Waterville Thursday night, so there was no other way she could get home.

"Thanks, Tom. I don't like what you're telling me but I appreciate it anyway. Doug, I'll give you a call when I get her home, if the phones are still working. The cell phone doesn't work at the lake." Jack looked over at Susan, who nodded her approval, then told Doug, "We'd better get out of here now. Thanks, again."

Susan hung up the phone, heaved a sigh of anguish followed by a few four-letter words, then slid down in her chair. Their long-planned weekend at the Benoit Lodge was just snowed out. "Damn it," she shouted as she banged her hand on her chair's arm.

Susan and Jack got into his Land Rover to begin the trip to Lake Lucerne . The roads were still in reasonably good shape as the plows were still able to keep up with the snow, but that would soon change. They got to Interstate 95 without any problems and with the four-wheel drive in operation, the driving was not too bad. There were only a few cars on the road, but suddenly a semi roared by them causing Jack to slow down his Land Rover because he couldn't see anything from all the snow it blew against his SUV.

Jack cursed the truck driver. "Those bastards should know better than to speed when the road's full of snow. I'd love to beat the shit out of him." He pounded his steering wheel as though it was the truck driver's head. "Damn! Damn! Damn!" he shouted.

Jack really wasn't looking forward to the weekend at the Benoit Lodge since he and Janet hadn't done anything together for months and the odds of this changing were not promising. In a kidding mode, he put a sexy nighty in her suitcase to see if this might help change anything so he could find out if there was still some attraction between them. He didn't believe it possible, *but what the hell,* he thought, *we're going to be in the same bed for the first time in months.* Maybe we can relive our earlier years.

He was also aware that Eric and Susan were not getting along together, but that had mostly to do with lifestyle and not love. Jack enjoyed the time he spent with Susan, but he didn't know if she felt anything similar.

As they continued the drive to Susan's house, she looked over at Jack with a worried look. "Jack, do you think Eric and Janet are OK? Maybe they got caught in this storm before they got there."

Jack tapped his hand on the steering wheel. "They left Augusta at about one thirty so they should have gotten to the lodge by about three thirty if the weather is no worse than what we have here."

"Yeah, but Siegel says the storm hit there first," said a worried Susan.

"I'm sure Eric's a good driver. If they couldn't get to the lodge, then I would think they'd stop at some motel along the way. And that would be interesting," said Jack with a cynical smile. He envisioned a romantic encounter between his wife and Eric Forster in some motel in the middle of nowhere where there would be nothing else to do but make love.

Susan shook her head and slinked back in her seat. "I can't believe how this weekend has gone to hell. It was so nice yesterday that I can't believe this is all happening. It's a nightmare!" *But,* she thought to herself, *maybe this will be a fun weekend anyway.* It would give her a chance to be alone with Jack Meacham.

But she was really looking forward to the weekend with Eric even though she insisted on inviting the Meachams. She had a love for Eric that was still strong, even though their marriage was in jeopardy due to a difference in lifestyle.

She looked out her side window at the snow that was falling even faster than when they left Orono. She looked back at Jack and smiled at him as he carefully drove his SUV along the Interstate. Susan had wanted to get to know him better ever since he came to Maine. His reputation as a professional football player impressed Susan as did his incredible good looks and muscular build.

She had formally met him at the University of Maine when he arrived from Boston. In those days Jack was not in a very good humor since his professional football days were prematurely over from his hip injury and he was still madder than hell about what happened.

Before leaving the Brewer area, Susan suggested stopping at the grocery store so they could stock up for the weekend. The store was full of all sorts of people filling up their shopping carts with enough food and water to last several weeks. It took Susan and Jack nearly an hour to fill their cart and to check out. They picked canned food and some fresh meat that they could stock outside in the snow if the power was off.

They got back on Highway 1-A going east from Bangor toward the coast. Much had changed in the hour they spent shopping as the road was now suffering from snow and drifts that the plows couldn't keep up with. When they got to the Upper Dedham Road off 1-A the road hadn't been plowed and the depth of the snow made driving very slow and treacherous.

"I hate this road," Susan said in a quiet yet angry voice. "It's narrow, it's hilly, there are no shoulders, and too many people have no concept of how drive on this road even on a clear day. I'm surprised more accidents don't happen here. The road has no shoulders so if you go off the pavement, your car would probably turn over."

She continued on about her anger over the road. "With all the traffic on this road, you'd think the message would get through to the town that they need to work on making this road safer." Susan let out another batch of four-letter words that somewhat shocked Jack. He laughed at her anger while stroking her leg to try and calm her down.

Susan continued. "Jack, maybe you'd better stay at our place tonight. I don't like the idea of you traveling alone up the hill." Jack lived in Bangor, about twenty minutes away on a good day.

He nodded his head in agreement. "I think you're right. I don't think I can get back to Bangor." Jack's SUV was sliding as it made its way up a fairly steep and curved section, but they made it to the top without any real problem. He turned in at Lodge Road and the interesting part of the trip was just starting. The wind was howling in the parking lot, but was held away on the road through the woods when he began the descent.

The road was recently blacktopped but it hadn't changed the very steep section that began shortly after they passed the lodge parking lot. A steep short turn to the right was quickly followed by what the residents called the toboggan slide. It was a long section that went straight down a steep hill and turned to the left when it hit the base.

Jack looked at the road in front of him that was full of unplowed snow. He lowered all his gears to the lowest level and slowly began his trip down the road. "Here we go, hang on," Jack said as he lightly pressed on the accelerator. "This road is a challenge even when there isn't any snow on the ground and I hope to hell no one is coming up."

Susan gripped the dashboard and in a panicked voice told Jack, "Eric has always told me to keep momentum up while going down this hill in weather like this. Only I can't see the road. Can you?" The road was completely covered with snow and tree limbs had bent over so they somewhat covered the road. It was like going through a car wash.

Jack didn't reply right away as he was trying to make out the road in front of him. He felt his heart begin to race. "I can see it fairly well, but the snow is clobbering the windshield and now it's starting to rain." The windshield began to freeze over from the rain, so Jack opened his window and stuck his head out so he could see the road. It was difficult to maintain a set direction because of the snow, ice, and wind, but by keeping the Land Rover moving it helped to eliminate the possibility of sliding off the road and into the woods.

About a third of the way down, Jack felt his SUV start to slide to the left and Susan gripped her hands on the dashboard and let out a cry. He increased his speed and pulled out of it. "Holy shit, Susan, how do you guys manage this mess all winter? It'd make me old before my time." His frustration on seeing nothing but snow and ice on the road increased his anger. "God damn it!" he shouted out the window.

"Eric loves it down here. I really don't like it. I'm glad you're staying with me because I don't want to be alone in this storm."

"We'll be OK." He placed his hand on her thigh to reassure her, and then pulled it off and put it back on the steering wheel. "Come on, you're a tough old broad. This shouldn't bother you." He laughed at what he just said.

Jack got to the end of the road and while turning left he felt the rear of the SUV sliding to the right. He gunned the engine and brought the SUV back straight again. He breathed hard. Susan looked at Jack and smiled. "The rest should be easier but be careful of the next section. It has a gradual decline, but nothing like the toboggan slide, and at the end of this portion of the road is a hard left turn onto a bridge over a creek." Susan related that all sorts of cars have gone off the road on this turn even in good weather, because everyone thinks the worst is over.

The ice-covered branches banged his SUV as he started down the next section of the road. "Well, I'd better keep it slow. You know, Susan, this is more nerve-racking than playing football. You guys are nuts living down here."

Susan smiled and patted Jack on his shoulder. "Tell me about it. I don't like it down here and particularly in this weather. It was Eric's idea to design and build the house down here, not mine. I wanted to be in Orono, closer to the university. And really I'd like to move out of this state. I just don't like living in Maine. It's too boring."

Jack felt his SUV gather a little more speed than he wanted so he gently hit the brakes causing a slight sliding to the left. The SUV still didn't slow down that much so when he got to the curve he accelerated, driving the SUV safely over the bridge and onto a more level part of the road.

The snow continued to fall, still mixed with freezing rain, and the frozen branches continued to stroke the SUV. Jack said to Susan, "Do you remember the movie *Dr. Zhivago*? Well, this looks just like a scene from it. It's absolutely beautiful. It's horrible but it's beautiful."

"Yeah, I was thinking the same," said Susan, looking out at the road in front of them. "But I'd sooner see this in a movie than in real life." Susan again voiced her concern about their spouses and where they might be. "God, I hope they're OK." She tried her cell phone again to call her husband and when that didn't work, she tried reaching the lodge, but she still could not get through. "These cell phones just don't work down here."

CHAPTER 6

"Now let's get out of this stuff." Eric helped Janet up and before walking into the Benoit Lodge after they tried without success to brush the snow off their jackets and pants. The snow was frozen onto the fabrics. As they walked in they were immediately impressed with the interior of the lodge.

The Benoit Lodge was about ninety years old and built of classic white pine. The interior was unique as it was wide open and three stories tall with an array of animal heads hanging from the walls.

The main lobby was wide with some twenty-four thick, three story-long white pine tree trunks that held the lodge together. It looked like a timber-framed church. On each of the second and third floors were wooden guard railings. The view from the second and third walk was that of the Benoit lobby where the furniture was also made from the same pine trees, but with comfortable green cushions. A large staircase to the right of the entrance led to the bedrooms that circled the lodge. An elevator was next to it. Farther to the left was a huge fireplace that was sending out warmth they could feel across the room. The registration desk was in front of them. The unique beauty of the Benoit Lodge caused Eric and Janet to stop and admire its design and construction.

Beneath the massive snowfall was a beautiful and challenging eighteen-hole golf course that would remain covered until at least April. For now snowshoeing and cross country skiing took place where golf balls flew in the summer. Beyond the golf course and hidden by the northeaster were the foothills of the White Mountains of New Hampshire; the view in clear weather was spectacular.

But it was the inside of the Benoit Lodge that impressed everyone who walked into the lobby. "Wow," Janet exclaimed. "What a beautiful place this is." They both looked up at the pine construction. It was unlike any building they had ever seen. "Oh, I'm looking forward to spending time here," Janet remarked, looking at the unique interior.

The people in the lodge's lobby eventually looked over to Janet and Eric and were somewhat shocked by their snow-packed appearance as they walked up to the registration desk, where owner Michael Craven was studying his computer with paperwork laid out on the desk.

Craven looked up to and was surprised to see Eric and Janet. "Good heavens," a shocked Craven said, looking at Eric and his snow- and ice-covered body. "Where have you been?"

"Your driveway. Our car went off the road so we had to snowshoe up the driveway. By the way, I'm Eric Forster checking in." Eric couldn't help grinning at Craven's question.

"How in the world did you get here?" Michael Craven looked astonished.

"We drove from Augusta, but I couldn't make the drive up your road, so I ended up off your driveway and into a bunch of bushes so we had to snowshoe up the rest of the way. So my car is off the road in some bushes down your driveway."

"You're kidding. The highway's been closed since three. No one's been allowed on Highway 2 since then."

Eric shrugged his shoulders. "We didn't realize there was a storm on its way until we made the turn off 27. Then it got progressively worse, but I couldn't stop." The ice and snow on their clothes were beginning to melt leaving a puddle beneath their bodies.

Mr. Craven smiled. "Well, whatever, welcome to Benoit Lodge. I'm glad you got here all right." He shook hands with both Eric and Janet. I'll send my grandson to get your luggage out of the car, but I don't know when we can get your car up here; I'll have him check it out." He rang his bell to alert his staff that a new guest had arrived. "Let's get your jackets off by the door so you don't flood the lounge." Mr. Craven giggled at his comments.

After they took off their jackets and toweled off their pants, Eric and Janet returned to the registration desk. Eric handed his credit card to Craven and signed the register. He didn't know what to do about Janet's name, so he put them down as Dr. and Mrs. Forster. Interesting, thought Eric. "Have the Meachams checked in yet?" asked Eric looking around the lodge's grand room for his wife and Jack.

"No, not yet, but if they do we've got a problem. We have only one room left because an elderly couple didn't want to attempt leaving here this morning, so if your friends show up you'll have to join up in one room. Given this northeaster, I don't think there's a chance they'll get here. After all, you and your wife were very lucky to get here when you did."

Eric looked surprised before he said, "OK. We'll take the room and give our friends a call to see where they are.

"Eric?" Janet looked at Eric with a concerned look.

Mr. Craven raised his hands. "Can't do. Our phone lines are down along with our power lines and cell phones don't operate very well in this area of the state. We're operating off our generators for light and heat, but we'll turn these off at nine tonight to conserve our fuel. We'll talk more about this at dinner tonight. My grandson John will get your luggage to your room. Let me know if there is anything else I can do." He smiled as he called for John. "Come sit and have a cup of coffee to help you warm up." Eric gave the car keys to his grandson, then headed for the comfortable-looking chairs in front of the fireplace.

Eric and Janet collapsed into the chairs by the fireplace while enjoying the heat from the burning logs. The taste of freshly brewed coffee was terrific. Janet broke the silence. "Eric, what are we going to do about the room?" She wasn't smiling about it.

"I don't know. Let's wait until we see it." The warmth from the fireplace caused Eric to nod off until Janet shook his shoulder.

"I'm worried about Jack and Susan. Where do you think they're at?" Janet had pulled her shoeless legs underneath her body as both sat on towels so they wouldn't dampen the chairs.

"I would guess that they never got out of Bangor. Jack probably dropped Susan off at our house and they have probably tried to reach us by phone." Eric leaned his head back on the cushion. "Man, I'm tired," Eric said, dropping his head back on the chair's cushion and closing his eyes.

About a half hour later, Michael Craven came over to quietly tell Janet that their room was ready. "It's 229, which is to the left when you go upstairs. Your luggage is all there but your car is stuck for now. I think we got everything you need. If not, let me know." He handed an old-fashioned metal key to Janet.

Janet looked over at Eric and smiled. He was sound asleep. *He must be tired,* Janet thought, *as he performed two operations this morning and probably didn't get a lot of sleep last night. Then he had to drive and snowshoe in this mess.* For the moment she was able to study Eric's features and was impressed with how handsome he was. His features were sharp with his hairline beginning to move up the head. His tall body and long legs seemed to be uncomfortable in his chair, but he slept, soundly.

Janet leaned over to Eric's chair, grabbed his left arm and shook it. "Eric, the room's ready. Eric slowly opened his eyes and looked around, confused as to where he was. When he saw Janet, he smiled and got his brain back in gear and followed Janet up the stairs.

Their room had one king-size bed, two wooden rocking chairs, a dresser and end tables on either side of the bed, a basic bathroom with a bathtub and shower, along with an operating fireplace that warmed the room. The walls were covered with a variety of Maine wilderness pictures. Eric smiled at Janet and said, "I can't sleep in these chairs, but we can share the bed." He looked over at the bed and was tempted to lie down on it.

Janet stared at Eric with a surprised look. "What!" She broke into a laugh. "Not a chance!" Janet plopped down on a chair with her coat still on while looking over at the bed. It had three pillows, a beautiful patterned quilt, and a feather comforter folded on the end of the bed.

"Come on. There's room for both of us. Where else can I sleep?"

"Eric, I'm not sleeping with you! Period!" Her eyes were flaming.

Eric replied, "We'll sleep, not the other sleep."

Janet walked around the bed to a chair next to the fireplace. "Right, and suddenly you'll drift over to my side of the bed and then..." She had a panicked look.

"What do you mean...then? Do you think I'm going to rape you?" Eric was smiling as he mentally undressed Janet, so her breasts were bulging from her bra. *Jesus Christ,* he thought, *what am I thinking?*

"See, you're laughing about it." She still had the panicked look.

"When was the last time I made a pass at you?" Eric was having trouble keeping a serious look.

"Well, we were never in a situation like this." Her panicked look changed to a "help me" look. Her hands remained on her lap as though protecting that area of her body. She looked into Eric's eyes with a pleading look and at the same time looked at Eric and his tall lanky body. She then looked over at the bed. It would be interesting to see what's under his clothes. She had wondered this for as long as they had known each other. Maybe this was the time. Her mind stopped and she thought, *Good grief, stop thinking.*

"Now, wait a minute. Maybe I should be afraid you'll make a pass at me. You're assuming I'm the threat. Maybe it's you." Eric laughed as he wrapped his arms around his body.

Janet stood up. "You've got to be kidding." Janet's blonde hair was tied off in a large ponytail that came down below her shoulders. Well-formed breasts were evident even behind her wool sweater. She wore small diamond earrings and was wearing ski pants, a wool sweater and a pair of sensible winter boots compliments of L.L. Bean. Janet looked like a model for Bean's catalog. She was truly a beautiful woman.

Now Eric was getting concerned. He walked over to Janet. "We've been planning this trip since November. It was going to be a fun time for the four of us. The weather's screwed up Susan and Jack's getting here, so don't blame me for all this. I didn't bring this storm. It wasn't even in the forecast."

Janet sat back down and gave a weak smile. "I'm sorry. You're right. I'm overreacting." She looked over at the bed with a worried look and thought of what could happen. "But, don't get any ideas."

"What ideas?" Eric gave her a smile.

"You know what I mean."

Eric nodded his head in agreement and continued smiling as though he was anticipating what might happen later this evening. "Really? Maybe I'll think of something later. But I'm getting hungry and in need of a drink. So, let's unpack and get downstairs."

"OK," answered Janet while getting up from her chair.

Eric said, "Yeah, remember they're turning off the lights at nine, so we'd better get ready for bed while it's still light and the room's still warm. I'll stack up the fireplace so it will keep the room warm for a while. Then we can cuddle in these down comforters. It should be fun." Eric smiled to himself, anticipating going to bed with Janet.

Janet ignored his comments and began to unpack her suitcase. On top was a sexy black negligee and she had no idea where it came from. It certainly wasn't something she bought. Her husband Jack must have put it in her suitcase. Then she tried to hide it before Eric saw it, but he was standing behind her, looking over her shoulder.

"You're wearing that tonight?" He looked anxiously at Janet.

She blushed. "No, Eric, it's a present from Jack, so it will have to wait."

Eric looked surprised. "Jack bought this?" Eric picked it up and held up the top portion, which was quite transparent.

"Yes, he did." Janet didn't like Jack's idea of bringing this nightgown since the two of them hadn't had sex together for several months. She realized that Jack had hoped her wearing it would excite the two of them. She didn't think it possible so there was no way she would wear it.

"Well, I could enjoy it just as well," Eric said as he held the top portion against her body.

"Yeah, right! Not in your fondest dreams." Janet grabbed it back from Eric and stuffed the negligee back into her suitcase. Eric envisioned Janet coming toward him wearing that negligee and he began to get excited again.

"Eric, I'd like to take a shower," Susan said, "so maybe you could wait for me downstairs?" Her look convinced Eric that he'd better leave the room.

Eric agreed, "OK, but are you sure you don't want me to wash your back?"

Janet didn't answer. She just pointed to the door while mouthing the word "out."

CHAPTER 7

Twenty minutes later, Janet found Eric sitting by himself in front of the fireplace. He was holding a magazine, but couldn't remember anything he had read. He was thinking of both Susan and Janet and how a fun weekend was turning out to be a lost weekend. He also wondered where Susan was and if she and Jack had to get a room in a motel or if they even got out of Bangor. Getting down to their house would be a challenge if the snow was as bad there as it was in Bethel.

He looked up as a smiling Janet sat down in the couch next to him. She was wearing a blue pants with a multicolored wool sweater that appeared to fit comfortably on her body without accentuating her figure. "Did you miss me?" Janet asked.

"You were gone?" a smiling Eric answered. She reacted by jabbing his arm. "Maybe I'd better go up and shower. Perhaps you could come up and scrub my back," Janet smiled and ignored his idea. When Eric returned he was wearing a pair of tan slacks with a blue pullover sweater. He sat down next to Janet and asked, "Do I smell better?" Janet nodded in agreement.

Eric looked around the lodge's first floor and was even more impressed with it than when they came in out of the storm. The entire lobby was a classic design so sitting here felt better than he had anticipated. It was as though nothing dramatic was happening outside though the strong wind could be heard smashing snow and ice against the windows.

They sat in front of the fireplace and Janet grabbed his arm. "Eric!" Janet had the panicked look again. "What if we meet someone who knows us?" She quickly gazed around the room. "How do we explain it?" The room was full of all the guests as there was nowhere else they could go except their bedrooms.

"Explain what?" He smiled at her while his eyes went up and down her body. "Did you want to tell someone about our sleeping together?" he asked in a kidding sexy voice. When she frowned at him he looked at her and told her he didn't recognize anyone; then he asked if she did. He told her they could honestly explain what happened. They both glanced around the room to see if a face looked familiar.

"Yeah, and how do I do that?" she asked with a cynical look. "Who's going to believe that we're here together and our spouses are somewhere else?"

Eric started to laugh, "Well, in that case maybe we should do it so we can really be guilty of whatever someone might think."

"That makes no sense, Eric." She frowned at him again as she crossed her arms across her chest.

Janet focused on a couple seated by a window. She looked back at Eric. "They look somewhat familiar but I don't know from where."

"Who?" Eric asked, looking at the same couple.

"Those two by the window," she said, turning her gaze back to Eric. "Are they looking at us?"

"Yep, I think they're going through the same scenario we are. We look familiar to them, but they don't know from where, so let's just ignore them and hope they forget about us."

There were four card tables with wooden chairs and several lounge chairs and sofas for those who wanted to read or just relax. There was a working TV turned to a local channel that was describing the storm for its viewers. It showed Interstate 95 full of snow and all sorts of cars off the road. The announcer said the storm would continue through Saturday with a possible accumulation of three feet, depending on where you lived.

Already they reported all sorts of power outages, particularly in the western foothills, and most roads in the northern half of Maine were closed.

The owner of the lodge, Michael Craven, came into the dining room and rang a bell to get the attention of his quests. Craven was a short white-haired elderly man with a matching beard and mustache and a concerned smile. He looked around the dining room before talking.

"I'm sorry about this terrible storm but it obviously wasn't forecast and even if it were it wouldn't have made any difference. Trees are coming down from the ice and snow and we're without power and phones and probably will be for several days. Cell phones don't work here. You're stuck here until they get us plowed out and we're probably way down the list. They're going to get the eastern part of the state opened before they get here. So, we'll do our best to make your stay as pleasant as possible.

"The roads were covered with ice before the snow began to fall. So far we're up to about eighteen inches out the front door and the forecast says that we'll get up to as much as three feet of snow before it leaves us. To make matters worse, the wind is drifting the snow so some areas of our driveway will probably get up to six feet deep, maybe more. Obviously this will prevent anyone from leaving here any time soon.

"The last major storm we had here was is 1998 that left us without power and phones for about ten days, but the roads opened up in about three." Craven stopped his thoughts and looked around the room at some very worried guests who all listened without comments as they tried to understand how much three feet of snow would be.

"Should the need arise, and I hope it won't, we can possibly get a helicopter from the Western Maine Hospital for a medical emergency. Please let me know if you have a condition that might need emergency attention."

Michael Craven smiled at his trapped quests and added, "We'll keep the fires going here and in your rooms. If you need help, let me or my staff know. We have plenty food and our stoves are gas so we will be able to cook. We also have generators that will keep most of our essentials going, but we'll have to watch this carefully so we don't run out of fuel. There will be running water, but only heat during the day so we can conserve our fuel. Lights and heat will go off at about nine. Any questions?" he asked, looking around the room.

A lady two tables away asked, "Is there any chance of getting out of here with a snowmobile?"

Michael Craven answered with a grin, "You could probably get out, but there's nothing to get out to. Everything's closed and it's still snowing hard out there. The weather report says the snow won't stop falling until sometime tomorrow afternoon...maybe...and underneath the snow is ice so even if they can plow the roads, the ice will prevent anyone from leaving here. So just enjoy yourselves." Craven smiled and added, "Pretend it's another honeymoon. Anything else?" Eric looked over at Janet, smiled, and patted her shoulder. She ignored him.

"How 'bout skiing or snowshoeing?" another guest asked.

Craven answered with a shrug of his shoulders. "I don't really know yet, but skiing probably won't happen any time soon. There's just too much snow. Snowshoeing? Probably, but not until the snow stops. It's just too dangerous to stay outside with this storm. OK?"

He began walking toward the kitchen and halfway there stopped to announce, "Dinner tonight is prime rib or lobster thermadore. Cocktail hour starts now." He started walking again to the kitchen but stopped after a few more steps and rang his bell again.

"I almost forgot. Most of our staff will be staying here tonight because there's no way for them to get home and since there aren't any extra rooms, they'll sleep on the furniture in the main lobby, so I need to have everyone out of the lobby no later than eight thirty."

He smiled, waved and walked into the kitchen.

A well-nourished and friendly waitress came to their table. "Isn't this exciting?" She smiled at them. "May I get you a cocktail while you're thinking about what to order?"

Eric looked at Janet and asked, "Would you like a cocktail or should we get a bottle of wine?"

"A bottle of wine would be nice, but only one, OK?" She had that serious look again as though she was expecting to be attacked by a drunken Eric Forster while in bed with him.

Eric ordered a bottle of Merlot and when it came, he said, "Let's toast the weekend and our friends who didn't make it."

"Oh, Eric, I so miss not having Jack and Susan here. Now I feel as though I'm on a date." Tears began to well in her eyes. "I'm really worried about them."

"I do too, but are you sobbing because you're stuck with me?"

"Of course not, but I'm probably worried about sleeping with you."

"Well," Eric answered, "you should worry because I will probably lose all my soberness and roll over to your side of the bed." He rested his chin in both hands and winked at her.

She tried not to smile, but couldn't stop it. "Ha! Ha! You're very funny," she said as she mimicked a laugh.

Eric grinned. "But, I still wonder where they are. Maybe they're stuck in some motel between here and Bangor, but I've a feeling they probably didn't get out of town. It's incredible that in these days of sophisticated communication we might as well be on the moon. Well, this is classic Maine. Anything modern is not available to its citizens because it might ruin the environment."

For dinner, Janet had the lobster and Eric the prime rib, rare. They ate in silence trying not to bring the bedroom subject up for discussion. After dinner they finished their wine, had coffee, and commented on how good the food was. Then, out of the corner of her eye, Janet saw that the couple by the window was headed over to their table.

"Oh, Eric...they're coming over to see us. What'll we do?"

"Let me handle them."

The man was short, heavy, and baldhead with glasses, while his female companion was a walking ad for cosmetics and jewelry. She too wore glasses, was short, and overweight. The man looked at Eric and said, "Forgive us, but we seem to think we've met you before and it was driving us nuts trying to figure out who you are so we took a chance on coming over to introduce ourselves. I'm Hank Lewis and this is my wife Margaret." She was checking out their fingers to see if Eric and Janet were married and was obviously disappointed to see they appeared to be husband and wife.

Eric stood up, held out his hand and said, "Eric Forster and this is Janet."

Hank asked where Eric was from. "Bangor, and you?"

"We're from Ellsworth. Where do you work?

I'm an orthopedic surgeon at Eastern Maine. Janet's a teacher in Bangor. And you?" Eric asked as he invited the Lewises to sit down.

"We own Hank's Hardware in Ellsworth. That's probably where we've seen you." Hank was frowning as his lack of who Eric and Janet were was bugging him badly.

Janet's eyes widened. She remembered where she had seen the Lewises. At the same time Hank Lewis snapped his fingers and mumbled, "I remember now," he said looking at Janet. You came into our store a week or so ago to get some bathroom fixtures, but I don't remember you, Eric. I thought there was someone else with her. Now I remember, it was the Patriots halfback, Jack Meacham," he related without thinking. His wife quickly changed the subject.

They joined them for a cup of coffee while they talked about the weather and their drives over to Bethel. Hank and Margaret told them they drove over in the morning and missed all the snow. Margaret stood up and said, "Hank, we'd better get to our room before the lights go out. It was nice meeting you and I hope to see you tomorrow." She grabbed Hank's arm and led him out of the dining room.

Eric and Janet laughed as Eric said, "Now they've got something to talk about tonight." They finished their coffee and Eric asked, "All right, Janet, are you ready for bed?"

"Yes and no," offered Janet while looking at Eric with an anxious gaze.

Before going to their room, they took a quick trip outside to see what was happening. The wind was still blowing hard and snow was still falling; everything seemed to be buried. All that could be seen in the parking lot were white snow-covered objects that once were cars.

"That's enough of that," said Eric as they quickly got back inside. "It'll be a nice night to cuddle in bed. Isn't this romantic? Stuck together in a beautiful lodge with snow falling and no lights. Wow!"

Janet whacked him in his ribs as she led the way upstairs to their bedroom. Eric could not take his eyes off her long legs, tight behind, and small waistline. *God, what a great body she has,* he thought as he began to feel some increases in a certain body part. *And now I'm going to bed with her. Wow! Stop it,* he told himself. *Don't ruin the weekend and the future for the two of them and their missing spouses, but, wow!*

When they got to their room, the bed was already turned down and the fireplace was burning several logs. The two rocking chairs had been placed in front of the fireplace. The drapes were closed, shutting out the miserable weather as the room exuded comfort.

Eric sat down on one of the chairs and stretched his arms and legs. "I had thought that maybe I could have moved up a couch or something, but with the staff needing these for sleeping it left me without any other option. So, you're stuck with me."

Janet said nothing and stared at the fire, refusing to look at the bed. She began to think of what could happen when they got into it. She was certain he wouldn't attack her, but she worried that his presence in the same bed would start juices flowing and heaven knows what might happen then.

Eric broke the silence. "I hate to bring this up, but time is running short and we need to get ready for bed before the lights go off. So, who dresses first?"

Janet didn't answer immediately. She was trying to figure out what would be the safest. "I'll go first," she offered, "but I don't want you to look at me when I come out of the bathroom."

Eric smiled anxiously. "You mean you're going to wear that sexy nightie?"

"Stop it, Eric." He continued to stare at the fire. "I have another pair of pajamas with me." She got up from her chair, pulled her necessities from her suitcases and marched into the bathroom.

"Don't forget that you have only twenty-five minutes before the lights go off," Eric added while watching Janet close the bathroom door.

She reopened it and said in a serious voice. "Don't look when I come out."

"Why?" asked Eric to the closed bathroom door. He felt fatigue setting in as he stared at the fire. He closed his eyes thinking of the night ahead and soon nodded off. He woke up when he heard the bathroom door open and without thinking turned toward the door.

Janet was walking toward to bed wearing short-legged pajamas with a loose top. Her blonde hair was free of the ponytail and covered her back. As she got into bed she said to Eric, "You weren't supposed to look."

"So, what's to see?" Eric asked. "I've seen more of you when you've come swimming at the lake." But, he thought, she looked incredibly beautiful with a great figure, but most important was that they'd be in bed together. She had pulled her covers up to her chin as Eric got up and went to his suitcase. "I usually don't wear pajamas," he said as he headed to the bathroom while trying not to laugh at her.

Janet's eyes opened wide. "Eric, you have to wear something!" she demanded in a panicked voice.

"Close your eyes when I come out," he said, mimicking her demands. She closed her eyes, but thoughts of him coming to bed without any clothes on both panicked and excited her.

She heard the water stop running and the bathroom door opened. She tightened her closed eyes and pulled her comforter over her lips.

"Janet, open your eyes," Eric said in a very calm, seductive voice.

"I will not," she growled while she turned her head to the other side of the bed. "Go away!"

"I'm here to stay," he said in a phony spooky voice as he walked around to the other side of the bed. Janet couldn't stand it. She turned her head and opened her right eye squinting at Eric.

"You've got pajamas on!"

"You're disappointed. Of course I do," Eric said with a laugh. "Did you expect me to let you stare at my body?"

Janet turned her head away and pulled the down comforter even higher.

Eric turned his head toward Janet and whispered, "Don't I get a good night kiss?"

"No!" The answer ended any further discussion. Eric turned his body away from Janet. They were both exhausted and sleep awaited them even while they were amazed that they were actually in bed together. As promised, the lights went off at nine.

"Good night, Janet."

"Good night, Eric."

Eric wondered if he should touch her, but thought he'd better not. No sense in scaring her. Besides, he was really tired. Janet lay with her eyes wide open, waiting for an arm to come across her body, but nothing happened. *Maybe he doesn't think I'm worth it.* Finally she heard him breathing deeply. He was sleeping, so she closed her eyes and joined him.

The storm continued as the cold wind rattled the storm windows. The fire in the fireplace was still burning, setting off a comfortable glow, but the residents of the room didn't hear or feel a thing.

CHAPTER 8

Jack finally got to Susan's driveway and backed the car in next to the garage. There was still reasonable light as it was only a little after four, but it would be dark in less than an hour.

Power was obviously out, as the automatic door wasn't working. "Do you have a generator?" Jack asked Susan when he stopped the car.

"It's in the garage. I don't know how to set it up, but our neighbor Paul Glidden probably does."

"I'll look at it after we get the suitcases into the house. I should be able to figure it out." They carried their luggage through the deepening snow and vicious wind to the side door. When they got in the house it was surprisingly warm, as though the furnace was still working.

"Where would you like to sleep?" Susan asked. " Upstairs in the quest room or here on the couch?" Jack was a little concerned about sleeping too close to Susan.

Jack looked at Susan and then to the living room couch. "I'll be all right here."

"Are you sure?" asked Susan. "There's two extra bedrooms upstairs. Jack thought about sleeping close to her, but decided against it. There was no need to push temptation.

"Yeah, I'll be fine. You know, I have a feeling the generator is operating because it is warmer in here than I thought it would be." Jack walked over to the thermostat and checked the temperature. It was about sixty. He then went over to the table next to the couch and turned the light switch on, but nothing happened.

Suddenly there was a knock on the door and she opened it to view a snow-covered man. "It's Paul."

"Hi, Susan. You didn't make it over to Bethel. I didn't think so when it started to snow. I'm glad you got back OK."

"Thanks, Paul." She turned to Jack. "This is Jack Meacham and, Jack, this is our neighbor, Paul Glidden." Susan was still affected from their trip down the hill. "Paul, it was an adventure getting here and now there's no way for Jack to get out at least for tonight, so he's going to stay here until he can." She forced a smile at Jack and Paul.

"Well, that makes sense," Paul offered. He also thought the two of them might have some fun together. "There's no way you can make it back out of here because the road is soon going to be covered with trees. In fact, you can hear branches breaking and trees falling. It's weird sounding

Paul changed the subject when he looked at Jack. "Aren't you the football player from the Patriots?"

"Yep," answered Jack. "At least I used to be." Jack quickly changed the subject. "Now, how about the generator?"

"I turned it on about an hour ago, a little after we lost power. There are all sorts of trees falling on the road and on the other side of our house. The ice and snow have already torn down some trees and a lot of branches have fallen on the power lines. You were lucky to make it down the road."

"So, how does it work?" Jack asked again with a bit of impatience in his voice.

"OK, come with me and I'll show you." Paul ignored the tone of Jack's voice and took them through the snow to the garage where they had to kick snow that had drifted against the door. When they got in he showed Jack and Susan the generator using his flashlight. "Eric has plenty of fuel to run the generator for at least four days." He then pointed to the fuse box. "This shows what elements in the house are working."

"And what's that?" asked Jack.

Paul pointed the flashlight into the box. "The well pump, the furnace, the microwave, refrigerator, some lights in the kitchen, and probably in the bathroom upstairs, also the hot water heater. The TV downstairs seems to be on this power. But you need to be careful not to have all these on at the same time. Since your stove is gas, you'll be able to cook without power. OK?"

Paul Glidden was an overweight middle-aged man with glasses who wore strange but warm clothing and a red stocking hat. He loved talking and was difficult to stop as he continued to discuss the merits of Eric's generator and how it operated. Most of this went over Jack's head, but he listened and hoped everything would work as described.

The working part of the generator was outside the garage on the house side, but it ran fairly quietly, its noise somewhat hidden by the wind.

"Paul, thanks very much," Susan said, walking back to the house. "We don't know where Eric and Jack's wife are. We were supposed to meet them in Bethel this afternoon, but we got stuck at the university until it was too late to drive anywhere but here.

Paul looked at the two of them and agreed. "Yep, there's no way you'd be able to get out of here tonight, cause there'll probably be branches and trees on the road. This is the worst storm I've ever seen. More snow, more ice, and this heavy wind will make a huge mess before it's done." He put his hat back on. "I'd better get back to Harriet. If you need anything, let me know."

The snow and rain were still hitting hard on the house from the strong wind. "I think we'll be all right, Paul, thanks." He headed out the door and disappeared in the snow. Susan looked over at Jack and said with a smile, "See, he's a real talker, but he's also a very nice neighbor and a very close friend of Eric's."

Jack sat down on the couch and figured this would be good enough for sleeping. He got up and followed Susan upstairs, carrying her suitcases. "All this for a weekend?"

"You can never have enough clothes," she answered, smiling at Jack. "Let me change my clothes and I'll be down in a few minutes. You can pour us a drink. The booze and glasses are in the dry sink. Pour me a scotch on the rocks. And see if you can start a fire in the fireplace. Everything you'll need is on the hearth." She closed her bedroom door so she could dress in private.

There was only one light socket working in her bedroom so Susan used her flashlight to search out some different clothes. She settled on a pair of khaki slacks and a red blouse and a white wool sweater that accentuated her breasts. She got rid of her boots and put on a pair of sandals. I'm not going anywhere, she thought.

She brushed her short brown hair and looked at her face in the mirror and hoped Jack would be aroused by her looks now that they were alone. She began talking to herself. "Now, behave yourself," she said aloud. "He might not like me as much as I like him." She had always been awed with his muscular body and athletic talent and now she was alone with him probably for the weekend.

The living room was a place of great beauty. The ceiling was twenty-six feet high with glass all the way to the top. It normally rendered a beautiful view of the lake but today the snow took that away. When she got downstairs, her scotch was ready and the fire was burning brightly so they took their drinks into the living room. Jack raised his glass. "Here's to our lost weekend and to our spouses, wherever they might be." They clinked their glasses and sipped the scotch. "This is our Benoit Lodge."

"Yeah, let's relax and enjoy our drinks," Susan said. "There's no rush because we aren't going anywhere."

Jack looked at Susan with an inquiring look, as he couldn't take his eyes off her body. He had always been impressed with Susan and her physical appearance, which was accentuated by the light from the fireplace. She put her drink down on the end table, walked over to Jack and hugged him, saying, "And thanks, Jack, for getting me home. I couldn't have made it without you." She kissed him on his cheek and held the hug for what seemed an eternity to Jack. He felt her breasts against his chest and her rapidly beating heart.

Jack had long been impressed with Susan for her athletic abilities in coaching the soccer team to several successful conference titles. Janet was never really overly impressed with sports, particularly soccer, which she thought was boring, or with football, which she thought was a money-losing part of Maine's athletic programs. Jack decided he was more impressed with Susan than his wife as he and Susan seemed to think the same thoughts about athletics.

They sat on the couch staring at the flames in front of them and the conversation turned to their athletic teams and the problems each was having in recruiting good prospects. Orono, Maine, was so far away from any large market that most good recruits looked elsewhere first, thus Maine usually got the dregs. The only exception was the hockey team that had won a couple of national titles in recent years and was the place where outstanding players wanted to come.

Soon they had all but forgotten about Eric and Janet. "How about another scotch, Jack?"

They settled back on the couch and Jack looked at Susan and said, "Forgive me, but you are really beautiful."

Susan blushed and said, "Thank you and I can return the compliment to you. You are truly handsome." She placed her hand on his thigh and began to stroke it.

Jack was about to react when Susan changed the subject. "I'm getting hungry. How about some pasta for dinner? It's quick and easy."

"OK, can I help?"

"Sure, set the table, light the candles, and get a bottle of wine out of the rack over there." Susan pointed to the back wall of the kitchen. All this time, the snow was still falling mixed with what appeared to be freezing rain while the wind was getting stronger. It was now dark outside and wind was battering the snow on the outside of the house.

The dinner was a romantic setting with the only light coming from the candles on the dining room table. The only other light came from the fireplace and a small lamp in the kitchen. Their discussion centered around their athletic jobs and what they hoped for the future. They both preferred to move to a larger, more athletic-oriented market.

Susan felt very comfortable being alone with Jack Meacham, more so than she could have imagined. Jack felt much the same and soon they began to forget about Eric and Janet.

After dinner they went back to the couch in the living room and sat staring at the fire and somewhat afraid of touching each other for fear of what might happen. Jack looked over at Susan and though she was talking he didn't hear anything. He was too enthused with her, and the scotch and wine had begun to do a number on him.

Finally, Susan spoke. "Jack, I'm really tired. I'm going to bed. I'll throw down your blankets and pillow. If you need anything else, let me know." She had a look on her face that seemed to be asking Jack to come upstairs with her, but he thought better of it and made a bed out of the couch and went to the back bathroom where he changed into his pajamas.

Jack quickly fell asleep, helped by the wine, scotch, and the drive down to her house, but about an hour later, he was awakened from a sound sleep by a loud and frightening noise coming from the large windows in the front of the house. The wind had changed direction and was now coming out of the southeast directly toward the front of the house. He could feel the windows moving with the wind and he saw snow coming through the bottom of the door. The noise was frightening. It sounded like the windows were about to crash into the living room.

He went back to the bathroom and got some towels to put on the floor at the bottom of the door to keep the snow and rain outside. He then heard Susan's voice upstairs yell in a panicked voice, "Jack, what's the matter?"

"Susan, the snow's coming in the front windows and the wind is actually moving the windows. I just hope they don't break." He stood back from the windows so if they did break the glass wouldn't cut him.

Susan came running down the stairs screaming, "I hate this place, I hate it, I hate it!" she screamed. She was in her pajamas, shaking while staring at the darkened windows. "Every time we have a storm the same thing happens. One day the whole house is going to crash." She stood in front of the window shaking. "Please hold me, Jack. I'm scared to death the window will crash."

He put his arms around her shaking body and tried to calm her, but she was shaking in fear. He moved her away from the windows and as he stroked her back his hand slid down below her waist. She was also moving her hands down Jack's body pulling him closer to her. She pulled her head back and stared at Jack. He kissed her and she responded in kind. He could feel her tears.

"Oh, Jesus, Jack, take me upstairs. I can't stand to be here. I need you to be with me." Jack put his right arm around her knees and his left around her back and picked her up with ease. He carried her up the stairs and into her bedroom with its king-size bed. A dim light was shining from the bathroom so Jack could see Susan. Since he first met Susan at the university he had dreamt about making love to her. Now he was alone with her and his body shook with anticipation.

He gently placed her on the king-sized bed covered with a large down comforter. He grabbed her pajamas at the waist and pulled them off. He then pulled up her top, exposing her breasts. *Oh, God,* he thought, *is this really happening?* He could barely control himself as she untied his pajamas and pulled them down. He had problems getting his feet out of the pajama legs while undoing his top. "God damn it!" he impatiently yelled as Susan's tears turned to laughter as she helped pull off his top while he struggled with his pajama legs. She marveled at his body that was still solid muscle from his years as a pro football player. There were no signs of any soft spots on either of them.

"Hurry, get inside me," Susan cried. She had wanted to make love to Jack for such a long time that she could barely control her body.

When the pajama legs finally came out, he buried his head between her breasts while she stroked his body and guided him into her. They both rolled around the bed like a pair of wrestlers, yelling at each other as they came together in record time and oblivious to the storm that had brought them together.

"Oh, God, Jack, Oh, God," she cried as she felt him come. The pleasure was more incredible than anything she could ever remember. She wanted this to last forever, not a few moments, as they both collapsed into each other's arms and lay together breathing deeply.

He stroked her body from her face to her thighs and everything in between. Her body was firm without any semblance of fat. Her workout ethic was obvious. He could not believe what had happened, happened. He placed both hands on her face, kissed her and uttered, "Susan, I'm so glad we didn't get to Bethel. Now we have a weekend together. I have wanted to have this happen ever since I first met you."

Susan cried out, "Oh, Jack, I have wanted you for so long that I can't believe you are really here with me." After they came, they fell asleep in each other's arms.

CHAPTER 9

Dawn came to the Benoit Lodge with the wind and snow continuing. Eric woke and for a moment couldn't remember where he was until he sat up and saw Janet sleeping next to him. *God, she is beautiful,* he thought and then wondered what would happen if he reached over and touched her.

Instead, he got out of bed, made a quick trip to the bathroom then opened the window drapes. The snow had really piled up. There was nothing to see but white as the snow was still falling while being pushed by the wind.

He crawled back into bed and turned to face Janet, who was still asleep, and he sat there waiting for her to wake up. She began to stir and suddenly opened her eyes with a panicked look. Janet looked at a smiling Eric and quickly sat up in bed, forgetting where she was. When she remembered, she slid back under her covers and stared at Eric. "How long have you been awake?"

About an hour," he lied while sitting up. Janet checked under her covers to make certain she was covered and looked up at Eric.

"You didn't touch me, did you?"

"Well, yes, I did. I made love to you at about six this morning, but you were too out of it to enjoy it." He looked at Janet with a straight face. Her blonde hair covered the pillow. Even in the morning she looked terrific.

She smiled. "Stop it, Eric, you'd didn't do anything. I would have felt it. You're impossible, but thanks for not doing anything like that."

"OK, but like what?" He raised his hand to her hair, but quickly brought it back.

"You know! I would have felt it if you did." She made a quick trip to the bathroom and then crawled back into bed. "It's cold in here. How about starting the fire?" Eric got out of bed, organized the fireplace, and lit the logs with pinecones, then slid back into bed. She would love to have him cuddle her to help warm her body, *but that,* she thought, *would lead to something else.*

"My dear, have you any idea what it's taking not to attack you?"

She smiled and said, "Yes, I think I do." She quickly changed the subject. "Now what do we do today, other than what you are probably thinking?"

"Well, it's still snowing and there must be a couple of feet of snow out there." In the distance they could hear loud cracks followed by thuds. "You can hear trees coming down, so it's a bit dangerous to be out in the country with all that happening. I guess we'll have to stay inside, read a book and maybe even talk to each other, unless you suddenly feel a mad passion for my body." He glanced at her, hoping to change her mind.

"Even if I did, I still won't. You have to remember that we're married."

"Ugh!" Eric looked over at her with a pained expression. "So, who's first to take a shower? And can I watch you?" Janet shook her head and patted Eric on the top of his head.

"I'm almost tempted to say yes to see what you'd really do, but you might suffer a heart attack."

"Probably. I'll let you go first, if you promise to be finished by lunchtime."

Janet stuck her tongue out at Eric and proceeded to the dresser to get her clothes of the day. She hummed an unknown song as she closed the bathroom door.

When finished Janet came back into the bedroom dressed in casual slacks and a sweater. Eric copied her thinking and after his shower came out of the bathroom in a pair of jeans and a sweater.

Breakfast was a monster buffet full of all sorts of delicious-looking food. Eric filled his plate with blueberry pancakes, bacon, sausage and eggs Benedict. Janet was a bit less hungry and settled for waffles with walnuts and a couple of slices of bacon. They both started with fruit and fruit juice and coffee. Eric was tempted to go back for more, but Janet stared him out of it.

They headed for the front door and walked out on the porch that had recently been shoveled. Snow was still falling but the wind and rain seemed to have stopped. "There must be a couple of feet out here."

A voice behind him said, "Actually we've had twenty-seven inches so far with possibly another foot today." The voice belonged to the lodge owner, Michael Craven. "We'll probably end up with about forty inches before it stops. The weatherman says we should see sunlight by tomorrow morning. Then we can get your car up here, but it's going to take a long time to plow away all this snow."

Janet asked Craven, "Can we go snowshoeing yet?"

Craven looked out toward the golf course and answered, "The snow is really deep and it's going to be difficult going even with snowshoes, but go ahead and try it. Stay on the golf course and away from trees because branches and trees are still falling down."

"Eric, I want to go snowshoeing, OK?" She looked at him with wide-open eyes like a child on Christmas morning.

"Have I a choice?"

"Of course not. I'm going to change clothes. Give me about ten minutes."

Janet left Michael Craven and Eric talking about the monster storm and the problems it had created. Craven said, according to the radio report, just about everything in the northern two-thirds of the state was closed down. Power and phone lines were down in most of the same region and help was coming from other states and Canadian provinces to help restore power. "This is the most snow we've ever had in Bethel," responded Craven. It's going to take a long time for the state to clear its roads and to get the power back to everyone. What a mess!"

Eric checked his watch and left Craven for his room to get dressed for snowshoeing while thinking of how it must be at home. He hoped Susan was all right wherever she was.

He ran up the stairs two steps at a time and burst into the room without thinking or knocking. Standing by the dresser was Janet with nothing covering her top. She quickly covered her chest but not before Eric had a good look. She let out a semi-quiet scream as Eric quickly turned his head and said, "Sorry 'bout that. I should've knocked." *Boy, she looked great,* he thought to himself. "Can I try it again?" She laughed.

Janet quickly put on a bra and sweater and told Eric she was dressed. He turned around and said, "I liked it better the other way. You got me all excited."

"Very funny. Now I can watch you change your clothes." She gave him a smile and stared at his chest.

"OK." Eric began unbuttoning his shirt while Janet grabbed her jacket and hat and ran to the door, leaving Eric to dress himself. He kept thinking about what he had just seen. *God, she is beautiful.*

As she walked down the stairs of the Benoit Lodge, Janet was beginning to feel compassionate toward Eric. He was really a very nice guy, different in so many ways than her husband Jack. He was more fun than Jack and not as serious. He was also considerably more gentle, *but then,* she thought, *that's not a fair comparison because of their different lifestyles.* In any case Eric was fun to be with even with his teasing.

CHAPTER 10

Jack and Susan were still asleep under the down comforter when she heard her door-knocker. *Who the hell is this?* she wondered. The clock said a little after eight so she got up, put on a bathrobe and went to the window above the side porch. It was still snowing but the rain and wind had left. On the porch was Pam Miranda, one of her neighbors from up the road.

"Hi, Pam," she said, poking her head out the window. It was still snowing and everything was completely covered except for Pam's footprints. Everything was white and snow was still falling.

"Good morning, Susan. Paul told us you didn't get to Bethel. Sorry about that. Are you OK?" Pam was a tall, slender lady with short graying hair.

"Yeah, I'm fine, but it's a long story on what happened yesterday. I got a ride from Jack Meacham but there was no way he could get out of here last night, so he's staying until the road clears."

"Well that sounds romantic," Pam replied while looking up at Susan and without thinking. Susan couldn't think of a reply so she just stared at Pam who said, "We're having a brunch gathering to talk about the storm and what needs to be done to help clear the road. So, if you can, come on over at about ten."

"OK, we'll be there. Can I bring anything?"

"No, just the two of you," Pam said. She was anxious to meet Jack Meacham as was her husband and probably everyone else on the road. *In other words,* she thought, *everyone down here is aware that Jack is with her.*

Susan went back to the bed where Jack was listening to the conversation. His naked muscular chest was exposed. Susan said, "Pam's a bit nosy so that's probably why she came here. I think we should go, but we have lots of time before we need to be there." She stood next to Jack's head and opened her bathrobe. He grabbed and pulled her into the bed. "Screw her," she murmured.

Later they showered without saying anything as they both were thinking about Eric and Janet. Their bodies were an advertisement for a workout center. They dressed in outdoor clothes and went downstairs for coffee. Then they checked the closed fireplace, which was still smoldering wood, so with new logs the fire started quickly.

"Son of a bitch, I've never had a night like that," Jack said laughing. "Now what the hell are we going to do about Eric and Janet? Maybe they did the same thing last night wherever they are." He laughed about that thought. "Somehow I doubt it. Janet's a bit of a forever virgin. She would drive Eric to frustration."

Susan ignored any thoughts about Eric and Janet, as she felt uneasy that she and Jack had sex together. "Jack, I loved last night. I've always had a feeling for you, but I never believed it would be this great." She looked passionately at Jack, then walked over to embrace him. "I don't like deceiving Eric, but I couldn't help it. I thought I was in love with you and last night proved it. You were fantastic!"

Jack ran his hand over her hair. "God, I can't believe how much I think I love you. I've wanted to get you in bed for the longest time and now that it's happened, I know I love you. Why in the hell did we wait so long?" They embraced to show each other they didn't want to part. "I think Janet would understand and if she didn't, tough shit."

"I love Eric," Susan said quietly as she stroked his face, "but I hate living down here and I know he doesn't want to move back to town. We're just not made for each other anymore for a whole bunch of reasons, but I'll miss him. I now know I love you more than I can say."

The snow was still falling as Jack went out to shovel the snow off the deck and the sidewalk while Susan worked at cleaning up the water that had seeped into the living room from the storm last night. As she began to mop the floor she stared out toward the lake and leaned against the back of the couch. She thought about what she and Jack had done.

While thinking warm thoughts about their sexual encounter, Susan couldn't avoid a feeling of guilt toward Eric and also toward Janet. Susan felt she had violated her marriage bond with Eric by making love with Jack yet she still couldn't believe it had happened and though there was a guilty feeling she still loved sleeping with Jack. It was greater than she could have ever imagined. Maybe it was time for Eric and her to end their marriage.

When Jack finished with his shoveling, he came back in the house to join Susan for a couple of cups of coffee. Then they snowshoed up the road to the Mirandas' house since the road hadn't been plowed. It was still snowing, but not like yesterday, and the wind had all but vanished.

Bruce and Pam Miranda lived in a large two-story house just off the road. They had a spacious kitchen with a counter in the middle where the neighbors were all gathered. The large living and dining rooms were vacant as everyone was in the kitchen.

Ron Dunham came over to hug Susan and to shake Jack's hand. "So, you're the new boyfriend Pam's been telling us about. Nice to have you here, Jack," he said laughing. Jack got the same reaction from just about everyone in the kitchen. They also talked to him about his years with the Patriots and about the potential of Maine's football team to do anything. They were all friends of Eric's and they missed not having him at this snowstorm event.

What a bunch of jerks these people are, Jack thought to himself.

They were all looking at Susan and Jack to see if something was going on between them.

"Have you heard from Eric?" Rob asked.

"Nothing," answered Jack. "We have no idea where they are. We can't get through to the Benoit Lodge and we can't get them on our cell phones, so we assume they're at the lodge but their phone lines are probably down."

Susan added, "The roads over there are in really bad shape, according to the radio reports, but we hope and pray they got to the lodge before the worst of the storm hit them."

Pam Miranda got in on the conversation. "If it's as bad there as it is here, it will be a couple of days before they can drive back."

Pam's husband changed the subject. "Well, guys, there are several trees down between here and the top of the hill that we have to move so the town can plow the road. We'll start after we eat. OK?"

Everyone agreed and they started working on the buffet full of lunchmeat, cheese and all sorts of makings for salads. After they had finished, the men started up the road on snowmobiles, taking with them three chain saws, a variety of axes, shears, and some pruning saws. Not far from the Miranda house was a large birch tree lying across the road. It didn't take long for it to be cut up and pulled off the road. The snow was still falling and there appeared to be some two feet of snow on the ground, but the wind was moderate and temperature was in the high twenties.

The rest of the afternoon was spent going up the road and clearing fallen trees and branches that would hinder the town's snowplows. It was still difficult to see any distance because of the ice-covered branches and small trees hanging over the road. Jack was amazed that there was at least an inch of ice on these branches. Regardless, the scenery was incredibly beautiful.

The snow finally stopped about two o'clock.

They quit working at four o'clock and headed back to the Miranda house. Jack had to admit that he enjoyed this different type of exercise. He was now thinking of getting Susan back to her house for some late-afternoon enjoyment. Instead Susan invited the group for dinner at her house. Six of them accepted the invitation, but the remainder begged off. Jack looked anxiously at Susan but she rolled her eyes and shrugged her shoulders.

CHAPTER 11

Eric and Janet began their walk around the Benoit Lodge's golf course. It was safe to do it this way as they could hear limbs falling in the woods when the tree could no longer handle the weight of the ice. It was snowing very lightly and the scenery around them was spectacular with the snow and ice glistening, even without sunlight.

"Maybe I should have brought my golf clubs," said Eric, swinging his ski poles like a driver.

Janet stopped to admire the course in front of them. The trees were covered with snow and ice so heavy the birch trees were bent to the ground. "Eric, isn't this beautiful? I'm so glad we got out of the lodge by ourselves." Her face had a red tint to it from the exertion and the cold weather, but she was smiling at all of it.

Eric answered, "This is why I love it down at Lake Lucerne . This time of the year it's quiet and you can get out and enjoy the snow and ice."

Janet asked, "Does Susan enjoy it as much as you do?"

"No, she's a house and gym person. She'd rather work out in a weight room than go for a hike in the woods. She has a problem with the lake as though something in her past is affecting her. That's why she doesn't go boating very often." Eric had a puzzled look on his face. "She rarely goes swimming and never without me."

"Yeah, Jack feels the same. I don't understand his reasoning but he really doesn't like the outdoors as I do, except for football. But I so enjoy taking advantage of what Maine has to offer. I almost hate seeing this weekend end."

Eric nodded in agreement. This was a thought he never heard from Susan.

They walked on for another couple of miles, then headed back to the lodge for lunch. Eric was very impressed with Janet's ability to handle this long walk without tiring. They both stopped on occasion to rest and admire the scenery. The trees in the forest were covered with ice and snow and the peaks of the distant hills were Christmas-card pretty.

Lunch was being served when they arrived back at the lodge so they went directly to their table after a quick stop in their room. They both were still somewhat red faced but they were feeling very good about the hike just completed and looked forward to the next outing. The remainder of the guests seemed to have stayed indoors as they gazed at Janet and Eric as though they were crazy to have gone outside.

Eric ordered a cheeseburger with fries and a glass of iced tea. Janet settled for potato soup and a Greek salad with a diet coke. Eric asked, "You're drinking a diet soda? I doubt you have a weight problem."

"Well, this is a good way to avoid it in the future. Besides, I like the taste of it." They toasted each other. "Here's to more snowshoeing." She smiled as Eric attacked his cheeseburger.

"There's nothing greater in the world of eating than a cheeseburger. Nothing!" Eric insisted while Janet worked on her soup. They talked very little during lunch but every now and again, looked at each other with great pleasure. Eric was so inspired with everything about Janet, that at times he had a difficult time talking to her. Janet in turn felt much the same. She was getting a very warm feeling every time she was near Eric, something she hadn't felt about her husband for a long time.

Eric asked Janet, "How did you ever meet Jack? I didn't think you were a football fanatic."

"It's a long story," she replied in a soft quiet voice.

"Well, we've got all sorts of time," Eric said, leaning back in his chair. They got up and went to the lodge's sitting room where they found a private couch.

Janet leaned back on the sofa and brought her feet under her body. She related to Eric how she'd first met Jack about six years ago while she was watching from the press box as the New England Patriots played the New York Jets.

She was a senior at Harvard and her father was an executive with Channel 2 in Bangor, Maine, who had come down to do a personal interview with the Patriots' star halfback, Jack Meacham. After the game her father took her with him to the Patriots' locker room for the interview, but before going into the locker room her father warned her of what she would be seeing.

"You have to understand," he'd said, "these are very different men, particularly after they've finished playing the game. So, just understand this before we go into the locker room. You have to realize that they just played a tough game and that they are still keyed up. They will not match your thoughts of what a guy should be. OK?"

Janet hadn't been certain about what her dad was saying so she had just nodded her head and followed him into the locker room.

Jack Meacham had been with the Patriots for the past four years and was considered one of the best running back in the National Football League. He had made the all-pro team for the past three years.

When they were permitted into the locker room, Janet could not believe the size and strength of all these football players. She had never seen anything like this. The locker room was full of monster-sized men in a variety of dress; most of them were full of sweat and all smelled badly. Their bodies had a multitude of black and blue marks along with all sorts of scratches and cuts. Since they had won the game there was a lot of noise emanating from the players, yelling and complimenting each other on beating the Jets.

Several of these players had looked longingly at Janet, wondering whose girlfriend she was. There had also been a mass of reporters interviewing players and a bunch of people who were there as guests. They walked over to Jack Meacham's locker where Dave Felty introduced his daughter to him. He was sweaty, bruised, and was suffering from some cuts on his face and body from being repeatedly tackled. He had taken off his jersey so his incredible physique was right in front of her eyes. It was all muscle. His face was full of black stuff under his eyes, he hadn't shaved, and his hair was wet and messy, but Janet thought he was still very handsome. She couldn't stop staring and eventually, Jack waved his hand in front of her face and asked, "Hello! Haven't you seen a football player before?"

She snapped out of her trance and answered, "Uh, no. At least not this close."

Jack Meacham had smiled and asked, "So, what do you think?" while he pulled off his shoes.

She had wondered how much more he would take off before she should get out. "I can't believe how strong everyone looks. My God, you guys are huge," she answered with an amazed gaze.

"Well, it's a game of size, strength and speed. Without any of these you couldn't be a professional player," he had answered.

"All right, Janet, it's my turn," said her father who sat on a stool in front of Meacham and began to ask questions about the game while his cameraman recorded the interview. Janet had continued to stare at Jack and he looked back at her. He was inspired with her looks and she was enraptured with him.

She wasn't listening to her father's questioning but instead was still amazed at the size of these players. Noise filled the locker room and she was constantly brushed by a variety of players and reporters. She had never seen such large men in all her life and she was intrigued by Jack Meacham's physique and looks.

When the interview ended, Jack had asked Dave Felty if it would be all right to ask his daughter out for dinner. Felty thought for a minute because he didn't like this combination, but Janet was old enough to make her own decisions. "That's up to Janet," he answered. Later he regretted saying that.

Janet was snowed. *A professional football player wants to take me to dinner. Wait till I tell my friends. They won't believe me.* She gave Jack her phone number and address and he replied by thanking her and shaking her hand with his huge strong hand.

On the way home Dave Felty had tried to discourage her from dating a professional football player. "Janet, these guys are so self-centered they live in a universe all to themselves. At times they are dangerous because of the nature of their lifestyles. If he does call you and invites you out, I'd suggest that you take another couple with you." He looked at Janet with a very serious look.

"Dad, thanks, but I think I can handle this myself. I don't think he'll take me somewhere and rape me. Anyway it would be fun to know more about him."

For several weeks she had watched the Patriots' games on TV and read about Jack Meacham in the *Boston Globe*, but she didn't get the promised phone call so she had given up hope he would call. Then one evening while she was studying for an exam, her phone rang. "Janet, it's Jack Meacham."

Janet answered, "Hello." She couldn't think of anything else to say.

Jack said, "I'm sorry it's taken this long to call you but we've had a tough schedule and our coach told us to do nothing but concentrate on the next game, but we've got next week off so I'm free to do whatever."

"That's OK," Janet said in a quiet surprised voice. She was basically speechless since she had given up hope he would ever call.

"Would you still have dinner with me?" he asked.

Janet thought for a while and finally said, "Yes, I'd like to."

"How 'bout this Friday?" he asked.

Janet thought for a few seconds and replied, "That's fine. Where will I meet you?"

"I'll pick you up about seven, OK?"

Janet agreed and gave him directions to her dorm. "Where are we going?"

"Don't know. Any ideas?" Janet couldn't think of any restaurant since she rarely went out to dinner in Boston.

"Not really," she answered. "You pick the place."

"You've got it. See you Friday." He hung up the phone before she could ask if she had to dress up. And she forgot to ask for his phone number. She was excited about the invitation so she called her father. Janet's mother had died in a car crash three years before and her father hadn't remarried; as he told Janet, he didn't think he ever would. He was both mother and father to Janet, though his girlfriend Sarah Johnson was a big help.

"Dad, he asked me out for dinner," she had said in a rushed voice. Doug Felty did not need to ask who had called.

"And what did you say?"

"Of course I told him yes," said Janet. "We're going out this Friday"

"OK, I guess," her father said in a voice that expressed his concern. "Now, remember, he's older than you; he's a professional football player who lives in another world and sometimes they forget they're human. He's also richer than hell. But, have fun," he added, chuckling to hide his concern.

"Thanks, Dad," Janet answered as though she hadn't heard anything he said.

On Friday before Jack Meacham showed up at her dorm, Janet had gone through a variety of dresses, trying to pick the one that would make her most attractive. Her roommate, who was looking forward to meeting this famous football player, had helped her. In fact, most of the dorm had been alerted about her date with him. With assistance from a variety of friends, Janet put on a pink dress that came down to her ankles with a red sweater that matched the dress. It was an attractive but conservative dress that didn't overexpose any part of her body.

At a few minutes before seven on Friday evening, her answering bell had rung and, as expected, it was Jack, announcing his arrival. She had rushed down the first flight of stairs then casually walked down the last set to show she wasn't overly anxious to meet him. Her roommate Cynthia had gone down with her to see Jack Meacham up close so she could tell her boyfriend about meeting him. The windows in the dormitory had been full of friends wanting to see Jack Meacham.

He was wearing a pair of khaki-colored pants with a blue blazer over a light blue shirt. He was even wearing a tie. Jack looked at her, smiled, and complimented her on her looks. Janet introduced him to Cynthia, who was at a loss for words. He held out his hand, gently grasped hers, then led Janet to his car. He drove a Mercedes sports car, indicative of his wealth

"I've made reservations at Locke-Ober's. I hope that's all right with you."

Janet had never heard of it, but smiled and replied, "That sounds wonderful."

The drive to Locke-Ober's was quiet with neither one knowing what to say. Finally, Jack said, "I was very impressed with your father and how he handled the interview with me. So many of the reporters who interview me ask stupid questions that are impossible to answer. But that's the result of being a professional athlete with a winning team."

Janet turned and thanked him. She had looked at him and saw he was completely different from what she had remembered from the locker room.

He noticed her gaze and said, "We do clean up fairly well," and laughed when she smiled in agreement. Janet was overwhelmed with the situation and didn't know what to say. It was as if her tongue was tied.

The drive to Locke-Ober's had taken about twenty minutes and the conversation began to warm a bit as Janet Felty became more comfortable with Jack. A parking valet took the car when they reached the restaurant. Everyone at Locke-Ober's seemed to know Jack Meacham since he was quite often on the front page of the Boston daily newspapers and, of course, on TV.

Locke-Ober's was a German restaurant with massive woodwork around the dining room. There was a large bar with three bartenders handling drink orders. The tables were massive wood structures and the accompanying chairs matched the décor. This was certainly a male-oriented restaurant and the famed section was for men only.

It seemed as though everyone knew Jack Meacham, or at least they wanted to know him. Thus he was given complete attention by the Locke-Ober staff. Jack pointed to photos on the wall of famous people who ate at the restaurant. There were several Boston Red Sox players, including Ted Williams and Carl Yastrzemski, Bobby Orr of the Boston Bruins and Bill Russell of the Boston Celtics. There was also a picture of Jack Meacham. It had impressed Janet that he was included with these very famous stars.

They were guided to a table in a corner of dining room, which served booth men, women and children so they could have some privacy. Janet understood this when a man came over to their table to ask for an autograph. Jack had refused in a very friendly manner, but the man was upset and stormed away from their table, swearing at Jack.

"God damn it," Jack had said back to the man. He turned his head back to Janet. "I'm sorry, Janet, but this happens every time I got out to a public place. If I agreed to give him an autograph, we'd soon have the entire restaurant over here. So instead I'm a conceited football player who doesn't care for his fans. No matter what I do, I lose."

"I think I understand," Janet had said. "It must be difficult to put up with."

"Thanks, it's something professional athletes must learn to handle. Now let's enjoy our dinner. Would you like a cocktail or wine or what?" asked Jack.

"I'll have a glass of wine, please. Merlot."

Jack ordered the wine and an imported beer for himself.

Janet had begun to loosen up as they talked about her, what she was studying, and that she planned to teach school in the Bangor, Maine area after graduation. He had listened intently to her and finally commented that he had never been to Bangor, Maine. "I don't even know where it's at," Jack answered with a shrug of his shoulders.

Janet giggled at that thought and told him, "Bangor is about five hours down east from here, which means that it's really north. There's not much north of Bangor. It's small, but it's a nice place to live."

"Well, maybe someday I'll take a trip up there," Jack had replied, thinking to himself that Bangor didn't seem to be that exciting. "At least to see you," he'd added while sipping his beer.

Janet answered with a smile. "That would be nice," she'd said while thinking there was no way he'd come to Bangor. Not with the excitement of a city like Boston. She'd added, "It's not anything like Boston. It's small and probably boring to those from large cities, but I love the area."

For dinner she'd had lazy lobster so she didn't have to make a mess opening the lobster's shells. The dinner was delicious and the waiters did a good job in keeping other guests from invading their privacy

Jack looked at his watch and said, "You may not understand this, but I have a curfew so I have to get back to my apartment within the next hour."

He took her hand and looked her in the eye and remarked, "I've really enjoyed this evening, Janet, and I hope I can see you again."

Her heart began to race as she agreed that she would like to see him again. At no time did he attempt to seduce her as her father had suggested. He was a perfect gentleman. He was extremely handsome, she thought, and he seemed to have a nice personality even though he got angry with the man who wanted an autograph.

The drive home to her dorm was somewhat quiet, as they both had run out of things to say to each other. When he led her out of the car and escorted her to the dorm, Janet didn't know what to do next so she grasped his shoulder and gave him a quick kiss on his cheek. "Thank you for a lovely evening. I really enjoyed it and hope to see you again." She raced through her words.

He'd laughed at her feelings, and then returned to his car, saying, "You can count on that. You're a terrific young lady."

❧

Janet eased back in her chair and looked over at a very impressed Eric. "So, that's how I met him. It was very exciting to say the least. I fell in love with him soon after our first date. He was a very nice guy even though he had a quick temper, but we got along just fine.

"I'll bet," answered Eric. "So how soon after did you marry him?"

"About eight months later he invited me to go with him to Nantucket Island for a weekend. There he proposed to me and I happily agreed. I really loved him and I think he felt the same." She rocked back in her chair as her mind flowed back to that weekend. She smiled at remembering it. "But two years later he got really hurt when playing against the Miami Dolphins. Somehow his hip was permanently damage when he got tackled."

"I remember reading about it," said Eric.

Janet continued her story. "I was at the game with Miami when he got tackled badly. He was carted off the field and sent by ambulance to a hospital. An x-ray showed the broken hip and the doctor who looked at it said he probably would never play football again. I met him at the hospital, but he was told he had to stay to get the hip repaired." She shook her head while remembering that day.

"He was in shock over what had happened, so he ignored my presence.

"Jack didn't believe this until the team's orthopedic surgeon said he could repair the hip but it couldn't be fixed so he could play again. His career was over just that quickly. Jack couldn't accept it. You would have to go back to his early childhood to find a time when he didn't play football and now that he couldn't play again became a situation he never realized would happen. He always felt he had several more years of playing before age and younger players forced his retirement. This he could accept, at least he thought so, but he just couldn't accept not being able to ever play again so quickly after the injury.

"He was horribly depressed and no matter what I said or did, he didn't get back to his former lifestyle. I wanted us to move back to Bangor so I could begin teaching school and so Jack could get on with his life. He would just sit and say nothing. It was as though it was my fault he got hurt.

"He became frustrated even when he became an assistant coach at the University of Maine. Our relationship began to fall apart and there was nothing I could do to get him back to what he was before the injury. He just plain missed the stardom he was accustomed to. That's why he gave me the negligee. He'd probably hoped we'd get back together again, but I don't think we ever will. There just isn't any love left between us. We haven't had sex for over a year now and I don't really care to try again. Maybe there's someone else. I just don't know. I'm moving back to Dad's house after we get back."

Her eyes began to tear up when she finished. She hung her head in her hands while hiding her face from Eric. He reached over, embraced her and brought her head against his. "Janet, I'm so sorry. I didn't know any of this. Now I feel badly about how I treated you since we've been here."

"Oh, no, Eric," replied a smiling Janet, "I've enjoyed being with you. You've been an absolute joy and I love you for it. I really needed this and I can thank the storm for letting me get away from my problems." Janet took Eric's hand in hers and smiled through her tears. "However, don't think this will change my attitude in our bedroom." She began to laugh while crying. "I'm still married, but there was no way I was going to wear that nightgown."

"Janet, I'm so sorry all this has happened to the two of you and I'm also glad we've had this time together." Eric felt very comfortable being with her.

Eric continued, "I first met the two of you when Susan recommended Jack to me when the pain in his hip got so bad he had difficulty walking. I told him the only solution was a hip replacement. I gave him the name of several people for him to call and check how the artificial hip would work. One of the names was Bo Jackson who was an outstanding pro football and baseball player. He hurt his hip on what appeared to be a simple tackle. Even after his operation to replace the hip, he tried to continue playing baseball, but that didn't work out at all. While you can walk normally, you cannot participate in professional competitive sports. For a professional athlete this is a very difficult thing to accept, particularly when you're in your prime.

"Even amateurs will have a difficult time playing these sorts of sports. The artificial hip or knee cannot accept this strain. Janet, I'm really sorry for all this but somehow it'll work out."

Janet smiled and put her hand across his arm and left it there for what seemed an eternity to Eric. He felt good being with Janet. Eric suggested Janet might feel better if she lay down for a while, "even without me."

She smiled away her tears. "No, I'm OK. I think I'd like to go back outside again and maybe go down to see where the car is. It's stopped snowing so it can't be any worse than this morning, unless you want to take a nap. I realize you're getting a little old for all this." She felt good for the first time since relating her life with Jack.

"OK, let's do it." Eric got out of his chair, stretched and followed Janet to the door. He had no idea that Janet was going through this horrible episode in her life. She didn't deserve it. She was a marvelous woman, a great teacher, and must have been a terrific wife.

The snow had stopped as they snowshoed down to the car in less time than it took them to get up to the lodge. They agreed that this trip was easier than yesterday's adventure coming up the road. The surrounding trees were full of so much ice and snow that the branches touched the ground. Bushes were totally covered in white and pressed into the snow. When they got to Eric's SUV they were surprised at how far it had gone off the road; it was now part of the scenery. There didn't appear to be any damage but they also saw that it would have to be towed out. There was no way he could drive it out, as it was too far into the woods and covered with too much ice and snow.

"Have we left anything in the car?" Janet asked as she peered into the window.

"I don't think so," Eric said, looking in the back window. "Mr. Craven's staff got everything out except our skis." These were still on the car's rack. A few minutes later they proceeded back up the driveway in a much better procession than they had yesterday; while the snow was deep, the snowshoes worked as promised.

When they got back to the lodge, they took off their snowshoes and headed into the lodge where they ran into Hank and Margaret Lewis. "How 'bout joining us for a drink?" Hank asked.

"All right, we'd be delighted," Eric answered before Janet could say anything. They followed the Lewises to a table to the left of the fireplace, ordered a couple bottles of wine and began to talk about the miserable weather and how each of them was affected.

CHAPTER 12

Jack and Susan entertained six of her neighbors: Pam and Bruce Miranda, Paul and Harriet Glidden, and Bob and Laurie Anderson. They each brought food and wine while Susan roasted a leg of lamb she found in her freezer.

Before dinner, they gathered in the kitchen for cocktails. The men all had questions again for Jack about his days with the Patriots and how Maine will do in the next season. He was a little tired of being asked about the Patriots and the Maine Black Bears who realistically were not going to do very well. Nonetheless he held back his frustration since these people were friends of Susan's.

Susan smiled at him as the three stimulated neighbors surrounded him. The guys were tired from the work they had done clearing the road and there would still be work tomorrow, but the worst was over and they could get the town's snowplow to clean up the road so they could get out of there. Jack couldn't understand how these people and Eric could enjoy living so far from town and down a treacherous hill. He thought the house was beautiful, as was the location, but only for a summer place, not a year-round house.

For dinner they gathered around the dining room table with several candles supplying the light. The conversation got around to where Eric and Janet might be. "Is there any way we can reach the lodge to see if they are there?" asked Laurie who was a beautiful, young lady that was constantly teased by Eric for being a vegetarian. She missed him not being here with his wife, Susan, but understood what the storm had done to all of them.

Jack looked at Susan and smiled. Pam Miranda saw it and thought there was something more involved than just a smile. Susan finally said, "I have no idea where they are or how we could reach them. Their power must be out and they must have gotten more snow than us so they probably can't drive anywhere. Cell phones don't work here and even if they did, I don't think they'd work in Bethel. So, there's nothing we can do until they come back, and God knows how long that will be." Susan threw her arms up in disgust.

Susan suddenly wondered if Eric and Janet might try to drive back and, if so, what she and Jack should do to avoid being caught in a compromising position. She couldn't handle a worried look that was caught by Jack and by Pam Miranda. Pam wondered to herself if Jack and Susan were having a romantic weekend together. Their togetherness indicated something was happening.

The party began to break up as the Gliddens left for their house followed by the Andersons. Bruce Miranda asked if it would be all right to have another glass of wine. Jack thought to himself that this jerk should get the hell out of here right now. Bruce pushed back his chair and raised his glass to Jack and Susan. "Thanks for a great dinner. We do appreciate it." Jack forced a smile.

Pam poured another glass of wine and Jack and Susan did the same since they didn't want to look too anxious to get to get rid of them.

"'How is your hip doing, Jack?" Paul asked.

"Really well. Eric did a terrific job. There's no more pain so it's better than it has been for the last couple of years. I probably should have had it done sooner," answered Jack," but I couldn't ever play football again."

Susan added that without the operation Jack would be living in constant pain and would be somewhat of a cripple. After a moment of silence Pam finally looked at her husband and said, "Let's get going. I'm getting tired and I'm sure Susan and Jack are as well." She smiled at Susan as though she knew what had happened last night and would soon be happening again. Bruce quickly drank the rest of his wine and went to get their coats off the second floor stairs. "Thanks again, guys. It was fun. We'll see you tomorrow so we can finish cleaning up the road. Hopefully, Eric will be back." He smiled again at Susan.

When they were finally alone, Susan said to Jack, "I think Pam suspects that we are doing what we're doing." She smiled and hugged Jack. "But, I don't give a damn what any of them think...do you?"

Jack frowned. "Hell, no! These are your friends, not mine, so it doesn't make any damn difference to me. I just want to be with you. OK?" He helped gather the dishes off the dining room table and took them into the kitchen where they washed the dishes and cleaned up the kitchen stove and counters.

"Jack, we also have to think about what we're going to tell Eric and Janet," she said with a worried look. She couldn't think of how she would tell Eric that she wanted out of the marriage, but then the two of them had discussed what would happen in the eventuality of a divorce, so it shouldn't come as a complete surprise; this was part of their agreement before they got married.

Jack stepped behind Susan and embraced her with his hands moving up and down her front. "I'm not going to think about anything right now other than to make love to you." He guided her up to the bedroom where they each helped the other remove their clothes, got into bed, and explored each other's body before they made love.

When they finished, they sat up and looked lovingly at each other. Susan still had a guilty feeling and asked, "Do you think they might show up tonight?"

Jack answered firmly, "Not a chance. If the snow's as bad over there as it is here, it will be another day before they can get back here. I don't think they'll be out of there before Monday, assuming they got to Bethel."

Susan had a worried look on her face and said, "I hope you're right, but what if they didn't get to Bethel and stayed in the Augusta area?"

Jack embraced her and answered, "Even if they did, they still couldn't get down this road until we get it freed from all these trees. No, we won't see them until Monday at the earliest." Susan frowned at that thought.

"Then we have to figure out what we're going to tell Eric and Janet," Susan said while leaning against the bed's headboard.

"Let's talk about it tomorrow. I'm too tired to think about it tonight." He wrapped his arm around a contented Susan and fell asleep.

CHAPTER 13

Eric and Janet tried to explain to the Lewises what had happened to them. "So you see, we don't know where our spouses are. We assume they're still in the Bangor area, but we can't reach them with our cell phones."

Hank replied without thinking, "So, you're living together in the same room."

"That's right," added Janet in a serious voice with a blushing face. There was no other place for Eric to sleep." She didn't offer that they were sleeping in the same bed.

"Right," murmured Hank as he gazed hungrily at Janet. He could envision what was going on between the two of them and was envious of Eric.

His wife changed the subject. "I understand you went snowshoeing this morning. How was it?"

Janet looked at Eric and replied, "We had a good time. It's not too bad out there even with all the snow and ice, and the snowshoes really work well. We just got back from checking Eric's SUV, which rolled off the driveway on the way up here yesterday. Hopefully they can get it up here by tomorrow."

Janet asked Margaret. "Are the two of you going to snowshoe tomorrow?"

"Not a chance," answered Hank. "We're staying inside and we'll sit, read, and relax. You guys go ahead and exercise and then you can tell us what you've seen." He laughed as he thought about what he just said.

Eric nodded and joined in laughing. "I understand."

The conversation with the Lewises continued on a variety of subjects, but no matter what was said, Hank was thinking about what was happening in their room.

Eric and Janet excused themselves, saying they had to get ready for dinner, so they left the Lewises and went up the stairs to their room. Eric whispered, "See, they expect me to be making out with you. How can you disappoint them?" He patted her shoulders when she looked back at him. Then she stuck her tongue out at him.

Janet laughed saying, "Good try Eric, but it still won't work."

When they reached their room, Janet said she wanted to shower; Jack volunteered to assist and was quickly turned down. "Do you want me to leave, or do you trust me not to attack you?"

"You can stay, but no peeking, all right?"

"You ruin all my fun," Eric said with a serious look. He sat on the chair in front of the fireplace and thought about what Janet had told him. He felt sorry for her since it seemed that Jack was treating her badly after the ending of his career. How on earth he could do this puzzled him. Maybe there's another woman.

Janet finished her shower and as promised Eric was not peeking. He could only imagine what he was missing. When she finally said OK he turned around, hoping to see her undressed again, and marveled at how attractive she was. He couldn't understand how Jack Meacham could toss her aside

She was wearing a maroon-colored dress that went down to her ankles with buttons traveling down from her breasts to her waist.

He took a quick shower and got dressed in tan slacks and a blue sport coat. He came out, hung up his outdoor clothes in the closet, and got ready for dinner. She put her book down and looked up at Eric. She was again impressed with him. "You look very handsome," she said looking at him, then asked, "Maybe we should invite the Lewises to have dinner with us. OK?"

"Whatever you want, my dear," he answered while smiling at her.

"You don't sound too serious," Janet told him. "If you don't want to do it, let's forget it."

Eric sat down next to her and began to laugh. "Forget what you think I meant. Let's invite them to join us. They are a nice couple and I'm getting tired of being alone with you."

She jabbed her elbow into his ribs while getting up. "Put it in gear, you miserable jerk." She headed for the door while he stayed in his chair trying to figure out if she was serious. He caught up with her as they reached the bottom of the stairs and grabbed her arm. She turned a smiling face at him, as Eric was again impressed with how beautiful she was and how great a personality she possessed.

"Now, let's see if we can find them." They caught up with Margaret and Hank in the lobby and invited them to dinner. They both accepted and the four of them went into the dining room where they started their dinner with a bottle of wine and all felt good about being together. Even Hank stopped thinking about what was happening upstairs as he enjoyed being with the two of them.

Hank related how his business was doing and Eric and Janet were impressed at how well Hank and Margaret were doing, even with a Home Depot fairly close to them. He related how he tried to match prices, but his most important factor was how his staff treated their customers.

After dinner, the Lewises headed up to their room while Eric and Janet took a quick trip outside. The wind had stopped and the moon was floating with half its body showing. There was still enough light so they could see down to the snow-filled golf course. The weather was now like they had planned.

Eric put his right arm around her shoulder. "Boy, it is really gorgeous out here. I'm almost tempted to go out snowshoeing, but without lights outside we'd have a real problem, so we'd better get ready for bed."

Janet enjoyed being with Eric as she accepted his arm around her. She felt very comfortable and agreed that it would have been fun to go snowshoeing, but it was getting too late and both were getting tired.

They headed up the stairs along with several other couples and Eric noted that most of the men turned to look at Janet to admire her beauty..

When they got into their room they sat down in front of the fireplace and both stared at the fire. "Well," Eric offered, "that was a nice evening. They're really nice people."

"Yes, they are" Janet responded as she continued to look at the fireplace. She was beginning to feel more comfortable being with Eric. He was unlike any man she had ever known, particularly her husband Jack. Eric looked over at her and began to feel more comfortable with Janet.

Janet got up and headed for the bathroom to put on her pajamas. She was feeling a little cold so she looked forward to getting under the bedcovers.

Eric stared at her and couldn't believe he'd again sleep with Janet without touching her. He got up from his chair and exhaled loudly, then headed to the bathroom to change into his pajamas.

He took a copy of an old *National Geographic* with him as he crawled into his side of the bed. He opened the magazine and held it above his head.

"Eric," she said with a smile, "It's a little difficult to read upside down."

"Oh," replied Jack looking at the magazine. "I'm so enraptured being in bed with you again that I lost my concentration." He burst out laughing. "See what you do to me?"

She slapped the top of his head while leaning over to give him a kiss. "This is your good night kiss. Don't bug me again."

Eric answered, "You mean that's all I get?"

Count your blessings," she replied as the lights went out. Good night, Eric. And don 't touch me."

"Good night, Janet, and I just might touch you while you're sleeping." He tossed the magazine to the floor and turned his head away and thought of sleep. Janet smiled to herself and knew she was not in any danger from Eric doing what usually comes naturally when a man and woman are in bed together. She thanked God for Eric.

CHAPTER 14

Dawn hit the Forster house with a long-lost sun peeking through the window. Icicles were already melting on the side of the roof as the cold spell seemed to have ended in a hurry.

Susan was already in the bathroom when Jack got out of bed and went over to the window to see if it was really warming up. He thought it was already in the forties. This should help clear the roads. The closeness of the ocean helped warm up the outdoors.

Jack turned as Susan came out of the bathroom dressed in her bathrobe and came over to the window to see what he was looking at. Susan was amazed that the icicles were melting.

"What time are you to go up the road with the guys?" she asked, still staring out the window.

She looked up at Jack, who was smiling at her. "Not for another hour or so. Paul's coming to pick me up on his snowmobile," he said, guiding her back to the bed.

For breakfast Susan fixed scrambled eggs and bacon with orange juice and coffee. When they finished they heard a snowmobile out on the driveway followed by a knock on the door. Jack and Susan had left the blanket and pillow on the couch so anyone coming into the house would assume this was where Jack was sleeping.

"Hey," Paul said, "it's warm out here. The snow is melting and the ice is coming off the branches. Maybe spring is here so let's head up the road to see if the other guys are already working."

Susan decided she should stay home and work around the house this morning, so she patted both Paul and Jack on their backs while slipping her hand under Jack's waistband. "Have fun," she said as they walked out.

Susan went into the living room, put a couple of logs on the fireplace, got out a book, and curled up on the couch while reminiscing about what had happened the last two days. The book soon lost her interest.

About a mile and half up the road, the rest of the neighbors were already at work. "Good morning, Jack," Bruce said. "Hope you had a good night's sleep." His smile indicated he figured Jack had done more than sleep.

You son of a bitch, Jack thought. *I ought to knock the shit out of you.* But instead Jack smiled and began to move logs off the road. To do otherwise would be to admit his affair with Susan. By noon they got within half a mile of the top of the hill where there were only a few trees, but lots of branches on the road. The snow was several feet deep and made movement difficult, but the sun was shining and the day began to feel good.

While the men were working on clearing the road, Susan was staring out the window, reminiscing on what had happened the last two nights. She began to feel uncomfortable about her violating her marriage vows to Eric and though she had some guilt feelings, she felt a great love for Jack Meacham and that took precedent over her casual marriage to Eric.

⚭

It didn't seem that long ago when she first met Eric Forster. It was after a soccer game in Orono, Maine, where she had scored two goals, the last a game winner. Her friend and teammate, Jane Anderson, had a date the night after the game and asked Susan to come along.

Susan had begged off because she didn't enjoy noisy parties and would sooner go work out at the Gold's Gym in Bangor. When she arrived there were only a few people exercising so she would have lots of time to herself to keep her body toned up. One of the exercisers was a tall, handsome, slender guy with short brown hair.

However, she was not here to flirt with someone; she needed to concentrate on building her muscles. She went over to the leg-lifting machine and the man went to the same machine next to her. He looked over at the weight she was lifting and it was the same as his, 120 pounds. He looked at her with a smile as he started his lifting. She somewhat ignored him, but she finally looked over at him and asked, without a smile, what he was staring at.

"I'm sorry," he'd said, looking at her eyes, "but I was surprised at how much weight you're lifting. My mother used to say girls should be frail and not try to compete with men. Man, was she wrong! I'm very impressed. Do you do this often?" Eric was also impressed with her good looks and athletic body.

Susan ignored his comments for a while, but finally said, "I do this just about every day. It keeps me in shape for playing soccer."

"You're a soccer player?" he asked. "I've never seen a game. It just looks boring compared to football and baseball."

That did it. Susan glared at him. "See, that's just the usual male response to a women's sport. You probably have no respect for women playing any sports. She continued to glare at him as she lifted her weight with a vengeance.

Eric raised his hands and got off the leg machine and went to the far corner of the room to work on his shoulders. *God, you bastard,* thought Susan, *get your ass out of my sight.* As Susan continued her workout she gazed over at him and suddenly began to feel bad about what she had said to him.

When he headed to the locker room, Susan went into the ladies' locker room and hurried with a shower so she could make it to the parking lot before he did. When she finished she didn't see him in the workout room so she ran to the door. She saw him over at the left and ran to his car.

He was not paying attention to her as he opened his car, so Susan called to him. "Please, wait a minute," she hollered. Eric looked around to see if she was calling to someone else.

When she got closer he held out his gym bag in front of his chest in case she wanted to hit him. When she got to his car, she was smiling, and to avoid another confrontation Eric raised his right arm at Susan and confessed that he treated her badly and needed to apologize. "It's probably my male chauvinistic attitude, although I didn't mean it the way you think I did."

"No, I just overreacted. I'm sorry I made such an ass of myself. By the way, I'm Susan Reddy." She came close to Eric as she held out her hand. "No, I'm not going to hit you! Besides you're bigger than I am." Susan looked again at the whole guy and was very impressed with his good looks and build. He was really tall. Had to be about six foot four.

He shook her hand while admiring its strength. "I'm Eric Forster. It's nice to meet you and let's forget about how we met inside."

"I agree," said Susan with a smile as she gently slapped him on his arm.

They stared at each other for a few moments before Eric asked her if he could drive her somewhere. Finally, Susan replied, "Well, I'm staying with a friend in at the Holiday Inn, but she's off on a date, so I was going to have dinner and then take a cab to the motel."

"Well, I can do one better," offered Eric. "I'll join you for dinner and then I'll drive you wherever you need to go. That's if you'd trust me."

Susan nodded, "OK! Let's do it, but you'll have to pick the place. I don't know Bangor."

"All right, let's see," Eric replied, scratching his jaw. "What would you like for dinner?"

"I'm game for anything, but since we're in Maine, how 'bout lobster?" asked Susan with an inquiring look. "I also need to tell you that I have to be back at the Holiday Inn by ten tonight. I'm on a curfew. God, I can hardly wait until the Olympics are over and I can get back to somewhat of a normal life."

Eric turned to her with a surprised look. "You're on the Olympic soccer team? I'm impressed." He stared at her, then said, "OK, hop in. We'll go to Cap Morrill's over in Brewer. They have the best lobster in town and now you've made me hungry for lobster." They talked about the Olympic soccer team while driving to the restaurant. "Now this isn't a very fancy place, Susan, but the lobsters are terrific."

Cap Morrill's was just off the Penobscot River and had the looks of a rundown building. The interior was much the same. It was noisy and full of the smell of boiling lobster. They got a table in the back corner away from most of the noise and they each ordered a beer, then toasted each other.

"Boy, does that tastes good," sighed Susan as she drank half the mug in one chug. "Now, Eric Foster, tell me about yourself other than being a male chauvinist pig." She had grinned at Eric with her elbows on the table and her chin in her hands, waiting for him to deny what she was saying.

"First, it's Forster, not Foster, and second I only treat miserable ugly women in the manner you thought I did." He'd had a tough time keeping a straight face. Eric moved his fingers up and down his glass while staring at Susan and waiting for her to throw something at him. Her look at him didn't change nor did she blink an eye. The restaurant was crowded and they had to talk loudly in order to hear each other.

Susan finally grinned and answered, "You know, you're right and I think I'm going to enjoy being with you. I can't remember the last guy I dated who acts the way you do."

"This is a date?" asked Eric. "I thought it was a lobster dinner with a beautiful young lady who nearly attacked me in Gold's Gym." He leaned back in his chair waiting for a reply. "I can't classify this as a date."

Susan threw her hands in the air. "I give. I need to start all over again." She'd smiled at him and leaned back in her chair while finishing off her beer. "You are a very handsome guy with a great sense of humor. I like that. However, you appear to also have the ability to anger women, especially me. Now answer that, Mr. Forster," she said with a grin. She was beginning to feel very comfortable with Eric, as he was obviously different from any man she had ever dated.

Eric took her right hand and gently pulled it across the table where he kissed her palm. "Now, Susan, I want to start our existence all over again." He looked closely at her and was attracted to her athletic build. Her brown hair was quite short, as though she didn't want it to interfere with her game playing. Her body was thin and trim and her breasts were the size a woman of her stature would have. "Please tell me about yourself, and would you like another beer?"

Susan had smiled and nodded her head at the idea of another beer. Eric waved to their waitress and order another set of beer mugs. In a soft but firm voice she answered his question. "I am a professional soccer player, or at least I'm on the team as a substitute." Susan moved her finger up and down the table as she spoke while glancing at Eric and the table. "I am now being approached by the University of Maine to be the assistant coach of their new soccer team and if I succeed I will possibly be offered the job as head coach. But right now I am in training for the Olympics in Sidney, Australia.

"I'm not married because I don't have time and I have never met anyone who I truly wanted to marry. So that in a nutshell is who and what I am, Eric." She leaned back on her chair and put her hands on the table while smiling at him.

Eric looked fondly at her. "First, I find it difficult to believe that you haven't found anyone to get serious with, because you are a very beautiful lady, even if you weren't an athlete. Nonetheless, Susan, I am very much in awe with you. You're quite a gal." He smiled and took her hand in his. "I'm glad you tracked me down in the parking lot."

"OK," Susan replied, "now it's your turn."

"Well I certainly don't have the interesting life you seem to have lived. I'm just an intern for an orthopedic surgeon in Bangor and by this summer I should have my license, so if you need a knee replaced you can come and see me." Eric patted her hand and then grabbed his beer and took a drink.

Susan's eyes opened wide when she heard of what Eric was doing. "I'm impressed! You're a doctor. I would have never guessed it. Most doctors I know are old and grouchy so it's nice to meet a young one."

Susan had a surprised look and laughed while asking him, "Are you young and grouchy?"

Their lobsters came after they gave Eric and Susan bibs to place around their necks. They immediately stopped talking and began eating. Susan marveled at how good the lobster tasted and she thanked Eric for bringing her to Cap Morrill's. "It was terrific," she said while waving her arms. "Thanks again. You made this into a fun evening, even after our adventure at Gold's Gym." When the waitress brought the bill she grabbed it and said they should split it since this wasn't a date.

Eric agreed, somewhat to her surprise, but admired him for being honest.

"Now I'd better get going before I miss my curfew." They headed out to Eric's car feeling quite content with dinner and their time together. She felt a great desire to spend more time with Eric. When they got to the Holiday Inn, Susan turned to Eric and asked, "Do you ever get to Boston?"

"Oh, yeah," he replied. "There are several courses I need to take at the hospitals down there. I should be down there in a couple of weeks and if it's all right with you, could I see you again?" he asked while placing his right arm on her shoulder.

"That's a dumb question," Susan said softly while looking out the front window. "I'd like to see you again to see if you're really as obnoxious as you appear to be." She threw her arm against his chest while grinning at him.

Eric moaned, "OK, I'd like that except that you probably just broke a rib or two." He reached over and pulled her to him. "Now, this is more fun." He gripped her head and quickly kissed her.

Susan was pleasantly surprised and didn't say anything, but went after him again, but this time with her lips and for a longer kiss. All Eric could do was say, "Wow!" and then he added very softly, "Give me your address and phone number and I'll call you when I am next scheduled to be in Boston. It should be in a week or so. All right?"

"Yeah," she replied, "I'd like that." She wrote down her address and phone number, kissed him again, and went out the door, yelling to him to not forget her. He wondered how he could possibly do that as he watched her go into the Holiday Inn.

Ten days later Susan still hadn't heard from Eric and was wondering if she would ever hear from him again. She didn't want to call him, as it would appear that she was overly anxious to meet him again. She wanted to play it cool, but she wanted to see him again to see if there could be something possibly going on between them.

That night her phone rang

"Susan, you may not remember me, but it's Eric Forster."

"Who? What's your name?" She sounded as though she had never heard of him.

He repeated his name, "Eric Forster from Bangor."

"Oh, you're the obnoxious guy I met in Bangor several months ago." She sounded serious.

"It was only a week or so that we had dinner after you attacked me," he tried to answer.

"Now I remember you," she answered, trying to keep a straight face. "You're the foot doctor or something like that, right?" Susan was having a ball working him over, but she hoped he wouldn't suddenly hang up. "So, what'd you want?"

She started to laugh while rolling back in her chair. It finally got through to Eric that he was being teased.

"You miserable broad, it's a good thing you're not close enough for me to whap you on your oversized ass." He was beginning to enjoy this vocal feud.

Susan changed her voice. "Hi, Eric, it's nice to hear you. I thought you forgot about me."

For the next several minutes they each folded their bodies back in their chairs and continued the conversation. "Before I forget, Susan, I'll be in Boston next Tuesday and Wednesday so if you're free, I'd like to see you." Eric doodled with his pen on a tablet of paper. Susan circled the phone wire around her wrist.

"No shit! Sure I'll be here," Susan said softly. "Do you want to stay here?"

Eric was at a loss for words. He did not expect Susan to ask that. There was no answer.

"Hello, Eric, are you still there? Or have you fainted? I have two bedrooms in my apartment and my roommate is out of town next week." She grinned at what he was probably thinking. Do you think that I was going to let you rape me? I don't think so."

"Oh, that's different," Eric replied, still shaking from the thought of spending a night with Susan. He was also amazed at her male-oriented language.

"In other words," asked Susan, "you're happier that you're not going to have to sleep with me? That's your loss because I have a great body." She curled her feet under her as she thought of how it would be with Eric.

Eric arrived in Boston the next Tuesday afternoon and gave Susan a call from his cell phone. "Hi, Eric, I'm here waiting for you. Where are you?" When she found out she gave him directions to her apartment. "You should be here in about twenty minutes. We have a parking garage, so tell them you're here to see me and you want to put the car in Jane Burger's space. That's my roommate."

Her directions were perfect and the garage attendant took the car while Eric headed to the elevator to go to the eighth floor.

Susan was looking out the window waiting for Eric to arrive when the doorbell went off. She pressed the entrance button and he came up the elevator. When he got to the eighth floor she was waiting in the hall.

"Hi, Eric. Welcome to Boston." She took his hand as he bent down to kiss her cheek. Susan had to stand on her toes to receive the kiss since there was about eight inches' difference in their heights. She guided him into the very nice apartment overlooking Boston harbor. Then she took him into his room where he dropped off his suitcase. She was wearing a pair of jeans with a short-sleeve white shirt. Her brown eyes were penetrating

When he returned to the living room again he looked out the window. "Boy, what a view you have here." There were all sorts of boats in the harbor from sailboats to ocean freighters. To the right was Logan Airport.

Susan grabbed his arm. "Hey, you're here to see me...remember?"

Eric turned toward the rest of the apartment. "Boy, what a great place you have here." The living room had a large semicircular couch and two matching chairs. At the end of the living room was a dining area with a table and chairs for six. On the walls were framed photographs of Susan playing soccer along with several paintings by some local artist.

The view of the harbor was such that you could sit looking at it all day. "Let's see, it's been two years now since Jane and I moved in here. I do love Boston." She guided Eric to a couple of chairs that faced each other and asked him what he'd like to drink. "Now, I'm cooking dinner tonight. Nothing fancy, just pasta and sausage plus a salad with a bottle of Merlot. OK?"

"Sounds terrific, Susan." He handed her a bag containing two bottles of red wine. "I'm still shocked you've invited me to stay with you. Maybe you're a little crazier than I thought."

Susan laughed while she stretched out in her chair. She had a difficult time sitting still, so she was in somewhat constant motion.

Their meeting in Bangor had been pleasant and she had looked forward to Eric's visit.

"Have you ever been in this area of Boston?" Susan joined him looking down at the waterfront.

"No, I haven't. I've heard much about it, but I've never been down here."

"Why don't I take you on a walk through the Quincy Market while it's still early?" she said while putting on a sweater. She grabbed his hand and walked him out of the apartment. It amazed Eric how quickly Susan walked. It was as though she were still jogging.

For the next couple of hours they visited several shops in Quincy Market and then toured Faneuil Hall, a historic building that went back to the founding of the United States. Eric was very impressed with this historic section of Boston. Later they came to a bar and Eric suggested a stop for beer. Susan agreed. They sat at a table overlooking the mass of people who were touring the markets.

"My God, Susan, I've never seen so many people in one spot since a visit to New York. Hell, there's more people here than in all of Bangor." He leaned back in his chair while looking at the mass of people wandering through the stores and food grills.

"Yeah, but I love it here," replied Susan in a soft voice. "There's always something happening. There's action all the time. Somehow I don't imagine this in Orono, Maine." Her eyes indicated a potential unhappiness with a move to Maine from Boston. "But then, you'll be there, so it can't be all bad." She grinned at him while she grabbed his right hand. "We'd better get back to my place so I can get dinner started."

"Today, I buy," Eric demanded as he took the check from their waiter.

Susan enjoyed Eric's company and wondered if there was someone else involved in his life. She hoped not, but then again she had to be realistic as he was a choice mate for any woman. He was handsome, tall with a great personality, and a doctor. *What else is there?* she thought.

When they got back to her apartment, Susan went into the kitchen to pour a couple of glasses of Merlot. She took these into the living room where Eric was again looking out the window at the Boston Harbor. He took the glass, toasted hers, and looked back out the window. "Your view is terrific. I love being on the water so if I lived here I would probably spend all my time looking out the window." He turned away from the window and said, "Of course, if you were in the same room, I'd spend more time looking at you."

He sat down on the couch as Susan came out of the kitchen and sat down with him. She stroked his head, as she felt very comfortable with him. "Thanks very much," she finally replied. "Now I have to be careful with you, otherwise I might not have to make your bed tomorrow." She quickly kissed Eric on his cheek and then got up and headed back to the kitchen.

Eric turned on the couch to look at Susan making dinner. "So, tell me about yourself," he asked as she mixed the pasta sauce. "Where are your parents and do you have any brothers or sisters?"

Susan tapped her spoon on the stove while shifting her gaze back out the window. "I really don't have any family. I never knew my father. He left my mother just after I was born. I have no idea where he might be and quite frankly I don't give a damn. My mother died of breast cancer when I was eleven and then my aunt raised me. I left her when I turned eighteen and went off on my own." She began to show tears in her eyes. "Damn it," she said again while her face turned into an angry look while she pounded her spoon on the stove.

Eric quickly got up from the couch and went into the kitchen where he grabbed Susan and held her close to him. "Jesus, Susan, I'm sorry I brought it up." He placed his hand on the back of her neck and caressed her neck.

She looked up at him and kissed his cheek. Her tears had turned to a smile. "I'm OK. Thanks, Eric. I'm sorry," she said softly. "Now you can tell me about your family but I hope it's a happier situation." She smiled as she stirred the sauce.

Eric leaned against the counter. "Mom and Dad are retired in Florida. I was their only child."

"So you're probably spoiled rotten," she murmured as she continued stirring.

"Hah, you'd have to know them, particularly my mother. She's a tough lady, but I love her very much," he offered as he gazed at Susan.

"Dinner's about ready, so pour us another glass of wine and then you can set the table. You know you have to do something to earn this dinner." She patted him on his rear.

When they sat down, Susan smiled at Eric and toasted him. "I'm glad you're here and I'm happier still that you attacked me at Gold's Gym. Otherwise you wouldn't be here tonight."

Eric smiled and murmured, "Yeah right, I attacked you. You were the one who started the fight. I was my usual nice guy." He smiled at Susan and then he savored the spaghetti and sausage dinner. "Susan, this is terrific. I'm really surprised at what a good cook you are."

Susan waved her fork at him. "Here you go again, Eric. You assumed since I'm an athlete, my cooking would be lousy. Shame on you!" She glared at him across the table, but soon turned it into a grin. "Now what else might surprise you, and forget what you're thinking. That'll maybe come later after I straighten out your chauvinistic thoughts."

Eric was at a loss for words, as he knew he goofed the minute he made the cooking comment. He braced his chin on both hands and searched for a reply. Finally he said, "I can't think of anything appropriate, Susan. It must be your beauty that causes these unreasonable comments." His eyes widened as he continued to gaze into her brown eyes.

"Oh, brother! Finish your dinner. You're the most incredible guy I've ever met." She smiled as she watched him eat his dinner.

Eric questioned her thoughts, asking, "Is that good or bad?"

Susan waved her fork at him. "It's probably good. Now finish your dinner and be quiet." She broke into a broad smile while shaking her head and as asked, Eric finished his dinner without further comment. She also felt very comfortable with him.

He finished his second helping then pushed back his chair. "Can I talk again?"

"It depends on what you're going to say, but I guess it's better to have you talking than sitting there quietly." She threw her napkin at him. "So, be careful what you might say next."

They spent the remaining time resting and talking while finishing the bottle of wine. At ten o'clock, Susan got up and announced she was going to bed...alone...as she had to be at soccer practice at eight in the morning. She went over to his chair, gave him a kiss on his cheek and left him before anything else could be started.

"OK," replied Eric, "I'll see you in the morning and tomorrow night let me take you out for dinner."

"I'd like that. See you in the morning." She headed for her bedroom while Eric finished his wine and then went to his room where he laid down on the bed and reviewed some documents for tomorrow's hospital session, but he found it difficult to concentrate while being so close to Susan. Instead he turned off his lights, gazed out the window at the harbor and thought of the beautiful woman in the next room before climbing into bed and turning off the lights.

They both woke up at about six. Eric heard Susan making coffee while he finished his shower. When he got to the kitchen Susan was still in her pajamas as though Eric were either a permanent resident or totally harmless. She tiptoed up to him and kissed his cheek while Eric wrapped his left arm around her shoulders. He could feel her breasts against his chest. That's as far as it went.

"Good morning, Eric. How 'bout a cup of coffee and some orange juice?"

"Sounds great." Eric chugged down the juice and took a sip of the hot coffee while leaning against the kitchen counter and looking at his hostess.

"What would you like for breakfast, Eric? I've got eggs and bacon or I've got some granola."

"I'll take the granola. Here, I can get it," he answered while reaching into the cabinet. They both ended up with fruit juice and the granola and talked about what they would be doing that day and what time they would be back at the apartment.

Susan was very excited with Eric, as he was comfortable to be with. He was good looking, had a great career in front of him and a fun personality. While she never had a family, he seemed to be what Susan would have liked a brother to be. Even though she was walking around the apartment with just her pajamas on, he looked at her as if she were fully clothed.

They agreed upon a restaurant for dinner but would have cocktails at her apartment before dinner. Susan arrived first and changed into a new dress she had bought a couple of days before. It was light blue with white trim. It went down to her ankles but the top was somewhat open so her breasts would be slightly exposed. She was very pleased with her appearance.

When Eric finally arrived he commented on her dress and gazed at her body. "I'm impressed," he said. "Certainly looks better than your soccer uniform. You really are a girl!"

She hit him on his arm as she turned away and headed off to the kitchen. "You are really terrible. I can't imagine why I invited you to stay here." Eric wasn't certain whether or not she was serious. Susan brought out a bottle of Merlot and a couple of glasses and gave them to Eric. "Here, do something worthwhile."

She then couldn't keep from smiling at Eric. "You really are a miserable bastard."

"Yep," answered Eric, "you're right, but I did mean it when I said you're a beautiful woman. I'm also glad I met you in Bangor." He reached over and gave her a hug.

To Susan, Eric acted differently from every other man she had dated. He seemed to enjoy life and had an incredible sense of humor even though he seemed to often push it a bit hard. He also didn't make sexual advances toward her as many others had done. She respected that.

"So," Eric asked, "where do we go for dinner?"

Susan selected Lucia, a restaurant in the Italian North End of Boston. They walked to the restaurant, as it was across the main drag in the northeast Italian district. Lucia was renowned for a variety of Italian dishes, the most famous being veal marsala. The restaurant was one of many in the Italian area. The dining rooms were small and you had to be somewhat intimate with your neighbors. They started with a bottle of Pinot Noir.

It was difficult to carry on a conversation because of the noise throughout the restaurant. Susan gripped Eric's hand and explained, "You see, Eric, this place won't allow you to make nasty comments about me. All you can do is stare or make faces at me while you're enjoying dinner."

Eric gripped his ears and with a grin shouted, "What did you say? I can't hear you. Maybe we should have taken lip reading lessons before we came here. However, if I do attack you, no one will be able to hear you calling for help. I can also tell you that you're uglier than hell and you'd never hear me."

Susan laughed at his comments and, partially hidden by her menu, gave him the finger salute. "Screw you, doctor. You've never had it so good."

They quieted down and held each other's hand while drinking their wine and ordering dinner. They both ordered veal marsala and did very little talking while enjoying the incredibly great dinner.

After dinner they walked back up toward the Boston Harbor through a mass of people going both ways on the road. When they got to the harbor they found an empty bench and sat down. The bench overlooked the harbor and its many boats. Eric broke the silence. "My ears are still ringing from Lucia, but what a terrific place. Thanks for suggesting it." He rubbed his ears. "Man, that was really great food. Now what?"

Susan stretched her legs and arms, then wrapped her left arm around Eric's shoulders while looking out over the water. "When are you going to be back here?" she asked, hoping that it would be soon.

"Don't know, Susan," replied Eric, "but I have a feeling that it will be in about two weeks. I'm schedule to assist in an operation, but a date hasn't been set so if it's OK with you, I'll let you know."

"You promise?" she asked while looking at him with worried eyes.

"I promise, for sure," Eric said quietly while stroking her leg.

"I'll chase Jane out of town again, so you can stay with me. OK?"

"I'd like that," replied Eric in a quiet voice. "I've enjoyed being with you."

They walked around Quincy Market to work off their dinners then headed back to Susan's apartment. It was getting late so the crowd of people had diminished.

When they got back into Susan's apartment, she grabbed Eric by his waist and drew him toward her. "Eric, if it was a different time of the month, I'd want you in my room. Maybe we can wait until you get back. OK?"

Eric was constantly amazed at how blunt Susan was in all her words and actions. It was as though she was telling the world to listen and pay attention to what she was doing so they would follow her. While she was a beautiful woman, she had many attributes of a male athlete.

They both went to their bedrooms and they both thought about the other and wished they could have gone to bed together. But it made both of them more aroused with what might happen the next time they got together.

Eric and Susan talked quite often after Eric returned to Maine. Finally, he called her to let her know he had to be in Boston the next week, but would be there just for the day and would be free only for lunch. "I have to be at the hospital on Wednesday for the operation so I'll be coming down late Tuesday. The only problem is that I've got to be at the hospital at six in the morning to get ready for the operation. So, I think I'd better stay there Tuesday night so I don't have to worry about being late. So, if you're free maybe we can get together sometime Wednesday around lunchtime.

"I'm never free and I can't be there at noon. I have practice most of the day and I can't afford not to be there," said a disappointed Susan. "I'll just have to wait until you get back down here the next time." She felt bad about not seeing him again.

Eric was disappointed, but asked, "How 'bout the weekend? I could drive down late Friday, but I'd have to leave early afternoon on Sunday."

I'll be here," answered Susan in a soft sexy voice. "I wouldn't want you to miss fixing someone's hip but come on down and stay with me. Maybe you can check my hip." When she finished his phone call she jumped up from her chair and worked her fist up and down as though she'd just kicked a winning goal. Eric was somewhat shocked at her comments, but they made his upcoming visit all the more tantalizing.

When Susan got back from soccer practice late Friday, she showered and put on a pair of denim shorts and a white T-shirt. She didn't bother with a bra or shoes. She felt very comfortable. While waiting for Eric her doorbell rang. It was the local floral shop's smiling deliveryman who handed her a bouquet of roses along with a card. It read: *I'll be there shortly to check your hip. Eric.*

She couldn't remember the last time anyone had ever given her such a bouquet and she grinned to herself as she put them in a vase. *God, they're beautiful,* she thought to herself. *What a nice guy Eric is!* She now wished he'd hurry up and get there.

A couple of hours later, her phone rang. It was Eric. "Hi, there! I'm stuck in traffic but should be there in about fifteen minutes. God, I can't believe the number of cars out here." He sounded exasperated while she smiled at the sound of his voice.

"Take your time, Eric. I'm not going anywhere. I'm actually working on dinner so we can eat in instead of going out," Susan offered as she was reading a recipe for sweet and sour chicken.

"OK, see you soon. Is there anything I can bring?"

"Just yourself."

Forty minutes later her doorbell finally rang. It was Eric. "May I help you?" she teased before buzzing him through the door.

"I'm beyond help," a voice muttered," but if you don't let me in now you're in deep trouble."

"Yes, sir! The door's open."

Susan met him in the hallway as Eric came up the elevator. She grabbed Eric by his waist as he bent over to kiss her on her cheek. "Damn," he said, "I can't believe how people can exist in that kind of traffic. You have to be nuts to drive in downtown Boston." Eric then smiled as he exclaimed, "Except if I was coming to see you. Now I need a drink, badly!" He grabbed her hand while carrying his suitcase in his other and walked into Susan's apartment.

He went into his bedroom and took a quick shower, then came into the living room wearing a pair of denim jeans and a T-shirt. He copied her dress code by not wearing shoes. Eric opened the bottle of wine and poured two glasses while Susan was working over dinner.

They sat down on the living room couch and toasted each other. Susan had her feet under her body while Eric stretched out his long legs.

"I almost forgot. Thanks for the roses. That was very sweet of you."

"You're welcome. It's the least I could do for your having to put up with me again." Eric put his glass down and hugged Susan around her shoulders. "I've missed you. No one's been around to yell at me."

Susan put her glass down and put her head against Eric's chest while he stroked her back. Then she pulled herself up on her knees and pushed Eric down on the couch.

He placed his hands on her cheeks and kissed her as she leaned over to return his kiss. Eric slid his hands down her face to her breasts and she gasped when he began to stroke her. Susan then told Eric, "Take me to my bedroom, but I'd better turn off the oven first."

Eric picked her up and carried her into the kitchen where she laughed while turning off the oven. "At halftime we can come back and eat."

When they got to her room, she pulled off her shirt, exposing her somewhat small breasts while Eric helped with her jeans. She undressed Eric, then grabbed and pulled him on the bed while he searched out her body. He took a long look at her left hip before announcing. "Your hip is just fine. All it needs is a massage." As he stroked it, he uttered, "God, you're incredible."

Eric was amazed at Susan's strength as they wrestled on the bed, raising the excitement of their lovemaking. She turned so she was on top and could initiate and control their action. He grasped her breasts then pushed himself into her. She was in constant motion and inhaled loudly as he entered her. "My God," she shouted, "you're big," then groaned until they both came. Afterward they lay together, thinking about what had just happened.

Eric stroked her hair as they lay side by side. "Maybe I should be late again if this is how I'm to be treated. You're something else," Eric said softly as he turned to face her. He couldn't get over her lean, strong body and what a great lover she was.

Susan turned to face him and stroked his head with her left hand. "I really enjoyed it. God, you are huge!" She pushed him aside. "Now, it's halftime and time for dinner. The second half can be continued later," she replied with a broad smile. She got up and began to redress, so Eric followed suit.

Dinner was delicious: sweet and sour chicken with rice and a mixed salad. She told Eric that she really wasn't much of a cook, except for a few items her aunt taught her. After dinner they sat in the living room finishing their wine and anticipating the second half of lovemaking.

"Eric, I'm ready," stated Susan as she finished her wine. She grabbed his arm and led him back to the bedroom.

"You're the boss," said Eric while pulling off his shirt. When they got back into bed, their lovemaking was slower and without Susan leading the way. This time it was Eric's turn and each wore the other out of breath. He grasped her head and pulled it against his cheek, then kissed her. "Oh, man, you're something else. I might die of a heart attack if I had to do this every day."

Susan straddled Eric's stomach while pinning his arms to the mattress. "Now that I have your complete attention I need to talk to you." She had a surprisingly serious voice.

Eric nodded his OK as he surveyed her body. "Whatever you want to do I'm ready," he said while grinning at her.

"I'm serious now, Eric, so listen to me!" She applied even more pressure on his arms as she lowered her head close to his. "I want to marry you, Eric."

He looked at her with wide-open eyes. He was at a loss for words.

She repeated her demand. "Did you hear me? I want to marry you!" Her voice was totally different from any conversation he'd had with her. She continued. "I'm going to be in Orono very soon and I dislike the idea of dating complete strangers with the idea that I'd find someone I might want to marry. I don't have time for that. With you I think I'll be happy. For you it's much the same." She rocked back and forth on his stomach.

"Good grief, Susan, we've known each other for about three weeks. Much as I like you, I'd need more time before I'd ask someone to marry me. You might be the perfect one for me, but I don't know," replied a shocked Eric. His eyes opened, staring at a grinning Susan with her eyes wide open while she stroked his chest. He still couldn't believe what she was saying.

"Eric, I understand, but that's how it's got to be," Susan answered while holding down Eric's arms again. "If you decide not to, then our relationship will be strictly platonic from now on. I can't let you screw me if there's nothing in the future for me other than being your mistress." Susan stared directly into Eric's eyes. "Do you understand what I'm saying?" She bounced up and down on his shoulders while trying to convince Eric that she was serious.

Eric grabbed her and placed her next to him. "Susan, I think I understand, but first, let's get dressed. I can't think with you naked next to me." He grinned and shook his head in disbelief at what she was saying. "When did this idea come into play?" asked Eric.

She quickly answered. "Well I've thought about this for a long time because it seems that every guy I date has my body in his mind and not any long-term relationship."

They quickly dressed and went back to the living room. "Eric, how 'bout another glass of wine?" she asked while smiling at him.

"You'd better believe I need another glass of wine, maybe a bottle." Eric went into the kitchen, opened a bottle of Merlot, and noted he was shaking as he poured wine into two glasses. They sat on the couch again, but this time their knees blocked the other from getting too close.

"Eric, I'm pretty sure that I'm in love with you. I've never been with any guy who I like as much as you, so in my mind I want to be your wife. I know it's really soon after our meeting in Bangor, but even when you were an obnoxious bastard I had a good feeling toward you. Don't know why, but I did." Susan reached out her left hand to him. "Now I know it's true."

Eric grabbed her hand and related his thoughts in a slow serious voice, as though he was talking to one of his patients. "I like you very much, Susan, but I'm at a loss for words. I'm not sure if I know what to say because marriage is the furthest thing from my mind right now. I've got too much going on right now, trying to get my medical license. We haven't spent enough time together to discover how marriage would affect us. I really don't know. I really don't," Eric said in a quiet serious voice as he sagged back down on the couch as though he were trying to hide. His mind was racing over what Susan was saying. He couldn't believe it as he looked into her eyes and he could tell she was totally serious about this.

In a low voice Eric had really never heard before, Susan said, "I don't want you to forget me. First, I want you to sleep with me tonight, but after tomorrow morning our relationship is going to have to change if our affair is to continue. Once the Olympics are over, I'll be moving to Maine. It's important to me that if we are to get married, it happens before I get there. If I'm not married I have a feeling that I'll be the target of all sorts of horny men who'd like to get a piece of my ass. I don't want that to happen. Do you understand?"

Eric nodded his head. "Yes, I think I understand, but I also think you're exaggerating what might happen."

Susan laughed at that. "Eric, that's a classic male response. That's so much bullshit that I'm surprised you said it. I bet a lot of your nurses feel the same way, but are afraid to say it." Her smile turned to an angry stare as she looked up and down his body.

Eric shrugged his shoulders and didn't reply to Susan's thoughts, because whatever he said might lead to an argument and that he didn't want. It was obvious to Eric that something had happened to Susan to affect her in this manner. She seemed to have a real problem in dating someone new.

Susan continued, "If the marriage doesn't work out or if either of us finds someone else, then we would have to be honest with one another and respect the other's thoughts. You don't know this, but when my aunt died she left all her assets to me and, while I won't tell you how much it is, it's enough to afford me a good living for the rest of my life, so I don't need your income and should we ever separate or get divorced I'll not expect anything from you other than a good-bye kiss. This can be put in a legal prenuptial agreement." She smiled at Eric. "So, you see, you can't lose." Susan stroked his arm while continuing to stare into his eyes. "Besides," she added, "who's better in bed than me?"

Eric's mind was racing with all that Susan had demanded. My God, he thought, all this has happened because he teased her at Gold's Gym. He really did like her, but he hadn't thought of marrying her or anyone else.

Susan kept talking. "I also don't want any children until I become more established as a soccer coach, so there is no pressure on either of us to take care of kids or, should we divorce, who would inherit them. And finally, I don't want a fancy wedding since I don't have any real friends in this area and certainly not in Bangor or Orono. I just want to marry you. It's that simple," she said with a smile while leaning toward him. From the tone of her voice and the look on her face, Eric knew she was serious about this marriage proposal.

"I just don't want to start dating prospective husbands, because most of them would just want to get between my legs so they could brag to their friends that they fucked me."

He shook his head in disbelief. He couldn't believe what he'd heard. God, she must have been mishandled by someone and now she is tired of it all. He could almost understand her feelings.

"Eric, I know this is very sudden, but I've felt this way since you were here two weeks ago and you didn't attack me when you could have easily done so. I also really like you and I like being with you. That also makes me want to marry you. Does this make any sense to you?" Susan asked with a very concerned voice.

Eric drew his hands across his face while shaking his head. "Susan, I can't believe what you're saying. How in the hell could I agree to any of this when we first made love and now you're going to charge me for repeat performances? Come on, you can't be serious."

"Trust me Eric, I am," replied Susan with a stern look on her face. "If you enjoyed screwing me, then all I'm asking is that we marry so repeat performances will be as husband and wife. What's so difficult about that? What's the big deal? Maybe it's because you've already got a girlfriend."

It took Eric a few moments to answer Susan's thoughts, but even then he was still at a loss over her demands. "No, I don't have someone else I'm even close to marrying, so that's not the problem. It's that you're threatening me if I don't marry you." He didn't mean to say that but he couldn't think of anything else.

Susan shook her head while placing her hands on his legs. "Eric, I'm not threatening you. God, that's the furthest thing from my mind. I'm just telling you that if you're not thinking of marrying me, I have to shut off my body from yours until you've made up your mind one way or the other. If you marry me I am yours and you're mine, but if you have no thoughts of marriage, then I become a sexless virgin to you." Each word was slowly said in her soft voice so there would be no unanswered questions.

Eric stared at her without saying anything because he couldn't think of anything to say. He didn't expect anything like this to happen. He finally replied, "All right, I think I understand what you're saying, but I can't possibly give you an answer now. Let me think on all this when I'm by myself and not persuaded by your presence. I will let you know as soon as I come to a decision, but I'm not going to pick a date. I just can't. OK?"

"Sure," Susan said, "take your time. I'm sorry if I have frightened you with my ideas, but I am serious about all this. I want to marry you. Period. I can't be more precise. I want to make you happy and I want us to have a long and successful marriage." She grabbed his head and gave him a long kiss, then looked back at him. "Is this so difficult to understand?"

Eric laughed, "That's a huge understatement. Usually it's the man who presses for the marriage, but with you it's different."

She began to laugh again. "That's right, but I'm different from most women. Maybe I've got some male hormones in my brain."

"That's also an understatement," Eric said while stroking her arm.

"Well anyway," Susan offered, "it's time for bed and your last chance, if you're up to it."

When they got into bed, Eric discovered he wasn't. Too many thoughts were roaring through his brain that couldn't be overcome by her naked presence next to him.

"Wow, see what I've done to you?" she said as she rolled up to him. You're deader than a doornail. I think our friend just died. Well, let's see what happens in the morning. It's going to be your last chance to make love to an unmarried Susan. Good night, dear." She kissed him, then turned her back to Eric while he laid there thinking about all that had happened this evening. He still couldn't believe what she wanted.

CHAPTER 15

He had difficulty trying to forget what had happened, but eventually he fell asleep and didn't wake until sometime after six o'clock. For a moment he forgot where he was, but reality struck quickly when he looked over to Susan's side of the bed. He didn't know what to do because he wasn't sure if she was awake.

Then she turned over toward him, smiled, stroked his head, and kissed his cheek. In turn he began to check out her body and was pleased to see he was finally reacting to her.

When they finished she laid her head on his shoulder. "Eric, I really loved having you, I really did, but that's the end of any sexual encounters until we marry. If not, you'll become just like the brother I never had."

The conversation at breakfast was about everything that didn't matter and nothing was said about Susan's requests. She hadn't bothered to dress and wore just a bathrobe.

Eric finally changed the talk. "I'm leaving for Bangor this morning and I don't know when I'll be back and even if I do, we have to figure out if getting together makes any sense. Your marriage proposal caught me off guard because it's usually the man that pursues this idea."

"Well," Susan replied with a serious look, "I'm different than most women, but I guess it's because of how I grew up. I had to handle my problems and I had to be strong enough to physically take care of myself. I'm not a lesbian, in case you're wondering. I like sex and I like to be in charge, but I also know that I have to be responsive to you. I don't have any problems with that." Susan looked at Eric and reached out for his hand.

She continued her thoughts. "The more time we've spent together the more I think I'm in love with you. I enjoy being with you more than I can describe and I want to marry you. Period!" She was emphatic. Eric understood.

"Susan, I still don't know what to say." He put his elbows on the table and kept his hands to himself. "I've really liked being with you, but your marriage ideas have sent me off to Mars. I need to talk with someone about all this, but I don't know who. Probably my father."

Susan threw her hands up over her head. "You mean you need to get your parents' permission to get married?" She had to force herself not to laugh at his thinking. He couldn't think of an appropriate answer.

He looked at his watch. "Susan, I've got to get going. I've got to be back in the office right after lunch." He hesitated, and then reached out for her hands. "I loved being with you and I'm going to miss you, but I need to think through your ideas. I think I understand where you're coming from, but I need time to think it through. I can't say yes or no yet. To say the least I'm confused." He kept referring to Susan's demands.

He got up, grabbed his suitcase, and headed for the door with Susan behind him. When he got to the door he dropped his suitcase, grabbed her in his arms, and kissed her lips. She hugged him with all her strength, hoping he'd stay.

"Susan, you're an exceptional lady. I've never known anyone like you. I'll call you soon even if I haven't made a decision. OK?" Eric really didn't want to leave her, but he had no choice, and he also needed to be alone to think through Susan's ideas.

He headed for the elevator without looking back and Susan went back into her apartment. She sat down and cried. She was afraid she had frightened Eric away and that she would never see him again. *Damn it,* she thought, *I've handled this stupidly! What a fucking jerk I am!*

Susan got up from her chair and went over to the front door and looked at the mass of snow on the trees, ground, and the house's deck. She smiled to herself over her memory of meeting Eric and how much she really loved him and how it came to be that he basically agreed to her marriage proposal. She remembered that phone call on Friday evening of the following week.

"Hello," Susan had said as she picked up the ringing phone. "This is Susan Reddy."

A strange drunken-sounding voice had asked, "Is this the horribly ugly soccer player who's about as sexy as a metal statue?"

Susan had reacted angrily, "You son of a bitch, get off this fucking phone!" She was about to slam down the phone when she realized the voice was somewhat familiar. "All right, who is this?"

The voice repeated his question.

She smiled and slowly answered. "You miserable bastard, Eric. Shame on you!"

"How did you know it was me?" asked the voice.

"That's simple. No one else would have said what you said. You should be ashamed of yourself." She couldn't help laughing. "You really are terrible. I thought you were some drunken jerk ready to attack me."

"Who would be that stupid? That's like taking a chance on further existence. Anyway, now that you figured me out, how are you?" Eric smiled at the phone.

"I'm OK...no, I'm terrific after knowing it's you on the phone. Where are you?" She'd sat down on the chair and brought her legs up to her chest while smiling at the phone.

"Actually I'm here in Boston. I just had dinner with some medical associates so I thought I'd better give you a call to see if you'd want to see me tonight."

"Oh, yeah," Sue answered in a hurry. "For sure! I was just about to take a shower. Where are you?" She talked faster than usual.

"Damned if I know, but I don't think I'm too far so it shouldn't be too long, so go ahead with your shower. I will certainly improve the apartment's odor." He hung up his phone before she could answer. Susan jumped up and down and danced into the bathroom.

Fifteen minutes later Susan was drying herself when the doorbell rang. She ran to it knowing it was Eric. She pressed the button to open the door and opened hers so he could get into the apartment, then ran back to the bathroom to quickly dry herself, brush her hair, and get a bathrobe on.

"Hello," Eric asked when he opened the door to an apparently empty apartment. "Is anyone here or have you all escaped?"

Susan came out of her bathroom dressed in her bathrobe and ran into Eric's arms. They kissed and held each other as though they hadn't seen each other for months.

"Hey, I've missed you," Eric said as he let her go. He decided he didn't want to let her go, so he embraced her again. "Your little body even smells good."

Susan punched him in his chest. "Now let me finish dressing. You can pour us a drink. OK?" Susan couldn't stop smiling, realizing how much she had missed him.

"You mean you don't have anything on under this bathrobe?" Eric asked as he touched her hip. She pushed him back then flashed open the bathrobe showing Eric her right breast.

"Eat your heart out!" Susan said as she went off to her bedroom. "I'll be back in a few minutes. You can fix me a scotch on the rocks. The bottle's in the cupboard next to the sink."

"OK," shouted Eric. "We also need to talk."

That comment made Susan hesitate as she put on a pair of denim shorts and a red and white shirt. What did he want to talk about? Probably why he won't marry her. "Well," she said to herself, "at least I tried."

Eric was pouring the scotch when she came into the kitchen. They took their glasses and went into the living room where they sat together on the couch. They toasted each other and took a sip. Susan was anxious but nervous about what Eric wanted to talk about, probably why he wouldn't marry her.

He reached his left arm over her shoulder and looked into her concerned face. "When I left here last week, I was totally at a loss as to what I wanted to do. To say that I was shocked would be an understatement. My mind was flashing so strongly that I can't remember driving to Bangor, but I do remember getting a ticket for going eighty-five miles an hour on the freeway. You see, this is what you did to me."

With a very serious look Susan told Eric she was sorry for causing that problem.

"Anyway, when I got home, I thought to myself that what you were demanding was ridiculous. What you were doing was trying to force me into a marriage before I had an idea that I wanted to do it. But then I thought about your concerns and why you wanted to get married, so I ran this thought past my father. At first, he said I was nuts to even think about it, but as we talked his mode changed, particularly because of the idea of a prenuptial agreement that would free either one of us financially from an unhappy marriage.

"He then asked me if I loved you and I answered that I thought I did. He ran this past my mother who told us that such a move was ridiculous since the only thing that was pulling us together was our time in the bedroom, but if I felt certain about it, I should go ahead."

Susan gulped a large portion of her scotch and fought successfully not to interrupt Eric's thoughts.

Eric continued without any change in his appearance. "So, I called a lawyer friend of mine and asked him about a prenuptial agreement as you described it and he indicated that this was not a problem, but it needed to be signed before the marriage took place.

"I checked one more friend, Sam Adams, the surgeon who got me to come to join him in Bangor. He is sort of my Maine father. He told me I was nuts to even think about such a marriage, but as we talked more about it he loosened his thinking and finally agreed that it could possibly work out."

Susan's hands were beginning to shake as she leaned back on the couch.

Jack took a drink of his scotch and continued his thoughts.

"I had one more person I needed to convince. If I couldn't, then such a marriage as you proposed wouldn't work. That was me." Eric stopped and took another swallow. "Time out, I need another drink!" Then he got up to fill his glass again. Susan gave him her glass and nodded yes when asked if she was ready for another. For once in her life she was speechless.

When he sat back down he took her left hand in his. "Now I need to tell you this. I was totally shocked at the prospect of getting married to anyone. I had thought about it but I never made any movement in that direction. I just wasn't ready to change my lifestyle. I enjoy being free to do what I want to do without checking with anyone else. To me a marriage would destroy that lifestyle."

Susan was beginning to feel defeated. Her thought of being married to Eric seemed to be quickly fading away from what he had just said. She sagged down on the couch and took another gulp of scotch.

He took another sip of his scotch, set it back on the coffee table and raised his arms toward the ceiling. "But then, the way you had demanded a marriage would seem to work with my continued freedom to do what I wanted to do and if that didn't work, I could say adieu to you.

"What I needed to determine was my feelings toward you in comparison to any other woman I had met. I find you are in a class by yourself. You're tough but surprisingly gentle and you seem to have found something in me that you liked. I know that there are all sorts of things that attract you to me. Certainly you are a terrific partner in bed, but you were also fun to be with when we spent time around the Quincy Market.

"So, I guess the next question is: Will you marry me under the arrangements we both want?" Eric stopped talking and stared at a silent Susan, who could not believe what she was hearing. When it finally hit her she jumped on Eric and hugged him with all her strength as she began to cry.

Eric lost his balance and the two of them fell off the couch, knocked over the coffee table and spilled their drinks. And while all this was happening, the front door opened and her roommate Jane Burger walked in. Not knowing what was happening, she hesitated before coming closer. "It looks like an interesting wrestling match. Who's winning?" she commented as she sat down and watched Eric and Susan untangle from one another.

Before their marriage they sat with their lawyers and worked out a prenuptial agreement that would allow either of them to end their marriage should they find someone else they'd prefer. Both lawyers had never heard of such an arrangement but since both Eric and Susan wanted it that way they didn't argue.

They also worked out a financial arrangement that would separate their current assets so either one could not expect any extra money should they decide to divorce each other. If they did have children then there would have to be a financial arrangement for them.

Their wedding took place in Bangor and as agreed upon it was limited to close friends and family. Eric's parents flew up from Florida to attend the wedding, and then flew back down the next morning. They weren't terribly pleased with the wedding, particularly Eric's mother. For their honeymoon, they went back down to Boston for a long weekend at her old apartment with a promise to take a longer honeymoon when time permitted it.

Susan could still remember that day as though it was just yesterday. She felt their first few years together were terrific but as time went on they began to drift apart. Eric wanted children and she wasn't ready for that. He loved Maine and she wanted to move to a large metropolitan area, and then when he had built his house on Lake Lucerne it drove them further apart because it took her forty minutes to drive to Orono. She also didn't like living on the lake because she had bad memories of a night on a lake at her aunt's place in Wisconsin.

While she knew Eric loved her, she didn't feel he totally appreciated her talent as a soccer coach. She still loved Eric, but the feelings between them had faded, or at least it seemed so to her. When she first met Jack Meacham, she was very impressed at his athletic achievements, his terrific body, and his tough manner. A couple of times she had caught him staring at her while they both worked out at the university. She felt her directions were the same as Jack's.

They got to know each other better one day when he was having a great deal of pain with his injured hip. She went up to him and asked how he was doing. "God awful," he had answered in a painful voice. "This goddamn hip is getting worse. I'm having problems even walking."

Susan could see the pain increasing in Jack's face, so she suggested to him that he go see her husband Eric to get an evaluation on his hip. Susan then met Jack's wife Janet who also encouraged Jack to see Dr. Forster. He finally did and Eric encouraged him to get a hip replacement as soon as possible. A couple of months later he had his hip replaced and a couple of months after that he was moving around without pain.

The two couples became friends and spent quite a bit of time together.

CHAPTER 16

The lake group finished clearing the road at about three thirty, making the road clear of trees and branches. Now all they needed was a snowplow to clear the road. The town told them they couldn't get down until Monday morning and since Monday was a holiday no one seemed to be disappointed. The power was still out and would stay out at least until the road was cleared so the electric people could get down and repair the fallen wires.

No one was offering dinner so everyone went to their own homes. Susan and Jack headed back to her house. Jack took a shower, then poured scotches for him and Susan. They sat looking at the fire without saying anything. Finally Susan broke the silence. "We have to figure out what we're going to tell Eric and Janet."

Jack didn't answer right away because he didn't have an answer. Finally he said, "Janet and I have not gotten along together for a long time, so I don't think she'll be too concerned about losing me, so we either tell them the truth that you and I are in love with each other and we want out of our marriages, or we can just pretend nothing happened and then work out later how to end it all." He shrugged his shoulders. Susan frowned at that idea as she still loved her husband even though they we not getting along as they had when they first met and got married.

Dinner was leftovers from the night before, preceded by scotch on the rocks. Their conversation was nonexistent as they both thought about what had happened between them. They felt so good together that they didn't want to let each other go. But what would they tell Eric and Janet? Whatever they did would be difficult and probably unpleasant.

After dinner they sat together on the couch in front of the fireplace. Jack finally broke the silence with a quiet, yet serious tone, saying, "I wish I had met you before I ever met up with Janet. Marrying her was the wrong thing to do, probably for the both of us, but I was intrigued with her because she was not overwhelmed with my football playing and, of course, she is a beautiful woman.

"This all came out when my hip got clobbered and my football career was over. I was finished. I felt screwed! Why in the hell did it happen to me? Why couldn't it have happened when my playing days were nearly over, not when I was still one of the top halfbacks in the NFL?

"She didn't seem to be as concerned as I thought she should be. She wanted us to just move back to Bangor and that was pretty horrifying. She wanted to start teaching school in Bangor. I liked Boston and the way people treated me. Most of my friends were there, but Janet was insistent on coming up here.

"She told me I had to get back to reality. The bitch! She had no idea of the pain I was suffering with and that my career was over. What was I to do?" Jack whacked his arm on the couch as though he was stiff-arming an opponent.

"And then I met you and you impressed me with your athletic ability. Most important, I like your great looks and active personality. I began to get hot for you, but I didn't want to jeopardize your marriage to Eric, because I have great respect for him for repairing my hip. But, now I know it's more than warm feelings. It's like a heat machine," he said while laughing. He pulled Susan over to him and embraced her with his strong arms.

"Wow, what a weekend! I'll remember this storm the rest of my life," Jack offered.

"Jack, I do love you...this I know for sure," Susan said, "but we still haven't figured out what to do about Eric and Janet. I'm sure they'll be back here tomorrow." She stared into the fire, hoping to find an answer while burying her head into his chest.

"So for now, this is going to be our last night together. I hate that thought," reflected Jack as he followed her gaze into the fireplace. He grasped her hand and sat holding it for what seemed like forever. They walked up the stairs to the bedroom where they undressed each other before lying down and making love.

Jack stroked Susan's hair and remarked with a smile, "At least I'll get some rest from you. My body probably can't handle much more than we've done this weekend. It's like playing in the Super Bowl." Jack flattened out on the bed and stretched out his arms and legs.

Susan laughed and returned his stroke. "You're just getting too old for this," she said laughing. She stroked the rest of his body, marveling at his muscular body.

"You'll find our little friend is dead," Jack commented with a frown when Susan tried to find some life in it. Nothing happened, so she suggested they wait for finality in the morning.

Susan placed her head on Jack's shoulder. "We have to make a decision tomorrow morning before we leave for Orono on what we're going to tell Eric and Janet," said Susan.

"OK, OK. I promise we'll figure this out tomorrow." He closed his eyes and tried to think what they should do. He fell asleep without coming to a conclusion.

CHAPTER 17

Morning came to the Benoit Lodge and Eric made a quick trip to the bathroom, then went and opened the curtains. *Remarkable,* he thought, *the sun is shining.* He built a fire and quietly crawled back into bed with a still sleeping Janet. Eric looked over at her and marveled at her good looks. Jack must be nuts to treat her as he did.

Finally she opened her eyes, then looked over at a smiling Eric. She looked down beneath her covers to make certain she was fully covered and adjusted her top to better cover her breasts.

"I'm sorry," Eric said, "I forgot to rearrange your top after I slid over last night. Don't you remember?" he asked, trying not to laugh.

Janet got out of bed, belted Eric on his head with her pillow and headed for the bathroom. On her way back she stopped to look out the window to admire the sunshine. "Boy, it looks nice out there. What should we do today?" She sat on the side of the bed next to Eric.

"Well, we don't have much of a choice," Eric answered, "We can't drive anywhere, we probably can't go skiing yet, so it leaves us with more snowshoeing or just sitting around in the lodge."

"OK, snowshoeing is fine with me. I enjoyed yesterday's walk. I'll get dressed first, OK? And, no, I don't need any help from you."

"You take away all my fun." Eric frowned and pretended to cry. All he got in response was another pillow in his face.

Janet came out of the bathroom wearing a pair of yellow slacks, a blue and gold sweater, and a pair of sandals. Eric took his turn and came out with a pair of jeans and a blue wool turtleneck sweater.

Eric held Janet's hand as they walked into a full dining room that surprised Eric. He thought since most of these people didn't go outside as Janet and he did, they would have stayed in bed longer. Maybe, he thought, they ran out of things to do in bed.

Breakfast was another buffet that Eric raided. Janet looked at him in amazement at the amount of food he had on his plate. Today it was two eggs Benedict, bacon, sausage, and a couple of English muffins, plus fruit, fruit juice and a glass of milk. She couldn't figure out where his body stored all that food.

Michael Craven came to their table with his usual smile in place. "You might want to try the woods trail today. It's warmer this morning and the snow is melting, but it should be beautiful. There shouldn't be any problems with falling trees or branches."

"Thanks, Mr. Craven. By the way, when do you think you can get my car up here?"

Craven took off his hat, scratched his head and looked out the window. "We're going to plow the drive and parking lot this morning and after that we'll get your car up here, so you'd better leave your keys at the front desk."

"Will you need help?" asked Eric.

Craven convinced Eric that his help wouldn't be needed, then left to go outside to supervise the snowplowing.

"Well, my dear. It's you and me all by ourselves in the snowy woods of Maine," said Eric. "If you want to go change, I'll make sure I don't walk in on you again...unless you insist."

Janet smiled at Eric while patting him on his arm. "You wait here. There's not going to be another striptease show this morning." Janet left for their room while Eric walked over to the door to check on the weather and to think about what he saw yesterday. It was surprisingly warm, as icicles were already dripping. Tomorrow, he thought, they could probably head back home.

He disliked the thought of not being with Janet. He had fallen in love with her, but how could he explain this to her and to Susan? His thinking continued in a variety of manners, but it all ended when he asked himself, "Now what do I do?" All the time he had spent with her at the lake reinforced his feelings toward her.

He suddenly felt arms around his shoulders. A sexy voice obviously belonging to Janet said, "I was waiting for you and you didn't show up. I finally had to get dressed." She laughed and hugged him tighter. She was not making it easy for him. "I even brought your jacket."

He turned around and in a disappointed voice told Janet, "Nuts, I thought it was the redhead coming to attack me. And it was just you." She whacked him with her gloves and headed out the door.

They sat on the porch and put on their snowshoes, admiring the quietness of the area. Except for a distant sound of snowplows, there was little else except for chickadees singing while coming back and forth to the bird feeders. The sun was shining for the first time since last Thursday and their sunglasses covered the brightness. The Benoit Lodge looked absolutely beautiful as the sun magnified its looks.

The trail into the woods was marked so no one would get lost. The scenery got more beautiful as they got closer to the foothills. Snow was still on the tree branches that were straightening out as the sun began to melt the snow. The only sound was that of their snowshoes crunching the snow and the occasional crackling of melting snow and ice.

They had been walking for about two hours when they came across a downed tree and Eric suggested they take a break. They brushed the snow off the fallen trunk and sat down. For a while they just sat enjoying the quiet of the woods. In the distance they could hear a woodpecker drilling a tree. Other than that the only noise heard was their heavy breathing.

Janet glanced over at Eric and said, "I love this area, even with all this snow. It's great fun to be away and I'm going to miss it when we go home." She looked up into the trees and leaned against Eric. "And I'm going to miss you too. It's been fun, even with your phony attacks on me." She grinned and put her head against his chest.

Eric put his arm around Janet and agreed that he would miss being with her, even though she was sexless. He couldn't help laughing as she pulled her arm from around his waist. She looked for something to throw at him and settled for snow. He got a face full. Then he retaliated by tipping her over the tree trunk and into the snow. They threw snow at each other, then suddenly stopped and looked at one another. Eric put his hands around her head and kissed her. She responded in kind. "Oh, Eric," she finally said, "I think I'm falling in love with you and I can't bear the thought of not being with you. I'm sorry. I shouldn't say these things and I'll deny them when we get in bed tonight." She was both laughing and crying with a face full of snow.

Eric stroked her head and said to her. "Janet, I was about to say the same. I've already told myself that I've fallen in love with you, but I've tried to put it aside because of Susan and Jack. We're married whether or not we like it and it wouldn't be fair to them if we did anything to violate those bonds. I was thinking that if Jack hadn't had problems with his hip I wouldn't have ever met you. I hate to say it, but I'm glad he broke his hip. That led me to you." Eric held Janet's hands and looked at her smiling face as she hugged Eric and again placed her head on his chest with its rapidly beating heart.

Finally they got up and continued snowshoeing along the trail. About an hour later they decided to head back to the lodge for lunch where the Lewises were waiting for them. They had invited Janet and Eric to join them and they were beginning to like the Ellsworth couple, as they were very nice basic people. Eric and Janet told them of their walk through the woods and the beautiful scenery they'd seen and recommended the Lewises take the same walk, but they were not outdoors-type people

Margaret Lewis looked longingly at Eric and Janet. "If you hadn't told us otherwise, we assumed you were married to each other. You're a fun couple to be with. Forgive me for asking but is there more to your relationship than just friends?"

Janet and Eric looked at each other, then back to the Margaret and Hank. Janet thought for a while before answering. "You're right; there might be more to our relationship than just friendship." She then went on to explain what was happening and not happening, including their bedding together.

Hank Lewis laughed and said, "I thought so and, Eric, you must have the patience of Job to not do what should be done in a bed between a beautiful girl and a handsome boy. I both envy and admire you." He patted Eric on his arm and brought a smile from Janet.

"Hank, mind your manners," said an embarrassed Margaret, frowning at her husband. She was at a loss of words.

"No, Margaret," replied Janet, "he's right. I am impressed with how patient Eric has been with me. We didn't plan this to happen. Maybe it's God's way of getting us together." Janet's eyes began to fill with happy tears.

Eric put his arm around Janet to comfort her, but she continued to cry. Then Michael Craven came over to their table to see what was wrong. He asked Janet if she was all right and she smiled and told him she couldn't be happier.

"The last time I encountered a woman both crying and being happy was when my wife told me she was pregnant," Craven said, thinking of what could make a happy Janet cry.

Janet laughed and wiped her eyes. "No, I'm not, but thanks for asking. I'm just plain happy and I often cry when I'm happy."

Eric and the Lewises joined in the laughter and this further confused Craven.

Michael Craven changed the subject. "Thought you'd like to know that the roads are being plowed so by tomorrow morning you'll be able to leave...if you want to. Check out time is noon, but I'm not going to get excited if you want to stay longer. And your car is OK and in the parking lot. The keys are at the desk."

They thanked Craven, who then went on to tell his other quests of the road conditions and to try and figure out what all the laughing and crying was about. The reaction of his other guests seemed to be one of great relief so they could get home to check on any possible damage the storm might have caused their homes.

Eric began to wonder what might have happened at his house and whether or not Susan went down to the house.

Eric and Janet decided to spend the rest of the afternoon reading in the main room. They both nodded off after a few minutes. The dining room bell woke them indicating dinner was a half hour away.

Janet wanted to change so she went up to the room by herself. Eric stayed, feeling better by not taking a chance at something happening between the two of them so soon after their encounter in the snow.

Eric watched Janet come down the stairs dressed in a beautiful green patterned dress that complemented her body. Her hair fell on her shoulders. The guests in the main room all seemed to stop talking and instead looked at her coming down the stairs. Eric got up from his chair and went to meet her at the bottom of the stairs.

"My God, you're beautiful," Eric murmured to her as he held out his hand for hers. She grasped his hand while smiling. "Now I'd better go up and get out of these clothes. I'll be back in a few minutes." He ran up the stairs two steps at a time. Ten minutes later he came down the stairs dressed in a pair of gray slacks and the light blue shirt.

"You do dress up pretty well," Janet offered as she took Eric by his hand and headed to the dining room where Eric ordered a bottle of Pinot Noir and then they toasted each other.

"I am so happy to be with you," Eric said, "I really can't handle the thought of taking you home."

Janet leaned over and kissed Eric on his cheek. "Thanks, Eric. I also don't want this weekend to end."

For dinner they had pot roast, a specialty of the lodge, and both agreed with that description. After dinner they sat finishing their bottle of Pinot Noir and coffee while reminiscing about the time spent together. Eric added, "You know I have the storm to thank for getting us together. If it hadn't happened we never would have been able to spend this time together." He reached over and held her hand.

Janet smiled in agreement and moved her blonde hair out of her eyes. She remarked, "Maybe it will storm again and make us stay here." Eric nodded in agreement as he stretched his arms over his head.

They went over to the Lewises' table to join them in a last cup of coffee before heading off to bed. As the clock approached eight thirty, Margaret wished them good luck in case they didn't see each other in the morning. Janet and Eric joined them in the walk up the stairs to their bedrooms.

Since Eric hadn't had a shower since returning from their hike, Janet suggested that the smell in the room would greatly improve if he did so. She didn't even look at him when she uttered those remarks as Eric turned to stare at her, and she was having difficulty keeping a straight face.

"I can't believe you said that!" Eric said in shock to her back. He retreated to the bathroom and when Janet heard the shower running, she undressed and put on her pajamas and a bathrobe. She waited in one of the chairs in front of the fireplace and thought about what would happen tomorrow when they would get back to the Bangor area. Where were Jack and Susan and what would they think when they found out about what happened at the Benoit Lodge?

She couldn't imagine Jack or Susan accepting the fact that nothing occurred between her and Eric. "Yeah," she said to herself, "we slept in the same bed for three nights and nothing sexual happened." She began laughing out loud just as the door to the bathroom opened and Eric came out dressed in his pajamas.

"You are a little goofy, aren't you?" he remarked as he looked around the room to see whom Janet was laughing at. "It must have been a joke you heard last week and just figured out." Eric was rubbing his hair with his towel while sitting down next to her with a strange look on his face toward Janet.

She continued laughing while relating what caused her it.

"Jack would probably hit you on your nose if he found out what you could have done, but didn't do. I don't think he'd buy into what really happened, but maybe he considers me sexless since we haven't done it with one another for a long time."

"Yeah," Eric thought as he envisioned a very strong Jack Meacham attacking him for sleeping with his wife. He already felt the pain. "Hmm, I didn't think of that. In other words, I'll be accused of something I wanted to do, but didn't. And I'm not certain how Susan will take this. I don't think that will be a problem since we had planned to separate, but I don't know." Eric stared into the fireplace while Janet put her arm around his shoulders. He couldn't take his eyes off her body while telling himself to behave.

Janet looked over at Eric with a puzzled look. "I don't quite understand how you and Susan are getting along. It always seemed to me that the two of you loved each other."

Eric laughed at that, but then turned his face into a serious look. "No, we do love each other, but we've had a strange marriage relationship and lately we've been drifting apart. Our lifestyles are completely different so there is no way I can see us staying together."

Janet gave Eric a peculiar look. "What do you mean?"

Eric chuckled and then related to Janet the marriage arrangement. She had a difficult time understanding it and shook her head when Eric finished. "Are you sure you're not telling me a story?"

Eric laughed at that thought. "No, it's really true. When I think about it now, the reason for our marriage doesn't make any sense, but at the time, we both thought it was a unique pairing. For a couple of years it worked just fine, but now it's not working because we each have a different lifestyle. I want to stay in Maine and have a family and Susan wants to move to some large city and she does not want children...at least not anytime soon."

Janet was confused by what she had just been told, but she still felt a love for Eric even though he still loved his wife. She shook her head and looked at Eric with a puzzled stare. She wondered if they got married sometime in the future, if Eric would set up some sort of marriage agreement.

Eric began to understand what was affecting Janet, so he reached over for her hand. "Now, don't get a feeling that I'm some sort of oddball in setting up the marriage agreement with Susan. If I had to do it over again, I doubt that I would have agreed to marry her, but as I said, we were quickly in love with each other when we agreed to our marriage, but things have changed and we're both happy we had set up our prenuptial agreement."

Eric frowned as he thought about Susan. "I think we're both sorry all this is happening, but we've enjoyed each other, even though we want to go off on our own. I don't know if she has a new boyfriend; she hasn't told me. Knowing how we've gotten along, I doubt that she is having an affair with someone else." He then tried to explain his feelings toward his marriage with Susan.

He stopped talking and thought for a moment about what might be happening with Susan and Janet's husband Jack, assuming they were together this weekend, but he doubted it. Susan had considered Jack a good friend.

Janet stared at the fireplace with an amazed expression before looking at a smiling Eric. "I've never heard of any arrangement like you and Susan have. I can't understand how you ever got involved with it."

Eric turned his head toward the fireplace and with a quiet voice tried to answer Janet. "Well, look at it this way. Susan and I are very good friends and probably will be for the rest of our lives. We're too much apart in nearly everything we do so there's no way we could have made a lengthy marriage work. She once told me that we were more like a brother and sister than husband and wife. Our separation really has nothing to do with a dislike toward each other.

"By the way, you do smell better," Janet said, putting her arms around his shoulders and placing her head on his chest. The lights went off and Eric sadly said, "It's time to go to neutral territory." They got up and went to bed.

Janet leaned over and kissed him. "Good night, Eric."

"Good night, Janet." He breathed deeply and quietly said, "I love you more than you can imagine." He heard her crying.

"Oh, Eric, I do love you too."

CHAPTER 18

They both slept soundly, reflecting on the activities they experienced on Sunday. Janet woke first and after a quick trip to the bathroom to brush her teeth, she went over to the window and looked out at a sunny day. She got back in bed and waited for Eric to wake up. Maybe I should touch him, she thought, but changed her mind when she realized she would be teasing him. Eric had been very patient in not pressing her for sex. If he had she doubted she would have resisted any advance he might have made.

Janet felt very comfortable with Eric, certainly a large change from their first evening together. She looked over at him and admired his good looks and wondered if getting together was going to be a serious option.

She suddenly felt something on her leg pulling her pajamas. She looked under her blanket and realized it was Eric probing her leg. Janet looked up at a smiling Eric who was still pretending to sleep. She pushed against his left shoulder and knocked him out of the bed. He groaned in agony as he bounced on the floor. Janet quickly went to his side of the bed to see how badly he was hurt.

He lay moaning on the floor as Janet fell to his side. "Are you OK?" she asked in a concerned voice, fearing she might have hurt him. Her blonde hair hung down to his head that was rolling in agony.

Suddenly he grabbed her and laughed, wrestling her to his side where he brought his face to hers. "Good morning, my dear. I think I'll sue you for attacking me while I slept."

"Yeah, and how do you figure that after you were grabbing me?" she asked, staring at his eyes with her intensely blue eyes. She avoided smiling.

"I'm obviously innocent of any such event. You're mistaken as usual," he answered in a serious tone. "I'll forgive you if you kiss me." He smiled at her while puckering his lips in anticipation

"Not a chance," Janet said laughing and pushing him aside. "Besides, you have bad breath. Yuck!" She grimaced. "Go brush your teeth."

Eric was enjoying the entire affair as they were acting like a couple of kids. He didn't want it to end, but soon they'd be on their way back to Bangor. He got up and headed for the bathroom to brush his teeth and shave. She waited patiently for her turn while enjoying these last moments with Eric.

Janet put on the same clothes that she wore over to Bethel on Friday. Jack put on his pair of jeans and a white shirt. As they went down for breakfast one last time where most of the people were also getting ready to have breakfast and then leave for their homes. Eric again shocked Janet with the amount of food he consumed. The amount he ate should have created all sorts of extra pounds on his frame, but for some reason it didn't. He knew what she was thinking and just smiled at her while stuffing his mouth with a waffle.

"I can't believe you don't weigh three hundred pounds," Janet said, looking at his plate full of food. "How do you do this?"

"Damned if I know," Eric offered. "It must be the activity I have with you that takes away all these calories. Besides, this stuff tastes terrific and it costs the same no matter how much I eat." Janet just shook her head and continued to marvel at his appetite.

The Lewises were not down yet, so Eric and Janet retreated to their room to pack and to get ready to drive back to Bangor. They were quiet as they emptied the dresser and put everything into their suitcases. When they finished, they sat down in front of the fireplace one last time and Eric suggested, "We'd better figure out what we're going to tell Jack and Susan, if we're to tell them anything."

Janet held Eric's hand and looked at him. "We need to understand what we are doing. I think I'm in love with you, but I need to know if this is just a weekend romance. I don't need to have another quick relationship as I did with Jack. I want something that will last the rest of my life and I think you are what I am after," Janet said with a firm voice devoid of any tears. She looked at him with an unusually serious look. "Does this make sense to you, Eric, or should we go back to our normal lives and consider this to have been a fun weekend, which it was?" She smiled at Eric while they held hands.

Eric finally replied after a long pause and he tried to say what he meant. "Janet, I think...no, I know I'm in love with you, but you're right in wanting to make it certain this wasn't anything more than a strange weekend where Jack and Susan didn't join us and where I let you remain a near virgin while sleeping in the same bed with you. What would happen if my friends found out that I didn't attack you? I'd be the laughing stock of Bangor." Eric began to laugh, but stopped and gripped both of Janet's hands.

"Unless there is something I'm missing I want you and me to be husband, wife, and parents. With all due respect and love to Susan, I know now it's you I want to be with, but, yes, we need to make certain this is what both of us want." Janet and Eric hugged each other in absolute joy.

When they separated, Eric gazed into Janet's blue eyes and suggested, "Well, you know they haven't made the bed yet so we can do a quickie before we leave." He had trouble keeping a straight face.

She answered by whacking him on his arm and sticking up her head to ignore him, but was unable to keep from grinning.

"I agree, at least I think I do. I don't know what else we can tell them about this weekend. As far as they know, we had two separate bedrooms and maybe we should leave it at that." She had a questioning look, and then broke out in laughter. "I feel like a teenager trying to explain to my parents what happened after the prom."

Janet added, "Maybe we should talk with my father. As tough as he seems to be, he listens well."

Eric thought for a while before answering. "It's OK with me, but how can he come up with a solution better than the one we agreed on?" Janet shrugged her shoulders as she shook her head.

Craven's grandson came to take their suitcases to Eric's SUV, now completely clear of snow. The driveway was still snow white but the ice had disappeared and the snow was melting. The forecast, if it could be believed, was for continued unseasonably warm weather for the next two days. At least this forecaster was not Tom Siegel.

Eric and Janet saw the Lewises in the dining room and went in to join them for a cup of coffee before leaving. They were also getting packed and ready to go, but not with the sadness affecting Eric and Janet. If fact, they were anxious to get back to Ellsworth to see their children and grandchildren and find out how their house and business fared in the storm.

Margaret had a good feel for people and suggested to Eric and Janet to be patient so everything could work its way for the best. "Don't do a lot of worrying. Just be honest with what you want to happen, assuming you do want the change to be made, and it probably will, if that makes any sense to you."

She smiled at both of them, and then kissed Janet and gave Eric a hug. Her husband joined the hugging and told both of them to "give us a call so we know what's happening."

A smiling Michael Craven was at his desk when Eric and Janet went to check out. There was a line of people anxiously waiting to check out so they could get home.

"Thanks for coming to visit us and I hope you had a good time, even with the problems the storm created. Please do come back to see us, but leave the storm behind." Craven laughed at his joke, then shook hands with Eric and Janet, while wishing them good luck and a safe drive back to Bangor.

They stood in front of the lodge and looked out on the snow-covered golf course and both felt good about the weekend together. Both were anxious to get back to Bangor but Eric had to stop in Waterville to see his patients.

Their luggage and snowshoes were in the SUV and the unused skis were still on the rack as Eric and Janet fastened themselves into their seats. They both looked back at the Benoit Lodge and commented on how much they had both enjoyed being there. Then they drove down the driveway to start their trip home. When they got on Highway 2 they were somewhat surprised to see other cars on the road, much different than it was last Friday, which seemed years ago.

The snow was piled deep on the road's shoulders so it was nearly impossible to see beyond the road except for the trees that were still covered with snow and ice. Birch trees went bent over to form arches. They probably would never straighten out again. The sun was shining and the day was ideal for driving back to Bangor.

Eric broke the silence. "I forgot to tell you, but I need to stop at the Waterville Hospital to check on my two patients. They should be well out of the operation mode so I need to check their legs to make sure all is OK. Besides, it's important to them that they see their surgeon. I also have to set up their physical therapy."

"Oh, sure," said Janet. "Could I go with you to see them?"

"Really?" replied Eric, looking over at Janet, surprised at her request.

"Yeah, I'd like to see them."

"OK, you're on."

The remainder of the drive to Waterville took an hour and a half and was without any significant traffic and little conversation between Eric and Janet. The two were doing a lot of thinking to themselves about the time they had spent together and the fun they had without getting involved with any sort of intimate relations. Both were wondering what was next and whether or not their relationship could transfer permanently to one another.

While they drove to Waterville, Janet spent her time going over her meetings in Augusta last Friday so she could properly explain the meeting to her other teachers. It seemed as though the three days were like three weeks.

Eric's patients were on the fourth floor of the hospital in downtown Waterville and when they arrived, the attending nurse greeted him warmly. The head nurse shook hands with Eric and Janet, who she assumed was his wife.

"It's nice to meet you Mrs. Forster." Janet didn't know what to say and left it by thanking Nurse Rita Parman.

Eric was reading the reports on his patients and everything seemed to be in good order. Both patients had already begun to walk with a therapist and a walker. "Any problems?" asked Eric.

"No, not really. Just the usual groans. Mr. Anderson is doing better with his new hip than Mr. Gladstone with his knee, but both are doing OK, at least until they see you," answered Rita with a tired smile. "We ran a little shorthanded this weekend because of the storm so most of us stayed here for the entire weekend."

Eric nodded his head, "I know what you mean. We were stuck in Bethel since Friday afternoon. You must be exhausted," offered Eric in appreciation for the tasks the nurses experienced in getting their patients' health back.

"That's an understatement, Doctor, "Rita offered with a gloomy smile. "I've missed being with my family during the storm but my husband handled the situation quite well. So," said Rita, "let's go see your patients."

Janet asked if she could go along. Rita and Eric looked at each other and nodded in agreement, but Eric reminded Janet to stay in the background. Janet agreed.

The first room they visited was John Anderson who'd had his left hip replaced. The room was quiet with Anderson sitting up in bed reading the morning newspaper. Anderson was an elderly patient in his late sixties, but with a much younger appearance and attitude.

"Hello, Dr. Forster. I see you've weathered the storm. And who's the pretty young lady by the door? Maybe she's here to replace the miserable nurses who have been abusing me." He had a difficult time keeping a straight

"Hi, I'm Janet, and I'm here to check on patients who have been abusing our nurses." Her smile won over John Anderson.

Anderson replied, "Well, you've got me. Now I guess I'll have to say nice things about Rita. I've asked her to marry me but she turned me down for her current husband." He looked at Rita with a broad smile. "I can't imagine why."

Eric had trouble keeping from laughing at this exchange, but asked John Anderson how he was doing. "I'm doing OK. I've been up and walking with the therapist, using the walker."

"How's the pain?" asked Eric while inspecting the incision.

"Not too bad. It's hurting less each day." John Anderson looked pleadingly at Eric. "So when do I get to go home?"

Eric sat next to John Anderson and told him that if all continues to go as well as it's going today, he could probably go home this afternoon. "However, you'll need to continue working with a therapist here at the hospital or in your home, whichever makes more sense, and you need to follow their instructions. If you don't, your recovery will take much longer than necessary.

Anderson smiled and gave his thanks for the good news. Eric threw out one more air of caution. "You need to follow the instructions on how to treat the hip while you are recovering. If you don't, you might dislocate the socket and I don't even want to tell you how painful that is. If it's icy outside you're not to leave your house. You can do the simple indoor exercises that will strengthen the muscles around the hip. Just don't do anything stupid. We'll go over this with your family so they know what you can and can't do. OK?" Eric looked John Anderson in the eye with a serious look so he would not misinterpret what he had just said. "You also need to memorize what's on our do's and don'ts list."

Eric pulled out a sheet of paper from Anderson's file and handed it to his patient. "You are to memorize what's on this sheet because if you don't you're not going home." There was a very serious tone to Eric's voice that surprised Janet after their fun weekend. Eric continued, "Here's a few of the items you need to be aware of. Don't cross your left leg over the right. Don't sit on low seats. Use a commode in your bathroom. Sleep with a pillow between your legs and don't sleep on your left hip. When you go up a step use your right leg first and when coming down a step use your left leg first." Eric continued with a list of things to avoid and was confident John Anderson was cognizant of what needed to be done to heal the new hip.

"One more thought. It's going to take about six months for your new hip to get back its full strength, so while it won't be painful, it's still weak and could come apart with little effort. I also want you to walk with the walker every day until the therapist moves you to a cane. But equally important, you need to rest. OK? Just remember that you've had very serious surgery."

Eric didn't want John Anderson to not realize the importance of following all these instructions so he stared at Anderson without a smile. He felt like he was chastising a child.

"Don't worry, Doctor, I don't want to come back here anytime soon except maybe to terrorize the nurses," replied Anderson, looking at Rita with a large smile. "And all kidding aside the nurses have been terrific, especially Rita."

The meeting with Phillip Gladstone went well, but Eric felt he might need an extra day before going home. Both operations were successful and both patients could look forward to pain-free walking.

Janet watched as Eric met with the nurses and physical therapists to go over the status of both transplant recipients. The people listened with intensity as Eric went over when the patients could leave the hospital and when and where therapy should occur. Janet could feel the respect the staff had for Eric and this was reinforced when Rita came over to Janet and said to her, "Your husband is easily the best orthopedic surgeon I've ever known. You're a very lucky woman."

Janet didn't answer. She just smiled and nodded her head in agreement. She was very surprised at how Eric changed his life style while dealing with his patients. While he was still friendly he remained serious about their conditions.

Eric next met with the families who were awaiting word as to when the husbands and fathers could come home. Eric patiently went through what restrictions must be followed by the two transplant recipients. He also set up appointments in six weeks for both patients. While being serious to both families, he was very friendly in his approach to what the patients could and could not do when they got home. He emphasized their staying indoors if the weather turned harsh like it just had. He didn't want either of them to slip on ice.

"I don't need to see him before the six weeks are up, but call me if he is having a problem," he told both families. He patiently listened to their questions and concerns and didn't end the meetings until all questions were answered. He added, "He'll see a huge improvement in walking without pain."

Eric said his good-byes to both patients and the nursing staff and went to meet a very pleased Janet. "Let's go have lunch and then get back to Bangor. OK?"

"OK", she repeated, reaching out for his hand. "Let's do it."

CHAPTER 19

Jack got up Monday morning at about six and went into Eric's study to see if there was something to read while waiting for Susan to wake up. He found a copy of *Vineline*, the Chicago Cubs magazine and came across an article on former Cubs players.

One of the players discussed was a Peter Forster who played third base in the sixties and was the youngest ever to play for the Cubs. He was an outstanding player, according to the story, and was listed as one of the top five third base men in Cubs history. Jack wondered if he was related to Eric since Forster was not a common name.

He didn't realize Eric was an athlete or from an athletic family. He'd never said anything about it. *Susan must know,* he thought, as he walked back to the bedroom and saw Susan was still sleeping. The sun was up and shining and melting more of the snow and ice. He crawled back into his side of the bed and wrapped his arm around Susan's breasts. She woke up and turned to a smiling Jack. Her hand caressed his face then slid down to his chest. "Good morning, Jack, how long have you been awake?"

"About an hour so I read for a while. I didn't want to disturb you."

"Aren't you sweet," Susan answered with a broad smile, anticipating another love match. She stroked his face then moved her hands down his body while Jack began to explore Susan's naked body. It didn't take long before they were rolling on the bed as though it were some sort of exercise.

When finished they laid together, breathing hard, while reminiscing about the incredible loving they had just experienced.

"Jack, sometime today Eric and Janet will be coming home and we need to figure out how we're going to handle what's happened," said Susan while Jack embraced her.

"I know, I know, but I don't have a damn clue as to what we should do," answered Jack while stroking her face. "Maybe we should leave it alone until they discover what happened this weekend."

"Jack, we can't do that. Damn it! That's like no plan at all," Susan answered.

"I realize that, but what are you going to say to them. Oh, Eric, Jack and I screwed each other all weekend," Jack said in an imitation of Susan's voice, "and now we want out of our marriages so we can marry each other. The only saving grace is that I'm stronger than Eric so he probably won't try to hit me." Jack sat up in the bed. "Besides, we don't know what happened to them this weekend."

Susan had to think this out and sat motionless for what appeared to be a long time before she spoke. "God, Jack, I don't know what to do, so let's go with your idea." She frowned as she spoke. "But somewhere down the line we're going to have to tell them what we want to do."

Jack answered, "I'll buy that idea. Janet and I haven't been getting along since we moved here after my hip injury. I think we still are fond of each other, but it's not the same as it was when we first dated. Probably the problem is that we have a different outlook on what we want to plan for the future. Maybe she wants a divorce, but then she'd probably sue me for most of my assets."

"Jack, that's too bad but I can somewhat understand. Eric and I still love each other, but our relationship is not that great. We have differing views on what we want to do with our lives. He's content to live here the rest of his life because he enjoys the outdoors so much, particularly the lake. I want to be close to the university and if I'm successful I want to go wherever necessary. Maine doesn't offer that much to me," Susan related as she crossed her legs and leaned against the bed's headboard.

Jack interrupted the train of thought by bringing up the article he read about a Peter Forster who played baseball for the Chicago Cubs. "Is Eric related to this guy?" he asked.

"That's Eric's father," she answered.

Jack looked surprised at this fact. "Well I'll be damned. I really never heard of Peter Forster but then I don't follow baseball. Where are his parents?" he asked.

"They live down in Captiva, Florida and they usually come up to Maine for part of the summer, but he still spends a lot of time in Chicago with the Cubs," related Susan, "and he works with the team in Arizona during spring training. He's a very nice man, but Eric's mother is something else. I've never gotten along with her." She rested her head on her hands. "She never thought our marriage would work out, and now I'm beginning to believe her."

Jack looked puzzled about her comments. "I don't understand her thinking. Was it something you did?"

Susan shrugged her shoulders and replied, "No, I don't think so. She just had a feeling that our marriage wouldn't work out. She also wants some grandchildren and I'm not to hot about that.

Susan looked at the bedroom clock and suggested that she and Jack had better get moving in case Eric and Janet show up soon. "I think Eric will probably spend the morning at the hospital in Waterville with his patients and then come back here later this afternoon." She turned to Jack and noted that they probably had time for one more adventure in bed.

Jack said," I've had more sex this weekend than in the past six months." He laughed as he reached out for Susan. "I'll need to rest for a week before I'm active again, and, yeah, how are we going to do this when they're back?"

Susan frowned since she hadn't thought of that. "Maybe we can get together at the U. Let's figure it out later," she said rolling on top of Jack.

CHAPTER 20

Eric drove Janet to a small restaurant in downtown Waterville where parking was still difficult due to the mounds of snow that blocked most of the street. When they got to the restaurant they found a table for two in the back of the restaurant so they could talk freely without interruptions. After they ordered, Eric stretched his arms and straightened himself out in his chair.

He broke the silence of talking about the past weekend and reached out for her hands. "Janet, I had a great time this weekend and forgive me for saying it but I'm glad Jack and Susan didn't make it."

Janet reached out and held his hands while looking in his eyes. "I agree," replied Janet. "I so enjoyed being with you that I can't explain it and now I don't know what to do."

Eric placed his left hand over her right hand and gripped it, not wanting to let go. "You're right; we can't make any quick judgments on a future together. We have to make sure it isn't the result of a weird weekend."

"What do you mean, weird?" Janet asked in a surprised voice.

Eric replied with a broad smile as he pulled her hand to his lips. "How much longer do you think you'd be safe in bed with me? It's weird that I didn't attack you. No, it's not weird. It's ridiculous. The next time you'll never get away with just a goodnight kiss."

Janet laughed at that description and threw her napkin at Eric. She was so enjoying his company that she wanted this relationship to strengthen. He was one terrific guy, she thought. "Maybe you wouldn't be able to do anything anyway and you're just faking it."

"Oh, you think so," Eric said with a laugh. "You say this now in public and not when we were alone this weekend. You're a coward!" he said, throwing her napkin back at her chest. The discussion would have continued, but the waitress brought their lunch, which they ate in relative silence with smiles of happiness transmitted back and forth.

While working on a chicken salad sandwich, Janet changed the subject. "I was very impressed with how you handled your patients this morning. How did you ever become an orthopedic surgeon?"

"Well, it's not a very long story. My father had hurt his right knee several times while playing baseball for the Chicago Cubs and eventually had to retire because it was just too painful to play. Many years later he visited an orthopedic surgeon in Chicago by the name of Dr. Sam Adams and he discussed options with Dad. There really wasn't any choice but to replace the knee so he could enjoy a normal life, but knee replacement was something fairly new.

"I was very young when I first met Dr. Adams and he impressed me by explaining what he was going to do to Dad's knee. After the operation, Dad was able to walk normally for the first time in years, all because of Dr. Adam's talent, so I decided then that I wanted to do the same. That's how it happened," Eric explained in a quiet yet serious tone while smiling.

"How did you ever get to Bangor?" asked Susan.

"When I graduated from Northwestern, Dr. Adams invited me to intern with him, but he wanted to move to Bangor, Maine, where he enjoyed the outdoors when not in surgery. So, that's how I got here and now I am delighted I came, more than you can imagine."

Janet was focused on what Eric was saying. "I didn't know your dad was a baseball player with the Chicago Cubs, but then I don't know much about baseball. Where is he now?" Janet asked, hoping she was not treading on a personal problem.

"Mom and Dad retired to Florida many years ago and on occasion he comes up to visit me, and when it's God-awful cold we go down to visit them. He was a terrific player and I think he is still the youngest guy ever to play for the Cubs." Eric smiled as he talked about his parents.

"How old was he?" asked Janet.

"Sixteen."

Janet had a look of amazement. She found it difficult to imagine anyone that young playing a professional sport. "You're kidding!" said a surprised Janet. "How did he ever do it?"

"It's a long story, but briefly, a scout for the Cubs saw him play in Jackson Park in Chicago when Dad was probably 14 and was so impressed he taught Dad how to play even better. The scout was a catcher with the Cubs in the thirties and said that dad was the best young player he had ever seen. He started playing with the Cubs in 1966 and played until 1978 when he retired. I was born in 1974 and dad had his operation in 1991, thirteen years after his retirement."

Relating this story always made Eric feel good as the new knee changed his father's outlook on life. He was now active again, playing golf and working with young children who wanted to play better baseball. He also helped out with the Cubs' spring training in Arizona.

"Did you ever play baseball?" asked Janet who was amazed that the two men in her life were connected to professional sports.

Eric laughed. "I tried, but I could never have been the player Dad was. I played in high school and college but I really wasn't very good, so I settled on becoming a good orthopedic surgeon. Dad watched me play quite often and while he encouraged me, he knew I didn't have the talent to follow him. If I ever have a son, maybe he can collect some of Dad's genes to become a really good player."

"Do you want children?" asked Janet with a curious look.

"Yes, I do, but Susan's not hot about being a mother. She enjoys her sports too much and doesn't want anything to interfere with it." After a moment of silence between bites of his cheeseburger, Eric asked, "I guess I should ask you the same."

"Oh, yes, I really do. I love children, but for some reason Jack and I have not connected. Before his injury we were going to have a checkup to see what the problem was, but that's been put aside. He says he wants to have children, but I don't know if he has the patience to be a father." Janet looked sad while she was explaining her problem.

"Enough of this," replied Eric. "It's time to get home."

Janet nodded, as she put on her coat "Eric, I really don't want this weekend to end I haven't felt this good in months." She grasped Eric's hands with hers and stared longingly at him. Eric got out of his seat put his coat on then hugged Janet before heading out the door.

CHAPTER 21

Susan and Jack showered together for the last time and Susan began to cry, as she didn't want the weekend to end. She couldn't figure out how to deal with Eric when they were alone tonight. *First,* she thought, *I'm aching and I hope Eric won't be looking for sex. I wouldn't be able to handle it. Second, anyone other than Jack would now be insignificant.*

She thought the world of Eric, but he was nothing like Jack either physically or sexually. *But then,* she thought, *how do I tell Eric?* They got dressed and checked the phones to see if they were working yet. They weren't and the cell phone never worked down at the lake.

Over a late breakfast they decided to go into town and back to the university to see what had happened since Friday. As they got into Jack's SUV, they saw that the road was still full of snow and there was ice just below the surface. The sun was shining and the plowed snow had narrowed the road so there was no longer room for two cars on most of the road. The trees had started to rise up to a near normal height, except the birch trees, which were permanently damaged by the snow and ice.

As they went up the road, they saw one of their neighbors, Rick Stephens, waving his arms to stop them. Jack rolled down his window and asked what was wrong.

Rick pointed up the road and told Susan and Jack, "There's a car off the road at the top of the hill and there's no way to get around it until we get it back on the road. We've got a tow truck coming, but I don't know how long it will take them to clear the road. She's really stuck in the ditch." Rick shook his head while describing the situation. "And I don't know how they're going to do it because it's off the steepest part of the curve."

Susan held back her anger over this development and asked Rick whose car it was. "It's Pam Miranda," he replied. "She just didn't get the car moving fast enough to get up the hill and it slid back into the ditch." The area of the road where this happened was at the top of the hill where a short section was so steep it was difficult for anything to move up.

Jack bounced his hand on the steering wheel to release his anger while Susan let go with a few words that surprised Jack and Rick. Susan was losing her composure. She was frustrated at the thought of staying at the lake for another day, even though she had thoroughly enjoyed her affair with Jack. She just wanted to get back to town.

Rick suggested that they back down the hill and wait at her house until the road became clear again. Rick informed them that they also needed to get more sand on the road before anyone tried to get out. Since he knew the road better, Jack listened to Rick's suggestions, then backed down to the curve at the bottom of the second hill and backed into the only section where he could turn around.

The car moved easily down the hill but it was still difficult to drive backward. He hoped he wouldn't meet anyone coming out because there wasn't room to pass. When he got to the big curve he carefully backed into a snowdrift, turned the wheels, and headed back down to Susan's house.

"Now what do we do until the roads clear?" asked a smiling Jack.

Susan grinned and hit Jack on his arm. "Jack, don't even say what you're thinking because it's going to take me a week to recover from this weekend. We can try to clear the snow off the deck and maybe some of the roofs. Heck, we can even go snowshoeing on the lake, but we're staying away from the bedroom."

They pulled back into the driveway and when Jack turned off the engine, they were awed by quietness of the area. Except for an occasional chain saw in the distance, there was nothing but silence. "Susan, maybe we should try to go snow-shoeing on the lake. OK?"

Susan nodded in agreement and they both went up to the bedroom on the second floor and changed into their outdoor clothes. She suggested to Jack that he move his clothes out of her bedroom and into the spare room, just in case Eric and Janet showed up.

While changing into their outdoor winter gear, Jack thought of making love one more time, but Susan's look changed that idea in a hurry. "If you touch me," Susan said with a smile, "I'll whap you where it will hurt the most. I can still accept a hug from you but no wandering of your hands."

"Susan," Jack answered, "your body tempts me more than you can imagine, but I hear you. Just a hug is all I'm good for right now."

They wrapped their arms around each other with the strength of two athletes. Susan pulled back her head and kissed Jack on his lips and then broke off the hug.

"It's time to go outside and use these snowshoes, "Susan suggested. "Maybe we should walk into town."

CHAPTER 22

The drive from Waterville to Bangor was slower than usual as the road was still covered with some snow and Eric couldn't tell if there was still ice. There was quite a bit of sand covering some spots on the highway and the fields and median strip were loaded with snow. While driving, Janet and Eric marveled at the number of cars and trucks in ditches and on the median. "These poor people probably had to spend a lot of time in their cars until someone finally rescued them," said Eric while looking to make certain there wasn't anyone left in these cars.

Janet turned toward Eric with a concerned look. "What a horrible storm this was." She remained quiet for a few minutes and then asked Eric. "We've avoided this subject, but what are we going to tell Jack and Susan?"

Eric shrugged his shoulders and didn't take his eyes off the road. "I don't know. Maybe the truth? That I slept with you for three nights and nothing happened. Do you think they'll believe that?" he offered as he looked at the road in front of him.

Janet pulled out her cell phone and tried to call Jack but got no answer at their house so she tried the university and still got no answer. She breathed deeply and looked at Eric. "I can't reach Jack, so maybe he's at the lake with Susan." She tapped on her cell phone and decided to call her father at Channel 2.

"This is Doug Felty."

"This is your daughter or have you forgotten me?"

"Where in heck are you and what's happened?" asked her father, who was relieved to hear from his daughter..

She began to explain what had happened but then stopped and told him that maybe she and Eric could stop by the station before going home and explain the weekend.

"OK, please do," answered a very relieved father.

She then asked her father, "Dad, did the storm knock out your power?"

"Yes, it did, but last night we got both the power and phone lines back. We're OK now."

"Dad, have you heard from Jack and Susan?" she asked while looking at Eric.

"Yeah, they got delayed on Friday and by the time they were ready to go it was too late to try to drive across the state, so Jack drove Susan home. I suspect they're still there. The snow was really coming down hard and I doubt Jack could have made it back up the hill. I've tried to call but got no answer so the phone lines are probably down. I guess they're still there."

About half an hour later Eric parked his SUV in the Channel 2 parking lot, which had piles of snow more than ten feet high, but the pavement was free of snow, as were the roads in Bangor. The temperature was in the mid forties so the snow and ice were melting.

Jill showed Janet and Eric into her father's office and the two of them embraced each other and traded kisses as though they hadn't seen each other in years. Doug shook Eric's hand with a very strong "thank you" grip. "God, I'm glad to see you two. Now tell me what happened in Bethel."

Janet and Eric looked at each other and then Janet began the description of the road to Bethel and the conditions at the Benoit Lodge. She didn't offer any comments on the fact that they were confined to one room and one bed. Such a situation never entered her father's thoughts.

As they were talking, Tom Siegel appeared at the door with a broad smile that must have been carried over from his success in identifying the storm. His being correct bugged Doug, as he really wanted to get rid of Siegel.

Janet repeated most of the trip story and how right Jim Siegel was in identifying the storm. She ended her story with a question. "How much snow did we get?"

"Here in the Bangor area, about thirty-one inches. Where you were, at least thirty-seven inches. There was also considerable freezing rain that further made a mess of the roads and ruined thousands of trees. The state is a mess and probably will be until spring when we finally get rid of this snow. It was the largest single storm since 1947. Next, we have to worry about flooding if it melts too fast."

Doug Felty ended Siegel's comments by thanking him for stopping by. After he left, Doug banged his fist on his desk. "Damn that guy. Now he's the local hero for correctly forecasting this storm. Of course everyone now forgets about his other lousy forecasts."

"Now, Dad," cautioned Janet, "be nice. He's little more than a trainee and if you're not careful you'll have heart attack.

"OK, OK," Doug said as he nodded in agreement, easing his face into a smile. "If Jack's stuck at the lake, do you want to stay at my place?"

"Thanks, Dad, but I don't know. She looked inquiringly at Eric, a look that surprised her father. "What do you think?" she asked Eric. Doug Felty saw something in their eye contact that told him something was going on between the two of them.

Eric looked at the clock behind Doug's desk and offered, "Maybe I should try to get down to the lake while it's still light. We've probably got another three hours. If we can't, I'll bring Janet back up to your place."

They all agreed with this idea, so Janet and Eric got up and walked out to the parking lot with Doug, who was pleased Janet was safe. She hugged her father again and told him they'd be in contact as soon as they found out if they could get to the lake. Doug grabbed Eric's hand and looked at him with a concerned look. *Something had happened at the lodge,* Doug thought, *but that might not be too bad since Janet and Jack were not getting along too well.*

It took about thirty minutes to get to the Peaks Hill Lodge parking lot. The drive was uneventful but the piles of snow impressed them. They both agreed they'd never seen this much snow. When they got to the lot, there were several cars parked close to the lake road. Snow was piled high in the back end of the parking lot and it looked like it would be the fourth of July before all this snow melted.

Most of the cars belonged to neighbors who were standing around talking. Eric figured something was wrong. As he walked to the cars, he saw Paul Glidden leaning against his pickup. "Hi, Eric," Paul said with a welcoming smile. "It's nice to have you back after we've done all the work clearing the road."

Eric gave him a finger salute and then commented on the number of neighbors waiting to go down the road. "So, what's the problem?" Eric finally asked.

"Well, you might not believe this, but there's been an accident on top of the toboggan slide. Pam Miranda slid off the road into a ditch and then, when they were trying to get her out, Jan Sutherland came down and panicked when she saw Pam's SUV. She braked too hard and sent the car off to the right. When she tried to compensate she hit something that tipped her car over. She's OK, but it's going to take awhile to get both these cars off the road and then get the road plowed again. So, welcome home," Paul said with a smile.

"You've missed a dandy weekend. Oh, and, yeah, the power's off as are the phones. I hooked up your generator and it's working just fine. You've got power for about one more day, but if you can't get down tomorrow, I'll find a snowmobile and take it down and put in more gas. OK?"

"Paul thanks a lot. I owe you big time for all your help." Eric shook Paul's hand. With all this, Eric shook his head in disbelief and looked at Janet, who could not believe what she was hearing. "Paul, how are Susan and Jack?"

"Well, they're OK as far as I know. We've had a couple of block parties and they both came to them and we had dinner at your house Saturday night. They tried to get out this morning but were told they couldn't. I understand Susan was madder than hell but it was probably just the frustration of being stuck at home."

Janet shook her head. *What else could go wrong?* She thought to herself. She then noticed a friend of hers, who lived down the road from Eric's house, and went over to talk with her. When she was out of earshot, Paul grabbed Eric's arm and peered at him with a serious look.

"Eric, I've got to talk to you. We've been friends a long time and I need to tell you that I think something was going on between Jack Meacham and Susan. Jack's a real asshole, but Susan seems to be enamored of him. I'm not the only one who has this same feeling, but I can't give you proof. We were told he was sleeping on the couch in the living room, but when I came by Sunday morning the pillow and blankets were folded as though they had never been used. I think he was upstairs in the bedroom." Paul shrugged his shoulders as his face turned sad. "I don't want to see you hurt. OK?"

Eric nodded his head as he tried to absorb what Paul was telling him. Paul had somewhat of a reputation for being the local gossip, as did many others on the road, so what he was telling Eric might be totally untrue. "Paul, thanks, but I don't know what to say." Eric also wondered what his friends would say had they known he and Janet had shared a bed for three nights; nonetheless Eric felt angry that his wife would submit to someone else that easily. He was also angry with his good friend Paul, who could have let this pass.

"Please don't say anything to Janet, OK?" Eric requested with a very serious look in his eyes. *Damn it,* he thought, *what do I do now? Should I tell Janet about this or let it pass?* Eric looked over to Janet, who was having a good time talking with a friend from high school. *I wonder,* Eric thought, *if she is telling her about our weekend together.*

"OK, Eric, you can count on it, and please don't say anything to Jack about me. I think he might come after me if he heard what I just told you." Paul Glidden had a very worried look, as he was afraid Jack Meacham would suddenly appear in the parking lot and hit him.

Eric walked over to Janet and told her about the accident on the road, but Phyllis Smith had already filled her in on the problem. Looking dismayed, Janet asked Eric, "So what do we do now?"

Eric leaned against Phyllis' car and gazed down the road to the lake. "Maybe we should walk down to where the cars are to see how long it will take to get this road opened." He leaned against her car and gazed down the road.

"OK," answered Janet, "Let's do it. Do we need snowshoes?"

Phyllis shook her head. "No the road is pretty clean and it's not that far to the mess. I'll join you, if that's OK," she replied. The three of them headed off to the first hill. They passed the Tucker house on their left and waved to Jim Tucker, who was out snow blowing his driveway.

As they came to the steep part of the hill, they moved off the road, which was beginning to get slippery, and went into the snow bank on the side. As they got to the top of the curve they could see the cars blocking the road. The first was Jan Sutherland's car, laying on its top, halfway down the first curve.

Down the road about twenty feet was Pam Miranda's car, backed into the ditch, with the car totally blocking the road.

"Oh, my goodness," said Janet with a concerned voice, "Phyllis, what a mess. Was anyone hurt?"

Phyllis shook her head. "They're both OK, but they both were scared to death, especially Jan, when her car tipped over." The three of them stared at the mess and figured it would take a long time to get both cars off the road.

Eric shook his head. "What a weekend. What else could go wrong?" He thought of going down the road to the cars, but thought better of it when he looked at the slippery steep road in front of him. He tried to figure out how they were going to get the cars off the road when it was so slippery. "They're going to have to put a ton of sand on the road before they can move the cars," he related to the ladies. He was also madder than hell since he couldn't get down to his house and Susan.

Phyllis assured the two of them that both ladies were all right, but scared to death. "Who wouldn't be if your car turned over while sliding down the hill?" The three of them went back up the curve to the parking lot where Paul Glidden was still standing. The weather was still above freezing and the snow and ice were melting.

"Paul, are you going to go back down tonight?" asked Eric.

Paul was still sitting in his truck seat. "I don't think so. I was hoping someone would be coming up on a snowmobile but if they haven't come by now, they're probably not coming until the road is cleared, so I'll probably go back to my store and stay there for the night." Paul had a furniture store in Bangor so he had plenty of beds to sleep on. "Harriet should be OK and if she needs help she can go over to your house and interrupt whatever is going on."

Janet came over to Paul's truck and asked what they had been talking about. She didn't get an answer from either one. They stared at each other.

"Janet, give your father a call and I'll take you to his house," Eric finally answered in a tone that bothered Janet. *Something is wrong,* she thought. *I've never seen Eric look like this.* Was there something going on down at the lake she didn't know about? She pulled her phone out of her jacket pocket and called her father at his office.

"Hello, this is Doug Felty."

"Hi, it's Janet again."

"So how were things at the lake?" he asked.

Janet explained to her father what had happened on the road. Then she assured him everything was OK, except that they couldn't get down to Eric's house.

Doug invited her and Eric to his house. "I've got plenty of room for both of you. We can go out for dinner or you can suffer with my cooking," Doug said while chuckling. "Actually, Sarah is doing the cooking tonight. I forgot to tell you before but, in case you haven't heard, schools will be closed tomorrow."

"I'll check with Eric, but I think we'll take you up on this and eat in with you tonight. When are you going to be leaving for home?" asked Janet.

Doug looked at his desk, frowned and commented that he was ready to go now. "I'll see you at the house."

"OK, thanks, Dad."

Janet turned to Eric, who was still in a daze. "All right, so what's the matter?" Janet asked in a quiet voice.

Eric played his steering wheel like a piano while avoiding looking at Janet. He finally turned to her and related what Paul Glidden had told her about Jack and Susan. "I don't know if I can believe him, but it's obvious that something may have been going on down here this weekend between Susan and Jack." He felt an ache in his stomach.

He banged his hands against the steering wheel as if it were someone's head. "If you and I could refrain from having sex with each other while in the same bed, why couldn't they do the same in my house? Damn them!"

Janet leaned over to Eric and agreed with him about what might have happened and added, "Eric, we don't know if this is true or just some storytelling from your neighbors. And if it did happen, don't forget it's my husband who's the other half. It takes two to tango and if all this is in any way true, then he's at least as much at fault. Maybe they've had something going on between them that we didn't realize. Let's not make any rash decisions before we have a chance to talk with them. OK?"

She continued her thoughts. "You know, if Jack and Susan heard that we slept together in the same bed for three nights, what do you think they'd say?" She then mimicked another voice. "You spent three nights in bed together and nothing happened? Give me a break!" Janet began to laugh while rocking back and forth on her seat.

Eric looked over at Janet and his mood totally changed, back to where it had been all weekend. He laughed, and then grabbed Janet without thinking the nosy neighbors might see them. At this stage, he didn't give a damn what any of them thought. "OK! OK! You're right as usual." He started his SUV and headed back to Bangor and her father's house.

Eric said. "I don't know why this is making me so mad because if this is true it will free me up to end our marriage. I guess it's that I feel abused.

All right, enough said, let's get to your father's house," he said while heading the SUV toward Bangor.

Janet reached over to Eric and held his right arm. "Eric, I think I need to tell my father what has happened and get his opinion on what our next move should be. Is that OK with you?" she asked him.

Eric looked over at a very serious-looking Janet and nodded his head. "Janet, no matter what, he is eventually going to find out about this past weekend, so it's better he hears it from you than from someone else."

CHAPTER 23

Jack and Susan sat in her living room staring out the window, watching layers of snow falling off the trees. They were quiet as both were angry that they couldn't get up the road and into town. Susan finally broke the silence while agonizing over her relationship with Eric.

"Jack, I think we need to tell Eric and Janet what happened this weekend. I just can't keep a lie away from Eric. I do love him, but in a different manner. We're really more like friends who happened to get married without thinking. I don't want to see him hurt any more than necessary. OK?" She held Jack's hand and looked straight into his eyes.

Jack Meacham looked back at Susan and nodded his head. "Yeah, Susan, I guess you're right. We can't keep this weekend a secret because sooner or later it's going to come out and I would sooner have it done now and get it over with. But we also need to make sure we want to be together."

Susan gave Jack a grimaced look. "Do you have any doubts about us? If either of us does then we need to reexamine right now what we plan to do. For sure, I thought I didn't want to stay married to Eric before this weekend and now it's for certain." She stared down at their feet as she waited for an answer while rubbing her face.

Meacham grabbed Susan around her shoulders. "I said it Friday, Saturday, and Sunday. I want us to spend the rest of our lives together. That hasn't changed, Susan, and it won't change. OK?"

Susan grabbed Jack's face with her hands and kissed him on his lips, then rested her head on his chest. "Jack, I do love you and I want us to be together. I want us to get married, but I don't know how Eric and Janet are going to accept what's happened. It's going to be tough as hell for them to understand our feelings for each other. I just hate the thought of what could happen."

Jack Meacham thought for a while and figured Janet could take a considerable amount of his football income for a divorce settlement. He'd still be all right but it could end up costing a lot of money. But this is what he wanted and the cost should not stand in their way. He felt bad about how he had been mistreating Janet, but the love he thought he had for her had faded away and his feelings toward Susan Forster outweighed any other consideration. There just wasn't anything left of their marriage so a divorce should benefit both.

After thinking about what could happen, Jack suggested that they meet with Eric and Janet at her house in Bangor sometime after work on Tuesday. It would be the closest house from work for all of them.

"That's fine with me," offered Susan. "I really just want to get out of this house. I want to get back to town so maybe I could move in with you if Janet feels it necessary to move out, and I think she will."

Jack grabbed Susan's hands. "That would be terrific. Would we have to sleep in separate bedrooms?"

Susan slapped her hand against Jack's chest and with a grin told him, "Don't even think of it."

CHAPTER 24

Doug Felty's house was in an old established area of Bangor, full of friends he'd known for years. While he hadn't married again, he did date a widow on the same block, Sarah Johnson, whom Doug invited to join them for dinner.

When Eric and Janet arrived at her father's house, the smell of meat loaf filled the house and increased their appetites. Sarah was in the kitchen with Doug, assisting him with the dinner. Janet went over and hugged Sarah. Janet felt a good deal of warmth for Sarah as she had assisted her father when her mother was killed in the car crash. She was also somewhat surprised that after all these years they hadn't gotten married. Sarah was in her sixties but was still active and very attractive. She was short and somewhat thin.

"Eric, how about a glass of wine and then we can sit down and you guys can tell us about your weekend," suggested Doug as he brought the bottles of wine and glasses into the living room. "The meat loaf is going to take another thirty minutes or so to get done so, Janet, you and Eric can tell us about your adventures in the northeaster."

Janet and Eric sat together on the couch and looked at him with a smile that started to turn into laughter. "Eric can tell you about the journey over to Bethel. What a drive!"

Eric then related the problems in driving through the storm to the Benoit Lodge and how for a while he wasn't certain they were going to make it. "I've never seen a storm like that one and I still can't believe it wasn't forecast the night before. Doug, we had virtually no idea the storm was coming until we got to a point of no return, but we made it, even though my Jeep ended up in the woods." Eric explained what happened when he tried to drive up the road to the lodge. Doug and Sarah were astounded by their adventure.

Doug offered an explanation of how this storm was forecast by Tom Siegel. "The jerk got this storm right but a lot of people didn't believe him because of past forecasts that weren't even close to being accurate, so a lot of cars ended up in ditches or on the median strip on

95. I've never seen such a snowy mess...ever! It was even tough driving home."

"So, how was the Benoit Lodge?" asked Sarah.

Janet rolled back and forth with her hands locked to her knees. "Well, that's another story," she offered while looking at Eric, who nodded in agreement about what she was about to tell her father and Sarah.

"Well, obviously Jack and Susan didn't make it to the lodge and the owner, Mr. Craven, was having a problem with rooms since several people couldn't leave because of the storm and the staff had to stay over in the living room," explained Janet while looking toward Eric to see if he wanted her to continue. He nodded again in agreement.

Doug interrupted his daughter. "Are you going to tell us that there wasn't a room for the two of you?"

Janet replied, "Oh, no, Dad, there was a room, just one room for the two of us." She grinned as she took a drink of her wine. "Mr. Craven thought we were married."

Sarah smiled at Janet and offered her timely thought. "Well, Janet, this is becoming more interesting."

Doug frowned at her. "Sarah, let her tell the rest of the story." Sarah had a pretty good idea of what was next so she sat back in her chair and sipped her wine.

"Well," Janet replied, dragging the word out. She looked at Eric and told him, "Maybe, you should continue the story."

"No, mine was the drive to the lodge. Yours is what happened when we got there." He slid back in the couch, smiled, took another drink of wine, then had it refilled by Doug. All this time Janet was silent while trying to think of a way to make the room story less sexy.

Doug hesitated for a moment before saying, "I don't know if I want to hear the rest." He glanced at both Janet and Eric, who were both smiling.

"Well, Dad, Janet continued, "there was only one double bed and there was nowhere else Eric could sleep so we shared the bed."

The room became silent until Sarah stood up and headed for the kitchen, "I think I'll turn the heat down on the meat loaf."

Doug stared at his daughter and then at a shrugging Eric and asked in a quiet, slow voice. "You slept together in the same bed for three days?"

"Yes, Dad, we did, but that's all we did. We slept together," Janet replied in a quick, smiling voice.

Doug looked over at Eric, who was working on his wine while looking at Janet. She had a serious look on her face and wanted to make certain her father and Sarah understood what didn't happen. He then looked at Janet then back again to Eric. The room was so quiet the ticking of the grandfather clock became very loud.

Doug stared with a quizzical look at both as he asked Eric, "Are you telling me that you were in the same bed with my daughter and nothing happened? I find that hard to believe. Unless you aren't interested in beautiful women or even women."

Eric laughed at that thought. "Doug, let me put it this way. It took everything in me to stop me from attacking your daughter. To say the least I was frustrated, but then we're both married and have an obligation to our spouses to honor our marriages."

Janet started to get excited and began talking fast. "Dad, we think we've fallen in love with each other and would like to spend the rest of our lives together, but we have to make certain this is true and we have to figure out a way to tell Jack and Susan. As you know, Jack and I are not getting along. And we've also heard that something may have happened between them at Eric's house this weekend. So we need your advice and help." Janet grabbed Eric's hand and looked up at him with blue eyes that were beginning to fill with tears.

Doug Felty waved his hand at his daughter. "Slow down, Janet!" he said with a serious look on his face. "Obviously you're old enough and mature enough to make the right decision, certainly better than when you agreed to marry Jack." Doug looked over to Sarah with a pleading "help me" look.

They all looked at Sarah as she came back into the living room from the kitchen holding a heating pad and a large spoon as she was still able to hear the conversation with Janet. She sat down in her chair and looked first at Doug and then to Janet. She finally spoke, "Janet, you've been unhappy for the past several years through no fault of yours. You're too young and too beautiful to keep hoping your husband will change his attitude toward you.

"But both of you are right in that you need to find out if you are truly in love or just good friends that had a fun weekend together. I've only met your wife once, Eric, so I can't make any comment on her, but if there are no children involved and if there is little or no love left between you, then it is time to make a change. Don't ruin the rest of your life just to keep a lousy marriage going. I'm sure your spouses may be thinking the same thing." Sarah smiled at Doug and went back to the kitchen, where she announced dinner was a few minutes away.

Then she yelled from the kitchen, "Janet, how could you sleep in the same bed with this very handsome man and nothing happened? My God, I've never had that kind of a chance. Wow! I sure as hell wouldn't have let him leave me alone." They all broke into laughter at Sarah's comments.

Doug replied in a surprised voice. "Sarah, I can't believe you said that!" He stood up and walked into the kitchen where he confronted his giggling friend.

Doug leaned against the door to the kitchen and related to Janet and Eric how he never did like the ideal of her marrying Jack Meacham. "There never appeared to be a significant love between you; rather it was like a mutual admiration society." He smiled and added, "but then you weren't about to listen to your father's wisdom. Jack's a nice guy, but he's focused on football and very little else. He obviously fell in love with you, but for some reason that ended when his hip was destroyed.

"Now he's no longer the guy who makes the sports page headlines and this has affected him. And the fact that he's here in Bangor and not Boston is a problem created by you, so you're to blame for everything that went wrong. He also may have found someone else...maybe Susan, who is quite the athlete and talks the same language as he does and, of course, they work together."

Eric finally broke his silence as he stood up and headed for the dining room. "I never thought that Susan had an interest in someone else, much less Jack, but anything is possible, particularly after this weekend. Janet, had you any thoughts about Susan and Jack?"

Janet looked at Eric and after thinking for a while said, "I'm not aware of any situation between Jack and Susan. The four of us have spent a lot of time together, but I can't remember any time that I thought something was going on between them. Maybe it was there, but possibly no one, including them, had an idea of what was in each other's mind until they were alone at your house."

Eric added, "What makes me mad is that they maybe had an intimate weekend at my house while we were respecting our marriages."

Doug broke in on their thoughts. "Look, if the two of you discovered a love for each other, what's the difference if Jack and Susan did the same? You know, you're not the only ones who can claim love."

Sarah added, "Doug's right. You're accepting your togetherness as true love while indicating that theirs is a nasty love. That isn't fair to them." She waved her serving spoon at them. "Come on, let's eat." The four of them ate the very delicious meat loaf while further discussing the past weekend's adventure and what will happen when the four of them meet tomorrow.

Janet laid down her fork and looked at her father, who was enjoying the meat loaf. "Dad, what would Mother think of all this?"

Doug was not expecting this question and hesitated before answering. He set his fork on his plate and placed his elbows on the table before answering. "Wow, I'd have to think on that." He stared at the other three, hoping to get help with this question. "I would think she'd go along with anything you'd decided on, but I think realistically that she wouldn't have encouraged your marriage to Jack Meacham. I don't think she would have been as comfortable with him as she would be with Eric. But this is only my opinion. Sarah?" Doug looked at Sarah, hoping she'd have some thoughts.

Janet looked at her father and finally asked the question she and others had wondered about for years. "Dad, why haven't you and Sarah gotten married after all the years you've been going together?" She hesitated, as she now felt bad about asking.

Doug looked at Sarah and held her hand in his. "Let me see if I can answer that." He thought for a moment and finally replied. "We've talked about this many times, but what has held us up is our feeling for your mother and Sarah's husband. We all had great love for our spouses and when they died it left a deep rut in our minds and bodies.

"We consider marriage to be very sacred and we found it difficult to start another marriage with each other because we had only one wife and husband. So, instead we've acted like we're married but we've done nothing formal about it. I love Sarah, as she has been a savior to me ever since your mother was killed in that car crash. I don't know what I'd have done without her, but I have had only one wife."

Sarah assisted by saying much the same. "Your father's a terrific man. He tries to be miserable but he's just the opposite. I love him, but I've only had one husband and unfortunately he died. So now we have each other and eventually we'll move into one house, but I don't think we'll ever marry. Instead we'll live in sin." Sarah squeezed Doug's hand, grinned, and added, "Now isn't that exciting?"

Doug quickly added, "Now don't feel guilty about what you and Eric are going through. It's an entirely different situation. You need to do what you think is best."

Sarah continued her smile and added, "I think you're on the right track. You just need to find out if this is really what you want and if it is, then do it."

Sarah looked over to a concerned Janet and related her thoughts. "I also agree with your dad. Your mother would be very happy to hear how you and Eric handled the weekend together and I'm certain she'd be all for a marriage between the two of you. I don't think she would have ever warmed up to Jack Meacham. He just wasn't her definition of a husband."

"So, guys," asked Doug Felty, "what are you going to tell Jack and Susan when you meet tomorrow?"

Eric and Janet looked at each other and tried to figure out an answer to her father's question. Janet finally said, "Dad, I really don't know. I think we have to be perfectly honest with Jack and Susan and maybe they'll be the same. I just don't know what else I could expect."

Eric bounced his fork on his plate and nodded in agreement to Janet. "I would think it best that we tell them exactly what happened and maybe they'll tell us what went on in my house. But first the four of us need to get together tomorrow and that will be interesting, to say the least.

"If they can get up the hill tomorrow morning I'm sure they'll reach us on one of our cell phones. I have to be in our office at least tomorrow morning, as I have several patients scheduled for meetings with me and I don't want to put them off since most are in pain."

When they finished dinner and the dishes were cleared from the table, Sarah brought on a cherry pie that caught Eric's total attention. He accepted the piece of pie with a wide grin and looked over to Janet, who was amazed again at how much he ate without adding any weight. She shook her head, but accepted some pie from Sarah. "Eric, when you turn fifty you're going to weigh three hundred pounds. Sarah, you have no idea how much he eats without gaining any weight. He almost ran the Benoit Lodge out of food."

Eric laughed at her comments. "She's just jealous that she can't keep up with me."

Doug finished his pie and threw his napkin on the table. "I hate to change the subject, but where are we going to put you guys tonight? I don't think I want the two of you in our doubled-bedded quest room. Eric, I could put you in our study, if that's all right with you."

Eric laughed at Doug's concern. "You're right. I'm not to be trusted for more than three nights in a row. The study would be fine. Thanks, Doug, and thanks, Sarah, for a great dinner. I'm not certain if Janet knows how to cook, so I appreciate being able to join you tonight." Janet's napkin went flying across the table, hitting him on his chest.

"Dad, why don't you put him in the garage tonight?" She stuck out her tongue at Eric.

CHAPTER 25

Tuesday morning at the lake was another day that would be above freezing so the snow continued to slowly melt and the sun was shining as it rose from the east. Jack and Susan looked out the front window over the deck that they had shoveled clean yesterday. It was still beautiful on the lake, but it didn't related what might be the problem on the road though the Andersons told them the cars had been pulled off the road late Monday night and the road should be open for traffic Tuesday morning.

They loaded Jack's SUV again with his suitcase and snowshoes, then looked around the house to make certain they didn't leave anything behind that might reveal what had gone on between the two of them. At a little after eight o'clock they headed up the road.

Near the top of the toboggan slide, where the two cars had gone off the road, the problems in getting both cars out had ended. This was obvious from the mass of sand and snow mounded along the edges of the area. Now Jack was able to easily get his SUV up the steep part of the hill without any hesitation. Even part of the asphalt was visible and with the sun and the warmer weather it wouldn't take long for the road to be clear of snow.

When they got to the parking lot, Jack and Susan both slammed their hands together as though they had just scored the winning goal. Susan then slammed her hands on the dashboard and shouted. "God damn, it's great to get out of here. I don't think I ever want to come back here again."

Jack stopped the car in the parking lot and looked over to Susan. "OK, but where are you going to stay? All your stuff's down here."

She looked at Jack, smiled, and sank into her seat. "I guess you're right...at least for now, so maybe I'll stay at your house?"

They then headed up the road to Orono and to their offices.

CHAPTER 26

Eric showered and shaved after Doug got out of the bathroom and headed off to the kitchen where Sarah was making coffee. Janet was nowhere in sight. "Maybe," Eric offered, "I should wake her up." Both Doug and Sarah nodded their approval.

He went down the hall to Janet's room and listened against the door to see if she was still sleeping. He heard nothing so he quietly opened the door. What he saw was a lump under covers. Softly a voice came out of the bed. "Don't bug me," it demanded. That was all Eric needed to hear.

He went over to the bed and sat on its edge. He addressed the lump. "You probably can't handle being in bed without me, so I'm going to take off my pajamas and hop in with you."

A blonde head suddenly appeared out of the covers and demanded of Eric, "Don't even think of it." She looked at him and discovered he was already dressed. "You're miserable! What time is it?"

"About seven thirty." He bent over to kiss her, and then pulled back his head from hers, "Ugh, you've got bad breath. You'd better go brush your teeth." He patted her head and added, "Now who does that sound like?"

She sat up in bed. "Don't bug me," she replied as she blew breath into his face. He collapsed on the bed. "Out, get out or I'll call my father," she yelled as Eric kissed her forehead and headed out the door.

About ten minutes later Janet came into the kitchen dressed in her pajamas and a bright red robe. She walked over to Eric and blew breath into his face. "Is this OK?"

"Beautiful"

She leaned over and kissed his cheek, and then greeted her father and Sarah. She grabbed a cup of coffee and sat down with the others. "Well, Eric, what do we do now?"

"Well, we can't do too much with your father and Sarah here." He banged his hand on the table while laughing about what he just said.

"Eric, stop that! She turned to her father and said, "Now do you see what a truly miserable guy he is? And I was stuck with him for three days. How horrifying!" She stared cross-eyed at Eric while pointing her tongue at him."

Doug shook his head and turned to Sarah, who couldn't stop laughing. "They're just like a couple of kids. They probably deserve each other." He couldn't keep a straight face.

"All right," offered Eric, "It's time to get serious. We do need to get in touch with Susan and Jack. I've already tried Susan's cell phone, but didn't get an answer so they are probably still down at the lake. Janet, why don't you try Jack's phone. If he's there then maybe we could all meet at your house about five. We can bring in pizzas and some beer and sodas."

Janet picked up her cell phone and dialed Jack's number. After three rings a voice came on the phone. "Janet, is that you?" asked Jack.

She looked surprised to hear his voice and looked at Eric while pointing at the phone and mouthing Jack's name. "Yes, Jack, it's me. Where are you?" Janet couldn't think of anything else to say.

"We finally got up the hill and we're in the Peaks Hill parking lot. We're headed for the university and should be there in about a half hour. Are you guys OK?" Jack asked the question very casually, as though he really didn't care how she and Eric were.

"We're fine, Jack. I'm at Dad's house and Eric's here. Is Susan there?" asked Janet.

"Yep, she's here. I'll put her on." Janet handed the phone to Eric, who was looking at his watch, as he needed to get to his office.

"Hi, Eric. I've missed you. Are you OK?" she asked in a concerned voice.

"I've missed you too," answered Eric. "We're both OK, thanks. I hate to cut this short, but I have to get to the office before I'm late for my appointments. Let me give this back to Janet so she can set up a time today when we can all get together." He looked at Janet then told Susan, "I've missed you."

"Thanks, Eric. I love you," replied Susan in a soft voice.

Eric looked at Janet and shrugged his shoulders. "I love you too, Susan, but I've got to go. Here's Janet." He passed the phone back to Janet, gave her a kiss and headed out the door to his car.

Doug followed Eric out to their cars and offered whatever help they would need before and after their meeting tonight. Eric thanked him, shook his hand and said Janet or he would be in touch with them.

Before starting his car, Eric began to think about his wife Susan and how much he did miss being with her.

The conversation between Jack and Janet was quiet and short. She wanted all four to come to their house at five. She would get the pizza, beer, and sodas. He asked Janet if she was OK and she told him she couldn't be better. She in turn asked how he was.

He quickly answered. "I'm OK, Janet. It was quite a weekend, but we can talk more about this when we get together tonight. I'll see you then." He hung up before she could make any sort of comment.

She turned to Sarah, who was sitting across the table. Janet related what Jack had told her and how he hung up before she could answer him. Sarah offered her thoughts. "I have a feeling this get-together at your house is going to turn into an unpleasant time for all of you, unless everyone is honest about what happened this past weekend. But these are just my thoughts."

Janet had a different perception of Sarah than she had before this weekend. While Janet used to be neutral about Sarah's relationship with her father, she was now very impressed with her. She was smart and had a good sense of humor that more often than not quieted down her father. They were an ideal couple.

Sarah offered a couple of more thoughts. "Assuming that everyone tells the truth about this weekend you may want to move out of your house sooner than later, so I'd suggest that you and I go over there, get your car and your clothing and whatever else is needed. Then you can stay here or at my house. How's that?"

Janet got up from her chair and went over and hugged Sarah. "Thanks very much. Let's do it, but first let me go over to the school to see what's happening there." Janet hit her hand on the table. "I forgot, my car isn't there." She looked at Sarah, who then offered to take Janet to school and then to Janet's house.

CHAPTER 27

As they drove toward Orono, Jack and Susan were quiet after their talk with Janet and Eric. "Well," Susan offered as she stared out the window, "this will be interesting. I just wonder what happened to them over the weekend. I doubt that they did anything out of order like we did." She turned and smiled at Jack.

Jack grumbled as he thought about Janet. "Well, we'll find out soon enough." Then they both began to concentrate on what was happening since they left last Friday. They couldn't completely stop thinking about what happened over the weekend.

Eric got to his office at eight thirty, before the nine o'clock patients arrived. He first called down to Waterville to check on those patients, and then went through a list of calls made to him over the weekend. His first patient came into his office a little after nine and by this time his mind was focused on his patients' conditions.

Sarah drove Janet to her school and went with her into Janet's classroom. The contents of the room reflected Janet's feelings toward her students. Impressed, Sarah gazed at the project illustrations hanging on the wall. She came away with an even warmer feeling toward Janet.

When they finished they headed for her house on outer Essex Street, a road with all sorts of large and expensive homes. Jack and Janet's house was a two story colonial painted white with dark green shutters. The lawn was large and the plantings around the house came from a dedicated gardener. That was Janet. She loved designing gardens, just as she did her classroom.

On the second floor were three bedrooms and it was obvious that Jack and Janet did not share the same room. Janet looked around her room with her hands on her hips. "I wonder what would happen if Jack came into my room before our meeting and saw my clothes gone." She glanced at Sarah and smiled in anticipation. "He'd probably be pissed off."

Sarah helped Janet pull out her clothes from her closet. She looked at the pile of clothes they had put on her bed. Janet brushed her hair with her hands and said, "I don't think that there's enough room in Dad's guest room for all this."

Sarah looked at the pile and laughed. "That's an understatement! Well, we can put some of these in my house. I've got all sorts of room." They took the clothes to the cars and tried to divide them between their houses. Next were the shoes. Janet had enough to start a small shoe store. These they also divided between the two houses.

"Is there anything in the living room or kitchen that you might want?" asked Sarah as the two of them sat down to rest.

Janet looked around the living room and shook her head. "Other than some of my books, I really don't need to take anything else. As far as the kitchen is concerned, I'll take my favorite cookbooks so I can prove to that miserable doctor that I can cook." She grinned at Sarah. "And there's some pots and pans that are mine."

Janet walked back and forth from the living room to the dining room, to the kitchen, and again upstairs to make sure she had taken everything she wanted. She came back into the living room, sat down, got up again, looked out the window, and then went back to her chair.

Finally, Sarah asked with a grin. "By chance are you nervous about your get-together tonight?"

"Oh, Sarah, I don't know what to think. I don't know what happened at the lake and I don't know what Jack's going to say about it. Yep, I'm really scared about tonight. I just wish it were over." She couldn't sit still so she walked around the room and then sat down again.

Sarah came over to the couch and sat down next to Janet and hugged her. "Janet, I can imagine what you're thinking, but don't let it get inside you. I can guarantee that Susan and maybe even Jack are going through the same feeling.

This is not an easy event, but it will work itself out."

"Thanks, Sarah," Janet replied with still a concerned look. "You're right, but I'm still not looking forward to telling my husband that for three nights I slept in the same bed with Eric without anything happening. It sounds ridiculous." She began to slide down as though she were trying to hide, then laughed as she reached the bottom of her couch.

"Yes," Sarah added, "but what did happen at Eric's house? From what Eric said, the neighbors seemed to think something was happening between Jack and Susan. If that's true, then they must be really nervous about tonight."

Janet thought for a while and then began to laugh again "Oh, God, what a party this is going to be." She couldn't imagine what was going to happen between the four of them, but she felt nervous about the end results.

Sarah quietly changed the subject and said, "For what it's worth, Janet, I think Eric is a joy. He has a great sense of humor and it's obvious that he thinks the world of you. It's too bad that your marriage to Jack hasn't worked out, but then Eric's with Susan hasn't worked either."

Sarah leaned up from her couch and shook her head while thinking of what to say, then said, "But I agree your need to find out if you're truly in love with one another or whether this weekend together was just getting away from your spouses and the problems with your marriages." Sarah then came up with a broad grin. "All you need is too much unnecessary guidance. You and Eric will work it out just fine and I'm betting that you'll find you're very much in love with each other."

"Thanks, Sarah. I hope everything will work out all right, but I'm still a little nervous about tonight. I bet Jack won't buy that nothing happened in Bethel." She glanced around the room to see if there was anything else she needed to take. "You know it's kind of sad that our marriage didn't work out. I remember how happy I was when we got married., but he never thought about it. He was still angry about his injury and the move to Bangor," replied Janet in a soft voice. "Now I don't want to take that same sort of chance again, so Eric and I will act like two dating people who want to see if there is a long-term future involving us. I don't want to make the same mistake again," Janet said in a serious, quiet voice.

"I want to have a family, but I first have to be absolutely certain Eric and I are made for each other. I think we are and I think Eric feels the same, but I felt the same way about Jack and look what happened," related Janet in an angry voice. "I think I loved him, but it all fell apart soon after we were married. So how do you know?"

Sarah patted Janet on her shoulder. "You're doing the right thing, Janet. It will all come out perfectly in the end. Just don't lose your patience and sense of direction. You and Eric have to take time to determine whether you truly have a marital relationship or just a fun twosome.

"Now, enough of this. I feel like I'm acting like a mother." Sarah got out of her chair and looked at the clothes stacked on the couch. She felt comfortable that Janet would come out OK with this night's meeting.

Janet thought this to be true. "You know, Sarah, you've been like a mother to me since Mom was killed in that car crash. I don't know what I'd have done without you."

Sarah thought for a moment, and then said, "You know, Janet, you've been a marvelous girl and now a great lady. Doug is very proud of you, even with your marriage to Jack Meacham, but he holds himself to blame for introducing the two of you at that football game." Sarah looked again at the clothes and said, "Enough talk, we need to get this stuff out of here and into my house or your dad's house. "You know, your dad's looking forward to having you stay with him."

Janet stretched out her legs and put her arms behind her head. "You know, Sarah, none of this would be happening if it weren't for the storm. If it hadn't happened, the four of us would have been at the lodge and I certainly would not have been in the same bed with Eric. But I'm glad it snowed like hell."

Sarah nodded her agreement. "That's probably true, but I have a feeling that you and Jack would certainly have separated and probably gotten a divorce, while Eric and Susan would have soon parted ways. Then you and Eric would possibly have gotten together since you've known him from visiting at the lake. You've always talked to your dad and me about how much you like being down there."

"That's true. I've always enjoyed the lake. And I like sailing and canoeing or just swimming off the pier. For some reason Susan doesn't like the lake so she avoids boating with Eric and when Jack and I came down to spend the day, Susan and Jack would go off biking or jogging while Eric and I enjoyed the water. I wonder now if there was something going on between them, but I doubt it because they never made that appearance." She thought that maybe she was wrong about them, but she didn't believe it.

Janet tried to remember anything she saw between Jack and Susan, but couldn't. The two of them enjoyed biking and jogging around the hills that circle the southwest side of the lake. If there were something between them, certainly it would have been obvious.

"Maybe there was something going on in their minds that burst out when they were alone. I just don't know and right now I don't care," emphasized Janet as she got up to help Sarah sort out her clothes. While she was angry at the thought of her husband having an affair with another woman, she was convinced that she and Jack could never get back to their former feelings, particularly after this weekend.

CHAPTER 28

Susan had a difficult time concentrating on anything as she waited for the day to end so the four of them could get together for the first time since the weekend. To Susan it felt longer than four days. While her feelings toward Eric hadn't change that much, she was totally committed to Jack Meacham. He was everything she had wanted in a man so she wasn't about to let him get away.

She still had a love for Eric, but it was more a friendly relationship, as she didn't know how he would take being separated from each other. She still recalled the fun times the two had together, but fun times began to drift away when they moved to the lake.

She looked at her clock, which seemed to be stuck. It was only eleven forty-two and time was moving very slowly, if at all. She tried to read her mail, but she immediately lost any concentration. So she picked up her phone, called Jack, and invited him to lunch. He quickly agreed and within minutes he was at her door.

"You know," Jack offered, "I'm uptight about our meeting tonight. I'm more nervous about this than I was playing in the Super Bowl. At least there I could somewhat determine my own fate, but what's happened between us is driving me nuts." He sat down across from her and frowned because he could not find a comfortable spot for his arms.

Susan watched all this and smiled to herself, as she was glad to see that he was having the same problems that were affecting her. Jack stood up and went over to her window and asked, "So, what do we tell them and who's going to do it?" He turned around and began to massage her shoulders. He leaned over and whispered in her ear. "Maybe there's time for a quickie on your desk."

Susan turned around and lightly punched Jack in the stomach. "Jack, stop that! What if someone came in the door?" She pushed herself away from him while smiling at the thought of sex on her desk. "Come on, we need to get some lunch and talk about what's going to happen tonight. We need a quiet place so let's go to Margaritas."

They took his SUV to downtown Orono, which wasn't much more than a block in length. In the middle was the Mexican restaurant, Margaritas, that was well liked by anyone who enjoyed that type of food. On the way to their table, they met and waved to several other coaches and a few players. Seeing them together was not unusual so no one would go back to the university with any type of rumor. He was still a very popular pro football player and all sorts of people pointed him out.

After they ordered, Jack again brought up the subject of the coming evening. Susan finally agreed that it might be best if she did most of the talking since it was her husband who had organized the weekend in Bethel. Jack nodded his approval and was glad he wouldn't have to relate what had happened between them on Friday night and the rest of the weekend. He could admit to Susan only that he was glad it had happened.

She wanted to reach out to him across the table, but there were too many acquaintances in the restaurant and if they gripped hands, the word would spread quickly that something was going on between them. Jack put his elbows on the table and rested his head in his hands while staring at her as she outlined what she wanted to do tonight.

"We also have to figure out where we're going to stay tonight. I'm sure as hell that Eric won't want us in your house," offered Jack, "and I doubt Janet will want to stay with me. I guess she'll go over to her father's house."

Susan thought about this for a while. "Well, if that's the case, then I could stay with you in your house, if that's all right with you." The grin on her face began to excite him as he quickly agreed to the arrangement. "If not, then I'll go back to my house. Maybe we should go down there now and pick up some of my clothes."

"You're right. Let me call the office." Jack pulled out his cell phone and dialed his office. When his secretary answered he told her he might not be back this afternoon so if anyone was looking for him, they could call him in the morning or on his cell phone. Susan then called hers with the same message.

After they finished lunch they headed down to her house to pick up her necessary items and enough clothes for the rest of the week. She decided against taking anything else.

The road was even cleaner than it was in the morning and the road had been widened so it was possible to pass another car. When they got to the house they discovered that the power and phones were still not working. After they finished they sat down in the living room to think if she had forgotten anything.

Susan touched Jack on his shoulder. "Before we meet with Eric and Janet, you need to know about the arrangement Eric and I had before our marriage." She told Jack about the prenuptial agreement between Eric and her.

To say the least, Jack was surprised at the arrangement between them.

"Who in the hell set that up?" he asked with a puzzled look on his face.

"We both did," Susan said softly. "I wanted to get married before I came up here and I really liked Eric and still do, but it guaranteed either of us the right to a divorce if either of us found someone else we'd prefer being married to. I didn't want to have to pay some expensive lawyer a fee for doing what we agreed to. I've found you so now; I want to marry you and free myself of Eric and this house. Do you understand?" she asked with a frown covering her face.

Jack embraced Susan and whispered in her ear. "I don't understand but I couldn't care less. I just want to marry you. I really do." He leaned back from her and added, "You certainly are a tough old broad, aren't you? Man, I wouldn't want to mess with you for fear I'd need a knee or something else replaced."

She whacked him in his ribs and pushed herself off the couch. "Thanks a lot," she answered with a frown that quickly turned into a smile. "Now we'd better get it in gear or we'll be late for the meeting."

The road was now relatively easy to drive and they made it up before anyone came down. "God, what a difference," mumbled Jack as they drove through the Peaks Hill parking lot and onto the Upper Dedham road. Jack looked at the car's clock, which read four thirty. "We've got half an hour before we need to be at my house and I don't want to be the first one there." He glanced over at Susan, looking for her ideas.

She thought for a while then nodded in agreement. "Anyway, Janet should be at home since there wasn't any school today, so it's no big deal if Eric isn't there at five. Patients often delay him in his office, so let's plan on getting there after five. I don't want them to think this get-together is minor. Understand?" She looked over to Jack who, without any expression, agreed.

Susan stared out the windshield. "We have to figure out how we tell them of our weekend."

Jack agreed. "I wonder if anything happened between them at the lodge." He squinted his eyes as though he were planning to run through the opponent's line. "I doubt it," he continued, "because Janet's not that sort of person."

Susan turned in anger toward Jack. "You mean I am? Is that what you think of me? That I'm an easy target! What else are you thinking?" She leaned back against her door and folded her arms around her chest while glaring at Jack.

He turned the car off the road into someone's driveway and put the transmission in park. "Damn it, Susan, that's not what I meant, so don't give me this crap. I love you! That's what I mean. I'm just telling you that Janet is a very quiet, almost sexless person, so I don't know how anything could have happened between them, wherever they were." Now he was getting angry. "She just isn't an aggressive type. You are! And there's nothing wrong with that, because I'm the same way."

Susan's glare lessened as he reached out with his right hand to her head. "OK, I'm sorry I yelled at you. I guess I'm just worried about what might happen tonight. I just wish we didn't have to go through with this," she said while looking out the car's side window.

"Susan, we have no choice. As you said, we have to let them know what happened between us, so we can get on with our lives. I'll let you do the talking, as you're better at this then I am." He could feel her calming down. "OK, are we ready to get moving?"

She reached over and grabbed his leg and put her head on his shoulder. His hand wandered over her breasts. "Maybe we've got time for a quickie." He laughed as she pulled herself away from him.

She grinned at the thought, but instead pointed to the road. "That maybe will come later. Let's get moving."

CHAPTER 29

Eric's last patient was due to arrive at four o'clock so he figured he would finish with plenty of time to get to Janet's house before everyone arrived. But as usual, when you're in a hurry, everything stands in the way. His patient showed up fifteen minutes late.

After a discussion about his hip Eric had his nurse Sandy take an x-ray. It was four thirty before he got the x-ray back and he took it into a medical room where the patient, George Gray, a short bald-headed fifty-year-old, was waiting.

"George, I'm going to need time to study this x-ray so I can see what has to be done," Eric said as he looked at the x-ray placed on the lighted screen. "In the meantime, do you have any great pain?"

"Of course I do," he answered. "Why the hell do you think I'm here?" George Gray's' face showed both pain and anger.

"I understand. I can give you a prescription for some pain medication or you can use some over-the-counter painkillers. It's your choice." Eric looked George Gray in the eye, trying to calm him down.

George gazed down at his hip and nodded. "Tylenol seems to work fairly well and I really don't want to spend a lot of money for a prescription drug." Eric could see that George was hurting. "Do you think I need the hip replaced?" he asked, looking at the x-ray.

"George, I don't know. I need to study this x-ray before I make a suggestion to you. In the meantime, go ahead and walk on it as long as it isn't too painful, but avoid any rugged activity like tennis or jogging. That could increase the problem and the pain."

George wiped his hands over his face and nodded in agreement.

"Sandy will set you up with an appointment for early next week. OK?" Eric placed his hand on George's shoulder. "If this gets to a point where you can't stand the pain, give us a call. I don't want you to suffer any longer than necessary." Eric opened the door and guided him out to Sandy, who took him to her desk to set up a time for the following week.

Eric then picked up the phone, as he saw that it was fifteen minutes to five, and called Janet.

"Hello, this is Janet." He smiled when he heard her voice.

"Hi," he said quietly. "I'm just leaving now. Are you all set?"

"As much as I can," answered a worried voice. "Please hurry!"

"I'm on my way." He hung up the phone and waved good-bye to Sandy and headed out the back door to his car in the parking lot. As he drove to Janet's house he wondered again about what had happened at his house over the weekend and if Susan and Jack would be honest enough to tell Janet and him what really occurred.

He wanted to get to the house before Jack and Susan, because Janet was obviously worried about their meeting. The more he thought about it, the odder it got. It's just a get-together between husbands and wives after a weekend of horrible snow that separated them. He felt somewhat guilty about all of it because it was his idea to go over to Bethel, but if he hadn't he would have missed the time alone with Janet.

Bless the blizzard, he thought. If a storm hadn't hit Maine, none of this would be happening. And if it had been forecast they wouldn't have gone over to Bethel. But it did, he thought, and we did, and the end result might be truly great for him and Janet and maybe Susan and Jack.

Janet had everything organized. The half-cooked pizza was in the refrigerator along with the beer. She had set the dining room table for the four of them. She and Jack would sit at the ends of the table while Eric and Susan were across from each other. Sarah had suggested this since it was Jack's house and he needed to be at the head of the table.

Sarah left about a half hour ago as she felt Janet needed to be alone to get mentally ready for their meeting. Janet put on a pair of denim slacks and a yellowish wool sweater. Eric had just called, and he should be at her house in about fifteen minutes. She was concerned that she hadn't heard from Jack since earlier today. Maybe he was too embarrassed to call.

She walked around the house, rearranging cushions and kitchen utensils. She tried to sit down, but that didn't last. She was worried about what was going to happen and how Jack would accept what had happened at the Benoit Lodge, and she wondered how Eric would handle the situation if Jack and Susan did have a romantic weekend. *God,* she prayed, *I wish this were all over. I can't stand it.*

She heard a car door closing in the driveway and she hoped it would be Eric. It was. Janet ran to the door and opened it just as Eric was coming up the stairs. She couldn't wait until he got in the door to embrace him. He felt her trembling.

"Come on," he said to Janet, "let's get inside." When they got in and he took off his coat, he asked her, "Are you OK?"

"I'm just nervous about tonight, that's all. I'll be glad when it's all over." She sat down in the living room and looked at the clock on the fireplace mantel.

It began to chime five o'clock. She got up and walked over to the front window to see if Jack and Susan were there yet. They weren't, but Jack's car was coming up the street

Jack drove up the street and saw Eric's SUV already in the driveway. He pulled up next to it and without speaking he and Susan got out of the car and headed up to the front door. Janet looked out again and saw Jack's Land Rover in the driveway and turned to Eric. "They're here."

Janet opened the door and went out to meet them. A light snow was falling. Janet looked at the snow and said for all to hear. "God, I hope this isn't the start of another snow storm."

Susan and Janet hugged one another as though they hadn't seen each other for months. Eric and Jack shook hands and asked each other how the other was doing. "That," said Eric in a serious tone, "is what we'll talk about."

Susan rushed into Eric's arms and gave him a strong hug then kissed him on his lips. "Oh, Eric, I've missed you. Are you OK?" As she asked him, she looked at him with concerned eyes. Jack calmly embraced Janet, kissed her on her cheek, then pulled back and asked how she was. She nodded at him and assured him she was just fine.

There was a sudden silence as Jack and Susan took off their coats. Jack put these in the hallway closet. Finally, Jack looked at Susan. "Have we anything to serve these guys?"

Janet answered that there was beer in the refrigerator and pizza ready to go into the oven whenever they were ready to eat. Jack looked at Eric and asked what he would like. "I'll take a beer." They all went along with a beer so Jack poured four glasses and he and Eric took them into the living room. Susan and Janet were quietly talking to each other on the sofa. Jack raised his glass and said, "Well, here's to the snowy weekend."

Eric raised his glass. "Cheers," he answered as they clinked their glasses.

Again the room became silent, as no one seemed to want to start relating the events of the past weekend. Finally, Eric looked quickly at Janet, and then turned to Susan. "Well, someone has to start this, so here quickly is what happened to us. Jack and Susan were glad to have Eric start the conversation.

He described the trip over to Bethel from Augusta and how they were not aware of a storm until they got fairly close to Bethel. "At that stage, I didn't have a choice beyond getting to the lodge. I hate to think what might have happened had we gotten stuck on Route 2. Then the walk up to the lodge after I sent the Jeep off the road was considerably more dangerous then I realized. But, we did make it and were surprised the two of you weren't there." He grabbed his beer and took a large gulp. He then continued describing the weather conditions in Bethel. After finishing he looked over at Jack and just by being looked at he knew it was his turn.

Jack described how they got hung up at the university and then had no choice but to head down to the lake. He described the trip down the toboggan slide and what a mess it was. "When we got to your house, the generator was working. Paul Glidden had started it so when we got there the house was reasonably comfortable." He shook his head and added "I can't imagine living down at the lake in the winter. That road is something else!"

Susan broke in. "Were there a lot of people at the lodge?"

Janet answered. "The place was full. Several people stayed because they were afraid to try and drive out. That was a no-brainer." She looked at Eric, who nodded, so he continued.

"There was only one room left for us because they had to let a guest stay. So, we had to share a room."

Jack looked surprised. Susan smiled at the two of them and slapped her hand on her thigh. There was absolute silence as Jack and Susan tried to understand what Eric had just said. Susan finally said, "That should have been interesting. Sleeping in a chair must have been uncomfortable, Jack," she said rather softly, while grinning at him and beginning to understand what might have occurred.

Janet looked at Eric first, then at Susan and Jack. "Well, that's not exactly what happened. There was no place for Eric to sleep other than the bed, so we shared the bed." She quickly added loudly, "For sleeping!" She began to feel very uncomfortable and was certain her face was turning red.

Suddenly the room became quiet, interrupted only by the ticking of the grandfather clock. A smiling Susan looked over to Eric and repeated Janet's comment. "Sleeping? For three nights, Eric? Sure you did."

Jack's face was becoming a little red from embarrassment and anger. "Let me get this straight," he said to Eric. "The two of you slept together in the same bed for three nights and nothing happened? Come on, give me a break!" His tone was getting angrier. "How damn stupid do you think I am to buy that?"

Janet stood up and headed for the kitchen. "Maybe I'd better heat up the pizza."

Eric got up from his chair and went over to the mantle. "Jack, you can believe it or not, but nothing happened between us other than a nice, fun weekend, even with the storm."

Jack couldn't stop laughing. "Come on, Eric, Janet's not that bad so I have a hard time believing you could keep yourself out of her while in the same bed. Unless, of course, you don't like women."

Eric looked at Jack with a deep frown while holding back his anger. "Very funny, Jack. Personally I really don't give a damn whether or not you believe me, but nothing happened. Period! We both had too much respect for you and Susan." Eric stared at Jack with an angry look, as the room grew silent again.

Susan began to laugh. "You know, Eric, I do believe you. But how in the hell did you do it?"

Eric grinned back at Susan. "Believe me, with great difficulty, but I thought of you. You're my wife so it would have been wrong to do it any other way. Understand?" His face turned serious.

Susan looked quickly at Jack then back to Eric. She was beginning to get a guilty feeling but she believed Eric. "Yeah, I do, and thanks for thinking of me. Now before we get to our experience, why don't we have another beer and the pizza?

They went into the dining room where Janet was setting the table. She let them know the pizza would be done in about ten minutes. Eric asked Susan why they couldn't leave Orono on time. Susan explained what happened and Jack told about his contacts with a football prospect that delayed the two of them. They didn't know about the storm until they looked out the office window and called Janet's father. By that time it was too late to try to get over to Bethel.

"So, I took Susan home and going down that road was an adventure. I don't know how you can do it every day."

Janet had the table set and after everyone sat down, the oven timer went off. She and Susan got up to pull the pizza out of the oven while Eric and Jack looked at each other, drinking beer but not talking.

When the pizza was divided everyone grabbed a piece. "Janet, this is great pizza. It hits the spot," said Eric. "It's not a cheeseburger, but it comes close." Janet smiled to herself, thinking about the lunches they shared in Bethel and on the journey back.

Jack looked at Janet while he worked on his slice. "You know, Janet, I still can't believe nothing happened between you and Eric for three nights."

Janet got angry and raised her voice while answering her husband. "It was easy since we haven't done anything together in bed for months. So why would it be so damn unreal if I didn't do anything with Eric? You're something else." She took a large bite of her pizza while glaring at Jack.

No one answered her so Janet continued. "Maybe you should tell us what happened at Eric's house." She turned toward Susan then back to Jack.

Jack glared at Janet. "It's none of your fucking business what happened at the lake."

Janet laughed at that. "Oh, I see. I'm in the spotlight for what Eric and I didn't do, but you're in the dark when it comes to telling what you and Susan might have done. You're fucking nuts!" Her language and tone surprised everyone since Janet was always known for her gentleness. She was madder than hell at what Jack was trying to do to them.

She continued. "Let me also tell you that I've moved my stuff out of here and am going to live with my father. I'm sick and tired of putting up with your shit!" The other three looked at Janet in complete surprise. None of them had ever heard her swear, so the room became silent as everyone wondered what Janet would say next.

Jack's face was turning red as he slammed down his pizza. "Good, I'm glad to hear it," he told her. "You've been a pain in my ass ever since I hurt my hip, so if you want out, be my guest." His face began to turn red and severe anger was evident. Janet was beginning to match Jack's attitude.

"Good," replied an angry Janet, who stood up and walked into the kitchen, slamming the door shut. She was shaking but was too angry to cry.

Susan stood up and looked with anger toward Jack. "That was totally unnecessary. She and Eric have been trying to be honest with us, but you've accused them of what we did."

There was suddenly complete silence in response to what Susan had just said. Eric looked at her in complete surprise. He hadn't expected to hear her admit to what had happened in such a casual manner.

Susan went into the kitchen where Janet was leaning against the sink, shaking with anger. Susan apologized to Janet and then tried to get her back into the dining room. "Janet, what happened was my fault so don't blame Jack." She convinced Janet to come back into the dining room where Eric sat somewhat dumbfounded about what Susan had just said. They all sat quietly looking at each other and not being able to start a conversation.

Eric finally broke his silence as he looked at Susan. "So, what did happen?"

Susan sat down and picked up her beer. "Eric, you know how much I hate your house. Well, on the first night Jack was sleeping on the couch in the living room when the wind shifted and came directly at the front windows. I was scared to death that they were going to break so I ran down the stairs and into Jack's arms. I pleaded with him to get me out of the living room and to my bedroom. I'm not going to describe what happened in bed, but we did have intercourse with each other."

"What happened was the opposite of how you and Janet handled yourselves. I guess I was somewhat sorry about it happening this way but I've had my sight set on Jack ever since he came to the university. But, Eric, there was never anything between us before this weekend. We might have been thinking of it, but it never happened. Honestly.

"We made love to each other several times over the weekend, but for what it's worth, there was guilt for what we did and I also figured our neighbors probably knew what was happening." She ringed her finger around the top of her glass while looking at a surprised and hurt Eric. "Remember when I asked you to marry me and I promised that if either of us found someone else, our marriage could end? I didn't think this would ever happen, but, well, it's happened. I found someone else who I do love more than you and who has a lifestyle more like mine. So, I want out of our marriage so I can marry Jack, assuming, of course, Janet feels the same way.

Janet had a sad look on her face as her gaze traveled around the group, then focused on Eric to see if he had any sort of forgiveness for what happened between Susan and Jack.

Jack finally broke his silence and glared at Eric. "Yeah, we did what Susan said, but I can't believe that you didn't screw Janet. There's no way you couldn't have done it when you slept with her." His anger increased, so he stopped talking.

A very emphatic Janet answered. "You bet I do. Our marriage is over. Period!" She slammed her hand on the table. "It's something I should have done a long time ago, but I had hoped we could save it. God, was I wrong!" She took another sip of her beer while glaring at an expressionless Jack.

Eric was surprised and disgusted at how casual Susan was when telling what had happened over the weekend. He didn't know what to say, as he felt violated that Susan and Jack had an affair over the entire weekend in his house and probably in his bed.

After remaining silent for a while, Eric was still in shock over Susan's casual way of relating her affair with Jack Meacham. In anger he looked at Susan. "I can't believe you're so indifferent about what you and Jack did in our house. You're my wife! You could have told me before all this happened that this was what you planned to do. I can't understand how easily you gave into Jack." He looked back and forth at Susan and Jack in disgust. Jack stared down at his plate while Susan gazed back at Eric with a sad look.

Jack Meacham finally glared up at Eric in and broke his silence. "Yeah, we did what Susan said, but I can't believe you didn't screw Janet. There's no way you didn't do it while sleeping with her. At least we're being honest about what happened."

Eric was losing his normal calm feelings as he thought about the enjoyment he had with Susan when they first met and then got married. He had never thought the love they had for each other would change, even though they had disagreed over all sorts of things.

In a very calm voice, Susan said to Jack, "Shut up! If they say nothing happened, then I believe it. Eric, I'm sorry all this happened, but it wasn't planned and it wasn't Jack's doing. It was mine. I made it nearly impossible for him to ignore me. I had been impressed with Jack ever since he came to Maine and when you and I began to drift apart, I felt I needed to know more about him.

Eric," Susan said, reaching out for his hand, "I still have a love for you that will always be. You're like a big brother to me and I hope we will always stay in touch. We've had a good time together, but our lifestyles are just too different." Tears began to well in her eyes. "I also feel that I violated our marriage vows, but I couldn't help it. I'm in love with Jack, even with his miserable temper." She looked over to Jack, who gave her a weak grin as he was beginning to feel bad about what he had been saying.

Eric slammed his right hand on the table. "I can't believe what's going on. Last week, we were all seemingly happy and looking forward to the weekend. My God, this storm really did a number on us. In three days it's wiped out two marriages because we were more interested in each other's spouse than our own. I just wonder what would have happened if I didn't organize the weekend at Bethel. Now I feel responsible for what happened."

Janet looked at Eric in surprise, as it sounded like Eric was not certain he wanted to end the marriage. Eric shook his head and asked Susan, "What I don't understand is why you have been so adamant about the lake. So what is there about it that has caused you to feel as you do? I'm having the front doors reinforced so that will never be a problem again. For that I apologize. I can understand how you must have felt when the wind hit the front of the house, but you've never liked the lake," said Eric with a puzzled look. "Why?"

Susan looked down at her legs and took awhile before she answered Eric. She then stared up at the ceiling and related her anguish. "When I was young my aunt had a summer home on a lake in Wisconsin where we spent most every summer. It was a fun place to live and I had all sorts of friends, most of them boys.

"One year, when I was fifteen, I was beginning to fill out and I could see my friends staring at me. I never gave that much of a thought until one night when three of us decided to go swimming off our raft. We had done this many times before and it was always fun to dive into black water. But my aunt got nervous about not being able to see us and, since we were getting older, she cautioned me to be careful of boys.

"After we were swimming for a while, one of the guys named Charley Douglas suggested that we try swimming naked. I have to admit that it sounded like a fun thing to do and it was so dark you really couldn't see each other, so when they took off their suits, I took off mine." Susan breathed hard while avoiding looking at anyone else. "But it was so dark that I could barely see myself.

"When I dove into the water it felt terrific to have the dark water all over my body. Charley followed me in and when he reached me he began to feel me up. I could tell he was getting carried away because his hands were going all over by body. Up and down on my chest, on my breasts, and down to between my legs and over my ass. I was beginning to get worried, but I still didn't think he'd do anything since we had been friends for many years. I told him to knock it off, but he didn't listen." Susan stared at Eric with a look that had hatred written all over it. It was as though the cage had been opened and her feelings began to flow out.

"I got up on the raft to get my suit back on, but he was right behind me. He grabbed my arms and pulled me down on the deck and began to feel me up again. Then as he moaned he kissed me. It scared the hell out of me. I shouted at him to leave me alone but he didn't stop.

"Suddenly I heard my aunt yell from the shore. 'Susan, are you all right?' He told me not to say anything or he'd hit me, so I yelled back to her that I was OK. Then I told Charley to get off me and let me go back to shore. I could tell that he was too far along to stop. I also was not strong enough to keep him off me. The other guy was too afraid of Charley to stop him. Then Charley ordered him, 'Hold her down!' He came over the top on my head and held my arms down while Charley opened my legs and raped me.

"It hurt like hell!" Susan stopped talking as she thought again about that night and the raping. She breathed deeply and then continued. "He came in a hurry and when he was through, he rolled off me and lay next to me. I was crying. Then he got up and asked me if I was OK. I tried to hit him but he caught my hands. I told him I was going to tell my aunt what he did. Then he got mad and told me not to tell anyone what happened or he'd come after my aunt and me. I believed he would. I was hurting and scared to death and the black water made it worse.

"I put my suit back on, swam to shore and went into our house. Aunt Jean was waiting for me to make sure I was OK. I tried to convince her but I don't think she believed me. I didn't want to tell her because Charley might have been right outside listening. Then I took a bath to try and get everything he left behind out of my body before I went to bed." Susan did not look sad about telling her story, but her anger was obvious.

"So I never went swimming in that lake again. I told my aunt that I wanted to go back to our house in Chicago. She agreed and we packed up the next day and went home. We never went back to that lake again.

"Oh, my God," said Eric with a very concerned look on his face. "Why didn't you tell me this before?"

"I don't know. I was just trying to wipe this out of my mind, but every time I'm near a lake I have a vivid recollection of Charley Douglas and what happened. I guess I should have said something sooner than this, but I just wanted to forget it, but I never could." Susan had an aged look in her eyes as she looked around the room.

Janet went over to Susan and wrapped her arms around her while pressing her head against hers. "Oh, Susan, you should have told us this sooner."

Jack broke his silence by holding Susan's arm. "Damn it, I'm really sorry. I don't know what else to say. What a horrible experience! Did you ever see that guy again?"

Susan's expression slowly changed to a weak cynical smile. "After that summer, I began to work out because I wanted to be strong enough to never go through being raped by anyone. I got to a point where I am today. About five years after he raped me, I ran across him in downtown

Chicago when I came back for my aunt's funeral. I didn't recognize him because he was fat and I think he'd been using drugs or alcohol because he couldn't talk straight.

"He called out my name and I recognized his voice. 'Susan, it's Charley Douglas,' he slurred. 'Don't you remember me? It's Charley!' He held out his hands toward me and I grabbed his fingers and turned them back against his hand. I think I broke a couple of them. He screamed. Then I hit him on his jaw and I know I broke it. He fell to his knees. I told him to never, ever come close to me again, or I'd kill him. He got up and ran up the sidewalk in agony. I've never seen the son of a bitch again. Several people approached me to see if I was OK and I assured them I was as I walked away. My hand hurt, but I really felt good about what I had just done."

The room was quiet. Everyone was shocked at what they had just heard. They watched as Susan bit into her pizza with a smile. "So, that's why I don't like lakes. Every time I'm near one I remember what happened to me and then I don't feel comfortable until I'm away from it. It's probably the only thing I'm afraid of." She looked at Eric. "I guess I should have told you this before we moved to the lake, but I knew how much you loved being on Lake Lucerne ."

Eric looked at Susan. "God, I'm sorry about that, but you should have told me sooner."

Susan looked at Eric with a sad expression. "Actually I was beginning to feel better about the lake, but then I realized it was probably too late to correct one of our problems."

Susan ran her hand over her head and leaned back in her chair. "Eric, I didn't want to stand in the way of what you wanted. That wouldn't have been fair since you told me early on that you planned to build your dream house on Lake Lucerne. This was all part of our agreement when we married."

He grabbed his hands together and softy replied. "Yeah, I know, but you still should have told me. Maybe I could have helped you forget about what happened to you. But I'm still pissed off about what happened between you and Jack over the weekend."

"Eric, I understand," replied Susan, while starring at him with a serious look. "I still love you and probably always will. We had a great time early in our marriage, but now that's history. I'm really sorry that I've hurt you. I didn't plan what happened, it just did. Now that's also history."

Jack and Janet looked at both of them and Janet began to feel left out of this conversation. Jack was also beginning to wonder if maybe Eric and Susan were trying to get back into their marriage. He didn't know what to say so he sat back and listened. He knew there was nothing he could do to fix his marriage with Janet.

Susan grinned at Eric and reached out for his hands. "I will always have a love for you, Eric, but I don't think it would make sense to continue our marriage."

I also don't like living here in Maine. It's just too boring." She looked over at Jack and said, "Jack agrees with me."

She walked over to Jack and smiled at him while still talking to Eric. "No, I'm committed to Jack and unless he has a different feeling toward me, I want to eventually marry him and probably move out of Maine. I just feel uncomfortable here and I know that this will never change. Do you understand?"

Eric looked first at Janet, then Susan. "Yeah, I think I understand. There probably isn't anyway we could make our marriage last, but I'm sorry it's ending this way."

Susan leaned back in her chair and ran her fingers through her hair before answering Eric. "What Jack and I did this weekend finished any possibility of you and me continuing our marriage. It's my fault it happened, because I'm the one who enticed him to make love to me. I made sure he didn't want to stop. I knew it was wrong but I wanted it to happen. The storm made it easy for me to win him over. Had we been in Bethel, none of this probably would have happened."

The room was silent until Eric gave a weak smile to Susan. "Well, this is the last time I'm ever going to organize a damn weekend get-together." All eyes were on Susan as she nodded her agreement with a weak smile.

"I'm really sorry it happened this way, Eric, but I couldn't help myself," said Susan again.

Jack looked over at Janet and gave her a weak smile. Looking at the others, he got up, said he needed another beer, and went into the kitchen. When he came back he stood next to Janet. "After all this I need to apologize to you, Janet, for how I've treated you. I wanted to blame you for my problems. I was wrong. I know it now and I'm sorry for how I've screwed up our marriage and how I've abused you." He went over to his chair, sat down, and took a drink from his beer bottle. "And it didn't take too much on my part to make love to Susan."

Janet was still mad and couldn't believe what was happening. She was finally able to tell her husband exactly how she felt. She looked at Jack Meacham and told him that she would contact an attorney and begin divorce proceedings. "I don't want anything from you. I just want out of our marriage." She was still angry and now she was concerned about Eric and whether or not he still wanted to stay married to Susan.

Jack nodded his approval. He still looked embarrassed and had a difficult time looking at Janet. His strength seemed to have faded. He was at a loss and felt as though he had just been tackled.

The dining room became quiet again as each of them went to work on the remainder of the pizza, but there appeared to be a lack of interest in eating. Then they all carried their unfinished plates and beer bottles back to the kitchen. Janet looked at Eric and told him she needed to get back to her father's house. She hugged Susan and ignored Jack.

When they let go of each other, Susan apologized to Janet for what had happened over the weekend. Susan told Eric that she had already packed up some of her clothes and would come back on Saturday to pick up the remainder. She told him she would be moving into Jack's house. Eric nodded and told them he would be going down to his house. "Janet, I'll call you tomorrow. I think we all need some time alone to get our lives back in order." He didn't touch her as they walked out the front door into a light snow that was still falling and headed for their cars. He was still recovering from what had happened between Susan and Jack.

Susan and Jack went back into the house as soon as Janet and Eric drove off. They hugged each other. Susan had a serious look and told him, "God, I'm glad that it's over. I think Eric is somewhat in shock about what we did down at the lake. Now I really feel guilty about it."

Jack hugged Susan and told her, "I'm sorry for what happened tonight, but I'm not sorry for what you and I did at the lake." He sat down and stared at his feet while trying to find the right words for how he acted towards Janet. The silence in the room was nerve racking to both of them. Jack finally looked up to Susan. "God, I really feel lousy about what I said to Janet. I just couldn't help myself. When I get angry I seem to lose control."

Susan came over to his chair, sat on his lap, and stroked his head. She was concerned about how he was handling the meeting with Janet and Eric. He looked as though he had just lost a key game. "Jack, you're really a wonderful person, but when you get angry you become someone else and that person isn't very good. Maybe you need some sort of anger management before something drastic happens."

He shook his head and wrapped his arms around her shoulders. "I don't know. I really don't. This anger seems to come on quickly and I can't get rid of it for a long period of time. Somehow my relationship with Janet ended with my anger." He looked Susan in her eyes. "You know, I really loved her but I screwed up our marriage when my hip got ruined. All I could think about was myself and not her. That I realize now, but it's too late for any good to ever come of our marriage, so a divorce is the only solution. Now I want to spend the rest of my life with you." He stroked her head while the room again became very quiet with guilt feelings overpowering their thinking. "I just don't want anything to screw us up."

Susan finally broke the silence. "It's time for bed."

They got into bed and embraced each other, but after the evening's meeting, they couldn't get excited about making love nor could they think of anything to say, so they fell asleep in each other's arms.

CHAPTER 30

Doug Felty and Sarah were playing a game of Scrabble while waiting for Janet to come home. They were very anxious to hear what happened, so they fought off their tiredness.

Doug's mind wasn't totally on the game as he wondered aloud, "I almost wish we were there to hear it all, but then maybe not because it probably was not a very friendly get-together."

Sarah nodded in agreement. "We'll soon find out, because I think it's her car pulling into the driveway."

A few minutes later, an exhausted-looking Janet came into the house where her father and Sarah were impatiently waiting to hear what happened.

Janet took off her coat, sat down, and stretched out her body. Her father became impatient. "So, what happened?" Sarah told him to be quiet and let Janet take her time.

When Janet finished relating what had happened to the silent pair, Sarah asked Janet, "How did Jack handle what happened?"

Janet answered. "He was a complete ass. He never admitted anything. Susan told us how their affair started and how they wanted to get divorces so they could marry. I also agreed to end our marriage and I told him I would contact a lawyer to start divorce proceedings. Jack never did agree to do anything, but he did finally apologize for being nasty to me." She looked at her father and told him, "I really don't understand how I could have ever married him." She shook her head in anger and repeated, "He's such an ass!"

Doug asked, "So how's Eric handling it?"

Janet hesitated for a moment then shrugged her shoulders before answering. "I think he was hurt by what Susan admitted to doing even though he probably thought it did happen, if that makes any sense. I'm sure he felt violated by their affair because it continued all weekend." Janet stopped talking while thinking more about him. "I feel sorry for Eric. He really loved or loves Susan, but he knows the marriage is over. They had some sort of prenuptial agreement so Susan is taking advantage of it."

Sarah looked surprised at that and wondered aloud, "Could there have been some sort of financial arrangement between the two?"

Janet slowly shook her head before answering. "I have no idea what's involved, but Susan kept saying that either could end the marriage if they found someone else. Sounds weird, but that's what they both said." She looked at both Sarah and her father hoping they'd have an idea.

Doug scratched his jaw and turned to Sarah with a wondering look. "I guess it's weird. Sarah, have you ever heard of anything like that?" Sarah thought for a while before shaking her head.

Janet was getting restless and decided she had to be alone to think all this out. "I'm pooped, guys. I think I'll go to bed. Maybe all this will work itself out in some sort of dream." She shook her head and looked at the two of them. "I was hoping all this would have worked out better, but I guess it didn't." She got up and headed for the stairs with tears beginning to flow from her eyes.

Her father turned toward her and said, "Don't let this get into your system. It appears your marriage to Jack is over and there doesn't seem to be anything in what Eric said that might change his mind about you."

Sarah got up and walked over to Janet. "Your father's right. I'm certain that Eric still loves you, but he was just overwhelmed by what Susan and Jack did with each other. It has to be hard for Eric to go back alone to his house and sleep in his bed where his wife and Jack made love. I think I'd burn the mattress."

Janet grabbed and kissed Sarah. "Thanks." She then hugged and kissed her father and headed up the stairs to her room still feeling confused over how much Eric was affected by his wife's actions. It was obvious that he loved her, but from what they told each other, the marriage was definitely over. Susan was committed to Jack and Janet didn't have a problem with that. She was just glad her marriage to Jack Meacham was on its way out.

When Janet got into her room, Doug and Sarah went into the kitchen with the empty coffee cups, but really wanted to discuss what had happened at Jack Meacham's house.

"Well," said Doug Felty, "it sounds like there are some unhappy people going to sleep tonight."

Sarah nodded her agreement and then sat down at the kitchen table. "I really feel for Janet. She obviously feels hurt about what went on tonight. She's really pissed off at Jack and now she seems to be feeling that Eric is not certain he wants to leave Susan."

Doug moved into his chair and threw his arms on the table. "Man, I can't believe all this has happened." He shook his head in disbelief. "It seems as though Janet is taking the brunt of all these people's problems. First, her husband acted like some jerk, then her friend Susan tells how she enticed Jack into bed with her, though I don't think he really fought it, and then Eric seems to be off in a different world."

They both remained silent for a while as each tried to think of what to do to help Janet. They both knew she was such a nice person and now she was caught in between all sorts of affairs. Finally Sarah spoke. "You know, it's probably best that we stay out of this. I feel certain that it will work itself out without any help from us. In fact, if we get involved it could mess things up."

"I don't know, Sarah. She's my daughter and she's having a problem adjusting to losing her husband and maybe her boyfriend. I have to offer my help.

Sarah nodded her head and looked seriously at Doug. "You're probably right Doug, but she needs to let us know if she wants us to get involved. She's a mature lady who is more than capable of making the proper decision. She's also aware of us so if she needs advice she can come to us."

"OK," replied Doug, who yawned and rubbed his eyes. "I'm bushed. I'm ready for bed."

In her bedroom Janet was staring at the ceiling before falling asleep and kept thinking about Eric and how she felt about him. The weekend was great fun and she began to fall in love with him. She hoped he still felt the same about her. She thought about the weekend together and how the trip back to Bangor seemed to solidify it. But after the gathering at her and Jack's house she began to feel concerned about what would happen next. She was also surprised and upset that Eric left her so quickly.

Before she fell asleep, tears welled in her eyes again.

Eric was glad to get back to his house on Lake Lucerne. The drive down was easy as most of the people were already in bed. He had always enjoyed this drive when it was dark. The light snow continued and made the drive more pleasant. His driveway had been plowed but a large mound of snow sat over the walkway to the house.

The power was still off but the generator was running so there was heat and water in the house. Eric went into the kitchen and checked out the refrigerator to see what sort of food was still there. There wasn't much, but enough for breakfast.

He grabbed a bottle of beer, opened it and went into the living room where he sat in the dark, looking out over the lake. He kept thinking about Susan and Jack making love in his house, not once but all weekend. He felt surrounded by what must have happened. He felt he needed to have the house cleaned and their bed thrown out. The thought of sleeping on it again sickened him, as all he could think of was Susan's naked body under Jack Meacham.

Why in the hell couldn't they have fought off the sexual encounter, as he and Janet had? God, he thought, he wanted to grab Janet when they were in bed together, but he felt it wouldn't be fair to Susan. Knowing that Susan and Jack had screwed each other made him madder then hell.

He was further hurt by the thought that he and Susan would never be together again after five years of reasonable enjoyment. Initially they'd had a great time together, but the last couple of years had begun to push them apart. When he built the lake house and talked about having children, Susan didn't want to listen to either but did accept the house. The thought of children turned her off, as she was too active in her soccer coaching. Susan also had wanted to move to a large city where there was more activity. Bangor and Maine were boring to her.

After finishing his beer, he headed up the stairs to the guest bedroom and prepared himself for a long-awaited sleep. But first he looked into their bedroom and got angry again about what had happened over the weekend in that bed. He felt as though Jack and Susan were like a couple of teenagers who couldn't control themselves.

While waiting for sleep to overtake him he thought about Janet and how she must be feeling. It had to have been a terrible evening for her. He fell asleep feeling very sorry for her.

When Eric woke up the next morning he felt much better. He was looking forward to getting to his office so he could get back to work. He checked the refrigerator again but couldn't find anything he wanted to eat for breakfast, so he got ready to go and eat breakfast somewhere in Bangor.

A knock on his back door surprised him because he didn't think anyone knew he was back. He opened it to Paul Glidden. "Nice to have you back, Eric. How 'bout coming over for breakfast?" Paul had his usual friendly smile warming his face.

Eric didn't hesitate. "Great, Paul, give me a couple of minutes to get my stuff ready and I'll be right there. And, thanks, probably to Harriet."

He put together his briefcase and drove his SUV over to the Glidden house. She gave him a hug as he came into their house. "How are you, Eric?" she asked, looking up at him with a serious look. It was as though he'd been away for weeks.

"Yuck!" he answered. "This storm certainly did a number on all of us." He sat down at the kitchen table and sipped his cup of coffee. He looked at Harriet, who was middle-aged and slightly overweight but not as bad as Paul. She was a terrific cook so it was understandable why they were both heavier than they should be.

As they sat down to eat breakfast, he related what happened last night. "Susan and I are going to end our marriage. She's already moved to Jack Meacham's house and his wife Janet has moved back to her father's house. Man, what a job that storm did to us." He shook his head in disbelief over what had happened during the weekend.

Paul asked Eric if there was something they could do to help. Eric thought for a moment, and then grinned at him. "Yeah, there is. I want to get rid of our bed and mattress. Could you haul it away and bring down a new one as soon as possible?"

Paul slapped his hand on the table and roared. "You bet! Anyway I can make money."

Harriet whacked him on his arm. "Paul, behave yourself!" But she couldn't help grinning. She delivered three fried eggs and bacon to the table and sat down smiling at Eric. "So, the rumors were right."

Eric nodded his agreement. "Yep, that's what happened. And now we're headed for a divorce, so the neighborhood should be informed before any other possible rumors start." His sarcasm failed to register with the Gliddens who were more interested in telling the others on the road that Jack Meacham and Susan Reddy did have a glorious sexual weekend.

While they ate breakfast the conversation stayed with the weather at the lake. Eric wanted to know how the Gliddens were doing without power. "It's really not been too bad," answered Paul. "Our generator is larger than yours and most of our house is connected, so we're not missing too much. We're even getting used to the noise. When the power comes back on, we'll probably have a tough time sleeping because it'll be too quiet."

Eric sipped his coffee as he held the cup in both hands. "So how is my generator doing? I forgot to check it this morning."

Paul leaned back in his chair while drinking his coffee before answering. "It's OK. I'll check the gas before I go to work but you should have enough to last most the day. I expect the power might get back on today 'cause the crew was down here most of yesterday and is up the road this morning." Paul continued his talking while Eric's attention began to drift toward Janet. He felt he should have handled his leaving last night more personally. But he didn't want to let Jack and Susan know how he felt about Janet.

Paul suddenly stopped talking and was waiting for an answer but Eric missed what he was saying. Paul asked again, "What kind of bed and mattress do you want?"

"'Hell, I don't know." Eric then thought about it. "Make it the same mattress and the bed should be something similar. You've got an interior designer working for you, don't you?" Paul nodded his answer. "Well, then," continued Eric, "let her pick one out. OK?"

Harriet got into the act. "Eric, let me help."

"Good idea, thanks. I just want to get rid of that bed for obvious reasons. The bed, sheets, pillows. Everything! I'm also going to need a cleaning lady when the power comes back on," said Eric while hugging her. "And thanks for breakfast." He patted Harriet on her back and headed out the door. "Give me a call if there are any problems. See you later." Harriet came to the door and told him she'd clean the house for him today and asked Eric if he wanted to come over for dinner. Eric stopped and looked back at her. "Thanks, Harriet, but I don't know what my schedule is so I'd better take a rain check. I'll give you a call when I get back." He waved and got into his SUV and headed up the road that was now clear of most of the snow and ice. Large deposits of snow and parts of trees lined the road but driving was near normal.

Eric was feeling alone without Susan, but he realized there was no way they could have continued their marriage, particularly after the Benoit weekend events. She obviously loved Jack. He again thought of Janet and how he left her in a hurry last night. He felt guilty about not reaching out for her, but what was done couldn't be changed.

When he got to his office he went over his patient list and began to concentrate on their problems. All his thoughts about the past evening were put aside.

CHAPTER 31

Janet got up early the next morning, took a shower, dressed, and got ready for school. As she sat at the kitchen table drinking coffee with her father and Sarah, she felt anxious to get back to her schoolroom so she could forget for a while what had happened over the weekend. In fact, she thought, it would be fun for each of her students to tell what they experienced over the weekend. That made her smile.

Doug got up and headed for the garage. "I've got to get to the office early today, just to make certain Tom Siegel isn't going to give some oddball forecast this morning. That's all we need." He bent over, kissed Janet and Sarah, and headed out the door, feeling good that his daughter was back home.

The kitchen was quiet while Sarah and Janet finished their breakfasts. Finally Janet took her dishes to the sink and came back to the table with a fresh cup of coffee and the pot to fill Sarah's cup. "You know, Sarah, I'm looking forward to getting back to my classroom. It seems as though I've been away for weeks. And I've got to rethink all that happened last night and all that didn't happen at the Benoit Lodge. I've got to see if there is really something happening between Eric and me."

Sarah was having a difficult time replying to Janet's thinking. "I really don't know what to suggest, but I think you've got to let Eric get back on track. I'm sure it was difficult for him to hear his wife admit to enticing Jack into her bed and then to be so casual about it. There obviously was love between Eric and Susan so it must have been difficult for him to accept it. Their situation was much different than yours, even though you initially were in love with Jack." Sarah shrugged her shoulders.

"Yeah, I was, but he sure turned around when he was hurt in that Miami game. He wasn't ready to stop playing football because he was still one of the best halfbacks in the pros. The end came too quickly. I don't think he'd considered not being able to play because he started playing football when he was in grammar school. Suddenly he couldn't play again. He didn't know how to handle it. You know, I felt very sorry for him, but there wasn't anything I could do to help him, so I convinced him to move to Bangor when he was offered the running back coaching job at the university. Somehow all that happened seemed to be my fault." Janet shrugged her shoulders in disbelief.

"Oh, well, it's best for both of us to divorce. I have no feelings to do anything else. As for Eric, I still love him but he's got to handle his feelings toward Susan by himself. I sure as heck can't help with that. I think he loves me, but right now he's trying to end his marriage and that doesn't appear to be easy." Janet looked at the clock and got up from her chair and said. "I've talked enough. I'd better get ready for school."

Sarah asked if there was anything she could do to help, but Janet shook her head. There were no tears, only a very concerned look, as she was worried that Eric may have changed his mind about her. As she dressed for school, her mind became focused on her students in the sixth grade. She thought they'd all have stories to tell about the past weekend, so she planned for a student description of how each of them made it through the northeaster

Jack and Susan were quiet as they got up and had breakfast before driving up to Orono for the day's schedule. Since it was the off-season, most of the work involved the recruiting of potential football and soccer players.

The temperature was above freezing so there was lots of snow and ice melting, which caused cars and trucks to spray each other with melting snow combined with sand, which made the cars get dirty, particularly the windshields.

They were quiet while driving to Orono, as they couldn't find anything to say after the get-together last night. They both felt uncomfortable about what had happened with Eric and Janet, but Susan still felt they were doing the right thing.

When they arrived in their building, other coaches who had stories to tell about the northeaster welcomed them. Jack and Susan didn't get involved with these discussions and headed off to their offices. Both agreed to themselves that it felt good getting back to work.

When Eric finished with his last patient, he was surprised to find it past six o'clock. He sat down in his office and checked over the list of phone calls made to him during the day. There was nothing from either

Susan or Janet, but then Susan rarely called him during business hours. He was a little surprised not to have heard from Janet, but as he thought about it she probably was waiting to hear from him.

He checked Doug Felty's phone number and dialed it. Janet answered the phone. "Hi, it's Eric. I'm sorry I'm so late in getting back to you, but I've been backed up with all sorts of patients."

"Oh, Eric, don't worry about that. It's just good to hear you." She thought for a moment while waiting for Eric to answer. "If you're not doing anything, come on over for dinner. Dad and Sarah have gone out to eat and then they're going to a concert downtown."

Eric smiled to himself when asked because of the comment he made to her about the dinner she made on Tuesday. "I'll be there in about twenty minutes. Are you sure you want to cook? I could take you out to eat."

Janet laughed at that comment. "You thought I'd forgotten about your nasty comment when you were here for dinner on Tuesday."

"Whoops. I'm on the way." Eric was all smiles as he hung up the phone and headed out the door, remembering that Janet had a good memory. Janet was very happy to have heard from Eric; she had hoped he would call and he did, but it took him longer than she expected. She had been planning to make her mother's goulash that was always a favorite of anyone who ate it. The recipe was easy and relatively quick so she began to cook the ground beef and other ingredients.

Eric stopped at a florist on the way to pick up a bouquet of roses, and then headed off to see her. He was excited at the thought of being alone with Janet, particularly after last night.

She answered the doorbell and smiled as she opened the door for him. She quickly realized how much she looked forward to seeing him again. He took off his coat and hung it in the closet, then asked, "Do I get a hug?"

"You bet," answered Janet, who put the roses on a table and walked over to Eric. "I was afraid you weren't going to ask." They embraced for a long period of time and then pulled their heads back and quickly kissed each other.

"Janet, first, I need to apologize for leaving you so quickly last night. I just wanted to get away."

"Oh, Eric, I understand. Don't worry about it." She ran her hands down his chest. "I can understand what you were feeling." She picked up the roses, took his hand, and guided him into the kitchen. "We can talk while I finish making poison for dinner." She said it with a straight face. She pointed to the kitchen table where there were two glasses and a bottle of Merlot waiting to be opened.

Janet went to the stove where she was mixing the goulash meat and seasonings in a medium sized frying pan. Eric opened the bottle and poured the wine while looking at a very beautiful cook. A colorful apron covered the front of her dress. He went over to the stove to watch her cook. "I guess I won't live that down for a long time."

"And what is that, Eric?" she asked with a very straight face while wielding a spatula.

"Oh, the comment I made after dinner last Tuesday about your cooking. I guess I won't live that down anytime soon."

"Really?" she answered, while barely keeping her face serious. She turned back to the stove as Eric wrapped his arms around her waist. "And what was that comment? Certainly it wasn't anything to do about my cooking, was it?" She turned and smiled at him then turned back to the stove.

"I guess I should apologize, but maybe I should wait until I finish eating...and what are you making?" She turned around again and told him what was for dinner. He became more curious and stood next to her while she finished stirring the meat. Then she went and stirred the spaghetti and took out a sample to see if it was done. "Can I help?" he asked, while enjoying the smell of dinner.

"Nope, this is all going into the oven for forty minutes so we can sit and relax with some wine. Then you'll be able to make comments on my cooking. Until then I won't say a thing." She snarled at Eric, who couldn't help but shrug his shoulders and grin. "So, let's go sit on more comfortable chairs in the living room."

Eric was beginning to feel as he did in Bethel. Janet was a joy to be with and he hoped they could work out a situation to bring both of them together for the rest of their lives. Janet guided him to her father's comfortable chair and ottoman while she sat down on the couch and pulled her legs under her hips.

"How was school today?" asked Eric

"It was terrific. All the kids had interesting stories to tell about the northeaster. But then, I didn't tell them about mine."

Janet took a sip of wine and changed the conversation to last night's get-together with Jack and Susan. "I had a feeling last night, that you were shocked about what happened between them. Were you?"

He stared at his glass of wine while thinking of how he should answer Janet. "Even though I was pretty sure something went on with them last weekend, I was really upset when she said she was the one who started the affair. He just followed along as any normal guy would, and then they kept it going for the entire weekend, while you and I avoided doing the same. I just didn't expect her to have initiated the affair. But then, knowing Susan as I do, I should have guessed it. Then I just had to get away from her, so that's why I left so quickly last night."

"You really love her, don't you?" The question startled Eric. He stared at Janet and took another deep sip of wine before he tried to answer. He shook his head and laughed as he began to tell Janet how he and Susan met and finally wed with the understanding that either one could end the marriage if they found someone else. Janet sat in awe while listening to Eric's description of his life with Susan.

After he finished he began to work on his wine. Janet looked amazed at hearing about the relationship. "I've never heard of anything like what the two of you agreed on. That's really weird. Now after all this, are you still in love with her?"

Eric looked down at the floor and told Janet. "No, I don't think so," Eric replied in a very serious deep voice. "I do love her, but I'm not in love with her." He emphasized the word "in." "Susan has often described our relationship as brother and sister, not husband and wife, and to some degree I'd have to go along with it. But our marriage is over. There's no second-guessing that fact, but I think I still love her. We did have a good time together for a couple of years, but that changed in a hurry." Eric looked at Janet to see if she understood what he was saying.

Just as Janet was about to answer, the bell went off in the kitchen indicating that the goulash was ready. "Come with me, Eric, and you can set the table while I finish making dinner. OK"? Their conversation changed toward the dinner. Eric was most impressed with the aroma coming from the goulash as it cooled on top of the stove.

She pointed to a drawer next to the table. "The silverware is there, the napkins are in the first door and the salt and pepper are in the next cupboard. There is Parmesan cheese in the refrigerator. Do you think you can handle all that?" Eric mumbled some unintelligible words as he followed her orders. When finished he filled each of their glasses with more wine. When Janet was finished making the salad she carried it to the table, then went back to scoop out the goulash.

The dinner started quietly as Eric was consumed by the great-tasting goulash. He finally looked up from his plate and grinned as he looked into her eyes. "What can I say? This is terrific. Can I have a second helping?"

"Just help yourself," replied a happy Janet.

As he filled his plate, a humbled Dr. Forster confessed he was wrong the other day when he asked about her cooking. On the way back to his chair he leaned over and kissed her cheek. "I apologize. You're a terrific cook. Now what's for dinner tomorrow night?"

Janet laughed at that question. "Maybe I should have you do some cooking to see if you're worth anything."

"That's nasty," said a phony injured Eric.

"You're right, so how does it feel?" she asked while making a face at Eric. She was beginning to feel as comfortable as she was while they were at the Benoit Lodge. "Finish your dinner while I watch. Don't forget your salad." Janet wanted to keep feeling as she did when they were in Bethel. There was something between them that made life so much more pleasant, particularly after her time with Jack Meacham.

Janet finished her dinner, cleared off her dishes and looked over at Eric, as she was concerned about his situation with his soon-to-be ex-wife Susan. "Eric, I don't know if I'm able to understand your feelings for Susan. You either love her or you don't and if you do, where does that leave me?"

Eric took his dishes over to the sink and looked into a worried Janet's eyes. He placed his hands on her shoulders and looked into her blue eyes. "My marriage with Susan is over. There will never be a change in that...never!" His voice was very emphatic.

He continued. "She's totally committed to Jack and nothing is going to change that. Once she makes up her mind, there is no alternative. I'm history and I understand and accept it. What made me mad was how they handled their stay at my house while we were in Bethel behaving ourselves. That made me madder than hell."

He took Janet by her hands to their chairs where he sat her down in front of her. "In fact I've asked my neighbor Paul Glidden and his wife Harriet to get rid of my bed where all the sexual activity occurred. There's no way I'm ever going to sleep in that bed again." He stopped talking and looked at a very worried Janet. "Do you understand what I am saying?"

Janet bowed her head toward her chest and breathed deeply before replying. "Yes, I do." She looked him in his eyes and grabbed his hands. "Thank you." Eric reached over and took her head in his hands and kissed her on her lips. She was beginning to feel better about their relationship.

"Now, what about us?" Eric continued. "I think I'm very much in love with you." He hesitated. "No, I don't think I'm in love with you. I know it."

"I do too, Eric, but I think we need to make certain we feel the same after a reasonable length of time. In other words, I think we should act like two young adults who are thinking about marriage. Besides, it might take awhile for each of us to get a divorce." She was hoping Eric would feel the same.

Eric felt very good about her thoughts and smiled broadly at her ideas. "I couldn't agree more. I don't want to make the same wrong decision again. I want us to be happily married for the rest of our lives and to have a family to enjoy. I hate to say this, but I don't want us to have a sexual relationship until we are certain our marriage will work." Eric thought for a moment. "God, that's stupid of me to say that; it's going to be difficult as hell to avoid attacking you." He stroked her hair and kissed her on her forehead.

Janet couldn't have been happier with the prospect of marrying Eric. She could hardly wait. She laughed when she replied. "You'll just have to listen to what I told you at the lodge. 'Don't touch me!'"

Eric grimaced at that thought. To not try to make love to her was near impossible, but it had to be done. "OK, I won't...maybe. And since we need to see more of each other, I'll invite you to spend a weekend with me at the lake." He grinned and added, "In separate bedrooms."

"Oh, I'd loved to do that. Maybe you can do the cooking while I watch. After all I have to determine is if you're worth marrying."

Eric stuck out his tongue at her. "Stick it in your ear!"

They both felt relieved and happy about their prospects for a life together and the need to make certain their marriage would work.

"One more idea," added Eric. "I'd like you to meet my parents, so maybe on spring break you and I could go down to Florida to visit them. I know they'd both like to get to know you."

"I'd like that," answered Janet. "Besides, it would be great to get away from this cold weather. But I really want to meet your parents and hopefully they'll accept me."

"Don't worry about that. You're going to be more than welcome." Eric looked at his watch. "I'd better being getting home and I need to stop at the grocery store to get some food. But let me help you with the dishes".

"Don't worry about them. I'll take care of it. There'll be plenty of time for me to get you to work in the kitchen."

"Thanks, Janet," he said as he pulled her to his chest. As he felt her body against his, he grinned and told her, "Well, maybe I've made the wrong decision about some sort of intimate relationship. Can I change my mind?"

She poked him in his back and pulled away from him, but not until she kissed him. "Good try, but it won't work." She hugged him again. "Now, get out of here."

Eric headed for the front hallway and put on his coat. "You're the same miserable person I stayed with over the weekend. Why do I suffer over you?" He kept a straight face with a great deal of difficulty. As he opened the front door, Eric looked back at Janet. "By the way, that goulash was terrific. Are you sure you made it?"

She pointed her finger at the door and ordered him out of the house. "And don't come back until tomorrow," she offered as she closed the door. She felt so good about everything, she could hardly wait until her father and Sarah came home.

CHAPTER 32

Jack and Susan had a quiet dinner at home on the first night after the Tuesday meeting in his house. They were happy to be with each other, but they still felt a little strange living together after being married to someone else for several years.

Finally, Susan broke the silence and asked Jack how the university would react to their current situation. "Susan, I don't think there will be any concern from anyone about what has happened. No one knows either Janet or Eric, but they know us so I wouldn't worry about it. I don't like to brag, but how many other teams have someone with my background?"

She nodded her head in agreement. "There's no question about that."

"And," Jack continued, "I've brought in a good bunch of reasonable prospects. But equally important is what you've done with the women's soccer team. You've done a terrific job and the results are showing how well the team is doing. They sure as hell wouldn't want to lose you. You're a great coach and eventually you're going to be approached by some other major university to take over their team. That I can almost guarantee."

"Yeah, I understand that, and I can hardly wait until we move out of here. I just don't like it here and now that I'm getting a divorce, it makes this even more important to me." Susan leaned forward with her head on her hands. "I also want to get far away from Eric. I feel uncomfortable around him now that we're getting divorced, even though I still like him." Susan had a sad look in her face.

"Well, I don't feel that way about Janet. I just want to get away from her and I would also like to get away from here, but I've made a commitment for the rest of the spring so I probably will stay until then unless they ask me to leave."

Susan was surprised at that comment since Jack was so very popular with most of his football players. There were always exceptions but most of the players felt honored to be coached by the great Jack Meacham.

Several weeks later, Susan was on the phone with a soccer prospect when her mail arrived. As she was talking on her phone, she leafed through a significant amount of correspondence. One letter caught her eye. It was from Doris Munson, the women's athletic director at Northwestern University in Illinois. She couldn't remember ever meeting her or anyone else from there but she met all sorts of people at various conferences and games. She put it aside so she could go over the other mail. As usual there were letters from prospective athletes who were looking to select a school for the coming scholastic year. She was impressed with two of the letters and put them aside for further review. She then picked up the letter from Doris Munson.

She slit open the envelope and pulled out the letter. It read:

Dear Ms. Reddy:

I will make this letter short and to the point. June Allard, our current women's soccer coach, has announced her retirement after this season as she wishes to retire to Florida with her husband. We shall miss her.

Therefore we are now actively seeking a replacement for June and I would like to interview you for the position if you are interested. We are fully aware of what you have done at the University of Maine and believe you would be an outstanding candidate for this position. June suggested I contact you.

The Big Ten is one of the finest groups of universities in women's soccer and the university has made a significant investment in our soccer program. I don't like to belittle other conferences, but I believe ours is the finest in the country and we at this university have made a commitment to be the best in the Midwest.

If you are interested in interviewing for the position of soccer coach please let me know. All interviews will be conducted by me and will be attended by June Allard and some other athletic persons, both female and male. At this stage we do not wish to have any agent involved in these discussions. That would come later if we select you as a prime candidate.

I certainly do wish you would give this your immediate attention and if you have any questions, please give me a call.

Sincerely,

Doris Munson

Northwestern University

Women's Athletic Director

Susan couldn't believe what she was reading. She read it again and then a third time. When it did register she began to shake with anticipation, as this is what she had been working to achieve ever since she started coaching. She began to feel a little dizzy, thinking about being the head coach for a team of Northwestern's caliber. Susan had to tell Jack so she could share her feelings.

She ran down the hall to Jack's office and barged in without knocking. Out of breath, she cried out to him, "Jack you've got to read this," as she held Munson's letter above her head. Then she realized Jack was on his phone talking to some unknown person.

He waved her off and pointed to his phone and then to a chair. Susan had a difficult time sitting still while waiting for him to get off the phone so she looked around his office at all his trophies and pictures from his playing days. It was an impressive array for an impressive athlete. Finally he finished his phone call. "Susan, what in the hell is wrong with you?" he answered with a scornful look.

Susan didn't bother to answer. Instead she flashed the Munson letter in front of him. "Read this!" she insisted.

Jack gave her a strange look as he grabbed the letter and began to read. Very quickly he got the gist of it and muttered, "Jesus Christ, I can't believe this. Oh, shit, this is incredible." He looked at a smiling Susan who was trying to stay calm.

"Oh, Jack, I can't believe this either. It's like a dream. They want to interview me for the soccer coaching job," she said as she began to sweat. "Isn't it terrific?" she asked, while looking at a frowning Jack.

"Yeah, it's terrific," answered Jack in a quiet serious voice, "but what happens to us?"

Susan didn't have an answer, as she didn't expect his question. It went over her head. In the excitement of getting this letter, she totally forgot about their plans for the future.

"Damn it!" she muttered as she took back at the Doris Munson letter from a frowning Jack Meacham and read it again. "I don't know. I didn't even think of it because I was so happy to get this invitation." She rested her head on her hands as she looked to Jack for some sort of an answer.

Jack leaned forward on his desk. "Look, Susan, forget what I just said. I was thinking selfishly. You've got to go after this job. It's what you've wanted," he said as he came around his desk to sit next to her. "Let's check with your agent to see if you're obligated to stay here. I don't think so, but you might be under a contract and if that's true, then you might have a problem accepting this job if it's offered to you.

Even if you are and they want you badly enough they can buy out your contract, so don't worry about it.

"Let's face it. Either one of us could have been offered something or asked to interview for a better job. Maine is kind of at the bottom rung for our sports, so it was just a question of time before one of us was approached by another school." He held Susan's hand then took his right hand and stroked her hair. "Besides, they might need a football coach."

Susan was still not down to earth, but she hugged Jack as he spoke. "Thanks, but I don't want to leave you."

Jack looked at Susan with a concerned smile. "Susan," he said, "What if the tables were turned and I was offered a job as head coach at some major university or pro team? I'd be charging after that as hard as I could and if an offer was made then I would have to figure out what to do. Besides, I have invested a lot of money from my playing days and from my insurance when I got hurt, so I am in very good shape financially. I really don't have to work, so I could move out there with you."

Susan repeated, "Jack, I don't want to be away from you."

He added, "And I don't want to be away from you either." He hugged her around her shoulders and added, "First, let's get you out there for an interview and take it from there. You have to be offered the position so whatever you feel, don't let this opportunity pass, as it may not happen again. You have to convince these people that you're the right choice. When they make you an offer, then it will be time to make other decisions. OK?" He stroked her hair as he added, "You know, I'm really proud of you." He kissed her on the forehead and he tightened his grip around her shoulders. Susan was still trembling with joyful anticipation.

Jack got up and went back to his swivel chair and looked admiringly at her.

Susan was in another world as she gazed at Jack and then went back to reading the letter once again to make certain what she was reading was correct

"Now how should I handle this letter?" she asked Jack. Susan brushed her hair back with her right hand and she began to think about coaching a first class college soccer team. "Wow!" she yelled.

Jack crossed his hands around his chest and drifted back in his chair and turned to look out the window while thinking of her proper approach to the letter. "I think I'd write a letter back to her expressing your thanks and telling her you are very interested. I'd do it right away so they won't think you're not interested. You could call," he continued, "but that might make them think you're really hot for the job and it might affect their offer." He turned his chair to look out his window. "Yeah, I think that might be the best way to handle it. What do you think?" He turned back to an excited Susan who probably didn't hear what he just said.

"OK", she finally replied, "could you help me with the letter? I've never really done anything like this before." Jack understood what she was saying and the mental condition she was experiencing.

He waved his hand in front of her face to see if she was still there. "Hello, Susan. I just want to make certain you're still among the living."

Susan shook her head to get rid of the distant thoughts. She finally came back to reality. "I'm sorry, Jack. I'm just so overwhelmed by the letter that my mind is running ten miles ahead of my mouth. I just can't get over the fact that Doris Munson wants to interview me. I was hoping that sometime I would have a chance to get a job like this, but now that I have it I'm sitting on a cloud. Wow!"

Susan got out of her chair and went over to Jack's side of the desk, threw her arms around him, and gave him a kiss on his cheek. "I'll start working on this letter so I can get it in the mail today. But I don't want to let anyone else know what's going on.

She left a smiling but worried friend in his office that while happy for Susan, suddenly felt he might be left out of her future. Jack looked at the photos on his office walls and the many trophies he had in a cabinet. Hopefully, he thought, he could help Susan fulfill her life's dream.

Jack got up from his chair and walked over to the window and looked out at nothing in particular as he was wondering what would happen next. He didn't want to lose Susan so if she got a job offer at Northwestern, he would go with her. He could always find another team like the Chicago Bears or maybe he could get involved with a local TV station as a football analyst. In any event he could leave Maine and move into a large metropolitan area. He also felt it would be a good deal to move away from Janet.

CHAPTER 33

A knock on his door brought him back to reality. Standing there was Sam Edwards, one of the team's running backs. He was a junior who the coaching staff thought would be an exceptional running back, but his performance late in the previous year and at the spring practice was so poor he lost his first string status to incoming freshman Joe Jones.

Edwards was dressed in a pair of pants that were about to fall off his hips, his shoes were large unlaced sneakers, his shirt a Maine uniform and his baseball cap was tilted to his right side. He wore large earrings, a heavy necklace, and had a ponytail that reached down below his shoulders.

"Hey, man," he slurred to Jack. "We need to talk."

Jack pointed to a chair and Sam sat down. Jack did too, holding his head in his hands, wondering how in the hell this young college student dressed and talked like some imported idiot from the slums of New York. "OK, Sam, what's the problem?" Jack asked.

"You know, coach, you dropped me from the first team. How come?" he asked, while settling down in his chair. His body slid down the chair to where he nearly fell out.

Jack rubbed his face before he answered Sam's question so he wouldn't say something he would later regret. He was angry as hell at the attitude and dress codes of some of these kids. Besides, it was difficult to understand what he was saying.

"Sam, you don't deserve the starting status after your performance late last year and spring training. Joe Jones easily outplayed you, so until you can win back your starting position he'll be the starter."

"Hey, man, I was the starter last year," Sam complained in a whining tone.

"You were a starter last year because you worked hard at being a good halfback, but when we lost a chance to become a candidate for a bowl game, you appeared to give up," Jack answered in a quiet tone.

"Hey, man, I didn't give up. I was hurting," Sam answered in the same whining voice while rubbing his leg.

Jack stood up and walked over to the window, hoping Sam would get up and leave his office. Jack turned around and found Sam still sitting on his back with an angry look on his face.

"You were hurting? You were hurting?" Jack repeated, raising the tone of his voice. "Everybody is hurting at that time of the year, but most don't whine about it. They go out and keep playing, trying to win! You gave up!"

"Yeah, man, but if I got hurt badly I wouldn't have a chance of making a pro team," Sam continued with his agonizing look.

Jack broke into laughter. "Sam, the odds on you making a pro team are minimal at best. I'm sorry, but you just don't have the talent needed to play pro ball and now you don't have the attitude to make you a successful college football player either."

Sam stood up and glared at Jack as he slurred out, "You've probably moved me off the starting team 'cause I'm black."

Jack turned around and whipped his arm across his desk sending everything flying across the room. He yelled, "You dumb shit! You've lost starting because of lousy performance and attitude. Saying that the coaching staff is against you because you're black is so much bullshit that it doesn't deserve an answer. You asshole, look around you at the makeup of the coaching staff and the players." Jack was becoming more furious toward Sam Edwards and he was losing control.

"No one gives a shit if you're black, white, or purple. If you don't perform you're not going to play. No one is picked because of color, but by talent and attitude. The coaching staff felt that you had talent when they offered you a scholarship, but then you didn't want to work hard to keep your position and you expect us to forget this and bring you back to the first string because you're black. That's too much bullshit.

"Besides you're getting a free four-year education of your choosing. Get your ass out of here before I belt you out." Jack grabbed Sam's arm and pointed to the door. His anger shocked Sam, so he quickly got to the door.

When he reached for the doorknob, he turned and glared at Jack Meacham. "Hey, man, I still say you're being unfair to me and I'm not about to forget it. I'm going to tell this to Mr. McCall." Tom McCall was the athletic director.

Jack's anger hadn't changed and he again told Sam to get the hell out of his office. Sam walked out the door and slammed it shut. Jack felt like going after him, but thought better of it. He went back to the window and stared out while trying to calm himself. He thought to himself that maybe it was time to get the hell out of coaching college football and stop putting up with football players who really didn't deserve a college scholarship, but got one anyway just because they were good athletes. He'd seen too many of these worthless kids.

About twenty minutes later there was a knock on his door and in came the athletic director Tom McCall. He had a serious look on his face. "Jack, what the hell happened with Sam Edwards?" He sat down in the same chair Sam had just left.

Jack shook his head and laughed at the question. *You've got to be kidding,* he thought. *That little bastard!* He then related what had happened.

McCall listened carefully and finally said, "Edwards came right to my office and told me you threatened him when he asked why he was not the starting halfback. He also told me that you criticized his race."

Meacham rubbed his face with his hands to try and calm down his temper. "Tom, I don't give a shit what that jerk is saying because I wouldn't criticize anyone being black, white, or whatever. Sam Edwards is worthless and doesn't deserve being on this team."

McCall didn't answer immediately but instead looked with concern at Jack. He had great respect for Jack Meacham and how well his players admired him. It was important to the Maine football team that Jack was the assistant coach given his all-pro days with the New England Patriots. They were able to sign players who might have gone somewhere else just because they could meet and work with Jack Meacham.

Finally he replied. "Jack, I don't know what happened but we can't afford to have bad publicity and if Edwards talks to the press that will happen."

Jack Meacham couldn't believe what he was hearing. McCall was telling him that that punk Edwards was going to be believed before him. "I can't believe that you would accept what Edwards says instead of me."

Tom McCall sat down and shook his head at Jack. "That's not the issue, Jack. We can't afford to be involved with the NAACP or any other organization that will bring us bad publicity. Maybe you need to go talk to him again and apologize for what you told him."

Jack looked at McCall with anger, knowing Tom felt he had dropped Sam Edwards to the second string because Edwards was an African-American.

McCall's comments bugged Jack to a point where he had to try and relax before he said something he'd regret later. He finally tried to talk with a reasonably calm voice, but that failed. "Tom, I'm not about to apologize to that jerk. In fact I'm pissed off that you had the balls to come in to my office and accuse me of something I didn't do. If I wanted to, I'd have knocked the shit out of Edwards, but luckily I didn't touch him except to guide him out of this office." He glared at McCall with a face that was turning red.

McCall stood up and leaned over Jack's desk. "That you even touched him on his arm while you were angry is the same as belting him. You can't do it. Coaches have been fired for the same sort of thing. The fact that he's an African-American makes it even worse."

Jack stared back at McCall not believing what he just heard. "I don't give a shit what he is. This guy, Sam Edwards, is a real asshole and to baby him is ridiculous. How in the hell can you justify it?" Jack slammed his fist on his desk and began to feel that he was losing it.

He hesitated for a moment and finally said in a quieter voice. "To hell with all this. I'm out of here. Find someone else who'll put up with these idiot kids who have no business being in college."

Tom McCall looked shocked at what Jack just said so he sat down and looked at Meacham to make sure of what he just said. "For God's sake, Jack, I don't want you to leave us. You've done too much to help our football program. That's not the issue." McCall was in his early forties, six feet tall, and slightly overweight with a half-bald head.

Jack sat down and was beginning to calm down. "Tom, this whole football program is getting ridiculous. When you offer a scholarship to someone like Sam Edwards, you're asking for trouble. He doesn't deserve it. There has to be all sorts of high school students who have worked hard at getting prepared for college, but they can't find a place to go because they don't have the money for tuition, so instead of us helping them out we buy these fucking stupid kids, who probably can't spell, and give them a free scholarship. It's wrong and Sam Edwards is a prime example of what's wrong with college football.

"When I got a scholarship I had to have a better than average scholastic standing to qualify, and when I was in school I had to do well with tough courses. This Edwards guy doesn't have a clue as to what he should be doing.

All he's thinking about is playing pro ball, but he doesn't understand that he's not even close to that caliber. He can't even understand that he's not able to be a starting halfback here. And then he accused me of being racist. Bullshit!" Jack slammed his hand back down on his desk and glared at Tom McCall.

Tom hid his face with his hands as he tried to answer Jack. He knew what Jack was saying was not too far from the truth. Now he faced losing an important part of his football coaching staff, one who was popular with players and fans. "Jack, I don't want you to leave. No one wants you to leave, but I think you need to get some help in controlling your temper. It's doing you no good at all."

"God damn it!" He slammed his fist back down on his desk. "Why is it that everyone thinks I have a fucking anger problem?" His voice had quieted down and he looked at Tom McCall for help. "Regardless, I'm resigning. I'm tired of putting up with idiots like Sam Edwards. I don't give a shit if he's black, white, or purple; he's an asshole who doesn't deserve to be on this football team, or even at this university, but that's not my decision."

While looking at a worried Tom McCall, Jack began to feel bad about what he was saying. He had great respect for Tom and what he had accomplished as athletic director for a university that found it difficult to get top-ranked athletes other than hockey players. Jack knew that his presence helped bring quality football players who wanted to be able to tell their friends the great Jack Meacham was coaching them.

Tom McCall stood up and looked down at Meacham. "Jack, take some time to think this over. None of us want you to leave. You've been too great for our teams, but you've got to go easy with these minority students."

Jack shook his head. "The only thing I criticize is how these players perform. Sam Edwards gave up on the team last year and doesn't deserve to stay on the team as a first stringer. If you want to change that then you do it, but regardless, I'm out of here."

"Please think it over tonight with Susan." Tom was familiar with Jack and Susan's relationship, but was not aware of her being considered for the head soccer coach's job in Evanston, Illinois. He got up and left Jack's room, feeling he was in a no win situation. He went down to Andy LaVoie's office. LaVoie was the head football coach and the one who helped bring Jack Meacham onto the staff.

When told of what happened between Jack and Sam Edwards, Andy hid his face in his hands, hoping all this was some sort of nightmare. To lose Meacham would be to negatively affect bringing quality high school prospects to Maine.

Back in his office Jack looked out his window and tried to calm himself down after what had happened. He had figured he'd be resigning soon if Susan got the soccer job at Northwestern University. There was no way he'd not be with her no matter where she went. He began to feel bad for the way he treated Tom McCall, but not Sam Edwards.

His door opened and a very concerned looking Susan came in,

closed the door, and went over to Jack. She threw her arms around him. "Oh, Jack, what happened?" She had buried her head on his chest that had a heavy beating heart. "Are you OK?" She had pulled her head back.

Jack embraced her and began to tell her the events of the past hour. "I don't know how it all happened, but it was tied to this Sam Edwards who was bitching about his demotion from starting halfback."

Susan sat down and looked at Jack with a very concerned look. She was worried that his anger problem was beginning to get out of control. She spoke gently to a confused Jack Meacham. "I'm going to call Doris Munson at Northwestern to see when I can get out there to interview for the coaching job."

"Are you sure?"

"Yeah! I think we both need to get out of here and start a new life. We also have to get you to some sort of anger management course. You can't go on like this. OK?" Susan had a very concerned look as she gripped his hands.

"OK," answered Jack in a very quiet but worried voice.

Susan reached across his desk and took his hand in hers. "I've checked the Internet and there's all sorts of courses and books to read on the subject of anger management. Let's go through some of these tonight to see what we can do to correct this problem. OK?"

"Yeah, OK," replied a very weakened athlete who felt as though he'd been crushed by a massive string of tackles. "I feel shitty!" He rubbed his forehead, trying to get the problem out of his system. "But I still feel pissed off at the Edwards asshole. He doesn't deserve anything."

Susan smiled at that and thought to herself that Jack also had a problem, but certainly not one of not trying hard to be a good athlete and student. However, they both needed help in getting their lives back in order. She got up, hugged him again, and told him how much she loved him, then left Jack alone. She then went back to her office to call Doris Munson to set up a date to interview for Northwestern's soccer coach's job and hoping she would be offered the coaching job. She also looked forward to living in the Chicago area.

CHAPTER 34

Toward the end of March, Eric called Janet for dinner. "I've made reservations for us to go to Florida over the spring break. Mom and Dad have asked the two of us to stay with them. Obviously they want to meet you since I've already talked to them about you." For a few moments there was no answer from Janet.

Finally she answered Eric. "Oh, I don't know, Eric. I'd love to go with you but maybe we're pushing it a little."

Eric was surprised at that comment. "What do mean pushing it?" he asked in a surprised voice, as he hadn't expected it.

"Well, where would we stay?" Janet asked with a concerned voice. "I thought we were going to avoid...you know what." Eric could see her looking worried about spending more time together in bed.

"My folks have invited us to stay in their house and they've got extra bedrooms where you could hide from me. Don't worry. You'll be safe. I might be frustrated again, but you'll come out of it in virgin territory."

Janet laughed at his comments. "OK, if that's how it's to be, I'd love to go to Florida with you. I would also love to meet your parents."

"OK, you're on. However, I might touch you when you're not looking."

"Not a chance, buster," she answered.

"Do you want to come down tomorrow and spend the weekend with me? I'll even fix dinner, but you'll have to do the dishes. Your bedroom door will have a lock on it, so you won't have to worry about being attacked."

The weekend turned out to be a fun time for the two of them. On Saturday they went cross-country skiing along the lake, which was still frozen, and that night, he invited his neighbors over for drinks and dinner. All of them showed up to meet Janet who thrilled all of them, and it was obvious they were looking forward to her being down here full time.

Then on Good Friday morning Janet and Eric boarded a Delta flight to Ft. Myers, Florida. The plane was packed with all sorts of families headed to the warmth of Florida. Remarkably the plane was on time at two in the afternoon. Eric's parents told him they'd meet them outside the arrival terminal. Eric had warned Janet that his mother was quite blunt about what she thought of Susan, so Janet was concerned about how she would be accepted.

There was a mass of people arriving from several jammed flights so the crowd around the terminal was monstrous and the traffic people were having a difficult time moving cars. As usual the luggage seemed to take longer to get from the plane to the conveyor than it did to fly from Atlanta. Janet had never seen so many people and so many suitcases in her life. One could barely move, and getting to the conveyor was nearly impossible. A half hour later their luggage finally arrived so they headed out the door to the terminal driveway full of a mass of people, this time friends and relatives greeting each other and packing suitcases into all types of vehicles

The immediate feeling to Eric and Janet was the warm moist air that felt so good after a long winter in Maine. Eric spotted his father standing next to his car with an open trunk while his mother, Margaret, had stayed in their car waiting for them to arrive. Eric went over to the trunk where his father gave him a handshake and hug. Eric quickly introduced Janet to him and to his mother, who had just come out of the car to greet them. She hugged and kissed Eric and then turned to Janet and gave her a hug. "My goodness," she said, "you're really quite beautiful. Whatever, it's nice to meet you, Janet. Come let's get out of this mess. Eric, get into the front seat with your father and I'll sit back here with Janet." She appeared to be very happy to be with Janet for the drive to Captiva Island.

Peter Forster stood about six feet tall with a small amount of gray hair around a baldhead. His features were much like Eric's. Margaret was also tall, thin, with gray hair and quite beautiful. Both were in their mid sixties and obviously in good health.

It took several more minutes before they could get free of the traffic jam in front of the terminal, so while waiting, Eric's father Peter asked the traditional question. "So, how was your flight?"

"It was good, but very crowded. We're happy to get off that plane and happier to get out of the terminal. They take longer to get luggage ready than any other airport I've been."

His father interrupted. "I know. I've suffered through the same problem. They're building a new terminal, but I doubt the luggage will arrive quicker. Anyway, we're glad to have you here where the weather is a heck of a lot better than in Maine."

Peter asked Janet about the change in weather. "Well," she answered with a smile, "after that storm we had in February, I'm happy to be where it's warm. I don't mind the winter, but ours seems to last forever, so when I breathed this warm weather coming out of the terminal it felt wonderful."

"Have you ever been down here before now?" asked Margaret.

"No, I haven't."

"Well, I think you'll love it here, particularly this time of the year." Margaret looked at her husband. "It'll take us more than an hour to get to our house on Captiva, depending on the traffic. "Do you need anything before we get home?"

Eric looked at Janet and neither could think of anything. "No, we're all set."

The drive to Sanibel was on a multilane road crowded with all sorts of vehicles. When they got to Summerlin Road, the traffic began to ease. The drive across to Sanibel Island was very attractive, as there were all sorts of boats along the drive. Pelicans flew along the edge of the road, looking down into the water for fish. Coming from a frozen Maine to a warm Florida was quite a pleasant change.

They finally arrived at his parents' house. Janet was very surprised at its size. It was two stories tall with an attached two-car garage and a lanai in the back of the house that included an indoor pool. The house was located on the Gulf of Mexico. Trees between the SanCap Road and house kept the house hidden from the public. Off the front of the house, facing west, was a gentle flow of waves coming up on the sand beach.

Janet could hardly keep her eyes away from the waterfront. It was a place she would thoroughly enjoy after the long Maine winter. The interior of the house had a large living room with, oddly enough, a fireplace. To the right was the dining room with a beautiful solid dark maple table with six chairs. A large cabinet stood off to one side.

On the other side of the house was a family room with the kitchen next to it and off to the side was an office. Upstairs was the master bedroom and bath, three other bedrooms, and two additional bathrooms. Each was reasonably large and decorated with Floridian pictures of birds, boats, and beaches.

Janet was taken aback by Eric's parents' home. She didn't expect anything like it. She looked at Margaret with widened surprised blue eyes. "Mrs. Forster, I'm very impressed. It's beautiful. I had no idea that your house was anything like this."

"Well, thanks, Janet. We bought this house about twenty-five years ago when prices were considerably less than they are now. But we love it down here even though the summers are pretty hot and humid. And, Janet, please call me Margaret or Marge, not Mrs. Forster. We're not that formal here."

Margaret continued her talking while Eric and his father brought in the luggage. "I understand you and Eric wanted separate bedrooms, so I've set two of them up for you. I guess I'm old-fashioned but I like your thinking. It's totally different from when his first wife came down here. I had trouble getting them out of their bedroom to do anything."

Eric just rolled his eyes and his father ignored what was said and headed up the stairs with Janet's suitcases. Peter then asked if they would like to change clothes and go for a walk along the beach. They both agreed. Janet was put in the bedroom overlooking the gulf while Eric was across the hall overlooking the back of the house. "We'll give you fifteen minutes to get ready," Peter said as he headed down the stairs. "We'll be out on the porch."

Janet looked at Eric in disbelief. "I had no idea that your parents had anything like this house. It's incredible. I'll see you downstairs," she said as she closed her door, adding, "and no peeking."

Eric was looking forward to this week with Janet and his parents. He put on a pair of shorts, a T-shirt, and his tennis shoes and headed down to see his mother and father on the deck. They had been eagerly awaiting their arrival since Eric had called them to see if he could bring Janet with him. When Eric came he walked to the edge of the deck. "After this winter, this looks better than ever."

His mother smiled and said they were also very happy to have him visit them. "It's early," she stated, "but I'm quite impressed with Janet. She's very beautiful, but she also appears to be a very nice person."

Eric came over to her chair and stroked his mother's shoulder. "She is a terrific person. I am totally in love with her. We are just trying to figure out if marriage makes sense for us. I don't want another quickie marriage."

"I'd certainly agree with that, Eric," said his mother. "You just have to take time to make certain you both are truly in love."

"Now, Margaret, let's not get involved in this. This is their decision, not ours," commented a very concerned Peter Forster. "From what Eric has told us, Janet's a very nice lady and they seem to be in love with each other, but after what happened in February they need to make certain before they make a final decision one way or another. Besides, they're both old enough that they don't need parents getting involved."

Margaret grabbed Eric's arm. "Your dad's right. But anything I can do to help either of you, please let me know." As she finished her comments, Janet came out of the house. She was wearing a pair of tan slacks with a green short-sleeved shirt and a pair of white sneakers.

She had a broad smile on her face. "Boy, it feels good to have summer clothes on. I'd forgotten what they're like."

Margaret looked at Janet with a happy face. "Well, come on, let's do a quick walk so we can show you what it's like down here." They headed up north and as they walked Janet was impressed with the number of different birds along the shoreline, particularly the pelicans as they dove after fish.

Most of the homes along the beach were newer than Peter and Margaret's since many residents bought an older house, then tore it down so they could build a larger, more modern house. The beach was relatively narrow but there was certainly room for beach chairs. The water was inviting but somewhat empty of swimmers.

As the sun began to set they headed back to the house where Peter offered drinks to be served in the leisure room off the beach. He raised his glass and welcomed his son and Janet to the warmth of Florida. Instead of cooking dinner, his parents took Eric and Janet to the Green Flash farther up in Captiva. The restaurant overlooked the Pine Island Sound and had several piers for those who wished to boat over to the restaurant.

"Dad, you can buy tonight, but we're going to do most of the entertainment costs. After all, the two of you are retired."

"We may be retired but we're too busy to sit around doing nothing, so now that you're here we've planned a couple of golf outings and we'll take our boat out for rides around this area. Besides I still help out with the Cubs' minor league players in Arizona during spring training. However, given what doctors charge, I'll go along with it. Thanks." He laughed as he jabbed Eric's arm. "Regardless, we're delighted the two of you are here.

Dinner was excellent and they all felt very comfortable with each other. Janet noted that there was a close relationship between Eric and his parents, much as she had with her father and Sarah. It made life so much more pleasant when there was this family love. It was something she never had with Jack Meacham, but now all that was in the past.

While they were finishing their coffee, Margaret asked Janet if she golfed. Eric had never thought to ask her before they came down to Florida. It never dawned on him that she played. He was surprised when she told his mother she did. "Well, in that case, we'll plan a couple of outings this week. Don't worry about how well you might do. Just come along and enjoy yourself. And I'm not really that good a golfer anyway, but I enjoy it. And don't worry about clubs. I've got an extra set."

"I'd like to," answered a very definitive Janet, who surprised Eric with her agreement to golf. "Thanks."

Peter Forster had set up a golf date for Eric and him for nine thirty the next morning. "Then we can golf with the women later this week."

Margaret looked at the men of her family and shook her head. "That's OK. Janet and I will soak up sun on the beach and then maybe go shopping." She turned toward Janet. "I'm looking forward to getting to know you better, so we don't need the guys around." She smiled and held onto Janet's arm. Her thoughts made Janet feel very much at home.

They headed home after they finished their coffee. Both Eric and Janet began to feel sleepy since they had gotten up early to make the flight, so they headed to their separate bedrooms soon after they got back to his parents' house. They hugged each other before heading to their rooms. Eric turned around and grinned when he suggested that she might want him to spend the night together in her double bed. All he got for an answer was a loud "hah" and a tongue sticking out at him.

Eric and his father left for the golf course slightly before nine the next morning and told the ladies that they'd be back after they finished the game and lunch.

"That's OK," replied Margaret, "we're going to spend some time on the beach so Janet can get the Maine winter off her body. Then we may go shopping and we'll certainly do lunch together. Have fun!" She kissed her husband and Eric, then shoed them out the door.

The two ladies finished their breakfast and then went upstairs to change into their bathing suits. Then they grabbed a couple of portable chairs and headed out the front door to the Gulf. "The sun gets pretty hot and it can do a number on your body so put some of this lotion on. I'll do your back."

When they got to the beach they took off their jackets. Margaret looked closely at Janet, who was wearing a conservative swimming suit, and commented in a quiet voice. "You certainly have the body that must drive men nuts. You are truly beautiful."

Janet was slightly embarrassed but she thanked Eric's mother for her thoughts. She sat down on the chair and applied her lotion as she savored the warm sunshine. It seemed to push away all the cold weather she and Eric had left in Maine.

Margaret was still very attractive even though she was in her early sixties. She coated Janet's back with suntan lotion and then sat down next to her. "Now, Janet, tell me about what's happened between you and Eric, and what happened to Susan?"

"Well," answered Janet, "It's a long involved story." Before she could continue, Margaret told her time was not a factor, so Janet nodded her approval and began to tell the story of the President's Day weekend. Margaret listened with complete interest and didn't interrupt as Janet described the entire event

❧

Eric and his father teed off at the scheduled time. The head of the pro shop let them play alone per Peter Forster's request. This way they were not obligated to wait on another twosome. Eric felt somewhat stiff since he had not played since last October except for an indoor driving range in Bangor.

"All right, Dad, how many strokes do I get?" His father laughed at that suggestion. The eighteen-hole course was in great shape with all sorts of ponds in places where they created problems for the golfer. Around most of the greens were a variety of sand traps.

Driving off the first tee was always an adventure to Eric since all sorts of golfers were staring at him, hoping he would hit his ball long and straight so they could soon start playing. The first hole was 450 years with a slight dogleg to the left. Remarkably, his tee shot went straight and long. His father smiled at that and said, "Eric, nice shot. Maybe I need a stroke." Peter took his driver and whacked the ball straight and farther than Eric's.

Eric shook his head. His father hadn't lost any of his talent to hit a golf ball just as he did with baseballs many years ago. It was going to be a long day on the course for Eric.

As they drove to their balls on the first fairway Peter told Eric how impressed he and his mother were with Janet. "She is a beautiful lady, and she seems to be a fun person to be with. So, what's the situation with her? And what happened to Susan?"

"Well, Dad, it's a long story. Let's wait till lunch and I'll fill you in on everything. For now I have to figure some way of beating you." He grinned at a smiling father. Eric's second shot was short and to the left of the green while Peter's landed just short of the green. Eric's next shot went over the green and into a sand trap while Peter's pitch landed about a foot from the hole. He got a par while Eric ended up with a six. *Damn it,* he thought, *this is a hell of a way to start the game.* Peter put his arm around Eric's shoulders and congratulated him on doing as well as he did on the first hole.

They finished just before one o'clock with his father easily winning the match, and then they went to a local restaurant that made terrific cheeseburgers. When the food arrived, Eric began to tell his father the events of the Presidents Day weekend outing. He prefaced it with, "You might have a difficult time believing all this, but trust me, it's true.

Peter sat and listened to what his son was telling him. He found it difficult to believe all that happened and in such a short period of time. He had a fondness toward Susan because of her athletic abilities, but he had to agree with his wife that her marriage to Eric didn't appear to be secure for the long run.

Eric related the events that led to the divorces and to his relationship with Janet. "You'd like her father, Doug Felty," Eric added "and his girlfriend, Sarah. They're just very nice people. As for Janet, I know I'm in love with her and I want to marry her, but both of us want to make certain of each other before we take that step. Both of us are scarred from our first marriages and we don't want it to happen again, so that's one of the reasons we're down here for the week."

His father listened carefully to what Eric told him and he was somewhat surprised to hear what happened with Susan. "Maybe she'll be better off with Jack Meacham," he offered, "because they are both heavily involved with sports and I can understand their feelings. But I'm really surprised she did what she did over the weekend. She must really love Meacham."

"Yeah, I'm sure she does," Eric said with a sad voice. "And I did love her too. I've had a hard time understanding why she did what she did."

"Well, Eric, let me offer a suggestion." Peter looked in his son's face with a serious look. "If you want to score with Janet, then I'd suggest you forget about Susan. She's gone and it doesn't make sense for Janet to compete with Susan."

Eric looked surprised at his dad's thinking. "I didn't realize I was."

Peter took a sip of his iced tea. "Well, what you need is a recording of your comments when you start talking about Susan. It sounds like she's still here and in a sense competing against Janet. And at this stage in her life, Janet doesn't need that crap. If you truly love her as I think you do, then you need to focus entirely on her. After meeting her, I wouldn't find that to be too difficult. She seems to be one terrific lady. Even your mother agrees with that."

For a few moments, they both looked at each other. Finally, Eric broke the silence and repeated, "I didn't realize I was doing that." They finished eating and headed back to the house with Eric concerned about how Janet might be feeling about him. When they got home the ladies were still out shopping.

Eric and his father each took a shower and met on the deck where they continued their conversation. "So, how are the Cubs going to do this year?" His father grinned at the question.

"Well we thought we'd win last year, but all sorts of things went wrong, so maybe this is the year. Finally! Look, if the White Sox and Red Sox could win, then it's our turn this year. We certainly have the talent." They continued talking baseball until the ladies returned from their shopping spree.

After dinner they sat in the living room and played a game of Scrabble. When they finished, Margaret snapped her fingers and announced, "I almost forgot. Your dad and I have a city council meeting to go to tomorrow morning. We should be back by early afternoon, so you're on your own till then. OK?"

"All right, Mom, don't worry about us, we'll find something to do by ourselves." He suddenly realized what he said and tried to change it, but it didn't work. Janet's face turned slightly red while his parents smiled at his thinking. He looked at all of them and with a smile said, "Well, I'd better go to bed. See you guys in the morning."

After breakfast the next morning his parents left for their meeting. Margaret smiled at Janet and said, "Watch out for this guy! We'll be back about two or so." Peter ignored the entire thought as they headed out the door.

It was suddenly quiet. Janet finally said, "I'm going to get my suit on and go down to the beach before it gets too hot. Do you want to go with me?"

"Yep, I do. I could use a little relaxing after yesterday's golf. Let's go get changed or do you want to wait down here?"

Janet smiled and stroked Eric's cheek. "No, I'm all right. We've been through enough of these situations." They headed up the stairs to change. Eric finished dressing before Janet and went down to the family room where he sat on the couch and began to read the newspaper.

A few minutes later Janet came into the room dressed in her two-piece bathing suit. It wasn't a bikini but it accentuated her figure. Eric hadn't seen her like this since last summer when she and Jack had come down to visit them at the lake, but he hadn't paid as much attention as he did today.

She stood in front of him and asked "Are you ready?"

Eric looked longingly at her and quietly answered, "You bet," as he reached up and pulled her down on the couch.

She didn't resist, but added softly when she slid down on the couch, "This wasn't what I meant, but here I am."

"God, you're beautiful", he said as he embraced her. They locked their arms around each other and kissed. He stroked her face and then his hand drifted down her body. She worked her hands down his back. They were both beginning to lose control and Eric was about to take off her top when the doorbell rang. He tried to ignore it, but it rang again, followed by a voice calling, "Mrs. Forster, Mrs. Forster, its Clara."

They quickly got off the couch, straightened out their swimming suits and hurried to the front door where his parents' maid Clara was waiting. "Hello, Eric. How are you?" Eric shook her hand and introduced her to Janet.

After a short talk with Clara, they headed off to the beach holding hands. They both felt a little guilty over what almost happened since they had decided weeks ago to not have sex together until they at least committed to marriage. When they got to the beach they laughed at each other as they embraced.

Eric looked over at a blushing Janet whose heart was still beating hard after the couch encounter. He thought for a moment, and then finally said, "Man, that was close. You really got my juices flowing."

She still felt charged up and rose up to kiss him. "I know. I did too, but it's just as well she showed up." She felt good about what almost happened. In her mind there was no question that she loved him, and she hoped he loved her as well. Maybe when Susan leaves town or gets married to Jack he would forget about her.

They spent most of the morning reading on the beach and then going for a walk up the beach while holding hands. He noticed that she drew all sorts of looks from nearly every man who passed them and that made him even more pleased that she was with him.

He guided her off into the shallow water and turned to her. "You know, Janet, I need to make it clear to you that my love for Susan is gone. It will never come back even though we will always be friends. I need you to understand this."

She reached up and kissed him on his forehead. "Eric, I think I understand. What bothered me was what happened after we all got together. You seemed to have forgotten me. I didn't think it was true, but it did worry me until we met again. I do love you, but we do need to give this some time before we decide we can stand each other as a married couple."

Eric didn't pay any attention to any of the people on the beach as he pulled Janet to his body and gave her a long kiss. "There," he said, "that should seal that question. Now let's get back to the house. There are more important things to worry about. Like, I'm hungry." She whacked him on his back as they jogged back to his parent's house.

Two days later, Eric's father set up a golf time for the four of them. Janet hadn't played since last fall and she felt she needed some practice, so she took a couple of clubs and went out to the backyard to practice her swing. Eric was watching her with his mother. "She's got a nice swing, Eric. You'd better watch out. She might beat you." Eric laughed at that.

She ignored his laugh and continued looking at Janet, who was concentrating on her swing. "Eric, I'm really impressed with Janet. She's not only beautiful but she's a very pleasant person. I'd love to have her as my daughter-in-law, so get busy and get this marriage going."

"Mother!" Eric exclaimed.

"What?" she replied, "This is an exceptional lady. I cannot understand how her husband could have let her go. He must be nuts!" She turned to look at Eric with a very serious face. "Your father and I have wanted to have grandchildren to love but we're getting older and running out of time. Understand?"

Eric put his arm around his mother's shoulder. "I understand and I'll see what I can do to convince Janet to marry me. I love her and she loves me, but we want to be certain that this is not going to be like our first marriages."

Margaret laughed. "There's no comparison between these two. Susan was a nice girl, but there was always something missing with her. Janet is just a super lady, so marry her and start making children," she pleaded as she wrapped her arms around him. "Now get out there and help her with her swing."

The next day they had a golf outing at ten thirty with lunch after the ninth hole. Both Peter and Eric were pleasantly surprised at how well Janet golfed even though she hadn't played in months. Her score was not too terrific, but she was enjoying the outing. Eric's mother never hit the ball very far but it was always straight and her putting was better than any of them, so her score was quite good. They all had a good time and decided they'd play once more before Eric and Janet had to head back to Maine.

On Thursday, Eric had a date with some orthopedic surgeons in Fort Myers for lunch. One of them, Jim Hagere, was a classmate of Eric's and they kept in touch with each other. Eric was shocked when he arrived at the waiting room where five orthopedic surgeons accepted patients, and he was amazed at the number of people waiting to see an orthopedic surgeon. There had to have been at least fifty people in the waiting room with many more in examining rooms or waiting for an x-ray. A TV was blasting away with some sort of soap opera.

He kept thinking that too many mistakes could happen with so many potential patients waiting for one of the five doctors. The place seemed to be a mad house with doctors and nurses running up and down the examining room hallways. He spent lunch with Hagere, who was very wealthy from his mass of operations. He suggested to Eric that he should consider moving down here to become part of this medical staff. There was all sorts of money to be made.

"Jim, not a chance. You guys must be so busy that there has to be errors made. How in the hell can you ever relax with this many patients? No, there's not a chance I'd work in a place like yours. I'm not exactly short of cash, but I can spend more time with patients than you do down here. Hell, it's like an assembly line."

Jim Hagere grinned at this thought. "Eric, this area is full of elderly people who have serious problems with their joints and more often than not, a replacement is the only way they can enjoy the rest of their lives. Believe me, we don't have to promote ourselves, but we do so we can offer a better lifestyle for them. Hell, all of Maine doesn't have as many people as there are in this area of Florida, and a great percentage of them are over sixty. Somebody has to take care of them."

Eric shook his head to acknowledge Jim's problem. "I think I understand, but I'm still shocked at how many patients you have waiting. How long does it take you to see them?"

"About an hour to an hour and a half." Eric was amazed at that since they had a policy at his place in Maine that no one would have to wait more than fifteen minutes unless there was an emergency.

"Do any of these people complain?" asked a very surprised Eric.

"Oh, yeah, we hear about it and every once in a while a prospective patient will walk out." Jim looked at his watch and told Eric that he had to get back to his clinic. They promised to stay in touch and Hagere reminded Eric to think about moving down to the Ft. Myers area.

While driving back to Captiva, Eric was still surprised at what he had just witnessed. Maybe, he thought, all other markets were similar to Florida's in that there were more patients than all these doctors could handle safely. Now he could hardly wait until he got back to his clinic and staff.

When he got back to the house, everyone was sitting on the beach soaking up sunshine. He got his swimming trunks on and went down to join them. After kissing his mother and Janet he sat next to his father and related what he had just witnessed. His father was a bit more understanding of what Eric described.

"You need to understand that this is a huge retirement area and as a result lots of people need all sorts of medical assistance. Just about any doctor's office is crowded with more people than they can possibly handle. It's a mess to say the least." Peter shrugged his shoulders as he spoke about it. "And when you watch TV you'll see all sorts of medical and lawyer ads, which in a sense tell the viewer to come see this doctor and if he screws up call the ambulance chasers. Thank God my knee is doing all right. Otherwise I might have to fly up and see you in your uniform."

They continued discussing the medical problems until the women demanded a halt to this discussion. Later they went back in the house for a glass of wine before dressing to go out for dinner.

On Saturday, they were scheduled to leave at noon and arrive in Bangor around seven. The drive to the airport was relatively quiet as they all didn't like the thought of leaving. When they got to the airport, they each hugged the other and Janet was really unhappy to leave, as was Margaret to see Janet leave. The two had become quite close during their time together as his mother was happy to have met Janet and sad to see her leave. Finally Margaret broke the silence. "Janet, I hope to see you again real soon," she said while looking at her son. Her message was quite simple. Marry Janet as quickly as possible.

The flight to Bangor was uneventful and close to being on time. Coming out of the plane they were stunned by the cold air. It would take them awhile before they got used to the Maine spring and to put away the warmth of sunny Florida

Doug and Sarah were waiting for them at the luggage area and their luggage arrived much quicker than in Ft. Myers. Sarah told them she had made dinner for the two of them and Doug invited Eric to stay the night...in a separate room, of course. Janet encouraged him to stay so they could tell her father and Sarah about their week in Florida.

Sunday morning Eric planned to get back to his house and Janet decided to stay home to get caught up on what occurred while they were in Florida. He held her as he told her how much he loved having her with him. Now he felt he was going to be backed up for several days with patients and operations. He had already scheduled another set of operations for Waterville.

"I don't know when I'm going to be free this week, but I'll stay in touch." Janet acknowledged his plans as she was beginning to feel their marriage was getting closer.

CHAPTER 35

Doris Munson was very pleased to hear from Susan Reddy, as she was hoping to hire her as the women's soccer coach. They agreed on a time for the following week and Doris told Susan she'd send her the airplane ticket. Susan told Jack about her coming trip to Northwestern University to interview for the women's soccer coach position and she planned to make the trip and interview by herself. Then she would call him to tell him about her meeting.

Doris Munson met her at O'Hare Airport in Chicago and they shook hands as they greeted each other with broad smiles. Doris Munson's initial reaction was very good. Susan Reddy was quick, direct, and to the point on just about everything she said without being overwhelming. This would sit well with her team players who had enjoyed playing under the direction of June Allard.

Doris was a fairly tall middle-aged woman with brown hair down to her shoulders and a thin body. She was attractive with a very vocal voice that immediately captured one's attention. She took Susan on a quick tour of the Evanston campus, the gymnasium, the soccer field and then headed back to her office. As they were talking about the school and the position of women's soccer coach, June Allard came into the office. Susan was very impressed with June's attitude toward her coaching position but wondered why she was looking forward to retiring; she didn't look that old. Susan was later told that June's husband was experiencing health problems and had to retire from his engineering job in Chicago. His doctor suggested a move out of the cold Chicago winters. June had somewhat of a serious toned voice. She too was quite thin and quite athletic looking even with hair that was turning gray. Susan immediately knew these two women were very close friends and that they both were saddened by June's retirement.

As the three-way conversation continued, June Allard asked about Susan's marital situation. Susan thought for a moment before answering and quickly decided she had to be truthful about her divorce and plans to marry Jack Meacham.

"Well," she said, "I've just gone through a relatively friendly divorce and am now planning to marry Jack Meacham.

June Allard's eyes widened. "Do you mean the Patriots' halfback?"

"Yes, that's who it is." Susan could tell they were both impressed with her proposed marriage to Jack.

"Will this cause a problem with you possibly moving here?" asked Doris, who hoped that it wasn't to be a hindrance in moving from Maine.

"No, we are looking forward to leaving Maine, and coming to the Chicago area is an exciting prospect." Susan's sincere answer convinced both June and Doris to push hard for getting Susan to join the Northwestern athletic staff. They discussed the entire program and how the team was looking for the next soccer year. Most important was the commitment the university was offering to the athletic department to improve the women's soccer program.

June Allard continued her discussion on the women's athletic programs. "Northwestern is the smallest school in the conference and is also the best of the bunch in scholastic excellence. There are those who don't seem to think we can compete with the other major universities, but we've done reasonably well. We're also more concerned about our students doing well with their studies as we are in winning games. That goes for both men and women teams."

Doris Munson continued the description. "Look, anytime you can get high quality students who are good athletes you're going to feel good about it. Any high school student athlete who cares about her future will understand it's important to get a degree from this university. We may not get the best athletes but we get the most intelligent ones of any other school in the Big Ten and many times the smart students end up playing better sports."

Susan liked what she was hearing. While Maine had some quality students and players, they were limited in competing with more famous universities. The more she listened the more excited she became about getting this coaching job. In turn, June Allard was feeling the same. She couldn't offer as much money or as much fame to Susan, but there was still to be exceptional results from joining up with a university like Northwestern.

Doris Munson got tired of sitting so she got up and walked over to the window and looked out at the campus. She turned around and placed her hands on her hips and told Susan, "Look, we want you to join us as coach. We felt this before you got here today as everyone we talked with about you came back with raving remarks." She lifted a folder from her desk and handed it to Susan. "This will officially explain our offer to you. We've given it a great deal of thought and all I can add is that I am very pleased that you came here to see what we are and whether or not you want to join us. Please take this with you and study it tonight, so we can talk about it tomorrow before you fly back to Maine."

Susan stood up and took the folder from Doris while June Allard stayed in her chair and indicated her approval with a broad smile. "Susan," June said, "I can't think of anyone who'd be better qualified for this job than you. And I don't think you'd find a more rewarding job than here at Northwestern. The place is full of good, honest and hard-working people and the students are exceptional. They have to be to get a scholarship offer. So I hope you accept it. I really do!" She emphasized the final words in a serious tone. She got up and walked over to shake Susan's hand and then walked out of the office.

"Now," asked Doris, "is there anything I've forgotten?"

Susan laughed at the thought. "No, you've done a beautiful job in explaining everything to me. Let me study this proposal tonight and I'll ask any questions tomorrow. OK?"

"You're on. Now we're going to have dinner together tonight, so if you're ready, let's get you checked into the motel and then we'll do dinner together so we can get a better feel for each other." She took Susan by her arm and led her out the door.

Dinner was at a small restaurant across the railroad embankment. Doris ordered a bottle of wine for the two of them while waiting to order their dinners. Then while waiting for their dinners to arrive, Doris had all sorts of questions to ask of Susan.

"Susan," asked Doris, "do you have a family?" Susan shook her head and related her past to June. She also talked about her years with Eric Forster and the admiration they had for each other. She didn't get into any details on what created the divorce but did emphasize her love for Jack Meacham.

June then asked what Jack was going to do if Susan accepted their offer. "Well, he's an assistant coach for the Maine football team, but he's about to resign. If I take your offer, he'll come with me and look for a job somewhere here in Chicago. He wants to continue with football, but he's not terribly happy with the quality of students he's had to coach." Susan then explained what had recently happened in Maine.

"Well, I can certainly understand his problem with some of the students colleges chase. Too many are just not ready for college and probably never will be. They're good athletes but lousy students. I don't see this changing anytime soon. Depending on how you look at it, we chase after a combination of quality athletes with quality students.

Doris changed quickly and quietly the direction of her conversation. "Susan, let me make this as clear as I can. I want you to be our soccer coach. June and I looked at several other prospective coaches but we kept coming back to you so I know we've made the right choice and I think the offer you'll find in that folder is very generous. If you have any questions you need answered tonight give me a call at my house. Here's the number." Doris handed Susan her business card after she wrote her home and cell phone numbers.

That evening Susan went through the proposal prepared by June Allard. It was better than she had anticipated. In fact anything would have been better than continued living in the Bangor, Maine area. She sat down on her bed, picked up the phone and called Jack who was impatiently waiting.

"Hi, Jack."

"Hi. So what happened today?" Jack was seated at his kitchen table reading the newspaper and anxious to hear from Susan.

"Well, darling, I had a great meeting with June Allard and Doris Munson." She continued by explaining what had been said between them and how anxious they were to hire her. "Jack, the offer they made me is terrific. I'm going to accept it tomorrow morning." She then related the offer as laid out to her by Doris. "I can hardly wait to get started." She told him about their discussion of Jack possibly assisting with their football teams.

"Well, I'm available if they want to put up with me. For sure I'm not coming back to the Maine football team. Now, when are you coming home? I'm lonesome. I need you."

"I'll be there tomorrow night. I need to spend some more time with June Allard and Doris Munson going over the program. Oh, Jack, I feel so good about this that I can hardly wait to get started." Jack fully understood her excitement in taking their coaching job. They talked for a while longer, then wished each other good night and hung up.

The next morning Doris Munson picked up Susan and took her back to Northwestern's athletic department. Susan told her of her decision and Doris was elated to hear it. She patted Susan on her knee. "You're going to really enjoy this school. It's full of terrific people who are doing a really good job in competing with the other Big Ten teams."

June Allard was relieved to hear Susan's decision and was all smiles as they went through the contract. Susan spent the remainder of time before her afternoon flight going over details and visiting some of the other coaches. Their football coach was Ted Bryant and he was most anxious to meet with Jack Meacham to see if there was a position that might interest him. He thought he could offer him an assistant coach's job that would utilize his talent. Ted Bryant envisioned Jack Meacham as their running back coach. This would impress high school prospects who would love to play under a quality halfback like him. Bryant had been a fan of Jack Meacham for many years.

Susan gave Ted Bryant Jack's phone number and suggested he call and talk with him to see if there was something he could offer Jack. She then called Jack to alert him on what might be coming and he was impressed with the possibility of moving to the Chicago area with Susan. He could hardly wait until she got back to Bangor so they could start working on plans to move out of Bangor.

CHAPTER 36

A few weeks after Susan got back from Illinois in early May, she decided to call Eric to let him know what was going on as she couldn't leave without getting together with him one last time. She still had a love for Eric that probably would never go away, but she had made a decision to marry Jack Meacham and was looking forward to it.

She found Eric alone at home. "Eric, I want to see you before Jack and I head off the Illinois this Friday. How 'bout dinner tonight?" There was silence on the other end for a moment, but Eric said he wanted very much to see her before she left Bangor. They decided on Cap Morrill's where they first had dinner. "Eric, I'll meet you there about seven thirty. OK?" she asked. He agreed.

While Eric drove into Brewer he began to reminisce about their first dinner at Cap Morrill's some five years ago. He remembered how impressed he was with her and how much he wanted to see her again. He never thought he'd end up marrying her, but he was glad he did. The first three years were fun as they both were young and heavily involved with their professions. But the last couple of years began to wear on both as their lifestyles were going in opposite directions. The love was still there but not the reality that was changing rapidly.

When he got to Cap Morrill's, Susan was already there with a bottle of beer waiting for him. There was the usual noisy crowd along with the aroma of lobster cooking. She got up to give Eric a strong hug and a kiss as he came around the table. She looked as good as ever and her smile was very bright. "Hi, Eric, how are you?" she asked, not knowing what else to say.

"Well, I'm fine, but I'm sorry to see you leave and I'm glad you called." He still felt somewhat out of place with her. "So tell me about your new job and when you're heading for Illinois."

Susan related what occurred at her meeting at Northwestern and then told Eric, , "The day after tomorrow we're driving out." She finally began to break up. "Oh, Eric, I'm going to miss you. I really, really loved you, even now, after our divorce is final. I enjoyed our time together, especially when we first met."

Eric took a drink out of his glass and smiled, remembering their first encounter at the gym. "Yeah, you were something else, but I did love you. Now it's different, but I'll miss you. What other woman could physically threaten me?" She laughed at that thought.

They spent the remainder of the dinner talking about their time together and laughed when they remembered their time at her apartment in Boston. She then began to tell Eric Forster more about her new coaching job. Finally they sat quietly looking at each other. Eric reached over the table to grip her hands. "Susan, I hope everything goes well for you and Jack and I know you'll do really well with your coaching. I'll be watching this and will cheer you on."

Susan's eyes began to fill with tears and she had a difficult time speaking, but finally remarked to Eric, "Jack is really a very nice considerate guy, but he does have a temper that needs to be controlled. He's not like you, but then there really isn't anyone like you. But, he's promised me that he'll take an anger management course. She got up from her chair as Eric walked around the table.

He hugged her and kissed her cheek. Neither wanted to let go. Those in the tables around them watched with great interest. Susan and Eric were not aware of anyone other than themselves.

It was cool out but neither of them acknowledged it. When they got to her car in the parking lot, Eric grabbed her again and held her tight, not wanting to let her go. "That's the last time I'll plan a weekend party."

She laughed at his thought. "Yeah, I know what you mean, but maybe you'll get together with Janet. I certainly hope so. She's a terrific lady."

"I know, Susan, I think Janet and I will be getting married. I'll let you know what happens. Right now I'm just sorry to see you go, but you've made the right decision." He held her as they got to her car. "Give my best to Jack and good luck in controlling his anger. He needs to be careful."

"Eric, I know that. I'll take care of him," she said with a quiet serious voice.

Eric laughed at that thought. "I bet you will."

Suddenly they both ran out of words and instead stood looking at each other. Simultaneously they ran their arms around one another as tears began in both their eyes. He opened her door and helped her into her car and she looked sadly back at Eric, then started her car and drove away. Eric stood staring at her car and said quietly to himself, "I love you." Now he felt alone as he got into his SUV and headed down to the lake.

The next morning he called Janet before he headed off to his clinic. "How would you like to come down to the lake over the Memorial Day weekend? The weather should be fairly decent so we can do some boating. There is also the pier putting-in party on Saturday. That's always a fun day."

"Do you mean that I won't see you until then?"

"I hope not, but I just wanted to have you stay with me for that weekend before someone else calls you for a date. And I'll behave myself. Promise."

"Yeah, I'm going to have to check out my calendar to see who wants to take me out over that weekend, but if not, you can count on me being there, particularly if you do behave yourself," she replied with enthusiasm. "When do you want to get together this week?"

"I have to go to Waterville tomorrow, so we can have dinner on Friday. OK?"

"You're on," she answered, "Where would you like to go?"

"You pick the place."

"OK, but no grumbling about my choice."

"Who me?" said Eric. "I'll see you then."

"OK."

"Janet?"

"What?"

"I love you." He hung up the phone before she could answer.

When Janet arrived at school the next day she walked in with one of the other grammar school teachers. During their conversation Carolyn Larsen mentioned that she was at Cap Morrill's last night and sat next to Eric and Susan. "I thought they were divorced, but they sure as heck weren't acting like it.

It looked like a romantic evening." Carolyn was aware of Janet's involvement with Eric Forster and thought she should be made aware of what might be going on.

Janet was shocked to hear what Carolyn had to say because Eric had told her many times that his involvement with his former wife was over. The more she thought about it, the unhappier she became, so when Eric called to see where they were going to dinner she said she wanted to stay home. She said she was too tired to go out.

"Do you want me to come over to your place?" asked Eric.

"No, I think I want to be alone this weekend," answered Janet in a very subdued voice.

Eric was surprised at her answer, but finally asked, "Is something wrong?"

"Yes, but you probably know yourself," she answered. Eric hadn't a clue as to what was wrong, but there obviously was something bugging her. She hung up the phone without saying anything else and leaving him with an empty phone on his ear.

Eric stayed alone at the lake for the weekend, wondering what was wrong with Janet. Eventually he thought that maybe someone had seen him with Susan at Cap Morrill's and had misinterpreted what happened. He couldn't think of any other reason why Janet had turned him off.

Janet was madder than hell as she told Sarah about Eric's dinner with Susan. "I can't believe he did it since he told me his relationship with her was over. If it was, then what was he doing taking her out of dinner and kissing her in public?" Sarah didn't have an answer.

After finishing his patients on Monday, Eric drove over to Doug Felty's house because he needed to talk with Janet. A very disgruntled Janet greeted him at the door and she didn't offer anything to him including inviting him in. He could tell she was very angry.

"Janet, what's wrong?"

"That's sort of a dumb question," she answered without changing her expression.

Eric was very concerned about what she might be thinking. "Janet, can I come in so we can talk about this?" She hesitated then opened the door and walked back into the house where she sat down on a single chair, as she didn't want him near to her.

A frowning Eric sat down across the living room and asked her, "Has this anything to do with my dinner with Susan?"

"Well, what do you think?" asked Janet

"OK, so that's it. Well let me tell you what happened. She invited me to go to a last dinner with her because she and Jack were leaving for Illinois this week and she wanted to meet with me one last time. I agreed with her because as I've told you before, we still have affection between us that will probably always be there.

"If I was planning to do something with her, I sure as hell wouldn't take her out to a public restaurant in this area. We had a good time remembering the past and talking about her new job as women's soccer coach at Northwestern University and my thoughts about you. If you don't believe this, then I don't know what else I can tell you." Eric was now getting mad at Janet for her thoughts about his dinner with Susan.

Janet's expression did not change as she listened to Eric explain his date with his ex-wife as she continued to glare at him. "Well, you kissed her in the restaurant.

"Of course I did. Where else should I have done it? In her house? My house? Or should I have just shaken her hand and left it at that? Remember she was my wife and we had a love for each other, and this was where we first met," Eric said, getting madder as he talked. He got up and walked out of Janet's father's house without looking back at her. "Good night, Janet," he said in a loud tone.

Janet was shocked at Eric's quick departure from her house and didn't quite know what to do. Suddenly she felt her relationship with Eric was slipping and she began to feel bad about what just happened. She sat alone on the chair trying to come up with something that would correct his anger.

CHAPTER 37

While Eric drove back down to the lake, his mind was on what had just occurred and now he was trying to figure out some way for them to get back together. He fixed himself dinner and watched TV for a while before going to bed. His anger had turned to concern over their confrontation over his dinner with Susan. Hell, he thought, it was no big deal, but obviously Janet didn't think so.

Doug and Sarah arrived home about an hour after Eric had come and gone. It was obvious to them that something was wrong since Janet was so silent. Finally, Sarah asked her. "Janet, what's wrong?" Janet looked sadly at both her father and Sarah, and then explained what had happened with Eric.

Doug and Sarah looked at each other after listening to Janet. Their concern was that they also might disagree with each other as to who was at fault.

Finally her father offered his thoughts. "It seems to me, Janet, that you might have overreacted to what Eric did. It sounds to me like they were just saying good-bye to each other from the place where they first met. And men and women generally hug and kiss when they part company. It sounds like this was exactly what Eric was doing." He looked over at Sarah, hoping she would not disagree.

Sarah nodded her head while looking at Doug as she basically agreed with his thinking. "Doug, you might be right, but it still has to have created some concern with Janet. After all, what's she to think when she hears this story from one of her friends who was at Cap Morrill's when all this happened?" replied Sarah. "There has always been a concern that Eric really didn't want to divorce Susan and his action while at dinner with her seemed to indicate it might be true."

Doug just shrugged his shoulders as he looked at his daughter, whose eyes were beginning to moisten. "I would have to ask whether or not Eric is in love with you, Janet. I don't think there is any question about that, but that's my opinion."

"Well, Dad, I do love him, but I was just upset that he went out with her and made advances at dinner," said Janet as she finally replied to the comments being made about Eric. "Particularly after they were divorced," she added.

"Yeah, Janet," said her father, "but he didn't make advances. He just said good-bye to her just as any man and woman would and now you'll probably never see or hear from her again. Part of your problem might be the concern you have about getting married again."

Janet looked surprised at her father's thoughts. "Oh, Dad," she replied, "I don't really think so." She looked at Sarah, whose expression seemed to agree with her father.

"Well," said Sarah, "your dad's probably right. You've put all sorts of pressure on yourself about your possible future with Eric and when you heard that he had dinner with Susan, it set off alarms. Then when you heard that they hugged and kissed each other, it must have set you off." Sarah reached out for Janet's hand while smiling at her.

Janet slid down in her chair as she rolled her eyes to the ceiling. "Oh, God, I think you're right." She glanced at both of them with a sad look. "Now what do I do?"

After a moment of silence, her father finally suggested that she call Eric so they could get together and forget what just happened. Janet looked at her watch and thought it was too late to call Eric tonight. Sarah offered that Eric was probably upset at what happened and probably had not gone to bed.

As Janet got up to phone Eric the phone rang. Doug answered it and handed it over to his daughter. He whispered that it was Eric as he grabbed Sarah's hand and headed off to the kitchen.

"Hello," said Janet In a quiet voice.

"Janet, I need to apologize for what I did tonight."

"Oh, no, Eric, It was my fault," she said as she began to wrap the phone cord around her left hand. They spent several minutes apologizing to each other for what had happened.

Finally, Eric began to laugh. "Janet, this is ridiculous. We're acting like a couple of high school students. Let's just forget what happened because Susan and Jack have left Bangor and I doubt we'll ever see them again."

Janet slid down on her chair as she grinned at the wall across the room. "No matter what you say, Eric, it was my fault for creating this nonsense. It's the last time I'm going to say this, but I am sorry for my actions." She emphasized the phrase.

"Ok" replied Eric, "it's over. Period. Now I've got to go down to

Waterville tomorrow, but I'll be back Friday morning and I'm still looking forward to spending the weekend with you at the lake."

""You bet. I'll be ready whenever you come down." They decided that on Saturday morning since he would be involved with putting in piers with his neighbors. After they hung up, Janet went into the kitchen to relate to her father and Sarah, what happened. They were both relieved to hear how it all came out and they promised to come down Monday morning.

Memorial Day weekend was warm and dry and the black flies were pretty well history for another year. Though the lake was still too cold for swimming for most people, Eric always planned to go swimming just to say he went swimming before anyone else. He also planned to get his boats in the lake, but now had to wait for the neighborhood pier party to get his pier set. Janet drove down in her car Saturday morning while Eric was tied up helping install the neighborhood's piers.

After all the piers were in, Eric got his powerboat and sailboat tied into their buoys. To get the boats tied to the buoys he had to swim them out. Janet watched him with concern because the lake was still quite cold. However, Eric was enjoying swimming as in his mind it signified the beginning of a new year for lake dwellers. Besides, he said, the water really isn't that cold.

Lake Lucerne was one of the more beautiful lakes in Maine. It was some three miles long with a large body on the west end. The water was extremely clear and quite deep. It was obvious that the lake was created centuries before by glaciers that dug the lakes and moved large granite boulders into the water. Lake Lucerne had several small islands filled with huge granite boulders and beautiful pine trees.

He swam back to the pier after he fastened his sailboat and invited Janet to join him. "Not a chance," she said shaking her head. She stuck her foot into the water and quickly pulled it out. "Eric, that's cold!"

"Well," he replied, "it really isn't that bad once you get in."

"You're nuts!" She got up and headed off the pier to wait for him to come out of the water.

"Well, this will give me an excuse to come and cuddle with you." He smiled broadly as he pulled himself onto the pier.

"Hah, that's a good try, but forget it. I'm not going to freeze my body just to please you." She looked at him as he stood up on the pier. He was still an impressive guy. He wasn't built like Jack but he still had an athletic-type body. There wasn't much fat even with his passion for cheeseburgers.

"You're a coward. I think I'll attack you now so I can get my body dry," he said as he walked toward her.

"Forget it," she said as she turned and began to run up to the house. He caught her at the top of the hill and she let out some sort of scream. "Oh, God, you're cold and you're soaking wet." She began to laugh at what was happening.

"Go away," she yelled as she tried to free herself from his wet arms.

"I'm cold and I need to cuddle." He finally released her from his grip. "My goodness, you're wet," he said looking at her damp blouse. "Maybe you should take it off so you don't catch cold. And maybe I can help," he offered, grinning at her.

"You're terrible," she said looking down at her wet blouse. "Don't even think of touching me. Maybe I'll call my father and tell him how you attacked me," she said, grinning back at him. "And I'm cold so I'd better take this blouse off before I catch a cold, she told him as she began to slowly unbutton her blouse while he stared at her.

"Oh, my God, I'll be put in jail for abusing you. I guess I'd better let you go." He gazed at her, then smiled and told her, "I can always sneak into your bedroom tonight." He looked up and down her body with a phony sinister look.

Eric waved at her and headed off to his bedroom. "I'm out of here." She followed him up the stairs and headed to the master bedroom to change blouses. When she finished she headed back out the door where Eric was waiting for her. "I want you to be aware that you're sleeping on a brand new bed and mattress. I had the other one thrown out. I couldn't handle the thought of sleeping on top of where Jack and Susan made love." He was very serious about needing to change beds.

"Well, it's a nice-looking bed. You did well in picking it out."

"Actually Harriet Glidden picked it out for me and Paul installed it. Yeah, they did a good job. Now I can hardly wait to have you and me together in this bed." He looked seriously at her hoping she would go along with his ideas.

She put her head on his chest, then rose up and kissed him. "Don't tempt me. We've gone this far so let's see whether or not we're meant for each other beyond a bed adventure."

Eric rolled his eyes and muttered, "I thought you'd say this. But you're right, so let's get out of here while I still can and have some lunch." They held hands as they went downstairs to the kitchen.

After lunch they went outside to finish Eric's basket gardening. He had already loaded a wheelbarrow with dirt, cow manure and peat moss.

They loaded hanging baskets and manger baskets with this mixture then attached the manger baskets to the deck. Next they planted geraniums, impatiens, and several different smaller annual flowers into the manger baskets, and then hung them on the sides of the deck.

In the hanging baskets they planted a variety of flowers. For those baskets that would be shaded they planted tuberous begonias and impatiens, and for the sunny areas, another variety of flowers beginning with petunias. It took them all of the afternoon to finish the project, but they were very pleased with the final results. Eric was also very impressed with how Janet seemed to enjoy gardening. It was a task that Susan never really liked.

The neighborhood dinner party was at the Miranda house and they were to bring salad for ten people. Janet put this together while Eric took a shower. They were acting like a married couple and this convinced Eric that there was no longer a question of whether or not a marriage between them would work. He thought he just had to convince Janet.

The dinner was preceded by a variety of cocktails. Eric and Janet stayed with red wine. It was a fun party since it was officially the beginning of summer for everyone on the block's waterfront. Janet was well accepted by everyone at the party, including some who knew her through her former husband Jack Meacham. Fortunately no one brought up his name for conversation.

Dinner was barbequed ribs with Florida-grown corn on the cob, baked potatoes and a variety of salads. Dessert was also a variety of items from brownies to pies. Since everyone at the party was involved in the pier assembly the conversations evolved around whose pier was the most difficult to put in. Eric easily won that honor, as his floating pier was the longest and heaviest on their side of the lake.

The party began to break up around ten so Eric and Janet headed home. The evening was cool but pleasant with a nearly full moon in the sky and when they got away from the Miranda's house, it became quiet except for the cry of the loons. Those birds never seemed to sleep. There was enough light from the moon for them to see their way up the road. They were tired from the long day and both looked forward to bed...alone.

Once in the house, they checked the phone for messages and the computer for e-mails. There was nothing urgent on either so they headed up the stairs to their bedrooms. They stopped, hugged and kissed each other, then headed into their rooms. It didn't take long for sleep to take over.

At a little after eight on Sunday morning Janet woke up and after a bathroom stop got dressed in blue slacks and a multicolored sweater, then headed down the stairs. Eric was already there, dressed in jeans and a sweatshirt, making coffee. He smiled at her and went over to embrace her. She was feeling very relaxed after a long Saturday and looked forward to a day alone with Eric.

"Boy, did I ever sleep. That's a very comfortable bed."

Eric grinned at that and told her she should thank the Gliddens for their selection. He also thought to himself how nice it would be if they shared the bed.

After the large dinner Saturday night, they settled on cold cereal, fruit juice, and a piece of toast for breakfast. After they finished eating they took their coffee and went out on the deck where the sun was shining making the outdoors reasonably comfortable. The lake was fairly quiet since a lot of the summer people wouldn't be there until later in June.

A variety of birds had congregated on the feeders...goldfinches, chickadees, nuthatches, purple finches and a beautiful pair of rose breasted grosbeaks. On tree branches around the feeder were birds waiting their turns. On the ground were several blue jays and mourning doves. Attached to a tree in front of the deck was a suet feeder where a couple of different woodpeckers came for food. On the deck in front of them was a hummingbird feeder that was populated by a couple of acrobatic hummingbirds.

Janet was spellbound by the variety of birds and sat in awe watching them feed. When they finished eating, they all disappeared into the woods. Janet finally broke the silence. "Eric, I've never seen anything like this. How long did it take you to get all these birds here?"

Eric laughed. "I think they were all waiting for me to put up these feeders because once I did they all seemed to come in from the woods. I have no idea where any of them have a nest but it has to be close to here. Whatever, I really enjoy watching them. It takes your mind off everything else." Janet voiced her agreement.

"So what's on tap for today?" asked Janet, while stretching out her long legs.

"Really nothing, but maybe we could go for a canoe ride this morning and then take the motor boat out for a longer trip."

"That sounds like fun. Let's do it," replied an anxious Janet. They went into the house to get ready for the canoe ride and into the garage for the paddles and lifejackets. The canoe was sitting on the ground next to the pier where it was easy to get in and out of the water. Janet got into the front seat while Eric held the boat to the dock. The water was fairly calm so it was easy to paddle along the shore and to see down into the water. There were some fishermen on the lake but the large and noisy powerboats were still at their docks.

Eric was impressed with how much Janet was enjoying canoeing. She obviously had paddled before and then asked her. "Oh, yes, I've done a lot of canoeing. I really like it, particularly on a day like this when the water and wind are calm. There's nothing more fun," she said, turning around to look at Eric. They paddled for over an hour up the narrows of the lake where there were fewer homes and quiet water.

After they docked the canoe, they headed back up to the house. Janet went upstairs to make the beds and then came down to wash the dishes while Eric went out to the garage to get his rake so he could clean up the front yard of all the twigs and branches that had fallen over the winter. Janet looked at the inside of the house and decided it needed some cleaning, so she looked around for the vacuum cleaner. When she found it, she began cleaning the living room.

Eric was raking the front of the house when he turned to look inside the house where Janet was vacuuming. He realized that they were acting like husband and wife and that he was totally happy just being with her. This was the same feeling he'd had at the Benoit Lodge. He just felt great being with her and while he desperately wanted to get into bed with her again, he was feeling exceptionally well just being with her. . There was no question, but that he wanted to marry her. He sat down on the deck and looked into his house and wondered why he had waited so long.

Janet finished vacuuming the living room and looked out and saw Eric sitting on the deck looking in the window. He had a peculiar look on his face and it concerned her, so she open the door and went out to see what the problem was.

"Are you OK?" she asked in a worried tone. He was looking at her with an odd facial expression. She sat down next to him and stroked the side of his face.

He continued gazing at her and thought how beautiful Janet was, but more important what a terrific person she was.

He reached out for her and changed his expression to one of happiness. "You know," he finally said, "we've been dating each other since February and I have become so in love with you, that I've been afraid to tell you for fear you might not love me as much." He hesitated for a moment, and then asked, "Does that make any sense?"

She shook her head and kissed him on his cheek. "Eric, how can you possibly not know that I've been in love with you ever since that weekend? I was worried for a long time that your love for Susan was going to keep us apart."

Eric took her hand and smiled as he told her. "I can understand that, because I was hurt by what she did that weekend and I couldn't understand why she was so casual about her affair with Jack. Even though we were having a difficult time I felt that I still loved her." He looked down toward the lake and hesitated before continuing. "It's over with Susan. It has been for a long time, but I refused to accept it. Susan finally convinced me that she was in love with Jack and that our marriage was over. Period! We're still friends, but that's all." He looked back at Janet, wondering how she was accepting this.

"Eric, I thought I was in love with you when we were together in Bethel. When we got back here, there was no question I was in love with you. But I was worried that you were still in love with Susan so I kept it to myself until I was certain your relationship was over."

The birds were coming back to the feeders and seemed to be singing songs to Eric and Janet. They stopped talking for a few moments as they looked again at the birds. Eric then placed his hands on her face and kissed her. "Will you marry me, Janet?"

Tears began to well in her eyes. "Oh, yes, Eric, I want to marry you. Oh, I do, I do." They gripped each other and fell onto the deck laughing with absolute joy.

Eric asked, "Why did we wait so long?"

Janet quickly answered, "Because we didn't want to make another mistake and now I know we haven't. Oh, I love you, Eric."

They kissed each other and stroked each other's hair. Then they heard a voice calling them. Paul and Harriet Glidden came around the side of the house and stopped when they saw Janet and Eric embracing. "Hey, I hope we're not interrupting something," Paul said, "but we'd like to have you join us for lunch."

Eric and Janet smiled at each other and sat up on the deck. He looked at the Gliddens and assured them they weren't interrupting anything, "But" he continued, "I need to tell you that Janet's agreed to marry me."

"Hey, congratulations," said Paul, while Harriet thought they should probably leave the two of them alone. "Now you can legally try out the new bed together." He laughed at his comments.

"Paul!" Harriet yelled. "Behave yourself!" Paul just laughed at her as she turned to Janet and Eric and told them how happy she was to hear that. "So, when's the marriage?"

Eric and Janet looked at each other and both shrugged shoulders. "I have no idea," Eric said, gazing at Janet. "We'll figure that out later. For lunch with you, yes, but we need to make a couple of phone calls first to let Janet's father know and for me to call my mom and dad."

Janet looked lovingly at Eric and added, "There's all sorts of things we need to get organized, so give us at least a half hour. OK?" The Gliddens nodded their approval and headed back to their house.

Eric and Janet headed into the house and when they hit the kitchen, Eric stopped. "Oh, my God, I forgot to get you an engagement ring."

Janet patted him on his back. "Don't worry about that. It's no big deal. Getting engaged to you is more important to me than a ring.

"Well, next week I'll take care of that," said a very embarrassed Eric. "Damn it! I should have gotten the ring first and then asked you to marry me. I'm sorry."

Janet grinned at him. "Well, what would have happened if I said no?"

Eric laughed and held her tighter. "No big deal if you had turned me down. You're ugly, overweight, a lousy cook and a woman who has no concept of managing a house, so I was your last chance!"

She pushed him down on the deck. "You're miserable!" Janet had a difficult time keeping a straight face.

Eric grabbed her again and pulled her down on the deck. "God, I don't even want to think of that." He ran his arms around her body and pulled her close to him. "I don't ever want to be without you."

CHAPTER 38

Janet first called her father and reminded him that they'd like to have him and Sarah down Monday morning. She didn't tell him about her agreement to marry Eric. Her father said they'd come down Monday morning.

Next, Eric called his parents in Florida. He got his mother on the phone as his father was out golfing. "Mom, just to let you know, Janet and I are going to get married."

"Oh, terrific," shouted a very happy Margaret Forster. "I couldn't be happier. I'm sure your father will feel the same. Oh, terrific!" she repeated. "Where's Janet?"

"Right here. I'll put her on." Janet and Eric's mother talked for quite a while. It was obvious that his mother was very pleased with Eric's choice this time. She could now envision grandchildren being a part of her life and she was only sorry that Janet and Eric weren't closer so they all could get together to celebrate their agreement to marry. Margaret wanted to know when the wedding was planned, as they would fly up to Bangor.

Lunch at the Gliddens was fun. The two of them always seemed to be fighting, but it was merely their way of enjoying each other. Eric and Janet left their house about three and headed back to their house. "Let's go for a boat ride," said Eric as they walked down to the deck. "It'll be the first of the new year."

"I'm ready," replied Janet, who took off her sweater as the day was warming up. Eric gazed longingly at her figure and began to laugh. "So what's so funny?" she asked him.

"Ever since we were together in Bethel I have been going nuts waiting to touch you without getting in trouble. Now I'm going to be able to do it, but I feel I should wait until we are married." Eric leaned back on the deck and gazed at the sky in anticipation of finally making love to Janet.

Janet leaned down next to Eric. "Well, I guess you're right and we can now legally get married since both our divorces are final. Now, you're going to have to put up with me for the rest of your life."

"Man, I can't think of anything better," answered Eric in a very soft voice, while he turned his face to hers and kissed her while brushing her blonde hair back from her face. "So, when should we get married?"

She grinned at him. "The sooner the better. School's out in two weeks, so we should wait at least until then. How about the fourth of July weekend? Or can you wait that long?"

Eric rolled over and groaned. "You mean I can't touch you until then?"

She sat up and looked down at an anxious husband-to-be. He groaned even louder. "Eric, be quiet. You'll scare the birds away," she said as she hit him on his chest. "And, yes, you can't touch me till then."

Eric continued his groaning. "How can I possibly do that?" he asked, reaching for her shoulders and then letting his hand slide down until he got his hand whapped.

"Hands off, buster," she ordered. To herself she had a hard time not letting him do whatever he wanted. She rolled over on top of him and bent over to give him a kiss. He was about to lose it when her hair fell over his face and her breasts began to penetrate his chest. "This will be a preview of things to come," she said in a sexy soft voice.

He grabbed and shook her arms. "You miserable broad! I can't believe what you're doing. You should be shot!"

She laughed at him while rolling off his body. "Eat your heart out," she said, while making a face at him. "Now that I've got your attention, let's go for a boat ride before you have any other ideas."

The lake was fairly quiet since most of the boats had yet to be put in the water. Eric asked Janet if she'd like to drive the boat and she immediately took over. Even though she had never driven a boat before now, she handled the steering as though this was an everyday occasion.

Eric worked up a calendar in his mind and figured it would be about five weeks until they got married. That evening they had dinner across the lake at the Lucerne Inn that sat high up, overlooking the lake. The Inn advertised itself as the most beautiful lake site in Maine. From the front windows they could almost see Eric's house. Janet was very impressed with the view of the lake and the hills behind it.

The food and service were excellent. They had to agree that this was one of the finest restaurants in the Bangor area. When they finished eating they sat drinking coffee and watching the sunset. It took about fifteen minutes to get back to the house and both agreed they needed to get to bed reasonably soon.

The next morning they got up early and after a cup of coffee, headed down to the lake to take a canoe ride while the water was calm and before the powerboats got onto Lake Lucerne. The weather was quickly warming up as the sun was shining. They were both dressed in denim shorts with short-sleeve T-shirts and they left their shoes on the pier, so they wouldn't get wet.

As they paddled in the shallow waters there were two loons with their baby out in the deeper part of the lake. The lake was lined with all sorts of granite boulders and in the shallow water there were huge ledges below the surface. The large boulders and ledges were very visible as were all sorts of fish, but particularly the smallmouth bass. A large bass went swimming by the front of the boat while Janet pointed it out to Eric. He told her it was a smallmouth bass.

She asked, "What's the difference between the smallmouth and largemouth bass?"

In a very serious tone, Eric explained, "Well, the smallmouth bass are males and the largemouth, females."

This didn't register to Janet as she initially nodded her head, but when she realized what he just said she turned around and splashed water on him with her paddle. "You're terrible, you really are, and now I'm supposed to be a loving wife to someone as obnoxious as you?" She sprayed more water on him with her paddle and Eric then beat his paddle toward her in return. As they were spraying each other, voices from the pier made them turn their bodies toward the shore which caused the canoe to overturn and send both of them into the lake.

The water was cold and got her attention in a hurry as it started to take away her breath. Fortunately they were a few yards away from the pier so Janet quickly swam to it where her father and Sarah couldn't contain their laughter. Right behind her Eric was pushing the canoe toward the shore and laughing at what just happened.

As Doug helped her out of the water and onto the pier, Janet couldn't help but join the laughter. "Oh, God, Dad, he's terrible. How on earth did I ever find him attractive? He's the most miserable person I've ever known." She shook her fist at Eric as he got the canoe out of the lake. She turned back to her father and Sarah and said, "Oh, by the way, we've decided to get married."

Doug reached down to pull Janet up and decided not to hug her, as he'd get wet, so he kissed her instead. Sarah followed, still shaking from her laughter at what happened to the two of them. Then Janet ran up to the house to get out of her cold wet clothes. Eric was not far behind.

Breakfast was a joyful time as Doug and Sarah couldn't have been happier now that Janet and Eric had decided marriage was the thing to do.

When they both got dressed they joined her father and Sarah in the kitchen. Janet came up behind her husband-to-be and hugged him while showing her complete happiness with him.

Sarah held Doug's hand, as they were so pleased to see Janet this happy. They had waited a long time, but now they were certain she made the right decision even though Eric and Janet often acted like a couple of teenage kids. During lunch they discussed when and where the marriage should take place and who should be invited.

Both Janet and Eric wanted the marriage to be informal with only close friends and family invited. They both felt they'd already had a large formal wedding and once was enough.

After the day at the lake, Janet followed her father and Sarah home, but not before Eric held Janet in his arms, not wanting to let her go. All he could think was that in about six weeks, they'd be together forever. He could hardly wait.

CHAPTER 39

They decided to have the wedding Friday morning, the first of July at the
Congregational Church in Bangor. The minister was Jeffrey Hancock,
a close family friend who had married Janet and Jack Meacham. Eric's
parents came up for the wedding on Thursday afternoon and stayed at
Eric's house. Other than their immediate families only close friends were
invited to attend. Eric's medical staff and Janet's teacher friends and
friends were invited. They also invited the Lewises from Ellsworth.

A friend of Janet's sang a few songs before the organist played the
wedding march. Eric waited impatiently for Janet to stroll down the
aisle to the altar, where he reached out his hand for hers and turned to
face Reverend Hancock, who welcomed them with a warm smile.

Eric looked over at Janet who, while smiling, had moisture in her
eyes. The formal ritual seemed to take longer for both of them as they
longed to get off by themselves as husband and wife.

When Reverend Hancock announced that Eric and Janet were
husband and wife, they turned and grasped each other, while giving a
long penetrating kiss. They pulled back their heads and looked out at
an applauding audience with a set of broad smiles.

After the nine o'clock wedding, they all met at the Pilot's Grill
Restaurant for a brunch since Janet and Eric were planning to leave
before noon. When the brunch was over, Eric and Janet said good-bye
to everyone and drove over to her father's house where they changed
clothing. "My suitcases are in the hall," she told Eric, as she was full of
happiness to now be Mrs. Forster.

"Janet, we're only going for the weekend," Eric commented as
he looked at the luggage and a set of golf clubs. He shook his head in
amazement at how much she was taking with her. "And golf clubs. What
are they for?"

She grabbed him on the sides of his head. "We've got a golf date
this afternoon."

"We what?" asked a grinning Eric. "Besides I didn't bring my golf
clubs."

"Oh, yes, you did," answered Janet. I put them in the back of your Jeep, under the blanket."

"OK, but how did you know we're going to a golf course?"

Janet walked around to her side of the Jeep. "Well, I called Mr. Craven to reserve a time for golf so now we have a tee time of three thirty this afternoon and an eleven o'clock tomorrow morning, after we finish what we didn't start last winter. I also figured that you would take the two of us to the Benoit Lodge. This is where it all started."

Eric shook his head in bewilderment. He thought it would be a surprise to go back to the Benoit Lodge for their weekend honeymoon. He got into the SUV and started the engine. "How did you know we were going to Bethel?"

"That's obvious. Where else would we go? This is where our romance started and I'm sure both of us felt we had to have some sort of climax in room 229. Right?"

Eric put the Jeep into gear and began the drive over to Bethel. He shook his head again. "You're impossible." He couldn't contain his laughter.

Janet was acting like a teenage girl headed for her first prom with the boy she'd been admiring for years. Her mind was full of anticipation over the weekend with the man she loved who was now her husband. She leaned over to hug Eric and to give him a kiss on his cheek. They both were all smiles. The two of them had been looking forward to this time since they were together last February.

It was summer and the traffic on 95 was heavy but most of cars were headed north. Janet had on a pair of light green pants topped by a multicolored blouse. Her blonde hair fell over her shoulders. Eric was dressed in a pair of khakis, boat shoes, and a yellow shirt. He had on his Chicago Cubs baseball hat and a pair of sunglasses. He didn't look at all like a surgeon.

As they drove west on 95 on the way out of Bangor, Janet leaned over and put her head on Eric's shoulder. He in turn caressed her thigh before announcing, "We'd better watch out or we're going to end up in the median."

She continued to lean on him. "That's too bad," she offered in a less than serious voice. As the seat belt began to hurt her, she moved back to her seat.

Janet sighed a deep feeling of relief. "I'm so happy to be going to Bethel with you that I can barely wait to get there. I also didn't bring my snowshoes, but then I didn't watch the weatherman either."

"Then what are we supposed to do all weekend if we don't snowshoe?" asked Eric. "I have to try out that bed again," Eric told Janet, "only this time you won't get away."

"Ha!"

Eric hadn't felt this good in many years. Just looking at Janet thrilled him. She seemed to have a perpetual smile on a face that was the most beautiful he'd ever seen. Her blue eyes penetrated his brain and her blonde hair made her model perfect. But it was her personality that affected Eric the most. She was a lady who loved people, especially children, and who also loved Eric above all else.

She smiled as if she had something secret. Eric finally asked, "All right, what's with the smile? What are you up to?"

"Nothing, you planned this weekend. Nothing," she answered, trying to keep a calm look. "I'm just here for the ride," she reiterated as she slapped her thigh. She had been practicing golf for the past week so she could be ready to compete with him. Eric was a better than average golfer with great strength with his drives, but generally did poorly with his pitching and putting. However, he was thinking more of bedtime with Janet than he was of being on the golf course with her.

"We can get in a game this afternoon before it gets dark, but don't worry too much about how you play. It's still early in the season so don't get disappointed if you don't play well." Janet thought Eric sounded like a teacher lecturing students.

Janet had been golfing since the end of winter and was feeling comfortable about playing with Eric. She and her father had played a couple of times at early opening golf courses and Doug was surprised at how well and how far she hit the ball. She was particularly good on and around the greens. Doug had to struggle to beat his daughter.

The drive up Route 2 was so much different than it was back in February that it didn't look the same. The road up to the lodge was beautiful. It was difficult to describe the difference between summer and winter in Maine.

The lodge looked the same as they entered and headed toward the registration desk. Mr. Craven was signing in guests, and as Eric and Janet approached the desk, Craven looked up and smiled at the two of them. "Welcome back Dr. Forster and Mrs. Forster. I hope you left the snow behind this time." He broke out in laughter.

It seemed to Janet that the President's Day weekend was longer ago than it actually was. Without the snow, ice, and wind it seemed like a completely different place. She also knew that her feelings were completely different than that weekend and she grinned to herself as she remembered the concern she had about sharing a bed with Eric. Now she could hardly wait until the time came again later today.

Mr. Craven handed the keys to Eric. "As you ordered, you've got the same room, number 229, that you had last February. Only this time the lights are on and the fireplace is cold.

The room was the same as when they left it in February, except there wasn't a fire going in the fireplace and all the lights were working. Janet began unpacking her suitcases making certain Eric was not peering over her shoulder. She was very anxious for the day to end so they could go to bed together without any reservations.

"Hurry up, Eric, we've got a golf game to play before dinner. Mr. Craven's reserved a three thirty start time for us." Janet was going through some stretching exercises, getting ready for their game. "We can probably get only nine holes in before it gets dark." Eric was just finishing unpacking when she demanded, "Let's move it!" He didn't see her smile as she whapped him on his butt.

She walked to the door, opened it and left an embattled Eric getting dressed for their golf match. After Eric changed he went to the clubhouse and signed in for a nine-hole match with Janet. He also was thinking of the night alone with her in the same bed they slept in last January.

When he got to the first tee, he found Janet practicing. Eric was impressed with her swing, but then, he thought, hitting is different then practicing. The golf course seemed to be in good shape, considering the effects of the winter storm.

"Ladies first," Eric offered, as he walked up to the tee box. Janet smiled, nodded her approval and picked out her driver from the golf bag. She made several practice swings after setting up her golf ball on the tee. The first hole was 410 yards with a slight dogleg to the left. For Eric the distance was 425 yards.

Janet teed off and drove her first shot about 150 yards down the middle of the fairway. Eric looked at Janet with a surprised look and didn't say anything to her smiling face. Eric teed off and drove the ball about 200 yards, but unfortunately it didn't go straight and ended up in the rough on the right side of the fairway.

He drove their golf cart to her ball and Janet promptly hit her second shot just short of the green. Eric's second shot did not go very far since he had to get out of the rough grass. His third shot ended up in the sand trap to the left of the green while Janet's third shot landed about ten feet from the flag.

Eric overhit his fourth shot and it went off the other side of the green and he had to chip up his fifth shot to within a few feet of the hole. As he came up toward the hole he threatened Janet with his putter. "Not a word out of you," he said, "there's still eight holes to go." They both sank their putts, Janet for a par and Eric for a double bogey.

His mind was on their action after dinner. He'd been waiting so long for this day that it had taken his mind off everything, except now when he didn't seem to be able to beat her in the golf game.

The next hole was a 150-yard par three for Janet and 175 for Eric. Janet came up short but had a direct shot at the hole. Eric overshot the green and went into the rough behind the hole. His second shot came within a few feet of the hole while Janet nearly holed out her second shot. Eric conceded her third shot and then lined up his shot. It missed by a few inches. He was now three strokes behind and she was shooting par after two holes.

When they got back to the golf cart he turned toward her and complained, "You've been practicing!"

Janet smiled, but didn't answer him. She put her feet over the dashboard and wrapped her hands behind her hair as they headed for the third tee.

Eric finally won the next hole by a stroke when both of them missed the fairway on a par five hole. It took Janet five shots to get on the green while Eric got there in four. Janet missed her putt for a seven and Eric won with a six, but he was still two shots behind her.

When they got to the ninth hole, it was getting a little dark as the sun was setting. Janet was still winning but by only a stroke. Eric had honors and promptly sliced his shot into the right rough, next to a large oak tree. Janet's shot went straight but didn't go too far.

Eric grumbled about his slicing the ball and when he found it he discovered he had to hit it back on the fairway, as there was no way he could aim for the flag. He was now shooting three from behind Janet's ball. His next shot came up short of the hole, but was still closer to the hole than was her second shot. "Would you like to concede the match?" she asked him as they drove to their golf balls.

"Not a chance, you miserable broad," he growled in reply. "It's never over till it's over."

"OK, whatever you want," she answered, trying to keep from smiling too much. "It's my shot!" She pulled out her eight iron and promptly put her next shot to within ten feet of the hole. Eric's shot came closer, about five feet from the hole. Janet missed her putt and ended with a five and Eric holed out for a five but still lost the match by a stroke.

By the time they got to the golf shop it was fairly dark as they were the last golfers to come off the course. Eric grabbed her left arm and pulled her toward him. "All right, when did you learn to play golf this good? You never told me about what a good golfer you are." He shook her body. "You set me up!" he roared.

"Tough bananas," she answered yanking her arm away from him. "You're just another overmatched male who can't handle losing to a woman." She laughed at him while feeling so good for having won their first time golfing together.

Eric was now smiling about the game. "Damn, you're really a good golfer. Next time I won't let you off this easy. Also, I had other things on my mind so I couldn't really concentrate."

She looked at him with a surprised glance. "Now, what could that be?" she asked.

"Well the next time is tomorrow," she offered, "you might want to practice before we tee off so you aren't too embarrassed." She leaned over to him and wrapped her arms around his shoulders and kissed his cheek.

"Don't try buttering me up. It won't work," he said, while kissing the top of her blonde head, "but I like it anyway." They headed to the grand room where they sat together on a couch in front of an empty fireplace. Janet tucked her legs underneath her thighs and leaned over to rest her shoulder on Eric's chest. He, in turn, wrapped his arms around her.

Janet finally broke the silence. "Isn't it nice to be here without all that snow? I never thought we'd ever see green grass again."

"Yeah, and you're a bit more friendly than you were in February," he answered with a broad smile.

"Well, you were about to attack me in my bed," Janet replied, digging her shoulder farther into his chest.

Eric broke out in a laugh that carried throughout the room. "Attack you? You've got to be kidding. I had to keep you away from my body. You were the attacker. Who got pushed out of the bed?" He caressed her hair with a gentle hand.

"Well, you touched my leg under the cover. I thought you were about to rape me."

"Right, not in your fondest dreams," Jack said, pressing Janet closer to him.

Mr. Craven came around the couch and sat down on the fireplace hearth in front of them. He still had his friendly smile surfacing off his graying face. "I understand you got in a little golf in this afternoon. How did it go?" he asked Eric.

"Yeah, Eric, how did it go?" repeated Janet to Eric.

"I have a feeling I've touched on a tender situation," replied Craven. He laughed at Eric.

Eric looked at Craven and then at Janet. He stuck his tongue out at her and then turned back to Craven. "She got a little lucky this afternoon, but it'll change when we play tomorrow."

Janet pulled away from Eric and sat up. "He just won't admit he lost to me, but he did. Mr. Craven, your course is in great shape considering the miserable winter we had. Where did all the snow go?" asked Janet.

"Well, we were lucky. The snow melted slowly so it didn't wash away any part of the golf course. And we didn't have much snow after that weekend. I'm surprised, but happy about the results. Now how are you two doing? The last time I saw you, there were tears flowing. Is everything OK?" he asked Janet in a calm and soothing voice.

"Thanks, Mr. Craven. Everything's just fine. No more tears from me. I couldn't be happier," she added, turning to Eric.

Eric smiled at the two of them and added, "One day I'll tell you the whole story, Mr. Craven; it would take a long time to explain it. But I agree with Janet,

I couldn't be happier." He wrapped his right arm around Janet's shoulder. "All I have to do now is to whip her hinder in golf tomorrow."

CHAPTER 40

When Janet and Eric went up to their room to dress for dinner, they both felt a nervous anticipation for the coming evening. It was their first time together in a single room for a weekend since the February adventure. There was very little talking. Both were anticipating going to bed together.

After dinner they went and sat in the lounge when they finished the last of their wine. It was nice not to worry about the weather and the lights going off at nine o'clock. None of the other guests looked familiar and none appeared to have been here at the January storm.

Eric looked at Janet and said that it was time to think about going to their room. Janet nodded her approval and they walked out of the lounge and up the stairs to their room. Eric again marveled at Janet's body and her long legs and slim waist. His body began to react.

When they reached their room they sat down in front of the unlit fireplace and opened another bottle of wine. After filling their glasses he held up his glass to toast hers. "May this night be one to remember for the rest of our lives." They clinked glasses and took a sip of the wine, put their glasses on the table and then hugged and kissed each other. Eric added, "I love you more than I can ever say."

Janet ran her hand down his cheek and kissed him again. "But not as much as I love you." Eric and Janet held each other with a tight grip, afraid to let go and both were smiling in anticipation of what was to come.

Eric then broke the silence. "This time I've brought my favorite pajamas." Janet started to question it, but then realized what Eric was saying.

"OK, in that case it's my turn to get ready for bed." She went to her dresser and pulled out a bag and took it with her into the bathroom. "And, Eric, you..."

Eric interrupted, "I know, I know, I can't look at you when you come out of the bathroom. OK!" She grinned at Eric and closed the bathroom door.

"No, Eric, this time you can look."

He turned off all the lights, undressed and got into bed waiting with horrible impatience for Janet to come out of the bathroom. It seemed to be an eternity before she opened the door. She said in a very soft, warm voice, "Now you can look, Eric." He turned his head toward Janet and sucked in his breath.

She was wearing a mesh chiffon two-piece nightgown she bought from Victoria's Secret for the wedding night. It was white and transparent. The bathroom light behind her body allowed Eric to see all of her as she turned slowly in a circle with her arms above her head so Eric could see her entire body, her long legs, her waist, and her breasts with her blonde hair reaching down below her shoulders, and her blue eyes staring at him.

Eric was speechless and was about to lose it as she walked over to their bed. As she got closer, her body amazed Eric. Until now he could only imagine what she looked like. As she got next to the bed she drew back the covers and checked his lack of pajamas. She took his head in her hands and kissed him while he viewed her entire body.

She crawled into the bed.

They silently looked at each other until Janet spoke with a quiet plea,

"Eric, please touch me."

ABOUT THE AUTHOR

A native of Chicago, Peter Sonderegger has published magazines, founded his own company, and served as vice president of various manufacturing firms. Now retired, he has revisited his writing background as a student of journalism at the University of Colorado to write LOVE STORM, his first novel. He and his wife of fifty years reside in Florida.

986173